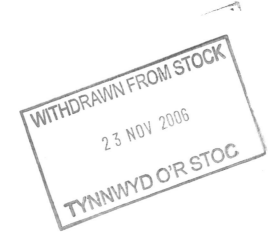

DARK
HEAVENS

Also by Roger Levy in Gollancz:

Reckless Sleep

DARK
HEAVENS

Roger Levy

GOLLANCZ
LONDON

First published in Great Britain in 2003 by
Gollancz
An imprint of the Orion Publishing Group
Orion House, 5 Upper St Martin's Lane, London WC2H 9EA

Distributed in the United States of America
by Sterling Publishing Co., Inc.
387 Park Avenue South, New York,
NY 10016–8810

A CIP catalogue record for this book is
available from the British Library

ISBN 0 575 07244 X (cased)
ISBN 0 575 07245 8 (trade paperback)

Typeset at The Spartan Press Ltd,
Lymington, Hants

Printed in Great Britain by
Clays Ltd, St Ives plc

For Tina, and Georgia and Alex

Quantum mechanics. Relativity. Mathematics. Chemistry. Physics. Science. Don't you see? Not one of them contains any of the letters G, O, D. How can you possibly believe that this has no significance?

Anon

And heaven? If God is not there, then what is?

Response, anon

PART ONE
ACTIVE

ONE

From the vantage point of the discreet Observer's balcony, with its data-monitors and racks of screens so new they still itched with box static, Auger gazed down over the crowded park beneath Alexandra Palace. He had forgotten to spray his face before setting out, and the atmosphere was starting to scratch at his cheeks and neck. There was a MagNet facility that he could have used to scrub the air on the balcony, but Auger didn't want the slight focus loss and the sense of distance that went with the Net. If he had to be here, he wasn't going to be anaesthetised against it.

Monsignor Arden was standing almost directly below him on his spidery pulpit, facing out at the congregation, as Auger was. Auger felt he could almost reach down and touch the top of the priest's head. He wondered what the hell was going on in that skull, to be doing this. It was insane. Auger leaned back, nauseous at the thought of it. And then leaned forward again, thinking, I'm damned if I'll flinch for him.

Arden's mirrorcloak, falling in slack folds to the ground, reflected the earth beneath him, so that to Auger he seemed to be sprouting from it, his neck and head erupting from the ground. His congregation wouldn't be seeing that, of course. They, before and beneath him, would see his face with its broad, earnest features merging with the sky. He would be part of that, to them. Of the heavens.

Auger ran a palm over the brickwork of the balcony. It came away, sand between his fingers, crumbling at his touch. Everything he touched, everything he looked at, it sometimes seemed, was fraying at the edges.

He let his gaze rove over them, the seemingly unending sweep of people down the slope and beyond it, falling out of sight, Arden's acolytes stretching away in every direction, every one of them dressed in the same rough, colourless, impregnated shifts. They stood, they coughed, they scratched at themselves in the abrasive air, and they waited with the infinite patience of the knowing. None of them was sprayed against the air, none wore a filter. They looked like shrouded phantoms.

Raising his eyes, Auger stared out towards the city beyond. Cloud shadows swarmed listlessly over the distant pitted landscape. He could imagine London the last deserted battlefield at the end of a lost war. The ash clouds could be the drifting smoke of bombs, the quaked and ruined buildings might have been ravaged by missiles. Auger took the wreckage in, his thoughts low, his mind wandering. Not a war, then, but something irretrievably lost. A lost cause. Even the sun above seemed lost, a tarnished, valueless coin.

As he tried to pull himself away from thoughts of lost causes, a small movement behind him made him turn. There shouldn't be anyone else. He should be alone up here on the balcony, the Observer. His hand went instinctively for the weapon at his side, and then he relaxed, recognising that flux of blonde hair in the doorway.

'Jay,' he said, and squinted for a second as she emerged onto the light-flooded gallery from the shadows of the steps, raising a hand to hood her eyes against the sudden brightness. 'What are you doing here?'

'I spoke to Wisch. He said it'd be okay. I didn't think you'd mind.'

She smiled and, despite himself, Auger chuckled. In that moment he could have been alone with her and all might have been well. He could pretend he didn't have to turn round again and be supervising this.

'Wisch said that?'

'I told him we'd had a fight. He didn't believe me, but he knows how you felt about getting the short straw for today. He said he'd rather it had been someone else. But that's the way of it.' She came up and took his hand, Auger feeling comfort in the warmth of her fingers.

She looked out over the balcony, and fell quiet. Then she murmured, 'So many. I never imagined . . .'

He didn't know what to answer. 'Are you sure you want to stay?' he said, his voice suddenly a rasp. He swallowed, trying to smooth some feeling into it. 'You don't have to.'

Her head tilted up towards him and for a brief moment the sun forced through the stained sky and a spasm of light hit the balcony, granting her a halo and making her hair more golden than seemed possible. Then the light was gone and she was human again. She reached up to touch his cheek, and he felt the tightness inside him ease a fraction.

'Do you want me to go?' Her voice soft. Perhaps she was his sun, warming him. She could always do that to him.

'Of course I don't,' he told her. 'But I'm the Observer. I have no choice.'

'And I'm going to be your wife. I'm not having you hold all this in, Cy. It'll destroy you. You're no good at standing back.'

She was right. He wasn't a watcher. Of the two of them, Jay was that. She knew what was going to happen here, and now she had taken in the scale of it and was okay about it. That was the difference between them. She was the scientist, he was the catalyst. That's what she had told him that night weeks ago, after they had decided to marry, had made slow love and then had sat up, talking, until the dogs howled and the dawn threw its queasy glow over the street outside.

'I have a choice,' she told him, her arm gentle at his waist. She swept a finger over the balcony's crumbled brick and blew it into the air like a breath of angel powder. 'I can stay with you, and I can go. I choose to stay, Cy. To be with you.' A nod of her head took in the sea of people. 'They have a choice too. Don't forget that. You're the only one here without that.' She paused. 'But then, you could leave CMS. Wisch can find someone else.'

She left that hanging in the air. For some reason, he took it up this time. Usually he just left it. 'I'll be in Active tomorrow. After today, after this—' he glanced out at Arden's flock '—in future this is going to be a Passive function and I don't need to have anything more to do with it.'

'So just be a functionary for once. For one day. Do the job, leave. Start in Active tomorrow. Forget Passive. It's not your department, won't ever be. End of story.'

She was right, he knew, but it always surprised him that she could be so objective. They talked about it in wine, at night, the wine smoothing their views, letting them believe there was common ground. She said her attitude was just acceptance of the craziness of humanity. 'Love the ones you love, Cy, accept the ones you don't. That's all. You can change nothing.'

The wine had swirled in his glass, its colour catching the light like the gloss of ripe plums, as he had answered her, shaking his head, 'But you can help, surely. Look at what *you* do, Jay. That helps.'

'Yes,' she had said evenly. 'It helps. It doesn't change things, though.' She had gestured through the window, at the street, the buckled paving, a dead dog being dragged away through the shadows by a pair of tiny, ragged rats. 'It's too late for change.'

With no answer to that, he had just drained his glass, swallowing the bitter lees. And Jay, as always, had looked into his eyes, leaned softly into him and kissed the taste away.

5

He was aware of a swell of sound beneath the balcony. The prayers were about to start. Auger had seen the text of the service. The catechism before the cataclysm, as the News Holohead had described it. Monsignor Arden called it a service of passage, a rite of joy and homecoming. CMS called it a Leaving. Auger had a name for it too, but he kept his mouth sealed on that.

From the pulpit, Arden raised his arms, spreading his open hands to encompass the congregation, and a wave of motion spread back through the mass of people as if the priest had sown a great wind. The surge carried on down the slope, taking Auger's gaze with it, and as it vanished like a waterfall out of sight, he saw the backdrop of stricken London again. It was as if they were pointing him towards what they were leaving, telling him why.

No, he thought. Even that's no reason.

Arden's voice boomed out. 'My people, hear me. Hear me now. We are the Long Pilgrims. We are the chosen. We are the seekers of another sky. And today is Our Day.'

He punched his hands into his chest. Auger heard the thump of them, the priest sounding hollow and empty.

'TODAY IS OUR DAY!'

Beside him, Jay whispered, 'There's nothing you can do, Cy.' She might have been reading his thoughts. Sanctioning this. Licensing it. This was not the job of CMS. Not Leavings. Not to be passive in the face of this.

Arden was still speaking, his voice softer now, pressing silence onto the congregation. He was telling them of God and of destiny.

'Who are they?' Jay said, pointing at the groups of men gathering at the peripheries of the crowd. They were far away, beyond the high e-fence that contained the Long Pilgrims, but they stood out with their bright yellow smocks, chatting idly amongst themselves, passing time. The Pilgrims were chanting now, their words and any meaning lost and distorted between the near and far. Many had linked hands. Some parts of the immense throng were swaying, some were standing like statues. Auger rubbed his eyes. Even to stare at them was almost to be mesmerised.

Auger looked down at the priest again. He was throwing his hands out, clutching, striking, pleading, working his sermon. He was preaching a message of destruction in a voice of hope. But he was their guide, and he would lead their way. If he didn't, Auger could halt the whole thing. It was the only thing there was to cling to. Thinking of that, Auger pulled up Arden's body function display. The priest was fine and dandy, all his readout spikes marching smoothly along like files of drilled infantry. He was just fine. But then communion was still to come.

'Cy?'

'Sorry.' Auger managed to shake Arden's voice away. He glanced at the distant teams of yellow-jacketed men. 'They're the clearers,' he said. 'The Pilgrims paid for them, and for the disposal. Conditions of the licence. There won't be any government funding for Leavings. The cult pays for their own psych reports and Understands, the hire of the park, they even pay for the licence. Hell, Jay, they've paid for me. In future these—' he let out a breath, controlled his voice '—these events will be funding the whole of CMS, both Passive and Active. That's the idea. Can you believe it?'

Jay didn't say anything. She let some time pass, listening to the murmur and swell of prayer while Auger checked his screens. The spikes marched on. The sine waves rolled like ruffled water. The priest was fit and well and in control.

'How many are there?' Jay asked eventually.

'Over three thousand. Three thousand, two hundred and forty-eight.' He indicated a data monitor. 'I can give you a breakdown by gender, by age, ethnic group, blood group, height, hair colour—'

'There won't be any pain,' she said gently, interrupting him. 'It's what they want.'

'Will it be what they expect?' He heard the harshness in his voice.

'Is anything ever what we expect?'

'These people are going to die, Jay.'

'We all are. Their deaths will be peaceful, at the side of the people they love. If they don't go where they think, they won't know otherwise.'

The swell of noise abruptly halted, and the priest turned round. He glanced up for a moment, and his eyes met Auger's. Auger noticed a spike miss a beat on one of the screens, at the periphery of his vision. There was a look of tranquillity on Arden's face that Auger hadn't expected, and Auger felt an odd pang pass through him and vanish. For that moment he felt unbalanced, and then the priest was out of sight, concealed by the overhang of the balcony. A moment later he was in view again, rolling a heavy, slatted barrel into place beside the pulpit. He swung the barrel upright and steadied it with some effort, and it rattled into stillness. The barrel had been painted bright blue; it was the blue of a perfect summer sky, the blue of hope and memory.

A further rumbling came now, as if of distant thunder, and acolytes dressed in that same blue came into view to either side of Arden, ten of them, each controlling a barrel. The barrels stilled and the thunder ceased. Auger couldn't help looking up at the sky. Grey and dead. There were no birds, but there were never birds.

With a flourish, Monsignor Arden released the round top of his barrel and let it spin to the ground where it settled in a faint drum roll. Then he reached into the barrel and brought out a tiny flake of something. He held it up between finger and thumb for the crowd to see. It was a wafer, a shining fragment of the same blue again, a flake of perfect sky.

'This,' he said, his voice a honeyed whisper, 'is our Communion.'

The word filled the silence. There was no echo, but it seemed to remain fixed there.

As he said the word, the crowd shifted. Arden lowered his hand, and from the crowd someone came forward and took the flake from him and walked back into the mass of people, brandishing it over his head. The priest brought out another from the barrel and gave it away to the next man.

The acolytes moved now. From their barrels they took trays of Communion and handed them out to the crowd to be distributed among themselves. The Long Pilgrims moved with purpose, passing the trays back, or else queuing for a wafer and a blessing directly from the hand of Arden.

There was no impatience, no hesitation or indecision. The time for that was past. Two hundred and fifty-three who had registered and signed their Understands had either failed to turn up this morning or else turned back at the e-fence. Auger's data monitors had all their details. It gave him little comfort. Those who remained were going to take their Communion. Auger felt blunted by their certainty.

He watched the congregation become suffused with shreds of glorious sky. It was possible to follow the progress of the trays by the blossoming waves of azure. After a few minutes, unable to continue watching it, Auger began checking the arrangements for after the Leaving.

He had almost forgotten Jay was still with him, and the unexpected touch of her hand jolted him. She had been as silenced by it as him. He looked up to see the congregation almost dizzyingly speckled with blue. The distribution was all but complete.

'What is it?' Jay said, making a gesture. 'Their Communion?'

'You really want to know?'

Jay nodded.

It had been explained to Auger and the rest of the team by the Medical Director the day before, just after Auger had drawn the Observer's

8

assignment. In the silence that had followed his speech the man had asked for questions, and Auger had just looked at him and said, 'You developed this? And you say you're a medic?' Wisch had quickly shouldered him out of the room, warning the Director with a stare to keep his mouth shut. Outside, Wisch had said he'd Observe in Auger's place, but Auger wouldn't have it. 'I drew it, I'll do it. But that's it, Wisch. Never again.'

Now he recollected it for Jay. 'It's a one-bite, two-stage process. Stage one's a neurotoxin, stage two a muscle relaxant. The whole thing's in a snap matrix. You bite into it to initiate it. Apparently it tastes like peppermint. After about ten seconds, your saliva releases the neurotoxin as a gas, which induces instant loss of consciousness. Then, only when you're out, the muscle relaxant kicks in. So you stop breathing, your heart stops beating, you die. Perfect and painless.'

Jay stopped him there. 'The saliva potentiates the neurotoxin *and* the muscle relaxant?'

'No. Just the neurotoxin. It's the snap matrix that activates the muscle relaxant. That first bite. It's activated instantly, before the saliva releases the neurotoxin. But the muscle relaxant's absorbed through the mucosal tissues of the mouth, which takes about a minute, so the neurotoxin kicks in first, knocking you out. That's the whole point, obviously.' He shrugged, seeing a faint frown on her face. 'You don't even need teeth, Jay. They've thought of everything. It's delicate enough that you can crunch it with bare gums.'

Jay said nothing, just looked at him. Then she said, 'Cy—'

'Hold on. This is it.'

The priest had raised the blue wafer in his hand. He held it there for a moment, gazing as if to take in every single member of his flock.

Auger held his breath. Don't take it. Don't let him take it. Please, please don't. He looked out over the crowd, Arden's flock, seeing individual faces for the first time in the almost painted stillness. An old man, sallow-skinned, a faint tremor in his raised arm. Across to his left a woman of maybe thirty, bald, her face and skull glittering with piercings, her mouth open, ready for the flake in her hand. Behind her a man in his prime, unshaven, his hair wave-dyed red and black, the muscles of his arm sharply defined. Further back a woman with a child on her shoulders, a little boy, both brandishing their wafers. The boy had to be fourteen to have signed his Understand, though he didn't look it. He was the spit of his mother, holding her free hand with his. Beyond them, another woman, another man, a family, another, another, another.

Don't take it. Please, don't let him take it.

Arden lowered his hand with the wafer. His voice needed only to be a whisper. 'I take Communion.'

The priest opened his mouth and placed the flake on his tongue. And then his mouth closed. Above him Auger could see the small convulsive movement of his jaw.

It was done. Auger felt something heavy in his own gut, as if death had lodged there. He felt himself draw a single breath and felt it depart.

Ten seconds exactly. Auger counted them out in his head. The medics had it right. The priest collapsed like a rag. His mirrorcloak billowed as he fell and followed him down, settling gently over the priest's body. Auger just stared. The cloak's reflections were a muddle of sky and earth, and amongst them was a tiny skewed image of Auger's own face, repeated and repeated.

He pulled back to scan the balcony's displays. On a screen he watched Arden's EEG jerk, smooth and ease away, just like it should. He was unconscious. Perfect, painless. In a minute the muscle relaxant would start slowing everything down, a few minutes later Arden would be dead.

It was done. Auger was aware of Jay tugging at his arm, saying something, but he had no time for her now. That was the last of the conditions fulfilled. The priest leading. There was nothing Auger could do now but watch.

The priest's collapse was a signal to the Long Pilgrims. Now he was awaiting them, and it was their time to go to meet him again. In the congregation, the blue specks jerked and disappeared. Watching, numbed, Auger saw an odd shuffling of feet among them, a meeting of eyes, a touching of hands. He felt a stinging in his eyes and knew it for tears and not the air's burn. Only the yellow jackets were for the first time silent and still.

Auger felt for Jay's hand and found it.

Ten seconds later, marked by ten faint amber pulses on the scanner at the periphery of Auger's vision, the land seemed to shift before him. The ground seemed to drop a few metres and then lock in place once more, to disconnect and catch again. It was like a quake, almost, but happening in absolute silence, and over instantly. There was no dust, no hysteria, nothing. Three thousand people, and silence. Auger felt dizzy with it.

No, he saw that not quite everyone had fallen. A few, scattered here and there, were still standing. Maybe thirty or forty people. Auger watched them, not understanding it. It shouldn't be. They knew it too, glancing around in clear panic, seeming as uncomprehending as Auger. One of them was the young boy who was kneeling, pushing uselessly at the slack arm of his fallen mother.

Auger looked around, spotting more of them, their uprightness and movement somehow horrifying in that deathly stillness. After a moment one or two of them began aimlessly to stumble over the bodies around them, tripping and rising again, and Auger thought, What the hell's happening?

They seemed to be moving for ever, those few, as if searching for something, as if in a stagnant dream. Auger fleetingly wondered whether it was a dream of his in which they were caught. He closed his eyes hard and opened them, and it was still there.

They were making noises, some of them, he realised, sounds that weren't words for Auger to comprehend. And then, suddenly, as if by joint decision, as if a signal had passed between them, they slowed down and fell first to their knees, and then toppled all the way. One or two of them half rose once more for a few moments, but finally all were still. Auger searched for the child again, but couldn't locate him.

He shivered and let out a breath, calming himself, working it out. They hadn't taken their communion initially. Something had stopped them, or made them hesitate. Nothing more than that. Their choice, like Jay had said. But they had made it in the end.

The child, though. Auger tried not to think about the child.

On the monitors, the priest's readouts were fading and flatlining. A long, diminishing Eeep, and then just the background hum of the instruments. Arden was dead now.

Beside Auger, Jay was pale and shaking. It had hit her harder than it had hit him, he realised. He was about to say something to her when she said, urgently, her voice rising, 'You have to find them, Cy. Those last ones. You have to get to them quickly.' She looked up at him. '*Now*, Cy.'

'Why? They're dead. They made their choice in the end. They're all dead, Jay. It's over now. Like you said, end of story.' Auger felt burnt out.

A second later she sighed once, hard. She looked at him, almost spoke, then looked away again. A long time seemed to pass. The screens nilled themselves, went to grey. Jay's face was like chalk. Her voice shook. 'Well, it's too late now. They're dead now. We'd never have located them.'

'What do you mean?'

She hesitated, started to say something, the beginning of a word, then bit her lip and wouldn't say any more. Auger didn't push it. It had sounded like she was saying 'Zero'.

After that, they watched as the clearers moved in, pushing the bodies into the centre of the slope with their foam-faced 'dozers, gathering the dead into a series of pyres and preparing to set light to them. The clearers were bLinkered, and Auger knew what they were seeing, piles of rags and rubbish and no more than that. No flesh, no faces. Auger wished he could be seeing rags too, instead of that desperate child pawing at his mother's arm.

Beside him Jay activated the MagNet, and Auger made no move to stop her, grateful for the substitution of clean air and a film of defocus for the fumes of the dead. The afternoon turned slowly into night, and with the pyres, the night turned into hell. Jay held his hand as the flames rose, the impregnated shifts of the willing dead creating a brief, pure sheet of flame that lit up the city beyond like the world's end.

A few hours later, nothing remained. Everything was consumed. The clearers began to rake the smoking earth. In the sky above them, ash added to ash. It made no difference. In the end, it was all pollution.

They left in silence, just before dawn, when there was beginning to be crimson in the sky. Auger was thinking of the few late suicides, troubled by the fact that he hadn't noticed their blue flakes still held aloft a few seconds after everyone else had swallowed theirs.

Jay hadn't talked about it for months afterwards. There had been two more Leavings since that first one, but Auger was in Active by then and not involved. The Communion of the Long Pilgrims had not been used again. Another Medical Director had introduced something else.

Auger still thought about it. But whenever he tried to talk to Jay about the Leaving, she changed the subject. It troubled him that she wouldn't discuss it, because she was the stronger of them. He wondered what she was holding away from him.

And then, one night, full of wine, she had said it. Not any night. She had chosen the night before their wedding.

'Xerostomia, Cy. Dry mouth.' She threw back her head and swallowed the wine in two gulps, then took the bottle and refilled her glass. She held it up and stared into it, holding the glass still against the pale glimmer of the overhead light. It looked like blood. 'The priest was calm, wasn't he? Most of them were, calm and ready. But not all of them. They were stirred up by it, the adrenalin was flowing. Maybe they were the ones who weren't quite so sure. So the saliva dried up on them. They

12

took their communion, but they were dry. The neurotoxin wasn't activated.'

Auger put his glass down carefully. He was half-drunk already, and afraid he was going to snap the crystal stem. In his mind he saw them there again, saw them standing surrounded by the fallen, and panicking. They had taken their sky blue flakes of death, ready for the next world, but maybe not quite ready, and maybe they had thought they were spared or something. Maybe they had even spat out the wafers, but it would have been too late by then. The muscle relaxant kicked in after a minute, and took two more to take full effect. Two minutes. Auger thought about it.

'Two minutes, that's it. And only then you start to die. Not a pleasant death, Cy,' Jay murmured. Her eyes were glazed, her head drooping. Freed by the wine, she went on as if to herself, her voice fading. Auger heard every word, though.

'You're fully conscious, but your lungs stop. Every muscle in your body relaxes. You can't move, can't even blink. Not blink, can you imagine that? Can't scream, oh, no. You lie in that great field of death and you can't yell, *Christ, here I am! Help me!*' She took a long, shuddering breath, and then giggled. 'Can't do anything but think, but feel. You're in hell, Cy. You die of slow suffocation.'

Xerostomia. Zero. As she filled her glass again, spilling it down her chin as she swallowed, Auger wondered whether Jay had seen the boy with his mother.

They hadn't said any more that night. They had finished the bottle and then two more before stumbling to their bed. Jay had rolled on top of him some time during the night and wordlessly urged an erection from him, and cased it in herself until he came. His orgasm felt like a small wave dying on a moonlit beach. She had fallen asleep then in his arms, but sleep wouldn't come to Auger. In the morning, touching his cheek with her lips, Jay had just whispered, 'I meant never to tell you that, Cy. I'm sorry. You didn't need to know it.'

'No secrets,' he had answered inadequately. 'Not between us.'

She took both his hands in hers and bit her lip, looking as if about to say something more. But all she added was, 'Oh, Cy. How I love you.'

And that afternoon they had been married.

It was strange, he sometimes thought, that despite their wedding day, the dream that woke him screaming, night after night after night, even now, two years and countless Leavings on, was one of paralysed suffocation.

Jay would have explained it. Jay would have helped him through it.

But Jay was out of his reach now, and out of the reach of everyone. No one could help Jay.

TWO

'Very funny,' Sweet said. 'Very, very funny. Jacko, that's not funny at all. No one's laughing. Our boy here isn't laughing.'

Sweet jerked his head away from Jacko. 'Auger, what do you think? You think he was bitten by a vampire, too?'

Auger looked at the emaciated body with its shock of lank red hair splayed out over the blue and white striped pillow. As if the hair was full of blood. Jacko was looking at Auger for help, but Auger wasn't going to get involved in Sweet's games. Not that he could have said anything more helpful anyway. It looked like airlock trauma to Auger, like the universe had drawn breath on the kid, licked out his contents and left him a husk, shock-white and lifeless. Airlock trauma in a warm, safe bedroom on the first floor of an air-conditioned student block at GenMed. Auger said nothing and Sweet turned his malice back to Jacko.

'Okay,' Jacko said, shrugging. 'Maybe he was an albino. How about that?'

'With hair like that?'

'Could be dyed.' As if he'd got one over on Sweet. And that was not a clever thing to do to Sweet, Auger thought.

Sweet said, 'What do you know about albinos, Jacko? Do you know one thing about albinos? No, I thought not. If you're an albino you want to look normal. You want to be invisible. You don't dye your hair red for a start. Give me your hand.'

He took his subordinate's hand, folding his own thick fist around it and pulling Jacko towards the bedside. He stretched out Jacko's index finger into a pointer and swirled it above the corpse's face like he was dowsing with it, circling until Jacko and his hand were relaxed. Jacko was chancing a smirk at Auger just as Sweet jabbed his stiff finger down hard into the corpse's open eye.

Jacko pulled away, swearing.

'Now tell me what that told you,' Sweet said when Jacko had finished wiping his finger on the curtain.

'Christ, Sweet.' Jacko shook his head, his face twitching like Sweet had stiffed him into a power point. He was staring at his finger, turning it over and peering under the nail.

'I'll tell you what that told you. That told you he wasn't wearing lenses. He has blue eyes. He's not an albino. And don't play with the curtains, Jacko. They could be evidence. Forensic won't like it at all. Auger won't like it either.' He grinned at Auger.

'Oh, no. You're not giving this to me, Sweet,' Auger said. Not here, he thought. Not at GenMed.

Sweet's grin broadened. 'This is the second one, Auger. Both the same, a week apart. Both med students here, no evidence of violence in either case. Both apparently exsanguinated. The first one looked like a solo, in the bath, but this time there had to be someone else, lugging the body onto the bed afterwards. Maybe a murderer, but maybe an assistant. You want me to go on?'

The knock on the door gave Auger an excuse not to have to agree with Sweet. He squeezed himself out without letting the waiting woman see past him into the room. Giving up on that, she looked at him sourly and said, 'I'm a medic. I won't faint on you.'

She didn't look like she would either. Cool green eyes flecked with grey, and cropped russet hair that reminded him of the colour of autumn leaves back when there had been autumns and leaves to fall. She looked only a little younger than Auger, but those lines around her eyes were probably no more than exhaustion. For a moment Auger wanted to smile at her and even apologise but, like she'd said, she was a medic.

He raised his eyebrows. 'I always thought the line was, "I'm a doctor, trust me."'

She looked at him emptily. He took a moment to realise she was returning him his own look, not backing down.

'Never mind,' he said. 'I'm sure that's equally reassuring. What is it?'

'Would you please tell Detective Sweet that the school governor would like to speak to him immediately.'

'Detective Sweet is no longer in charge of this case,' Auger said. 'I'll be needing to speak to Mr Ferec anyway. You can tell him I'll be with him shortly.' He waited for her to leave, but she held her ground.

'You are Detective . . . ?' She let it hang there. She had skin so clear

Auger could almost see the delicate bones of her cheeks through it, and she was looking at him like he was contagious.

'I'm not a 'fist. I'm with Consensual Mass Suicide. My name's Auger. You can tell the governor this is a CMS case as of now.'

He left her standing there and went back inside the room. 'Okay, Sweet,' he said, cutting to it. 'I want all the case notes downstreamed to me, this one and the last. Everything you've got, Sweet.'

'I've got Jacko, Auger. You want him too?'

Jacko looked up from his nails and shot a glance at Sweet. Auger said, 'You'd better keep him, Sweet. He's the only thing ever makes you look like you can tell the devil from a dustsheet.'

Heading for the governor's office, Auger made his way down GenMed's long colonnade with its two-hundred-year-old Doric columns. To his right were the neuro wards, and he couldn't bring himself to look there, so he looked to the other side where the research wing had been built. It had already been there four years ago, when he had begun to know his way around GenMed, but now it looked unfamiliar. It wasn't just time playing with his memory, he was sure. He had been here almost daily, visiting Jay when she was working in the wing. And then later, after the wedding, he had still kept visiting her for a while following her transfer across the colonnade. Not any more, though. It was too much for him to bear, the sight of her like that.

He walked on down the long colonnade. The black glass façade of the research wing showed him himself flicking between the columns. In the reflection the columns looked quite different, and it took Auger a moment to realise that he was seeing their unprotected side, nibbled and etched by the malevolent atmosphere. He slowed his pace on the worn flagstones and moved to the colonnade's edge until he could feel the unsafe air hurling itself at the MagNet's curtain.

That was it. Of course. The research wing had been raised two storeys. The Dirangesept floors. Everyone knew that. They had just been completed when Jay . . . No. The thought and the memory behind it wouldn't be acknowledged. He reformulated it. When she had stopped working there.

He looked up. The reflected sky in the high glass was skewed and troubled, dark clouds skipping beats as they shifted across the surface. Auger stopped, staring, thinking he could see a face in the clouds, a small, steady face gazing down at him from behind the expanse of dark glass. He put the palm of his hand against a pillar, surprised briefly to find the

17

stone warm, and squinted up. The face remained there for a moment, then the cloud skidded away and he lost it in the ashen sky. Maybe a Vet in there, he thought. A Far Warrior. Maybe something more, if the stories were true. Jay had never talked about it, brushing the subject away, and he had never pushed her, appreciating that she never pushed him about his work either, if he didn't want to talk about it. That was how it had worked between them. Maybe he had been her escape, just as she had been his. Not any more, though.

He looked at the dust on his hand and tried to rub it away, but the dust simply distributed itself between the two hands. And now the work that he had been trying to escape from had become the escape.

A movement at ground level distracted him, and a medic came out of the wing, his white coat flapping in the scouring breeze, a filter held tight to his face. He dashed the few metres to the colonnade and jumped through the MagNet on to the flagstones. His coat fell instantly limp. Ahead of Auger he pocketed the filter and resumed a steady walk over to the neuro wards on the other wing. On the neuro side of the colonnade, Auger noted, the Net was extended to cover him. It was as if the research wing was deliberately set apart from the rest of GenMed. Dissuading visitors. Quarantined, maybe.

The medic glanced back at Auger from the entrance to neuro, reacting to Auger's casual attention, and Auger found his eyes momentarily and uncomfortably held by the man who paused in mid-stride and stared as if he knew Auger. His face seemed mildly disfigured, maybe scarred or burnt. Auger felt himself redden. Perhaps the stare was a challenge to Auger to gaze on or avert his eyes, but then the medic broke the eye contact before Auger could look away or make out what the disfigurement was, and shot through the doorway to disappear into the neuro wards.

Auger walked on towards the governor's office, his heart pounding. He was sure he'd never seen the man before. He put his filter to his face, as if he'd just breathed some bad air.

There was a glass bell jar on the governor's desk, and something foetal suspended in the murky, speckled green fluid. Its shrivelled flesh was almost the colour of the liquid. Auger could hardly make it out. He moved his head around, the curve of the glass swelling and stretching what was inside, giving it the illusion of movement. Its splayed toes seemed to be paddling and it appeared to be following Auger with its tiny squinty eyes.

18

'Yes, Mr Auger, it is watching you. It is alive. That isn't formaldehyde. That's its universe.' Ferec tapped the jar with his knuckle and the thing inside began slowly to move its head towards the stimulus. 'It's the consequence of an experiment that failed. I keep it here as a reminder.'

'A reminder, Ferec? Christ. A reminder of what?' Auger looked away from the thing, feeling faintly dizzy.

'Of my responsibility, Mr Auger. Of the importance of humility.'

Ferec waited for a reaction, smiling neutrally, looking at Auger.

Auger let him wait. Ferec didn't look much like a medic, but that still didn't incline Auger to trust him. He'd heard about Ferec. He guessed the man saw GenMed as a platform to power, and that was all. The governor could have been a second-tier politician, already accustomed to corruption and its fruits. The shoulders of his pale blue suit were as square and sharp and creaseless as his features.

'Humility,' Auger said. 'You keep it alive for that? You're sure it's not just to scare the natives? Not just an executive pet?'

The governor rested the flat of his palm against the glass and said mildly, 'We're getting off on the wrong foot here, aren't we? I understand the death of Rudd Merchant is now being investigated by CMS. I have to say I'm rather puzzled by that.' The head in the jar shifted to nuzzle beneath the shadow of Ferec's hand.

'Both deaths.' Auger was conscious that he was in danger of losing control. Ferec was needling him, trying to prod him into an outburst. He said, 'The death of Neffer Haenson last month will be re-examined.'

Ferec sat back, withdrawing his hand from the jar and leaving a brief fogged print of his palm on the curved glass. Beneath it, the thing's mouth half opened in a slow swirl of liquid.

'Haenson simply committed suicide,' Ferec said slowly and firmly, nodding the statement home with jabs of his head, a hammer sinking a nail. 'That was never in question. The post-mortem was carried out right here. He slit his wrists in a warm bath.' The governor mimed it, right hand to left, the indicated cut lengthways down the arm, the neat efficient way a medic would do it. And at the same time showing Auger he knew more about it than Auger did, that this was his territory and not Auger's. He straightened his perfect cuffs again, taking his time, and smiled at Auger.

'Maybe so,' Auger said stiffly. 'I haven't examined the notes yet. But I can tell you this much, Ferec. Haenson *looked* like solo suicide, Merchant *could* have been assisted suicide. But they both slit their wrists. There's a connection by *modus*.' Auger used the word deliberately, letting Ferec

19

know he could forget the Latin. Auger knew enough about medics. And Ferec was worse than just a medic, as far as Auger was concerned. He was an Administration-appointed medic. 'If they were both suicides, we may have consent or collusion by the victims. Two may be a rolling snowball, and with a possible ritual element as well we could be seeing the lead-in to a non-registered consensual mass suicide. CMS. My job's to prevent that, Ferec, not to document it.'

'Don't tell me that. You look for cults, Auger. I know how you work at CMS. Do you have any idea how much damage it could do to the hospital if it got out that you were prowling around here?' He paused, then backtracked, as Auger knew he would. 'Ritual element? What ritual element?'

Auger stood up and squared his shoulders, trying to ease away his tension. 'I'll be in touch, Governor.'

Ferec held up a hand. 'Wait. Wait, Auger. You'll need an autopsy on Merchant. I'll arrange it for you. I'll do it myself. You'll have whatever you need. GenMed has nothing to hide. Let's just get this cleared up as quickly as we can, eh?'

'Thank you, Governor. But you needn't worry about the autopsy. It'll be carried out by an independent pathologist.' Auger glanced at the thing in the bell jar and turned around, but Ferec called out and stopped as he reached the door. 'Auger.'

Auger pulled the heavy door open before glancing back at the governor, not letting go of the brass doorknob. 'Yes?'

'Auger. Auger. Should I know that name?' Ferec had meshed his fingers and made a temple of them. He was frowning and staring hard at Auger.

Auger hesitated. Then he said, 'I don't know, but maybe you ought to remember it.' And then he walked out and closed the door solidly behind him.

Walking out of the building, his filter on, Auger turned first towards the colonnade and then away again. Once through there was enough for one day. He left GenMed by one of the back gates, feeling irritated with himself. Ferec was a bastard with stuff to hide, but he had probably been right. This wasn't a CMS case. Ferec was just worried about collateral damage to GenMed during a CMS investigation, the incidental uncovering of negligent deaths, drug misuse, the exposure of hospital corruption. Ferec wanted the 'fists because the 'fists were, first, case-focused, and, second, incompetent.

Auger trudged through the shadows of the narrow streets with their tall terraces shouldering away the dull sky. He should have stood up to Sweet. Probably would have if it hadn't been for that woman medic and then the shit of a governor. And that thing in the bottle. Auger shivered to think of it.

Without any conscious intention, he found himself turning in the wrong direction for his office and crossing London Bridge. There was a slight breeze coming off the water, its taint of acid and rot faintly penetrating Auger's filter. Auger put his head down and carried on, not bothering to glance over the broken and rusted railing that topped the parapet. The river had no beauty, no aura of raw nature. It was simply a matrix for what floated there, the orange blobs of waste visgel, the scraps of plastic and wood, and the small salvage boats that bumped and ground their way through the undulating wreckage, picking the pockets of the floating dead, dredging the silt for what little might be recycled.

On the far side of the Thames, the City was almost completely deserted now, the mostly collapsed financial buildings just an Ozymandian monument to a brazen past. In a world concertinaed by disaster, financial markets had no meaning any more, no existence. The only markets that mattered now were the real markets, the food markets.

The cracked redundant buildings hung over Auger, swallowing the light and making dusk out of the early afternoon. The ash here was thick and Auger adjusted his mask, raising the filter level until he could almost taste the carbon. The 'dozers seldom came to clear these streets any more. No priority. Auger didn't mind at all. He liked the City like this, with its silence and emptiness. It was where he used to come after visiting Jay at neuro. It had always cleared his mind, the sight of something at peace, even if it was only a graveyard peace.

Walking on into the ash, Auger nilled the alert on his mobile tasker and slid it back into his pocket. He wondered why he hadn't told Ferec about Jay, especially when the governor had been so close to it. Maybe he hadn't wanted Ferec's false sympathy. Or else he'd just wanted that last jab at the man. That hadn't been necessary, any more than the crap about a ritual element to the murders. It had been a stupid thing to say. But that thing in the jar had really shaken him. Alive, Jesus. And the way it had seemed to be staring at him.

He thought of the bloodless kid dead on the bed. He'd been intending to go back and tell Wisch he didn't want the case after all, but maybe he would take it. He hadn't seen Jay for months now, unable to face the changelessness in her, the terrible, haunting memories, but perhaps if he were on a case at GenMed it would be easier to walk across to the neuro wards and start seeing her once more.

Auger sighed, the filter's resistance turning the exhalation into a sharp snort that gave him a start. And being at GenMed, he thought, would give him an excuse to wander through the City again.

He stopped and rubbed his forehead, easing a finger under the mask's seal over the bridge of his nose, worrying at the score it had made on his skin. Looking at the ash-blurred Bank of England with its splintered columns and fractured steps, he realised how much those walks had meant to him. He noticed that the ash on the steps was sitting unevenly, as if the building had recently been visited. Squatters, maybe, or would-be looters.

He tried to picture Jay's face, and found he couldn't. That gave him pause, and he felt guilt digging at him. He'd left it too long. The woman he had married, and he couldn't remember her.

He moved on. Maybe it was a good thing, though. Maybe now was the time to finish it, to cut away, start again. He toyed with that thought as he walked, knowing, as he had always known, that he could never do that.

So maybe now was the time to open it again, to deal with who was responsible.

Coming out at last on to the Strand, he eased back his filter level and headed back towards the office.

Auger knew something bad was up by the big grin Roke gave him from the desk as he came into the building.

'Hey, Auger, you been a bad boy again? Wisch wants to see you.'

'You're only mad because no one ever says they want to see you, Roke,' Auger told him. But something had to be up. Being ignored by Roke was a good sign. Being sworn at was a better one. Roke's attitude to Auger was the general response that Auger got from the 'fists. Geniality from him was very bad.

And finding Wisch's office empty and the door open was bad too, doubly bad. Wisch grew anxious beyond the security of his room. It had to be something serious to flush him from it. And Wisch was a closer of doors.

Auger went straight to his own office. Wisch was waiting there, looking no happier than he ever did in the open.

'What is it that you do, Auger? What exactly do you do? I don't mean here, I mean . . .' he sighed, deflated. 'You know what I mean.'

Auger said nothing. Maybe it was nothing after all. Wisch would cool down. He always did in the end.

'I've been looking through your caseload.' Wisch's fingers were fanning over the keys and Auger suddenly couldn't remember whether he had carried out his shutdown routine before closing down the system last night. Wisch was making to twist the screen so that Auger could read it too, but then he paused and pulled it abruptly back towards himself.

Shit, Auger thought. He craned his neck but his angle on the screen was too acute. All he could see was a faint blur of text laid over the reflection of the door to his office, the double-reversed lettering on the frosted glass that should have read CY AUGER. CMS DEPT. PLEASE CALL AGAIN LATER. He noticed for the first time that everything after his name had been neatly wiped and over-etched SAD FUCK. PLEASE LEAVE ME ALONE. Thank you, Derace Sweet, Auger thought. He wondered how long that had been there. Wisch hadn't even mentioned it. Months, probably.

'What's this?' Wisch muttered. Auger bent further but still couldn't make out the screen. He could just read SAD FUCK more clearly. He wasn't sure if Wisch was talking to himself or to Auger.

'What? Let me see,' Auger said warily. He began to reach out to the monitor.

'No.' Wisch batted him away. 'Jesus, Auger, what the hell are you playing at?' He swung the monitor round and pointed. 'Records, Auger. Trail of logic. What the hell is this? This is a mess. How the hell do you function?'

'You know how I function, Wisch. I function in the real world. Paper.' Auger jabbed at the screen. 'You know how I am with these things. I don't understand them. Let me see . . .' He miskeyed a few times and then pulled up an options readout. He punched the board again and the words came, blue ice letters on a backcloth of ash.

'Here we are,' Auger said, sitting back.

```
The Church of Final Hope.
  File status: Active.
Subfiles:
  1. preacher
  2. theology
  3. church location
  4. congregation analysis
  5. termination risk analysis
```

After a minute, Auger said, 'So there it is. Exactly what is it you want to see, Wisch?'

'That's fine. It wasn't that.' Wisch pushed a key and an untitled file blinked into view. 'This. I can't access it.'

Auger frowned and punched it a couple of times. It wouldn't open. An error message flashed up. 'Damn,' Auger muttered. 'I don't know what happened there.'

Wisch sighed. 'Auger.' He played with the keyboard for a moment and then gave up on it. 'I don't suppose you have any idea what file that was.'

Auger shrugged. 'Something dead. You know all I've got. You allocate me, remember? It'll all be on paper somewhere. You need it now? Is this what you're here for?'

Wisch glanced around at the piles of paper jammed into every corner of the office. 'No. I just had a call from the governor of GenMed.'

That was it. Auger began to relax. 'Ah. Ferec. I'm not surprised. He's the sensitive kind.'

Wisch rubbed his forehead. The creases didn't go away. 'I think this is a record even for you, Auger. Between seeing the corpse and getting back to the shop.'

Auger nilled the monitor, watching the words melt slowly away and night consume the ash. 'He wants CMS out of GenMed? I wouldn't blame him for that. I'd want it too.'

'Maybe he wants that, but that's not quite how he put it. Sensitive he may be, but delicate he isn't. Ferec wants you gone first, Auger. Priority Alpha. Immediate.'

'Me? Why?'

'Jay. He says her presence at the unit there would distract you.' Wisch settled in his chair and looked at Auger. His voice dropped a notch, slowed down. 'How is she? Did you go to see her?'

Auger scratched at his chin. He needed a shave. Ferec hadn't wasted any time. He'd probably upscreened Auger and found Jay there before the door had even closed behind him. 'No, I didn't. I didn't feel like it. After seeing Ferec I wasn't in the mood.' He looked at Wisch's sagging cheeks and hangdog eyes, and sighed. 'I don't know how Jay is. Except that nothing's changed. It never changes, does it?' Auger felt helpless. He was angry with Ferec for Wisch asking him the question. 'Ferec's wrong. If she's there and they've got a problem, then I'm going to be focused, aren't I?'

There was a silence. Auger knew he should try to smooth it over but his voice was coming out rough. The silence extended, seeping into the corners of the room, and Auger let it settle, not knowing what else to do.

Eventually Wisch said, 'She's been there how long now? Two years?'

'And three, no, four months. It's what, February?'

'It's April, Auger.'

Auger looked at the wall. 'Time goes,' he murmured. It goes, he thought. Not for Jay, but it slides by for me, though. He stared through the open door at the corridor with its curling posters of blank-eyed murderers captioned with their rewards. The same pictures had been there as long as Auger could remember. It was all pointless. No one was going to give those men and women up for money. No one wanted money now. They wanted a future. Certainty. Auger sighed. April, he thought. A line from a poem came fleetingly into his head. It seemed to fit. The dead land.

Wisch stood up. 'Okay. I want you on another admin course, Auger. I don't like inaccessible files. And don't point at that pile of goddamn paper.'

'You're not taking me off this case, Wisch.'

Wisch gestured towards the dead screen. 'You've got the Final Church. I shouldn't even have let you take that. How's it going? When did you last update me?'

'Let me have this one too.'

'Hell, Auger, I thought I was doing you a favour here. According to Sweet, you didn't want it.'

'I changed my mind. It looks interesting.' He shrugged.

Wisch sat down again. 'I don't understand you at all, Auger. I've looked at Sweet's notes. I glanced at the other death, the Haenson case. There's obviously a connection, but at this stage CMS is a stretch.' He swung the chair in a big circle, slowing to face Auger again. 'Ferec was bleating about some ritual connection between the deaths that you'd thrown at him. I went through everything Sweet had and there was nothing except this vampire crap of Jacko's, and if that's pointing anywhere it's pointing to murder, not suicide, and that's a Pacifist matter. Which takes it right back up the corridor to Sweet.'

'Sweet didn't think so.'

Wisch made a noise that Auger didn't recognise for a moment. He'd never heard it from Wisch before, and he took a moment to work it out. Wisch's lips had stretched and he was actually chuckling. It seemed to have surprised Wisch too.

'Well, well, that's a flag, that really is. Cy Auger covering Derace Sweet's ass.' Wisch leaned forward and lowered his voice, and said, 'Sweet's a lazy bastard, Auger. You're not the only one to know that. But Ferec's got a point, from what I've seen. I can't justify a CMS investigation on this. It's too thin.'

He stood up again, straightening his trousers with the palms of his hands. 'Look, I'll tell you what. I can block GenMed for one more day, but you're going to have to come up with something hard to let me justify CMS involvement. In the meantime I'm going to be as chummy as I can with Ferec and accept his offer of an autopsy at GenMed.' He glanced at the palms of his hands. 'I can't justify taking that away from him. What the hell was that about, Auger? GenMed's not under suspicion. And we haven't the funds for an independent pathologist anyway.' He shook his head at Auger. 'It's Ferec, isn't it? That's all. If Ferec hadn't shoved his snout into it, you'd be in my office begging me to pull you off the case. I'll bet you'd even be telling me you wanted to stay clear of it because of Jay.'

He made for the door, but turned round when he got there. 'Oh, by the way, Auger, is your tasker working? Have you checked your messages this afternoon?' He pointed to the monitor. 'I couldn't help noticing. Some-one's pretty keen to talk to you.'

Auger let the door close on Wisch and flicked on his mobile tasker. He hadn't checked it since leaving GenMed. Walking through the City, thinking of Jay.

The screen blued, beeped at him and carried on beeping as a rack of two-liners scrolled down the face. Identical, thirty-four of them timed between two-twelve and five twenty-two. When the scroller hit the rack's base, the beeping stopped. And then the tasker beeped once more as he watched, and the lime green two-liner replicated itself one more time.

URGENT. FLY.

Shit, Auger thought.

THREE

Fly wasn't answering his doorbell, so Auger let himself in. It was easy enough, despite the laser-bolt Fly had fitted a few months ago after his third break-in inside a week. There was nothing at all wrong with the bolt. The trouble was that the door had warped with the climate swings, and with the constant rifts and terrashifts the frame wasn't true any more either. Even at the best of times you just had to lean hard in the right place and the door surrendered. On particularly wet days Fly had to leave it unlocked altogether and trust in the apathy of thieves.

Today a smack on the lock with the palm of his hand was sufficient to get Auger inside. The technology worked, he reflected, closing the door behind him. It was the fabric that was screwed. That and the people. Everything else was just fine.

He closed the door and looked around. The room was almost bare. Just Fly's holozone hardware and a small table and two metal frame chairs. Bare floors, bare walls. No imprint at all. No clues to Fly. After a few months of knowing him, Auger had just stopped looking for them. It was easier that way.

He went to the window to stare out at the street below. The sofglass was set to semi-trans and Auger could see himself faintly projected onto the world. The image made him uncomfortable and he moved back into the room, settling down in one of the hard chairs to wait.

After half an hour Fly came through the door and threw a short glance at Auger. 'Where the hell were you all day? I hope no one followed you here.'

'You aren't all I've got, Fly. And no one followed me. Don't worry.' Auger shook his head. 'You look like shit. No, you don't even look that good. Where have you been?'

'I thought I had a tail. I panicked. Are you sure you weren't followed?'

'Calm down, Fly. It's me, Auger.' Auger wondered what was so urgent, but he knew not to push Fly. Maybe it was Fury at last, but maybe it was just Fly needing to dump some paranoia on Auger.

Fly was at the window, looking out. Auger wondered what he could see that Auger hadn't. What the same things meant to him. Something wasn't right inside his skull but, then, who was to say nothing was wrong inside Auger's? Just different faults, he supposed. But, then, our faults define us. We're all the same template, just with different bugs.

He stopped that thought in its tracks and headed for the kitchen. 'You want a drink?'

'Coffee,' Fly called after him. The man was so twitchy he used caffeine to flatten it off a bit. Auger poured what was left in the coffee jar into a mug, and looked through the doorway while he waited for the water to boil, to see Fly standing in the centre of the room bathed in curdled green light. He had his eyes closed and seemed to be swaying there, washed from head to foot by emerald shadows. The chitter and hum of insects and the calls of birds came into the kitchen, and the green glow shaded the doorframe and blurred the edge of the flooring.

'Nil it, will you?' Auger said as he entered the zone, handing the mug to Fly. The walls had receded and the program had sent broadleaved vines across the doorway to the kitchen so that the neon-lit room was as distant as far memory.

Fly drained the mug and set it down on the litter of leaves that had been a table before the program had kicked in. Insects swooped above it.

'This is a Dirangesept environment, Fly. Isn't it?'

Fly looked away towards the window, which was a gap in the trees through which Auger could make out a distant sunlit plain. A small herd of animals moved there, grazing, a cloud of drifting points. Staring out at them, Fly murmured softly, 'What if it is?'

'You're not getting involved, are you?'

Fly turned around slowly. His face was oddly free of expression. He seemed to look right through Auger, as if Auger were the illusion here. 'I was always involved. I just never told you. But I think you knew, Auger. I think you knew all along.'

In the distance the sun was sinking beyond the plain. The animals filtered through a scattering of tall trees and disappeared. Auger didn't know what to say to Fly. He wondered if it was the truth. Had he known all along?

'Tell me, Fly,' he said, picking up the empty mug. A beetle crawled over the lip and flopped to the ground to crawl beneath a drift of glossy leaves.

Auger swore and dropped the mug. A faint clatter of china on tile penetrated the programmed rustle of dry leaves. 'Can you nil this god-damn program, Fly? Talk to me.'

Fly rubbed his eyes. 'Are you prepared? I think it's going to be tomorrow. The past few services have been getting more extreme, and last time he told us all to be there tomorrow for a special event. He told us to be ready for the Leaving. He's taking us there. Dirangesept.' Fly closed his eyes and licked his lips with the word. Dirangesept.

Auger felt a cold jolt of adrenaline. 'Fury said that? You're sure? He said the Leaving?'

Fly nodded.

'He say anything about registering with CMS? About Understands?'

Fly raised his eyebrows. 'Are you kidding?'

'Okay, I had to ask. I'll check it later anyway.' Auger felt the thump of his heart. All this time spent waiting, and now it was here he felt unready, knocked off balance. He made himself think, be logical. 'Look, Fly, I don't think you should be there. I'll find some way to bug the place, something else. I want you safe and clear when it goes down. You've done your part. It's mine now.'

Fly gave Auger a tight smile. 'No,' he said.

'What do you mean, no?'

There was a small silence before Fly said, softly, 'It's not *for* you, Auger. It was never for you. I don't know exactly what's going to happen tomorrow, but I'm going to be there. I'm telling you this now so that you know. So that if something goes wrong you can make sure he doesn't get away with it. I know you've been using me, Auger, but I'm using you too, so you shouldn't feel too bad about it.'

'Fly—' Auger began, but he could see there was no point. Fly had already half turned towards the plain again, where now the trees had shadows longer than themselves, and the rich ochre of the earth beneath the low sun had the transient intensity of a dream.

He had been using Auger? How? How could it be that way round?

Auger looked back and tried to see it. It couldn't be. Fly had contacted him a few months ago, saying he'd got himself involved with the Church of Final Hope and it was worrying him, the preacher talking about a fast track to Dirangesept; no CrySis, no rocket ships, and no risk from the beasts. Auger's ears had pricked immediately. Father Fury, at long last. Fly told him he'd heard the stories of cults, of mass killings dressed up as suicides, so he'd come to CMS, not knowing what else to do.

Auger had known about Fury for as long as he could remember, Father

29

Fury and his Church of Final Hope. He'd been after him for years, but nothing had ever stuck to the preacher. The stories were never quite proved, the suicides never connected to him. Fury had once even approached CMS voluntarily and told Auger that he was no more than a poor preacher of the Word of God, and God loved his flock and would never harm a single hair of a single one of them. Auger had listened to the words and recognised the light in Fury's eyes, and it wasn't the light of the Lord. But the preacher was as clean as chrome and knew it. He knew his way around all the rules of Faith. He knew the regulations better than he knew the Ten Commandments. Auger had stared into Fury's livid eyes and known that Fury's God was a god of hate and burning hellfire, and by the preacher's smile he'd also understood that Fury wanted him to know that.

And they had faced each other politely in Auger's office, each knowing these things and knowing the other's knowing, and then Auger had stood up and thanked Father Fury for his assistance, for coming into the department, and Fury had thanked Auger for his understanding, and left, smiling. That had been just weeks before Auger had married Jay. Fury had even known about that somehow, wishing Auger all the happiness he deserved from the door. He had even named the day. Fury. Father Fury.

So when Fly had arrived in the department a few months back, an insider in the Church of Final Hope, it had been like a gift to Auger. A gift from God.

How could that have been Fly using Auger?

'There is something I haven't told you,' Fly said, interrupting Auger's thoughts. 'Something else.'

Night was falling on the plain now, the rich colours fading.

'What's that?' Auger said, not really listening, thinking instead of the light in Father Fury's eyes, of Jay. Of retribution and revenge.

'I think you should know that my father was on the second Dirange-sept project.'

Auger took a minute to process that. 'Your father? On D2?' He automatically shook his head. 'No. That isn't possible.'

There weren't any dependants. The Far Warriors were all unattached, childless. Of course, everyone knew there were babies born in the months after the Warriors left on their eighteen-year frozen journey, but those babies were all removed from their mothers and anonymously adopted, never knowing, never told. Auger considered the alternative for the infants, growing up fatherless and then meeting your father off the ships, your father young enough by then to be your son. Your father who in thirty-seven years had aged just that single, terrible year the Warriors spent out of CrySis, that year on Dirangesept getting the hearts and souls ripped out of them by the beasts.

But Auger thought he knew everything about Fly, and one of the things he was absolutely certain of was that Fly was fifty-two years old. He would have been five when the Far Warriors set off, and forty-two when they returned. But no one with a five-year-old child would have been accepted for the project.

Auger stood staring at him, working it out, trying to make sense of it and hoping it made none. 'It would have been picked up,' he murmured. 'Someone with a kid, they'd never have let them go.'

Fly reached down to turn over a leaf on the forest floor. Something bright scuttled away in a blur of stubby legs, searching for better cover. 'The Administration misses nothing, huh? Bullshit. Listen to me, Auger. My father was fifteen years old when I was born. He was twenty and I was five when he left. No one outside our families ever knew I was his son. That's why it wasn't picked up by the Project.'

'I still don't—'

'My mother was nine. That's why. She was born a synDorphin dependant thanks to her own mother, went through puberty at eight, died at home of heart failure in childbirth having me. No one even knew she was pregnant until then. Everyone thought I was food-poisoning until I dropped out of her. If the truth had come out, I'd have been taken away. So my mother's parents registered me as their own.' Fly shrugged. 'SynDorphin metabolism. No one even questioned it. My grand-parents brought me up as their son.'

Fly had a faraway look in his eyes. 'But I found out he was my father. They told me when I was fourteen, when the ships were halfway to Dirangesept. He left to find me a better world, a place where I could play, where I could grow old and die of nothing but age. And when he came back he had failed. But he hadn't failed for me, Auger. He came back exactly as I had remembered him. He hadn't changed at all, except in his head. I didn't want a new world, you see. I just wanted my father.'

Fly seemed abruptly small and lost in the green forest. Softness mellowed his voice. 'You know, Auger, that's a strange thing, being an adult and then meeting your father like that. But it was worse for him. He knew how much I loved him, but he couldn't accept seeing me. All I reminded him of was his failure.'

Auger touched Fly on the arm, not knowing what else to do. Fly didn't seem to notice the gesture. He was somewhere else entirely.

31

'Two months after he came back, Auger, he joined the Final Church. And three weeks after that, he killed himself.'

Auger took that in. 'I'm sorry. You should have told me this before. You should have said.'

Fly let out a small sharp noise that lost itself in the jungle, and said, 'Really? And what would you have done?' The brief softness was gone from Fly. He didn't give Auger a chance to answer. 'I've thought about it. One of two things. Either you would have withdrawn me as psychologically vulnerable, and lost your key to Fury, or you would have tried to forget I'd told you anything at all about my father, so you could carry on with the case. But you'd have felt bad about that and you'd have lost your edge. You're a good man, Auger, and those are bad choices. I didn't want you to have to make that decision.'

Fly looked around at the zone, the world that had taken his father, and said, 'This way it suits us both. Now it's too late for either of us to back out.'

'No, it's not,' Auger began, but he knew Fly was right. Auger wanted this as much as Fly did. He swallowed, his mouth dry. 'Okay, Fly. I just need to know you're sure about it.'

'Never more, Auger,' he said. 'Never more sure.'

Auger nodded. Then he looked towards the window and took a long breath, drawing with it the moist pungency of the jungle. It felt that he was inhaling time, time that stretched back centuries. For the first time in years, he was relaxed. He was about to turn back towards Fly when he felt a stinging sensation just behind his shoulder, and simultaneously the slap of a hand there.

'What was that!'

Fly was staring at his palm, frowning. 'I don't know. Some sort of wasp? Big. Maybe a hornet. I think I must have missed it.' He turned Auger round and ran the flat of his hand over his shoulderblade.

'Hey!' Auger flinched.

'I guess it got you, whatever it was. Is it painful?'

'When you do that. Leave it.' He tried to reach it with his own hand, but couldn't quite get there. He rolled his shoulder and felt a mild, fading discomfort.

'You're not allergic, are you?'

'No. Whatever it was, I'm not going to die from it.' The pain was almost gone already. Maybe it had only been Fly's slap in the first place and nothing more. Just this crazy man seeing things in his zone.

He shook his head to clear it. 'I'll have to go and start setting it up, then. Tomorrow morning's not far away.' He paused stupidly, wanting to say something more to Fly but finding nothing, and in the end he just settled for, 'I'll see you back here afterwards. We can talk then.'

Fly reached out a hand towards Auger and said, 'I would have done it anyway, you know. Remember that. Just like you. So don't feel anything bad. And another thing. I didn't choose you lightly, Auger, remember that, too. Our coming together wasn't coincidence. I did my research on you before I contacted you in the first place. I knew what I wanted from you, and I needed to know how you'd react. I think I know you pretty well.'

He waited for Auger to get to the door before adding, 'I live in this room, Auger. And this zone, and somewhere else my father went. I want you to know something, in case I don't see you afterwards. Listen to me. Listen. I want you to know that everything that's important to me is right here.'

Auger looked at Fly in the centre of his jungle, his arms spread to encompass the zone, the pale doorway to the tiny kitchen and Auger himself, and didn't know what he felt except a gnawing sense of approaching disaster. But he knew he would have done it anyway. Fly was right. Auger wouldn't have pulled him out even if he had known that Fly was a Far Warrior's child. Auger had his own personal reason for wanting Fury, and he didn't feel like telling it to Fly just now.

But, then, Auger wasn't the one about to put his life on the line.

Fly abruptly smiled at Auger, relaxed and easy, as if the whole thing was a story they'd concocted between themselves and now the game was over, instead of just beginning. He said, 'Tell me, Auger, do you have a child?'

'I thought you said you'd done your research on me.' Jay came into his mind, and he squeezed his eyes against the memory. 'No. No kids.'

'No. That's what I thought. No child.' The jungle seemed to close around Fly, camouflaging him in green shadow. He seemed to be waiting for something else from Auger, but Auger didn't know what it could be. Sometimes Fly was beyond understanding.

Auger gave up. 'I'll see you after it,' he said.

'Yes,' Fly told him, turning away into the zone. 'I'll see you after.'

FOUR

Wisch stood up at the head of the room. He was tall enough not to need the extra height but those joints needed the exercise, the flux of movement. He stood there for a few seconds, staring around the room slowly, as if not believing who was there, and then went back to stare again at Sweet, presumably for Auger's benefit, and then once more, harder, at Auger. Also for my benefit, Auger thought. Not even Wisch did anything for the benefit of Sweet. Everything Sweet did was for himself, and that was more than enough.

'Okay,' Wisch said, his lilt stretching the word out into four syllables. Then crisply, like snapping a lock on it, 'Hyde Park.'

The words crystallised a map onto the screen behind him, the density of trees etched in umber, the grass in the palest of jades. The rift that ripped from the Serpentine to the Mall was a fat slash of jet black lightning. Wisch pointed up the tiny, innocuous square of daffodil yellow scored beside the rift's jag.

'The Church of Final Hope,' he said, and paused. 'Used to be called the Final Church, some of you may recall.'

Standing at the back, Auger looked around the room. None of them would remember that. They were too young. They didn't even remember when their autoids would have had three legs, why they were called trigs in the first place. They didn't remember the past or what it meant, any of it. To Auger it sometimes seemed that the past was all there was. To them it meant nothing, just five minutes more of Wisch.

'Auger, you want to take over?' Wisch was moving aside, sliding into his chair. He looked disjointed, his head rocking on a flurry of shoulders and elbows. Auger nodded towards him. There hadn't been any time to talk about Ferec and GenMed, which Auger was happy about. Wisch had set up the briefing with the 'fists within an hour of Auger bringing him up

34

to date with Fly's information. He could think later about what he wanted to do with the case at GenMed. Now it was nearly midnight, and Fury's service was set for nine a.m.

Auger started down towards the front, aware of the atmosphere changing as he came through them, the 'fists shifting their chairs only enough to make it possible for him to stumble past, not to make it easy. They tolerated Wisch, who was the head of CMS, because he had honorary Pacifist rank, but not Auger who was pure CMS. Even though Auger, unlike Wisch, had one time been a 'fist. That was 'fist logic. Wisch was an outsider, but Auger was an outcast.

'Father Fury,' Auger began. 'Preacher of the Final . . . of the Church of Final Hope. It's been a closed sect for a few years. We've had it on Amber for several months. Fury has a past, but nothing we could ever stick on him.'

Saying that, Auger tried not to think of Jay. They weren't interested, anyway. Sweet was casually cracking his knuckles, others were leaning over and whispering to each other. Auger tried to move on, conscious that it was as much his fault as theirs. He looked for something to fix them back on him. 'My information is that Fury has a high-quality zone, a Dirangesept mimic. And I mean very high quality. It's probably an unauthorised clone of the training zone they're using for the D3 project, except it's been sterilised, so there's no beast software.'

He looked at the dozen kids who were Sweet's crew. Most of them, most 'fists now, were D3 rejects, resenting any reminder of it. It wasn't important for Auger to be giving them the background, and he wondered why he was bothering to tell them. It was just how he always conducted a briefing.

'Father Fury was a veteran of the second project. When he came back he became a biblist and set up the Final Church. He preached hellfire and damnation. We were all damned and the Earth was to be our hell. By Fury's logic, escaping to 'Sept was against God, and so the Far Warriors had defied God. The D1 and D2 Vets were his congregation. Under his ministry there was a plague of self-mutilation and suicide. It seems he also got his hooks into a games company called Maze, and there's some indication that the director fell under Fury's influence and killed himself along with most of the Vets on the research team. But nothing was ever proved against Fury.'

Auger waited in case anyone had a question. Sweet stared straight at him and opened his mouth wide in a long, audible yawn. Jacko giggled.

None of them remembered it. It was hardly spoken of. Four years back, the Maze/Fury case had ripped the guts out of CMS. Its chief investigator, Madsen, had resigned and then vanished, and Wisch had been moved in from Faith and Auger from Pacifism. Then Faith had decided to license Leavings and split CMS right down the middle into two wings. Active and Passive. Now Active was just Wisch and Auger, and Passive was a vast complex teeming with clerks.

Auger often thought about Madsen. He heard rumours and occasionally saw the name on old files, though he never came across anything solid on the Maze/Fury case. Wisch said the notes on that were vaulted, which Auger knew was Wisch's way of saying it was Sodom and Gomorrah, look back at it and you'll be a pile of salt.

Auger shifted his feet and went on. 'After that, Fury went to ground for a few years. Then he resurfaced, claiming to have been reborn.'

Auger stopped abruptly, Jay in his mind, Fury wishing him well for his wedding, knowing about it and making sure Auger knew that. Fury the only suspect and nothing ever proved. It had to have been Fury, but Sweet had screwed it up.

Silence in the room. Auger cleared his throat, avoiding Wisch's eye. 'And it seems that now Fury has access to a clone of this zone, and he's putting it over as true access to Dirangesept.'

'Fuckin' dingdong,' someone sniggered. Jacko.

'I don't know. They say it's possible,' another voice said. 'You know the D2 Vets came back with tagalongs. Beasts in their brains. They say the beasts can take 'em back there any time.'

'They say you can walk Oxford Street without a filter,' Sweet sneered.

'But you said Fury was a Vet, Auger. Maybe he's got a beast up there.'

'Or maybe he's just got a bat in his belfry, like Auger here,' Sweet added, jerking a finger at his skull.

'It's a zone, Oswell,' Auger said, identifying the previous speaker. Auger knew him a little. Oswell had a few years on the rest of Sweet's crew. He even acknowledged Auger when they passed in the corridor. 'Forget about the beasts.' He was aware of Wisch's head turned to look at him. He tried to pull the whole thing back together, forget about Jay. Sweet was grinning lazily at him.

Auger pushed on. 'It's just a zone, but that's the track Fury's riding, and those are the rumours that built him a congregation of about five hundred. I've got a man inside, and he thinks Fury's got a Leaving set for the next meeting. Which is tomorrow morning.'

'He's a preacher, Auger,' Sweet drawled. 'They ain't all lookin' for a short cut to heaven.'

36

'I don't believe Fury's changed,' Auger said. 'I think he's going to tell them today's the day and he's taking them all to Dirangesept. That's what he's been holding out to them all along.'

Auger waited for silence and didn't get it. He had to settle for a low murmur. 'This isn't just a hunch. I've just been checking his time scales, the recruitment and decay rate of his congregation. He's been building this one for about a year. He's hit peak and just starting to slide down the other side.' Auger hesitated, wondering if it was worth it, then plunged on. 'There are recognised patterns with cults, with the sort of mass psychological subjugation that's Fury's special skill. A thing like that needs momentum. But promises have to be made, and without their fulfilment there eventually comes a point when the congregants start to think for themselves, to question the whole thing. The questioners start talking to the still loyal. They sow doubt. If this continues, the movement falters and starts to fail. That's when the cycle breaks down into dissident factions or violence.'

Auger paused. 'Fury's close to that point. He's made his promises. He has to provide fulfilment or he'll see his church fail, and he isn't the type to let it all go. He has to take them to Dirangesept, and I don't think the mode of transport he'll be using will be prayer. It'll be suicide. Mass suicide.'

Sweet said, 'Fine. He registered for a Leaving?'

Wisch stood up, interrupting. 'No. As far as we know, Fury's had no psych tests done. He hasn't even requested any Understands from the department.'

Sweet jerked his head towards Auger. 'He asked Fury his intentions?'

Wisch glanced at Auger, then sat again, gesturing Auger to answer.

'We don't know where he is,' Auger said. 'Fury can't be contacted.'

Sweet looked around the room slowly before drawling, 'You tried knockin' on heaven's door?'

Auger waited for the laughter to die. 'The church is locked. And I can't get a break-warrant on the information I have.'

Sweet's grin told him he'd already guessed that. Damn, Auger thought, seeing what was coming. Sweet paused and nodded seriously before saying, a smirk on his face, 'That's the sort of weight you carry, Auger.'

Wisch stood up sharply, breaking up the catcalls from Sweet's crew, but that was it for Auger. He boiled over. He leaned forward and let it go. 'If you were any good at your goddamn job, Sweet, Fury wouldn't be out there now.'

Wisch raised his hand, but Sweet stood up, fists bunched. 'There was zip on him, Auger. There was no case. You can't accept that, it's too bad. You're just as fucked up as your fucking wife.'

'Sweet, that's enough,' Wisch shouted. 'Auger, you too. Now, go on.'

Auger took a few breaths as Sweet slowly sat down again. 'My information is that Fury intends to go ahead with it tomorrow. There's a dawn service at the church. He'll be going for suicide, but if he can't take his congregation with him voluntarily, I think there's a strong risk he'll try to murder them all.'

'But if he's giving them a choice, why would he kill them if they don't take it?' It was Oswell again, shaking his head.

'Like I said. One, he hasn't registered a Leaving. Two, we have no indication he intends to get them to do their Understands,' Auger said slowly, trying to stay patient. Oswell was the best of them. 'If he's urging suicide as a route to Dirangesept, it's fine, sure, as long as it's registered and they do their psychs and Understands. But Fury has to believe it too, Oswell. In order to register a Leaving with CMS, he has to take a psych test himself. I think he knows what that test would tell us.'

Oswell wasn't looking convinced, and Auger sighed. 'Look, you're turned over by a priest who believes what he's selling you, that's fine. It's religion. But if he's an atheist and you end up down on the deal, it's fraud. In this case, you're face down and the fraud's terminal. So for it to be anywhere near legal we need the paperwork. We have to believe they will have choice and that Fury believes what he preaches. And that means he has to intend going with them.'

'Maybe he does,' Oswell said. 'And this is all a waste of time. So why don't we just let them all kill themselves?'

Sweet raised his hands and clapped them above his head. 'Yeah! Hallelujah and Amen. Yee-ha!'

Auger waited for the laughter to die away again. Wisch getting awkwardly to his feet and sitting down again didn't hurry it up.

'No. What Fury's preaching now,' Auger said, 'is the exact opposite of what he used to preach at the Final Church. He used to say it was a sin to go to Dirangesept. Now he's *taking* them?' He shook his head. 'No. I don't believe it.'

'Maybe he's seen the light,' Jacko said loudly, glancing at Sweet for approval.

'Maybe,' Auger said. He felt his patience running out. 'More likely just the fires of hell. They must be bright, Jacko. When you go, you'd better go with your glaregoggles on. Otherwise you'll never locate Sweet down there, and then where will you be?'

38

Wisch stood up again quickly, giving Auger a baleful glance. 'We'll call that it. I think we've covered it. Sweet, I want your bLink team ready at three a.m.'

Auger was turning to go when Oswell caught up with him. 'Auger?'

'Yes?' Auger was aware of Sweet's attention on Oswell and himself. Oswell was going out on a limb, one of Sweet's crew voluntarily talking to Auger, and doing it right in front of Sweet, too.

'One thing,' Oswell said. 'You didn't mention the ceremony in the park next week. You think that has anything to do with it? I mean, Fury's going to have to give up the church then, isn't he? He'll have to start all over again somewhere else.'

Auger said, 'What?' He felt almost dizzy, as if he'd just had a bad bLink. His hands felt shaky and his scalp tingled. 'God, the ceremony,' he murmured. He fleetingly wondered if it was just the associations of the word, the memory of Jay, but he knew it wasn't. Oswell was right. Of course, the ceremony. That was it. That was the clincher.

'You know. The rift fill. Nugel.' Oswell was frowning. 'Auger? Are you okay?'

'Yes. Yes,' Auger managed. Christ, how could he have forgotten that? The church, Fury's Church of Final Hope, was sitting on the edge of the great rift in Hyde Park. Fury had originally built it there as the Final Church for that very reason, all those years ago, to use the associations of that terrible symbol. It had been the first major rift of the cataclysm this side of the Atlantic, and now, in less than a week, that immense symbol of destruction was to be the world's first great symbol of regeneration.

The rift fill. The Ceremony of Regeneration. That was the final confirmation of Fury's intentions. And it shouldn't have taken Oswell to see it.

Sweet was walking away, Jacko as always at his side like a dog. Sweet glanced back and said. 'Hey, Oz, boy, don't you get too close to Auger there. He looks like he just caught something nasty. Don't catch it off him or we'll have to quarantine you too. And you wouldn't like that, Oz. Could get pretty lonely.'

Auger felt the blood flush his cheeks again. 'I owe you for that, Oswell,' he murmured. 'Thanks.'

FIVE

They met every Tuesday evening in the student hall. It was about all Astrid knew about them. She stood in the open doorway, ready to change her mind and leave, looking in but seeing no one she recognised. A girl, young and blonde and freckle-cheeked, came up to her as she was about to turn and go.

'Hallo. Please come in,' the girl said. Astrid guessed she was a first-year medic. Maybe she was twenty. She had a pleasant enough grin. Astrid looked past her at the chairs arranged in a semicircle.

The girl spread her smile even wider. 'My name's Sola. Is this your first time with the group?'

'Yes. I was invited along by a friend. Is that okay?'

'Sure it is. Great.' Sola looked around eagerly. 'Do you see him . . . ?' She hesitated, her eyes returning to Astrid, and said, 'Or her?'

'No. His name was Rudd Merchant.'

'Oh.' Sola's voice collapsed. 'Oh, I'm sorry. Poor Rudd.' She obviously didn't know what to say after that and looked around helplessly, her smile, as if touched by salt, shrinking away.

'Thanks,' Astrid said. 'It's all right.' The girl's awkwardness gave her some confidence. She touched Sola on the shoulder and walked into the hall, wandering around for a few minutes until Sola and a couple of other people began ushering the crowd into seats, and then she found a chair towards the edge of the semicircle. A man was holding court in a small group to the side of the hall, and once everyone else was seated he gestured the rest of his group to sit, then took his own seat at the focal point of the arc.

Astrid looked at him. So that was Troy Gordo. It had to be. She looked at his face, remembering what Rudd had told her about him. She had assumed Rudd had been exaggerating when he'd described the man to her, but he hadn't at all.

Gordo allowed the silence in the hall to deepen for a few seconds. Arrogant, she thought. He knows he can wait, he won't lose their attention too quickly. Rudd had said that about him. He'd said charismatic, too, which had raised her hackles even more.

She glanced around again, vaguely recognising a few people from around the hospital. Medics, students, a few nurses. There was no one she wanted to talk to, though. She really didn't know why she had come this evening. It was pointless. She wasn't going to discover anything here.

Gordo nodded his head in greeting and said, 'I see a few new faces this evening.' His eyes ranged around the room. Astrid tried to make her face neutral, to sink into the audience, but his gaze stopped at her, and she felt herself registered. 'Welcome to TNM,' he said, as if just to her. He smiled, and she forced herself to return the expression. Her smile was stiff and she knew it had to look false. Holding it there, eye to eye with Gordo, she wondered that someone who looked like he did would so actively court attention. His confidence had to be a hard-learnt front, his charisma the result of a burning need to overcome repulsion. Astrid didn't trust charisma, and she didn't trust Gordo.

His eyes held her, though, challenging her and forcing her to keep looking at his ravaged face. The skin of his face pitted with acne and dotted with deep, thick knots of stubble rooted in crevices beyond a razor's reach. Shadows gathered like spiders in the furrows of his cheeks.

But as he held her gaze, she suddenly saw such a deep rich brown in his eyes that they made her forget the rest of his face altogether. She flushed and felt she'd at the same time passed a test and received her reward. She relaxed her smile, and his gaze moved on. Watching him slowly and meticulously cover the room like that, she wondered whether, after all, he had stared at her longer than at anyone else.

She looked around the hall once more. There were probably about fifty people there, and she guessed from Gordo's scan that about five were first-timers like her. She couldn't put names to anyone. GenMed was big, though.

Gordo had completed his survey of the hall. He waited a moment longer, then said, 'My name is Troy Gordo. Many of you know me. Most of you know of me, even if you've never seen me before.' A few people laughed easily, and Gordo smiled with them. Astrid found herself smiling too. He was good, using in his favour the initial reaction he must always draw. She'd asked Rudd why he didn't have surgery if he looked like that. Rudd had just told her he didn't need to.

'For the benefit of our new members, I'd like to say something about the society. I'm sure you've heard stories, but most of them are fantasy. If we in TNM could do a fraction of what I've heard we can . . .' He grinned. 'Our philosophy, in brief, is this. We believe that the human brain is a device of undiscovered potential. It's not just a computer. It's a control device. And more than that. We believe that its potential can be explored and even exploited, using neural software in combination with what I describe as transneural meditation. Or, for short, TNM.'

Astrid looked around. There was a silence in the room now. The new people were, like her, less than focused on the speaker, while the rest were hanging on every word. Transneural meditation, she thought. Jesus.

'We all know that there are thousands of quacks claiming miracles, so I won't waste any more time before showing you something of what we have achieved so far.' He unbuttoned his shirt and peeled it off, handing it to a man sitting a few yards to his left.

Gordo had a good body, Astrid saw, his major muscle groups well developed and defined. An exhibitionist, of course, overcompensating for his acne.

He reached to his side, where there was a small, low table with a red velvet tablecloth, and picked up a small oval case, holding it out towards the audience. Astrid had the sudden strange feeling that she was watching a stage show. An exhibition of magic. Gordo opened the case towards the audience, using the tips of his fingers, tipping it to expose a set of bLinkers lying on a cushioned bed of exactly the same velvet as the tablecloth. The bLinkers were bright against the matt velvet.

The evening was going to be a waste of time. Without much enthusiasm she tried to feel for the signs of illusion. She looked for grain and blur, but everything was sharp. She scanned the walls for projectors, but she knew somehow that this was going to be too good for that. The projectors would be hidden, any dead spots covered by careful lighting.

She felt mildly disappointed. She had seen a magic show as a child, and when she had discovered how it was done, the disillusion had left her crying for days. The way the magician claimed the bLinkers he put on were the source of magic powers, when all they did was shield him alone from the holos projected within the theatre. Astrid had never forgotten that promise, the beautiful, empty promise of her childhood.

Gordo lifted the bLinkers clear of the case and set the case back on the table. His fluid movements were a magician's, Astrid was sure now. This was going to be a scam of some kind. She felt cross with herself for coming here. Gordo's eyes had promised something more, and she'd almost believed it. But she remembered the sincerity of the magician on the stage, and his promise too. And the birds flying from his opened jacket to flutter into the rafters, singing. So many birds that there was nowhere for them to perch, and they streamed in clouds over her head, making her duck and scream deliciously until he had summoned them all back to disappear impossibly again, in their hundreds, into the folds of his jacket. And then the snakes spilling endlessly from his sleeves on to the floor of the stage to slither out among the screaming audience where they turned to streamers, rising into the air and catching light, becoming wonderful fireworks in the suddenly dark auditorium. And all lies.

Gordo held the bLinkers before him in the cups of his palms, and closed his eyes. Astrid looked at him, watching him fake the entry into a trance. His breathing, audible in the perfect silence, became deep and slow, and his shoulders relaxed.

Now that his eyes were closed, Astrid expected him to appear less attractive again. But somehow the acne that cracked his face simply made him seem vulnerable. It struck him that she couldn't tell how old he was. He could have been twenty or fifty.

The sound of his breathing was hypnotic, achieving a rhythm that mellowed her thoughts. So he was a fake. What had she expected? She felt herself relaxing too, and felt the pattern of her breathing merging with his. Their joined breathing sounded louder than it should, and she was so tranquil that it took her a few moments to realise that the whole of the audience was breathing together, the breathing of everyone in the room dependent on the breathing of Troy Gordo.

Astrid found herself staring at him. His shoulders were rising and falling gently as he breathed in and out, and his raised cupped hands were moving almost imperceptibly, as if stirred by the tide of the room's breath.

Just as she felt herself drifting away, Gordo's breath caught fractionally, and with the breaking of the rhythm, she jerked forward, instantly alert. The whole room moved with her, and she thought, Quake. She looked around to see the same expression on everyone's face, and turned with everyone to stare at Gordo.

Gordo was leaning slowly forward, lowering his hands so that the bLinkers were clearly visible. The neural tendrils were in spasm, and he smoothly took the bLinkers between a finger and thumb and tipped his head back to slide the delicate device down over the bridge of his nose. He began to take in a long breath, and Astrid felt herself joining him, along with everyone else in the room. But his breath kept drawing, and Astrid's lungs were full and then bursting. As she let out the air in an unwilling, racking sob, the room around her filled with an explosion of coughing and wheezing. After the long rhythmic tranquillity, she felt disorientated.

The noise gradually settled back and Gordo became the focus of attention again. Somehow he seemed still to be drawing breath. Astrid had no idea whether it was the same breath. Half an hour ago she would have been sure it wasn't. Now, she only thought maybe. And she'd given up searching for the projectors. It was hypnosis, that was all. Troy Gordo wasn't even a magician. TNM was a personality cult. The evening was a waste of time. Feeling sapped of strength, she stretched and leaned forward, ready to push herself up and leave.

Troy Gordo was holding his right arm out, directly in front of himself, palm out. Astrid thought for a moment that he was gesturing at her to stop. She sat back abruptly.

Gordo was still again. The smooth convex bLinkers over his eyes made him look like something carved. His outstretched arm began to shiver, and then as Astrid watched, it was motionless again. His shoulder and elbow seemed to have locked, and the contours seemed to have changed almost imperceptibly, and the stillness somehow wasn't just muscular control. Gordo's arm was set like stone. His hand began to shiver next, and then it too became equally still.

'Now I need someone,' Gordo said. His voice was suddenly slightly different, a fraction deeper, and full of calm. His arm was moving, but the movement was just a rocking with the movement of his chest as he breathed, a ship rolling the tide. His hand was frozen, fingers splayed and rigid.

Astrid wondered whether she was hypnotised, or whether he was. Or maybe he'd given himself some muscle freezant before the meeting and it had just kicked in. That was all it would be. After the meeting Gordo would be selling the bLinkers with their software, and then there would be the endless courses to learn to use the useless program. And its inevitable failure would be their fault, not the software's.

Without considering, she stood up. 'Yes,' she said. And immediately thought, Stupid. Drawing attention. It was how she'd been as a student in the med lectures, always volunteering, knowing that she'd remember it better if it was connected with touch, with her senses.

'Come up, then,' Gordo said. With the words and the movement of his head and chest, the rigid limb rocked towards her like a dowsing rod on

44

its target. Astrid made her way through the chairs until she was standing in front of Gordo. She looked at his open palm with its spread fingers. She glanced at Gordo's face. The bLinkers, she saw, were only semi-opaque. He was looking at her through a dark sheen. He could see everything. She had the sense that he could see right into her with that still, calm, bLinkered gaze. Behind the bLinkers his beautiful eyes were clear, his pupils wide, black.

'Touch it,' he said.

Astrid raised her hand, conscious of her own fingers as they approached Gordo's. Hers were trembling. She made a soft fist beside his hand, and rolled her fist over. Then she opened her hand again and splayed her fingers in imitation of his, and touched fingertips with him.

She almost pulled away. She had half expected it to be ice cold, thinking unconsciously of rigor mortis, but it was like touching blood-warm metal. His hand was so rigid that she noticed only the shaking of her own fingers. She was not aware of him but of herself. Touching the hard flesh, she had a sudden sense of vulnerability and danger. Feeling lost, she looked back into Gordo's eyes, and he whispered, 'Push it. Move it. Experiment.'

Tentatively, she leaned against his palm. The hand and arm were as unmoving as a somehow solid snapshot of itself. It was as if time had stopped for the limb, as if it was frozen not just physically, but in a fraction of time that needed only to move forward for the arm to move again. She felt slightly dizzy for a moment, then realised that she had lurched forward without realising it, that Gordo had moved, but from the shoulder, his torso bending back fractionally, and she had lost her balance.

Behind her she heard sounds of approval. They had seen this before. Astrid took a breath. It gave her confidence to know she wasn't the only one being duped. And at least she knew it was a scam, even if she didn't yet know how Gordo was doing it.

She took his wrist, feeling for the pulse. It was there, but like the faintest chuckle of water through a shallow rock channel. His pulse wasn't even slow. If anything, it was fast. She glanced at his face and saw a smile spreading there in the mess of his face. It was a thin smile, telling her that he knew what she was thinking. A medic observing a medic. He knew all the questions, so he knew he had all the answers.

'Try to bend it,' he said, and grinned at the expression on her face. 'Don't worry, nothing's going to snap.'

45

She tried to bend his wrist, and couldn't; then his elbow, and couldn't; and then his fingers. Each time, all that moved was his upper body. He showed no pain, not even any sign of awareness of her attempts to flex him.

She was beginning to feel angry now. She could feel his smile on her. He wasn't showing any sign of tiredness from what had now to be an immensely uncomfortable position. Astrid let her fingers drift up to his biceps. Trying to be methodical, she felt his skin carefully, and realised that his epidermis moved against the connective tissue beneath it. She went back to his fingers and it was the same. There was a small degree of yielding there. So the fixing wasn't total. Troy Gordo's arm was just rock from the connective tissue down.

Gordo was smiling more broadly. 'Go on,' he murmured. 'You're doing well.'

Astrid knew she was being sucked in by the illusion. He was selling her the idea that sense might be made of this. But she couldn't help it. She had to know, as she always had to know. It was why she'd become a medic, having to know why her father had died despite the reflexology, the iridology and all the other quackeries that had failed to turn back the cancer consuming his lungs. He had been put off by the doubts of the medics and seduced by the certainties of the quacks. And that had made her his reverse.

She turned round to see everyone in the room leaning forward, watching her and Gordo, and felt her anger rising further. Ten years ago her father had died, and now GenMed taught its students the quackeries because it was the only way to sneak real medicine through. And people like Troy Gordo preyed on the medics themselves.

A sheath of some sort. That had to be it. Some form of ultra-thin transparent casing for the entire limb, whose molecular structure could be altered by electrical impulse under bLinker control.

'You're wearing some form of sheath,' she murmured. She kept it low, unaccountably feeling guilty for exposing it, but he laughed and repeated it aloud for the whole hall. 'Not bad, but are the hairs part of the sheath, or are they poked through, each one individually?'

Astrid pulled at a few hairs on his arm at random. His epidermis lifted the tiniest fraction with each hair. She scratched at his skin with a fingernail, and he complained mildly. 'I never claimed anaesthesia,' he said, to the hall's laughter and applause. Then he quickly added to Astrid, 'I'm not mocking you. It was a good theory. I've had worse guesses – someone suggested wholescale venous enlargement and circulatory rechannelling, so my arm was like some great erect penis. And most people can't suggest a thing. Are you done?'

She shook her head, looking at him, expecting him to call a halt regardless.

'Okay,' he said, though. 'Go on.'

She moved her hand up to his shoulder. It was as rigid as his arm. Then she moved across, and felt the stiffness gradually begin to yield. She took her hands over his shoulder and continued to feel the transitional area. There was something odd about it, and she searched out the muscle groups feeding from the mobile to the fixed areas.

Gordo couldn't twist his head to look at her. 'Ah! Well done. Got it?'

Astrid didn't want to say it. It made sense, and at the same time it was quite impossible. She looked round the room again, searching for projectors, even though no projection could be this real. And it wasn't hypnosis.

'Say it,' Gordo told her. In profile the bLinkers he was wearing were jet black. He was unreadable.

'It seems,' she said, knowing that if she was hearing someone else say it, she'd be thinking them a fool, 'that every muscle group that has an insertion or attachment to any part of the arm and hand has become frozen. Like bone.'

Gordo nodded lopsidedly, his arm tipping in the movement. '*Very* good. And now, if you would like to grip my biceps again, I'll reverse the process.'

Astrid was feeling like a magician's stooge, but she had to know what would happen. As he went into his trance again, she made herself breathe irregularly. She felt a shuddering of his flesh, and the flesh slowly began to yield under her grip. His fingers curled like petals, and Astrid moved a hand to his wrist. His pulse was faster now, but as the softening of his flesh became complete, it slowed again. His arm sagged gently until she was supporting its weight. She guided it gently into his lap.

Gordo raised his other hand and let his head nod forward, carefully removing the bLinkers. He returned them to their case, and sighed. He seemed abruptly tired. The man who had been holding his shirt handed it back to him and he shrugged it on with some difficulty. The arm that had been frozen was obviously still slightly stiff. He had some trouble working the buttons closed, and Astrid wondered whether that was for her benefit.

Gordo leaned towards her and murmured, 'What's your name?'

She replied automatically. 'Astrid Remarque.'

47

'I thought so.' He rubbed at his shoulder, working his fingers into the muscle. 'You were a friend of Rudd's, weren't you?'

'Yes. How did you know that?'

'He mentioned you once or twice. He said he might bring you along some time. He wasn't sure you'd accept, though. He said you were a sceptic.' Gordo paused, turning his hand over, flexing the fingers, and said, 'I'm sorry about Rudd, he was a nice guy. Didn't seem the type to do that. But, then, few do. It's always a surprise, even if you expect it.' Gordo held her eyes. 'I'm glad you came, and that I had a chance to show you that TNM isn't just another cabal of chicken's blood and chanting. Will you come again?'

'What happens if I do? Is there a magic show every time?'

Gordo shook his head, but with a grin. 'I see what Rudd meant about you. No. The core of TNM is experiment and research. What you saw today was the limit of what we can do at the moment. I only do this every now and then. It's mainly a morale raiser. People get dispirited when they bLink and nothing happens, and most of the time nothing does.'

At least he admits it, she thought.

He held up the bLinker case. 'The software only monitors neural activity, nothing more. Biofeedback, it's hardly a new track. The meditation focuses it. But, really, we have no idea how it does what it does. And as you saw, it does work, for some of us, and to varying degrees.' He looked away for a moment, catching the eye of someone across the room and nodding briefly. 'Look, if you're interested in finding out more, why not join us? I'm sure Rudd would have been pleased if you did. There's nothing to lose.'

Astrid smiled at him. 'I pay for the bLinkers, do I? And what about membership? How much is that?'

Gordo looked surprised. 'No. There's nothing to pay. We're financed by GenMed's research unit. They even generate the software for us and provide us with the bLinkers. It's quite free, Astrid. No catches. Maybe you don't believe it, but what you saw did happen. I know how to do it, but I don't know exactly what I do, or why it works. I want to find out. GenMed is interested enough to think it worth backing us.' He took her hand. His grip was warm but tentative, as if the musculature wasn't quite under his control. 'Does it interest you at all?'

SIX

Auger sat at the observation console in the Command Room and watched the wall monitor fizz to life. He'd had the cam set there in the park the day after Fly had first come to him. He'd set it in plain sight, fixed and focused on Fury's church, half hoping the preacher would make a complaint or even attempt to sabotage it. But he never had. It crossed his mind now that maybe he'd underestimated Fury. He wouldn't be the first.

But, then, Fury didn't know about Fly. Fly would be Auger's salvation, and Auger would be the agent of Jay's retribution at last.

The display rocked and stabilised, and Auger leant forward. Beneath the endless night there was nothing yet to see except shadows, the possibility of motion at the screen's edges, dark rubbing up against darker. Auger punched HighLight and substance emerged, the revealed shapes of trees cloaked in a powdery sheen to the sides of the cam's view. And in the centre, like a fist brandishing a fat blade at the sky, the Church of Final Hope.

Auger felt a punch of adrenalin. And then beyond the church, on the far side of the great rift, he saw the machinery that would be used in the plugging of the rift, bulking like elements of a dark and distant mountain range. They had been setting it up all this time and Auger had ignored it, just seen the foreground. Stupid, he thought. Stupid. He wiped sweat from his palms. It changed nothing, though. Fly was his edge over Fury, and today was the day.

At a sound behind him, Auger twisted round. Wisch was there, shaking his head. 'I've got good and bad. And you won't like the good enough to make the bad any easier.'

'Go on,' Auger said. The harsh overhead light wasn't kind to Wisch, making a sunken-eyed skeleton of him. Auger wondered what it made of himself.

'You want the good or the bad?'

Auger shrugged. 'I want Fury. Don't play games with me, Wisch.'

'Okay. We can hold Fury. But only on sight.'

Auger rubbed his forehead. The palm of his hand was like ice. He glanced back at the HighLit church on the screen. Its spire was a sliver of jet, seemingly immune to the HighLight. 'On sight? What the hell use is that? You told them about Fury?'

'I told them Fury hasn't emerged from the church for a month. Why should he now?' Wisch made a little conciliatory movement with his shoulders. 'Of course I told them, Auger.'

Auger let out a long breath. 'Shit, this has been building up too long. I should have guessed it earlier.' He thought of Fly again and wondered how much use those extra hours might have been if he'd picked up the first of Fly's urgent messages instead of wandering through the City's ashen ruin. But no point thinking that. 'What's the good news, then?'

'That was it, Auger. That was the good news. The bad's that we still can't access the church, and we can't seal it off either. Insufficient evidence. They said you don't get those powers on history and a hunch.'

Auger swore. 'Who said that? Who did you go to, Wisch?'

'This is straight from Faith, Auger. From Maxenham's office. They actually woke Maxenham. It's final.'

'Great. So unless Fury comes out, the service runs. There's nothing we can do.' Auger shook his head.

Wisch glanced at the screen, at the waiting church. 'It's two a.m., Auger. Why don't you grab a few hours' sleep? Sweet's team will be in place by four, and no one's going to be getting to the church before seven. There's nothing to do now.'

The clock on the wall said it was three-thirty, and Auger hadn't slept at all. He'd spent the time thinking of Fly and Father Fury, and now he felt unprepared. He threw the dregs of his fifth mug of coffee of the night into the sink where the thin grounds formed a question mark against the stained green plastic, then turned the tap hard to flood it away. There were more than enough questions already. He rinsed the mug and filled it with cold water, tilted his head back and sluiced his face, then yawned and raised the shutters of the Command Room to see the world. It was still dark out there, the high half-moon a bowl tipping with ashes. Auger wondered whether Fly had slept at all.

He sat down, turned on the monitor and winced. The screen was still set to HighLight, and the park was blindingly bright, the church a pale grey silhouette against it. Auger punched default and stared at the muted image.

An early morning mist was settled over the grass, the church rising out of it as if it were founded on thick air. Beyond it the mist was ebbing away into the chasm, flowing around the building like water around a rock. Auger checked the time again. It was still a few hours until dawn. He panned the cam around, searching for the trigs of Sweet's crew. There was no sign of them, and he swore. He left the room and walked down the corridor to the trig room and stood feeling stupid at the door in front of the ABSOLUTELY NO ACCESS WITHOUT AUTHORISATION sign, with Sweet's scribbled 'So Fuck Off' beneath it.

Auger knocked. It was a moment before the door opened. Oswell stood there, and Auger was grateful for that.

'Are you set in there?' Auger asked him. 'My cam doesn't show—'

'I'm here, Auger. Wouldn't miss this for anything.' The door swung wider and Sweet was standing there, grinning. He shouldered Oswell aside, and behind him Auger could see the rows of recliners. Most of them were occupied, Sweet's crew flat out and bLinkered, probably still walking their trigs to Hyde Park from their overnight stations.

'You should be in place by now,' Auger said tightly. 'It's time.'

'We'll be there when we're needed. Now, I believe you aren't authorised here.' Sweet shoved the thick door hard in Auger's face, but it was too heavily damped to do anything more than fail to insult him.

Four-thirty ticked into four thirty-one on the Command Room clock, and Auger turned around from the monitor at the sound of the door opening. He'd been staring at the screen too long, and a residual image of the Church of Final Hope faded over the shape of Stimson.

'Auger,' Stimson said, breaking the word up with a yawn.

'You were supposed to be here half an hour ago,' Auger said, turning back, moving his shoulder, testing it for the faint ache he still had from that insect bite, or whatever it was, back in Fly's zone. Then he rotated the cam to see Sweet's trig coming straight for it. The trig raised its HardHand and tapped the lens lightly, rocking the image. 'Asshole,' Auger muttered. He swivelled the cam, and Sweet moved in front of it to block it again. The comms unit on the desk console shivered alive.

'Trigs ready, Auger. My team's waiting for action. Hey, I hope we haven't missed anything.'

Auger didn't bother to answer Sweet. Stimson sat down beside him, chuckling. Stimson was one of Sweet's men, detailed to the Command

Room for the operation. Auger would have preferred to take the whole thing alone, but Wisch had cut that out.

'You done your stuff?' Auger said to Stimson.

Stimson nodded without looking at Auger.

'Okay. This is the picture. Service is due to start at nine, congregation will be arriving from any time now. Wisch tried Faith last night, and they said we can't put a man inside, but my informant will be wearing a cam and a patch so that once he's bLinkered in there I'll have a sensory link. That will provide our only information from inside the church. But it's in-traffic only, what my informant sees, hears and says. No outgoing comms from here. We can't risk Fury spotting us. Which means my informant's alone in there.'

Stimson shrugged and started to run his console checks.

Auger cut away to concentrate on the monitor. On the screen the image of the church was obscured and then cleared, and the shape of a man was past the cam and walking away towards the church. Auger watched him into the building through the great open doors. There were two sharp phased flashes of light as he passed through and into the darkness inside. The first congregant had arrived.

'Security,' Stimson murmured. 'Some kind of ID check.'

'Multiphase imaging,' Auger said. He'd got that from Fly. 'Retina, hair, body density, palm print and a few others. All of them early technology, way out of date. Each one easily fooled, but it's a rock-hard short-term combination. Simple to fix if you've got a full template, but time-consuming. Days.' Auger glanced at Stimson. 'I thought you'd done your stuff.'

Stimson reddened. 'I knew that. Don't worry.'

More people were arriving now, filtering past the cam, ignoring Sweet's trigs stationed in plain sight at the edge of the trees. Beyond the church, across the rift, Auger could clearly see the heavy machinery gathered ready for the ceremony of rift-fill. He wondered how he could have failed to register their significance before. Fury had known. Fury was ready. Auger had been focused on the preacher, and the preacher had been focused on his Leaving. Fury was way ahead of Auger.

The congregants were queuing to enter the church, one by one. It would take them hours to get through the security, each one passing through the double flare of light.

Auger checked the clock again. Eight-twenty. He hadn't realised the time had passed so quickly. But it was light now, the day had arrived.

And Fly was supposed to be there about now.

As the thought was in his head, Fly's face was on the monitor. Auger picked up the small case from his desk and removed the single bLinker. He palmed the tiny cup over his left eye and then closed his right.

It was working fine. Auger allowed himself a small smile. With his left eye he was now in the park looking at the monitor cam on its smooth grey metal stalk. The image from the tiny cam in the corner of Fly's eye wasn't great, though, neither was the clarity of Fly's voice as he said, 'I hope you're there, Auger, because if you aren't, this could all be one great glorious fuckup.'

Auger opened his unbLinkered right eye and closed the left, flicked back and forth a few times until he had it straight. Now he was in the Command Room seeing Fly in the monitor, and now in the park seeing the monitor through Fly's eye. Right eye, left eye. Command right, Fly left. He felt slightly disjointed, connected neither with Fly nor himself. Right-eyed, he jerked the park's cam up and down twice. Then he went left, back to Fly.

'And once more so I know you can hear me as well as see me,' Fly said, his hand over his mouth so Auger couldn't be lip-reading from the cam.

Auger did it.

'Okay, let's hike. I'll nil the eyecam to go through the doors, then I'll reactivate it once I'm inside. If it's like before, they'll give us bLinkers once we're in. See you soon. Or whatever.'

Fly turned around and joined the steady flood of people heading for the Church of Final Hope. Auger watched him diminish and disappear amongst them. Fly's eyecam went dead, and Auger wiped sweat from his palms. He continued to watch the flashes of light at the church's door, feeling nervous until he was sure Fly had passed through, and then even more nervous still.

'What makes you think they won't pick up the eyecam at the door?' Stimson said.

'It's biochip technology. The security they've got, as long as the cam's not broadcasting, all they should register is he's got a medical implant. But, then, you know that.'

Stimson didn't respond for a long time. 'Five hundred and twenty through,' he eventually said. The doorway was finally clear. 'Which is about max. And no one's arrived for ten minutes.' He leant back. 'I guess that's it.'

The church, silent and forlorn by the side of the chasm, looked too small to hold so many souls, Auger thought. Smoke and dust drifted up from the pit beyond, and the small building, with its corrugated roof and its walls of sheet metal in overlapping scales like the skin of a serpent, looked like a way station to the boiling depths. Like the last bastion of heaven, or the first of hell.

It was eight fifty-five. The doors of the church moved silently closed. Auger touched the cup over his left eye. Fly's eyecam was still dead.

'Stimson, I'm not getting anything from Fly. Are you sure there's no blocks in there?'

'Nothing,' Stimson said. 'I checked. I checked everything like you said.'

Auger's left eye suddenly came on again, the image swinging round and up from the ground, Auger catching views of feet and legs, and then the backs of heads, a background of candlelight and high ahead a great pulpit holding the vast bulking shadow of a man. Auger felt his heart start to race.

Father Fury. Auger was back with Fly.

'Sorry, Auger.' Auger could hardly hear the whisper. 'It's a bit crowded in here. I didn't want to draw attention. I had to pretend to drop something.'

There were heads turning in front of Fly, and Fly's hand reached out to take a handful of bLinker packs. He kept one and passed the rest back. When he turned forward again, Auger could see the preacher hold a pack high in the air and burst it open. He brandished it over his head and shouted out, 'Today, I give you Dirangesept. No more words, no more promises. I offer you your salvation. If you would take it, if you are with me, then come with me now.'

Fury brought the bLinkers down towards his face. In the uncertain light of the thousands of candles, the eyeLids were like something the preacher had conjured from the smoky air, barely a compaction of the gloom surrounding him. Auger had a sudden sense of the man's immense power, and along with it, a feeling of dreadful foreboding.

'Don't bLink,' Auger heard himself whispering to Fly. But, of course, Fly couldn't hear it, and Auger wondered fleetingly whether he would have said it if Fly could have heard.

Fly's head was tipping up, and the darkness of the church's high ceiling was overlaid by the oval shadow of the left eyeLid of the bLinkers coming down like a coin over his eye.

There was nothing. Auger was blind until the eyecam patched into the bLinkers and Fury's zone went live.

Still nothing. Auger waited a moment, then switched to his right eye, to the Command Room. On the monitor the church was just squatting there at the edge of the rift. It looked deserted. There was no sign of life. The sky stirred with thick drifts of grey cloud. At the edge of the screen the narrow access bridge, thrown across the rift a couple of days back as an aid to the workers, dropped into the chasm and disappeared, visible again as it rose to meet the rift's far side twenty metres away. A few people were crossing it now, seemingly walking down into the chasm and walking back out again as if they were negotiating no more than a dip in the ground. They began to gather by the great machinery over there, preparing for the day's work.

'Sweet?'

'I hear you, Auger. Can we go home now?'

'Don't you move a goddamn inch, Sweet.'

Auger tried left again and was taken without warning into all of Fly's bLinkered senses. He almost jerked back in the chair. Fly wasn't saying anything, and Auger just let himself be seized by Fury's zone.

Even with the scratched gossamer that overlaid Auger's secondhand view of it, the zone was astonishing. Even through two eyes, Auger had never seen a bLinkered image like it. The sweeping plain and the deep green horizon of forest made him almost ache to be there.

Fly was still glancing around, speechless, and Auger wondered what he was feeling. Fury's zone made the projected Dirangesept zone in Fly's room look like a pencilled scrawl. As Fly slowly moved his head, taking it all in, Auger could see the rest of the congregation assembled there, standing in scattered groups on the grass, waiting patiently beneath the pale blue sky with its warmth that Auger could almost feel. No wonder the Final Hopers believed in Fury.

As if aware of Auger's thoughts, a voice thundered, 'Now, at last, as I promised you, we are truly here. Our hope, our Final Hope, is realised. We are, in spirit, on Dirangesept. We are coming to our Far Home. All that remains is finally to sever the last slender thread that binds us to our dying world.'

Auger flicked back to Sweet, checking he was there. Fury was very close, but he wasn't there yet. This wasn't enough to justify sending Sweet in. Fury had to tell them plainly that they had to kill themselves to get there.

To get there, he thought, realising what he was thinking. To get where? On to a simulation of a world eighteen years of sleep away. And *how* would they all kill themselves in there? Because Auger was sure there was no way Fury would let them leave the building now, even with the intention to kill themselves elsewhere.

There was something Auger had missed. There had to be. 'This is going sideways,' he muttered. 'I don't trust him. Are we sure the building isn't some way toxic? Has he got gas in there, chemicals, anything?'

'We're sure,' Stimson said. 'There's nothing. No drugs, no weapons, no source of, or indirect access to power beyond what little Fury needs to run the software. Nothing's going to happen in there today. It's just another meeting. Like last week, the week before, a month ago, a year back. They're all just bLinkydinks.'

'Sweet tell you that?' Auger looked up at the map above the live screen, scanning the ring of pulsing pinlights. He buzzed the orange leader. 'Sweet, what can you see?'

'I can see the whole fucking day going down the pan, Auger. I can see a total waste of fucking time. Only thing keeping me awake's composing the complaint I'm gonna make about you first thing I get back there.'

Auger cut him off and went back to Fly. There was Fury up ahead, standing on a small grassy mound, speaking. His black cloak caught the breeze and seemed to raise him higher.

'It is time. It is time for us to leave our world behind, to come to a new world, a place of dreams and wonder. The Earth is cracked and broken, a gutted fire swirling with ash. There is nothing back there for us but misery and slow death. We must rise, rise from the embers and fly to our new birthright, our new world, our new Eden.' His cloak flicked up at his shoulders and took off like wings, its darkness somehow catching the sun and glinting silver. The breeze grew, the silver gained. Scales of silver turned to silver feathers. Fly couldn't look away. Auger couldn't close his eye. Fury was transforming himself. Now he was a devil, now an angel.

Eighty per cent, Auger found himself thinking. Fury was that good. If he said, right now, Who wants to come, to kill themselves and take the risk? Auger reckoned he'd take eighty per cent. The other week Fly had estimated sixty, and up until now Auger just might have raised him a couple of per cent. But this was good.

It was a long way too good. This felt to Auger like the final push, the end of the ramp. But Fury still hadn't said it. And how was he going to do it anyway?

The stims in the zone seemed to be stepping up a few points, more colour seeping into it, the audio and visuals significantly sharpening. Fury was juicing up the zone somehow. Fly was looking around at last, he'd obviously picked up on it. Hell, of course he had. If Auger clicked on it one-eyed and secondhand, it must be hyper to Fly. Everyone else there was shifting their feet, glancing around. Some of them kneeling to touch the grass, running their fingers over it. A few smiles and riffs of nervous laughter. Even Auger felt he was there, the furred glass between his eye and Fly's pulled aside, the zone tautening, reeling him into Fury's vision.

He forced himself to come out. The Command room seemed flat, as if he could poke a finger through anything solid. His own voice sounded like a sluggish echo. 'You *sure* there's nothing toxic in that church, Stimson? No extra power source?'

'Nothing. It's safer than your mother's tit. If something's going to happen – and it isn't – it's not going to happen in there. He'll have to bring them out.'

Auger said, 'I don't think so. I'm not waiting any longer. We're going in.'

Stimson frowned. 'Fury said the words?'

'No, he hasn't. I don't know. There's something—'

'If he hasn't said the words, he's done nothing wrong. And the place is sterile. You've got no grounds. Wisch'll kill you.'

Auger made to speak to Sweet, then hesitated and returned to Fly instead.

Fury was almost screaming at the congregation. His arms were spread wide, palms open, lifting. His cloak was blinding, moving with him as if it were part of his flesh. It was beckoning, urging, pulling at the congregation. 'By the pure and perfect power of the Almighty Lord I am *with* you now in Dirangesept. We are finally ready to discard the illusion. We are finally prepared to emerge in glory in the true land. Tell me, can you *see* it? Can you *see* the true land?'

Around Fly the words began to come, muttered and murmured, in belief and disbelief. 'We can see it.' Fly was casting his eyes around and Auger could see everything somehow hardening into certainty, becoming better defined, becoming perfect.

'Can you *hear* it?'

More powerfully, more positively, 'We can hear it.'

Fury's voice was booming now over the great green plain, raising distant birds into clouds of flight. 'Can you *feel* it?'

And shouting now in exuberant response, the congregation united. 'We can FEEL it.'

Auger wanted to go back to tell Sweet to go in, but he couldn't tear himself away from Fly's view as Fury held up his right arm and said, with abrupt calm, 'Even with the help of the Lord, my power is limited. I am only able to hold us all here for a few brief moments.' His cloak was poised and almost without motion, a great banner behind him. There was bird song all around him. Even Auger felt it, the hope, the aching promise of glorious life. Fury brought his arms in and cupped his hands as if holding something magnificent and at the same time delicate, then threw out his hands again as fists, shaking them wildly, and cried out, 'Then *seize* that moment. *Choose* the Lord. Choose *now!*'

Forcing himself to bLink out, Auger glanced briefly at the Command Room. It looked even more washed-out and pale, the steel surfaces as insubstantial as if he could stare only a little harder and see right through them.

He went back to the monitor and examined the church again. There were no windows in the building other than the tall holo of stained glass beneath the spire with its naked Christ lashed to the hull of a rocket, bearing his crown of stars.

'Now, Sweet,' he said. 'Now. Go in now.'

There must have been something in Auger's voice, because for once Sweet said nothing, just stepped forward out of the ring of trees and into the clearing. Five more autoids moved into view to either side of Sweet, and Auger saw the final pair of Sweet's crew standing on the grass beyond the rift.

'Okay, Sweet, break the door. Get in there.'

'Something happened?' Sweet sounded almost disappointed.

'Just do it. Now.'

Auger went back to Fly, who alone in the crowd had moved a pace forward. He was saying to Fury, 'I don't know about this. What exactly do you mean, *go* there? We are there, aren't we?'

He knows it too, Auger thought, the back of his neck prickling. This wasn't just another prayer meeting. Fury had promised something special last time and this was it to the max.

Auger said to Stimson, 'You're *sure* the place—'

'One hundred per cent,' Stimson said after a pause.

'Sweet, what are you doing? You should be in there by now.' Auger could feel sweat rising on his forehead, or maybe it was Fly's sweat, Fly's forehead. It sure wasn't Sweet's. Sweet wasn't giving a damn. Fly wasn't Sweet's connection.

Fury was saying, 'It is time to depart now. The door is open. The Lord awaits you in his Far Home.'

'Wait. I want to know exactly what we're saying yes to. What exactly do we have to do?' Fly's voice was rising, not quite in control, but it was Auger's question. Auger had given it to him, for Fury to damn himself.

Fury smiled easily, looking directly at Fly, and Auger had an uncomfortably sharp sense of the priest. 'Among you, I know, are

58

unbelievers. Those who think that this is a game. Those who disapprove of me.' He paused, still staring at Fly. 'You are all welcome, though.'

He knows, Auger thought. Does he?

'You are welcome, whoever you are and wherever you are,' Fury said. His voice was low, and he was talking only to Fly. He seemed to be staring right through him, at Auger, eye to eye. 'There is a place in the new world for all. You ask what we are saying yes to? My friend, we are saying yes to life.'

'Auger, get your men in here, for Christ's sake,' Fly screamed. Out loud, breaking cover. Auger could feel Fly's fear like salt in his skull.

'I'm coming,' Auger yelled. 'Hold on.'

He came out, knowing Fly hadn't heard that, and caught Stimson looking at him, a what-the-fuck look. But he'd had to say it. 'Sweet! What's happening?'

'Something wrong here, Auger. This is supposed to be steel and corrugated iron. What the hell is it?' Sweet's voice was slow, and then it was rising a little, but not like Fly's. Fly was seeing death. Sweet in his head was just seeing Auger grinning at him. Auger imagined Sweet squirming a little in that room down the corridor, bLinkered, here-and-there. Another time it would have given him some satisfaction.

'I don't give a damn, Sweet. I don't care if it's TiCo three. Get in there now.'

He went back to Fly. Everyone around him was looking uncertain. A few metres from Fly, someone said, falteringly, 'Yes, Father. I am ready.'

Fury hadn't reacted at all to Fly's outburst. He'd known. He'd known it all along. Auger felt ice in his veins.

'Ready for what?' Fly said, his voice cracking. 'What's going to happen?'

Fury ignored Fly. 'Do you choose Dirangesept?' he said to the man who was ready.

'I . . . I choose Dirangesept.' And saying it, the man crumpled to the ground. Fly was heading for him at a run, kneeling and reaching out, picking up the slack hand, fingering the wrist. He let the hand fall, and Auger knew there was no pulse.

He won't really be dead, Auger told himself. It's just the zone. Just Fury provoking a reaction. He came out, needing a moment to think, but Sweet's voice intruded, too loud, splintering. 'It fucking *is* TiCo, Auger.'

At Auger's side, Stimson muttered, 'Something's happening.' He was tugging at Auger's sleeve, but Auger was with Fly again, who was standing among the crowd of people. A few more had fallen now.

59

Auger was trying to work out what was happening to the fallen ones. Assume it was real and they were dead. It wasn't poison or gas. If it had been, everyone would be down. Those bLinkers were sensory only, there was no motor override like with the 'fist trigs.

He came out again. 'Stimson, are you *sure* there's no auxiliary power source in there?'

'There's none.' Stimson's voice was tight and defensive.

'Check the area. Check everything.'

Back again. Beside Fly, someone else murmured, 'I choose Dirangesept.' And with the words, they fell to the ground.

The exact same words. An Exitline. Shit.

Auger came out fast.

'Sweet. Listen to me. Fury's jacked into the bLinkers' Exitline function. I don't know how, but he's turned it toxic. You understand me? They say this line, it kills them. So there's a power source somewhere and it's connected to the bLinkers. You've got to locate the power source. It has to be somewhere in the church.'

'I'm not a goddamn electrician, Auger.'

Auger left him. 'Fly, you've got to hang in there. We're coming.' As if Fly could hear him. Men and women were collapsing to the ground all around him, folding silently into the grass. Fury was still tall on the mound, holding a hand up to Fly as he advanced at a run, the priest's palm out in a gesture both definite and ambiguous. His face with Fly about to reach him was serene, as if Fly were illusory.

Auger took Fly's view down to 2D left retina and simultaneously squinted with his right eye at Sweet's display. He was between the two, with both and neither. Images fused and parted. Auger felt dizzy. He shouldn't be doing this. He knew he was in danger of losing it. 'Fly, ignore him. Use your own Exitline and take the damn bLinkers off. BLink out, now.' Screaming the words. 'Damn it, will you *listen* to me? Sweet, what the *hell* are you doing? Get into that goddamn building *now*.'

Looking at the massive doors of the church, struggling to pull his voice back level, Auger turned to Stimson. 'Exactly who was it checked the building?'

'I did.'

'Checked it how?'

'I, uh, I checked the plans.'

'You checked the plans. Oh, great. That go for power sources too, everything else? You checked the *plans*?'

Stimson nodded. 'But I'm sure there's no power source. I'm sure of it.'

'Christ in a bucket. Sweet, how're you doing?'

He didn't catch the answer. Fly was only a few yards from Fury and Fury hadn't moved an inch.

'Fly, don't touch him. Just stop, back off slowly and bLink out. Use your own Exitline. Can you *hear* me? We're coming in. We're coming in.'

'Auger, are you crazy? He can't hear you,' Stimson said, staring. Auger looked at him, the 2D Dirangesept zone drifting over him. Auger closed his left eye, not liking to leave Fly even for a moment now. But he had to keep control. Stimson was right. Keep control.

Stimson cleared his throat and added, 'I think they mostly said yes.' He hesitantly pushed a readout at Auger. 'Five hundred twelve out of five twenty, located and confirmed.'

Auger opened both eyes again, he had no choice. Dirangesept and the Command Room swam there, layered and merging, both of them out of Auger's control. 'Fly, get *out* of there.'

'Come with me,' Fury was saying gently.

Fly had stopped now, standing at the base of the mound, looking up at Fury.

'We can go there together, you and I. To paradise, to our new Eden, from this world to the next. Only come with me. Take my hand and come. On Dirangesept there will be neither pain nor sorrow. Only everlasting peace.' Fury raised his arm. 'Take my hand.'

'They're dead,' Fly screamed. 'Look at them! What have you done to them?'

'They are now without their fleshly bodies. They have abdicated them, as will we. Come.' Fury took a slow, easy pace down the mound towards Fly and the few remaining congregants.

Auger managed to leave Fly for a moment. 'We don't even know they're dead,' Stimson was saying. He was looking oddly at Auger. Keep control, Auger thought. Keep it separate. Right eye, left eye. Don't stay with Fly too long.

'I said we don't know they're dead,' Stimson repeated.

'We don't know the church isn't made of goddamn cheese, you asshole,' Auger said, trying to control his voice. 'If you can think of anything else we don't know, don't tell me.'

The thump of explosive sounded in his right ear, then a scream. Sweet said shakily, 'Trig down, Auger. It's Royle. The walls are charge-reactive.'

Auger was aware of Stimson dropping his head into the cradle of his palms, and heard running in the corridor, medics on their way to the cubicle where Royle was still screaming, the nearby screams not quite in sync with the screams Auger was getting via the monitor in the park. Sweet was now grinding into the titanium cobalt alloy of the church doors with his sharplight and getting nowhere, but carrying on anyway. Sweet didn't know what else to do.

In the zone Fury was pacing around the bodies, touching hands and faces with the tips of his fingers as if blessing the dead. There were about half a dozen people left standing, who hadn't chosen Dirangesept. Ignoring the others, Father Fury came face to face with Fly again, and said, 'You would truly remain on Earth? On this planet of damnation?' He shrugged lightly, his cape stirring gently. 'Then stay. I have no hold on you. Leave us, and be at peace.'

Auger looked through Fly's eye at the preacher, wondering, uncertain, then went back to the monitor. There was hardly any activity across the rift, he noticed. The machines were standing idle, workers walking around, moving from machine to machine, talking, gesticulating.

That wasn't right, he thought. They should be up and rumbling by now, the crabs and the spinners. It was well past nine. The machines should be going by now, jetting Nugel into the rift as they had done every day for weeks without Auger even registering it. Carrying on the great task of filling it with the material that would be the saviour of the planet, would safeguard it until D3 secured Dirangesept for the great emigration.

But nothing was happening. And when he went to Sweet's comms Auger was hearing a jarring background hum that he hadn't noticed before.

That was it.

Auger leaned forward, yelling. 'Sweet, he's leeching power from the generators across the rift. Get them to cut it. Cut the power.' He stopped, making himself think. 'No, take too long. It's the bridge. He must have a line over the bridge. Blow the goddamn bridge, Sweet.'

Auger changed eyes. Fly was kneeling down at the side of a dead man, a palm to his cheek. He looked up at Fury. 'What did you do? I know Carris. He wouldn't want Dirangesept. He wouldn't have said it.'

'I?' Fury arched his eyebrows. 'I did nothing. We are each of us responsible to himself, and that alone, and no more. We make our own choices. Where they take us . . .' He shrugged. Behind him another man fell.

'Oh, no,' Auger murmured. 'Oh, no, no.' He stood up, then sat down again hopelessly. 'Fly, don't exit. Whatever you do, stay in the zone. Don't say your line. Just wait there.'

Fury wasn't going to let anyone go. No one was going to leave the church alive. Those who declined Dirangesept were choosing simply to exit, but Fury had their own individual Exitlines linked to the same end. If they rejected suicide, they would have murder.

'*Fly!*'

Auger left him. He ignored Stimson's look.

Oswell's voice was coming over on the comms system. 'I'm getting through,' he was yelling through a grinding screech. 'I found a plasma cutter on the other side of the rift.' Auger could see Oswell's trig on the monitor now, the trig barely supporting the massive cutter that was screaming into the wall of the church. There was a jet of sparks, then a sudden ball of brown smoke that flared to enclose the trig.

'I'm through. I can see—'

'What, Oswell?'

'There's a lot of smoke. That was probably me, the cutter. Wait, it's clearing.'

'What, Oswell? Talk to me.'

'Bodies. A few people standing, not many. It's difficult to tell. Hold on. I'm going inside. Maybe I can bring them out.'

On the monitor the smoke cleared and Auger saw the trig vanish into the church. Swinging the monitor cam round to cover the bridge, he had a sense of everything moving even further out of his control.

Sweet was standing beside the bridge this side of the rift, the trig brandishing a great loop of red and green striped cable high in one claw. Behind the claw the fat cable fell to disappear beneath the slack bridge, and in front it vanished towards the church, hidden in the long grass of the park. Sweet was whooping and yelling. 'I've got it. I've got the bastard.'

'Hold it, Sweet,' Auger said. 'Fury might have it booby-trapped. Oswell's in there. Just give him a chance—'

Sweet dropped the cable and raised his sharplight, firing a long burst across the bridge and the cable.

Auger shouted, 'Oswell, get them out of there fast. Sweet's blowing the bridge.' Then he returned to Fly.

Fly was looking around. There was only him left standing in the zone now, apart from Father Fury. Fury said mildly, 'The decision is yours, my friend. But remember that God is your judge, not I. And remember Matthew eighteen, verse nine.'

As if to himself, Fly murmured, 'Remember what's important, Auger,' and as he said it, slumped to the grass. Auger's left eye view went to black.

He bent forward over the table, feeling sick. Fly was dead and he had failed. He sighed hard and then looked up again. It's over, he thought. All over.

It wasn't, though. On the monitor the bridge was sliding into the rift. As Auger watched it slither down, a generator over the other side exploded into life. An orange knifeblade of honeycomb Nugel arced into the air from an unsecured nozzle, the thin jet expanding a hundredfold, ten-thousandfold as the uncontrolled recoil raised it high. The nozzle whipped left and right, out of control, and the gel fanned, still spraying, swelling to engorge the sky with orange. Above the trees, the wind took the ultra-light gel, lifting it up towards the clouds. High in the sky it began to set hard, and the wind-sculpted bubbles began to drift back towards the ground.

Auger felt numb as he watched the vast bubbles come down. They fell gently against the church, bouncing off the spire and tumbling to the ground. He almost expected them to burst there, they seemed so light and fragile, but instead they collected on the grass in great clumps.

'Oswell?' Auger said, trying to pull himself together. Maybe he was out of the church now. It was impossible to tell. The church was vanishing behind the huge orange globules. All of a sudden it seemed tiny and in- nocuous, a model of itself.

The generator was abruptly nilled, and for a moment there was perfect silence, nothing in Auger's ears or on the monitor but the sky filled with billowing Nugel and the ground covered in great shining bubbles and the church spire, which was the only other thing visible, the jet-black spire of the Church of Final Hope.

And then out of that peace and silence erupted an explosion that deafened Auger. The spire's tip, the messiah lashed to its symbolic rocket, cracked like a black bolt and spun away, soaring in a high arc before descending again to disappear into the rift.

Before Auger could react, a second blast filled the echo of the first. The church itself burst outward. Orange flames and fragmented gel filled the screen, and then the huge bubbles of Nugel splintered away and the black church was there again, revealed for the briefest moment in skeletal form, the bare struts and pillars all that remained, but nevertheless recognisably Fury's church.

At Auger's side, Stimson let out a small whimper. And then the earth split with thunder, the ground before the church cracking, and the phantom church seemed to shudder and lurch once, violently, before it and the earth that held it broke away in one piece and tumbled slowly backwards into the great rift of Hyde Park.

Auger watched it vanish. A brief low rumble came from within the rift, then a longer, diminishing groan, and then silence.

Auger felt hot and cold with sweat, drained of energy, of everything. On the monitor, smoke was rising out of the rift, and above it clouds of vaporised Nugel rolled and swarmed in the heated air. Auger felt he was staring at hell, and knew that this was what Fury had intended all along.

He pulled forward in his chair, realising he was completely soaked in sweat. There was movement beside him.

'Stimson,' he said. He had nothing else.

'You lost it, Auger,' Stimson told him, standing up. His voice was shaking. 'You lost it, didn't you? You should have kept focused. It was your fault. I saw you.'

Auger felt a surge of anger and couldn't hold it back. He swung at Stimson, but Stimson swayed back easily and Auger overbalanced, fell off the chair and on to the floor.

No perspective vision. He was blind in one eye, the bLinkered left eye, the eye in which Fly had died saying his Exitline. Auger felt like crying, knowing that he was part of Fly's Exitline. Knowing he was that important to Fly, and that he'd failed him.

Lying on the floor at Stimson's feet, Auger reached up to remove the bLinker. Blood was dripping steadily to the floor from the knuckles of his hand where his fist had smashed wildly into the edge of the table after missing Stimson. His hand was throbbing now, but he hardly noticed it. He pulled himself to his knees and let the bLinker fall into his cupped palm, and stared at it, thinking of Fury's last words.

Matthew eighteen, verse nine. He didn't need to look it up. He knew it well enough. The cults loved it.

If thine eye offend thee, pluck it out and cast it from thee.

SEVEN

She was coming off a night duty in Emergency, and her head was still burning with it. She wasn't aware of Troy Gordo until he was at her side and matching her, pace for pace, along the colonnade.

'Astrid,' he said. 'Busy night, huh?'

She looked blankly at him until he pointed at her white coat. Then she looked down at the mess of swirls and blotches that covered it. The coat was a Rorschach of blood. She saw shapes in the red and white chaos, and wondered exhaustedly what they meant to her.

Death was the answer, and Troy Gordo could obviously see that in her face, cutting the subject and just saying, 'Can I buy you a coffee?'

'Sure,' she told him. 'That would be good. I haven't had a break for fourteen hours.' She rubbed her eyes. 'You know what the night's high point was? A midnight crowd of would-be revenants. I think they'd been playing some game. Been sharing bLinkers, they all had chronic eye infections. Anyway, they brought a woman in, dead and rigored, and wouldn't accept I couldn't bring her back for them. They'd already had their own try, of course, they said it had to be a dud batch of newts' balls or some other crap.'

Troy shook his head. She brushed at her coat where a few flies were gathering at the blood. 'That was okay,' she said. 'That I could cope with. It was when one of them lost patience with me and decided he'd go over himself right there and then to fetch her back. Just to show me.' She stopped for a moment, thinking of it. 'Swallowed a capsule right in front of me, some neurotoxin or other. He was flat and gone before I knew. And you know what? I almost laughed. Tell me, what sort of a world is this?'

'You want an answer to that?'

She sighed. 'No, I want a coffee. Thanks.' She shrugged the white coat off and balled it up, tossing it into the burnbox at the door of the café. The wake of flies circled above the bin for a moment, then hissed to nothing in the swift blur of heat. 'There,' she said. 'Finished. New day.'

She smiled at Gordo. His face was as cratered as before, but maybe she was getting used to it. His eyes were as beautiful as she recalled, nuts of deep brown.

'Actually,' he said, 'I was hoping I'd bump into you.'

'Hoping?'

He laughed. 'I looked up your duty roster. I didn't want you disappearing after your first meeting and never coming back.'

As he steered her into the café, she wondered whether he meant as a member or for himself. She wondered what Troy Gordo was really like.

He ordered them both coffee, then brought a pair of bLinkers from a pocket and laid them on the table. She looked at them and felt disappointed for a moment, then tried to shake that away, thinking of Rudd. It was for him that she was doing this.

'I think you're probably still sceptical,' Gordo was saying. 'I was for months, I wasted a lot of time disbelieving. But I think you'd be a great person for TNM. I know you only came along because of Rudd, but he was serious in asking you. Maybe you could keep your mind open for him, if not for me?'

She couldn't help smiling. 'Go on.'

'I thought I'd show you these. These are the bLinkers I wear to meditate. I know you still think it's a trick, but I want you to see it isn't.' He picked them up and put them down again. 'These are just a sophisticated aid to the process, that's all. They provide a form of feedback to the meditation, so that with practice I can boost the blood supply to specific parts of my brain and increase the work rate. They also provide feedback to neurological activity. There's a brain map, so I can focus on the area I want to affect.'

He saw her face and backtracked. 'Okay, I know meditation sounds like mumbo-jumbo, but there really isn't a better word for it. Look at it like this, then. It's like I've found a gun and discovered that if I pull the trigger, whatever it's pointing at falls over. But I don't know what happens in the gun, between the trigger and the target. It still falls over, though.'

She saw him register her frown.

'Look, do you want to try them? You'll see what I mean.'

'Okay. Why not?' She sipped at her coffee, then took the bLinkers from the table. They were lighter than she'd imagined, and when she held them to the light she saw the neural tendrils, slender as silver thread within their gel casing.

She tipped back her head and bLinked. The shed gel slid like tears down her cheeks as the tendrils crawled home. She gripped the edge of the table, but the transition was smooth, just a moment's dizzy dislocation.

The eyeLids were translucent, as she remembered them over his eyes the night before. She could still see Troy Gordo and the café, but laid like a limpid sheet over everything was a plan of a brain, and beneath that, a sexless bodymap. As she watched, the bodymap swam and fixed into an image of herself, sitting exactly as she sat, but floating in a void. Unconsciously she straightened her back, and saw it happen to the femunculus. She smiled at herself, smiling back at herself in miniature. Impressive, she thought.

Gordo's voice intruded. 'It's easy to navigate,' he told her. 'Look through the menus. There's a retinal register. Just hold on anything with your eyes and blink twice to select, once more to confirm.'

When she was looking at Troy, the bodymap was a phantom. And when she looked at the maps, Troy Gordo was the ghost in the background.

She left him a ghost, clicked on neural blood flow and watched her excitement pulsing there. She'd seen visualisation bLinkers before, but only as teaching devices. She played around for a while, blinking and scrolling, then found an anatomical menu, blinked on her left foot, then selected musculature and found the tiny area of her brain responsible for it redlighted on the brain map. She tried to make it pulse harder, but nothing happened.

Gordo was tapping at her arm. She bLinked out and set the bLinkers on the table, feeling faintly dizzy.

'What do you think?'

She picked up her coffee and recoiled at its cold touch on her lips.

'It grabs you, doesn't it? You've been in there half an hour,' Troy said. He searched out a café attendant and summoned more coffee for them both.

'It's quite something,' she told him.

'Like I said, it's not much more than a sophisticated biofeedback vehicle. You have to learn to drive it, and it isn't easy. I can focus better than anyone else in TNM, that's all. I started with the tip of a finger, found I could harden that, and worked up from there.' He coiled the bLinkers into a sterilSac and slid them into a pocket. 'The thing is, we usually have a pretty fast turnover of members. They get disillusioned by the fact that nothing happens fast. They expect miracles. To recruit at all, unfortunately, you need something special, which is why I bring out my party trick. But then everyone expects to be doing it themselves first time. Unfortunately that's how we live these days. Like with medicine. Cures have to be instant. You'd maybe expect medics to be more realistic, but that isn't how it works. The ones you recruit are generally the ones who want miracles. There isn't much you can do about it. Your friend Rudd, he was a sticker. I got on well with him.'

'Did Rudd get anywhere with it?'

'A little. Did he ever show you?'

'No.'

'Good man. Same applies to you, if ever you get it. We're a serious group. It isn't for playing around.'

'I understand that.' She felt that she'd accepted something by saying that, and Troy seemed to think so, too. He drained his cup and smiled.

'How do you get by, Astrid? Pay the rent? Not easy as a medic, is it? You make the potions?'

She frowned, then realised he was talking about the quackeries that a lot of medics shifted on the side. The cures for warts and incurable cancers that did nothing, but that the sick and the desperate would pay anything for.

'No.'

'I thought not. Your friend Rudd was the same. Me, too. There are a few ethical ways of supplementing your pay, you know.'

'Yes?'

'Joining research projects.'

'Isn't TNM a research project anyway? I thought you said GenMed finances the group?'

'That's different. The project's all ours. I designed the software. They just had the bLinkers made up and they get to see our results in return. They don't pay us anything.' He made a face. 'Be nice if they did. No, what I'm talking about is a different thing entirely. But you do get paid, and pretty well.'

'For what? Being a guinea pig?'

'Yes, but the projects are tightly controlled. I'm doing one myself right now. They're looking for a few more subjects, if you're interested.'

'What's the project?'

'Neurological research. That's all I know about it. There's a psych test to start with, then they carry out a sequence of monitoring procedures. It's no sweat.'

'Did Rudd do this?'

Gordo frowned. 'Actually, yes.'

He was looking curiously at her, and she quickly said, 'Well, if he did, and you do it too, and you think it's okay, I'll have a look, at least. Where do I have to go?'

'Just over the colonnade from neuro. The research wing.'

She lifted the cold cup from the table, leaving a dark circle on the dirty green plastic, and replaced the cup to overlap the mark, linking the circles. 'Isn't that where they keep the Dirangesept Vets?'

'Yes, but don't worry, you won't ever see them. They're kept in isolation.' He grinned at her. 'Are you worried about those stories of them having parasites? The beasts of Dirangesept?'

She shook her head. 'Intrigued, that's all.'

'Yeah. Me, too. I'm sure there's stuff we don't know about. Especially with the third project readying to go. I guess they must be trying to analyse the beasts. Maybe they've already worked out how to kill them. How to clear the way.' There was a look of longing in his face, a faraway look. Astrid recognised it. The Dirangesept look.

Her fresh coffee arrived. The waiter took the old cup and wiped the table with a sweep of a cloth, removing the chained circles before setting down the new cup. She sipped at the hot coffee. It smelled good and tasted almost okay, but it had the usual odd aftertaste. She wondered what it might be like to live on a clean planet, where the food wasn't engineered, where you didn't have to treat the skin of your face for filter sores, your body for environmental cancers, your skull for craziness. Where you could start again.

But if it were ever to happen, it would be years away. Eighteen years for the ships to reach Dirangesept, say a year to subdue the planet, she'd be forty-three by then.

She sipped at her coffee, letting its heat suffuse her and thinking. What was the alternative, though? To remain here, waiting. To believe the Administration's claims that the Earth might be regenerated. To keep drinking coffee that tasted of rancid rust.

She put the cup down. There was another alternative. To accept the dying world and live for the people who mattered to her. To be in some small way moral.

Not to let Rudd's death go unchallenged.

'Are many of the guinea pigs there TNM members?' she asked Troy.

'Not many, no. Not everyone's suitable. To be honest, Astrid, they pay me a small finder's fee. I'm their first filter. The project isn't that well funded, they can't afford too many rejections. It's worth it to them to know they're less likely to be wasting their time with the initial tests.'

'So what makes me a good bet?'

'Can't tell you that. It'd screw the tests if you knew.'

He was looking at her suspiciously again. With a smile she said, 'And if I knew, I could start recruiting myself, and that wouldn't be so good for you.'

He relaxed. 'Okay, tell you what. Finder's fee's worth the price of a meal for two. How about we spend it together? That is, if you don't turn out to be just another crazy and they decide to take you.'

She pushed her coffee away, and smiled again. 'Done.' For Rudd, she thought. And maybe just a little bit for herself, too.

EIGHT

His fist bloody and stinging, Auger got to his feet and stumbled from the Control Room, ignoring Stimson's yelling. He couldn't block out the pictures in his head of Hyde Park. All he knew was that he needed to be anaesthetised. He needed noise and people.

He walked into the daylight and carried on walking blindly, not conscious of time or where he was heading until he found himself at midday outside the holo of Parliament. It looked like ancient weathered grandeur today, but Auger had seen it when the satellites had been down and the reality of the squat black, windowless Administration buildings had blurred through. Big Ben told him it was nearly midnight, but it had been that time for years now. Blood was dripping from his hand.

Trafalgar Square, he thought lethargically, looking towards Whitehall. There were always people in Trafalgar Square, watching the government holos, the skycast state-of-the-planet news. That was what he needed. Crowds. He pushed on.

Whitehall was clogged as far down as the HardVeil shutters of Downing Street, and Trafalgar Square was a solid clot of humanity. It must be good news today.

It took him half an hour to force himself through Whitehall. At the periphery of the Square he kept going, heading for the epicentre, wanting an oblivion. His hand was throbbing now like a distant heartbeat. He was hardly aware of it.

He pushed himself on into the crowd until he could move no more, and finally, wedged so tightly in the knot of people that even his breathing was regulated by the bodies around him, the guilt and sense of failure that was swamping Auger began to transform into a comforting numbness. There were no decisions to be made here. There was nowhere to go any more. Auger had no choice but to submit to the motion of the mass. The only movement was a steady, almost tidal shift, as people were washed in and out at the edges of the shoal. Auger felt all thought drain away and let himself float and be comforted.

After a time he became aware that everyone around him was staring up into the sky, and he raised his head with them to see a vast holo shimmering against the ashen sky. The skycast was starting.

It was glorious. The vision caught him like a hook lodged in his skull. It was Eden. He couldn't help himself looking at it. Nothing could be that green, that vibrant. He stared, and the crowd around him seemed to vanish. He was no longer with them. He had had been taken up.

Thank you, Auger thought. For these few blessed moments Father Fury was erased and his head was empty except for the vision of beauty above.

Almost immediately the eye contact locked him into an audio cast, and the commentator was telling him that it was 09.46 on a brilliant morning on Dirangesept, a slight sprinkling of rain expected in the lowland forests, while the mountain plains would be experiencing warm sun throughout the eighteen hours of daylight.

Dirangesept. Auger almost laughed with the irony of it, of coming here for oblivion and seeing this. He couldn't escape Dirangesept. First Fury, and now this.

He tried half-heartedly to move, but there was no escape from it. Auger had deliberately wedged himself at the core of the crowd.

He had no choice. He surrendered to the skycast.

'We will now overlay a simulation to demonstrate the effects of cultivation upon the environment. This simulation is at plus five years. Please imagine that five years have passed since D3, the successful colonisation of Dirangesept.'

The voice faded away. A gentle wave of defocus rippled across the landscape and in its wake the plains were suddenly regulated, blocked out into squares and rectangles of deep green, with speckled orchards and tiny clusters of village communities.

'Please remember that this is, of course, only a simulation.' The cam zoomed down and began to track across the Simaged countryside, slow enough that Auger could catch glimpses of men guiding silver-jawed ploughs through the fields and see the threads of woodsmoke lingering above rough brick chimneys, and children running through meadows, their heads thrown back in laughter so that Auger could see their perfect teeth.

Utopia. Well, at least Fury wasn't there, Auger thought. He wanted to bring his eyes down and see who around him was buying it, but he couldn't pull away from the seductive vision.

He stared on. Maybe Utopia was an option. Everyone else seemed to think so.

The cam settled down to follow a single child, a little rosy-cheeked girl with blonde hair. She was yelling something at the kids behind her but there was no sound to the images. She leapt across a small bright stream and ran on into open pastures. A silent wind swept the grass into a gentle tide that swirled around her knees. The cam, still moving with the girl, panned back to show the other kids falling behind, coming to a halt in a sprawled, confused group on the far side of the stream.

Auger shifted his feet. Around him the crowd moved. He felt a part of them now. His hope mixed with theirs, his fears linked to theirs. He couldn't tear his eyes from the projection of the perfect little girl running laughing in the sun away from her friends and towards the edge of the forest.

The cam zoomed forward towards the rising bank of trees, dropping behind the girl's shoulder as she slowed down. Her shoulders were heaving as she caught her breath, and there was an abrupt flash of movement in the trees, and the commentator's voice was back in Auger's head.

'You are going to die now.'

This wasn't the commentator's voice, though. This was harsh and full of hate, and Auger flinched with the child as the beast emerged slowly from the trees. It was some kind of animal, four-footed, moving easily into the open. It seemed to shimmer between wolf and bear, although as Auger focused on it, he saw that there was no symmetry or fine beauty to its features. Its head was bulbous and misshapen, and as it moved, shadowy slabs of muscle rolled beneath the dull and dirty fur of its flanks.

A few paces clear of the trees, it stopped, sat on its haunches and lifted a forefoot. A rack of silver claws slid out and the beast inspected them with narrowed, glittering eyes. It raised its head to stare with those eyes at the defenceless girl. At Auger.

The child stepped back as the beast leaned back on its haunches and tensed, teeth bared and slavering, preparing to spring at her. Auger was holding his breath, conscious of total silence around him. Then he could hear someone breathing sharply and whimpering, and it was the little girl way up there. He wanted to do something but there was nothing he could do as the beast launched itself at her, claws extended and jaws wide. He heard a scream and almost immediately a terrible animal cry, and then the image seemed to burst apart in a blinding flare.

The cam moved in to settle above the beast's blasted corpse, and then panned back again to the child who was sobbing onto the smooth shining carapace of an autoid. There was no clue to its weaponry, and no indication of how it had arrived there. The machine was as motionless as a lizard in the grass, and the reflections of sun and sky that drifted over its silver skin seemed for an instant to be radiating from it, as if the world sprang from the machine.

The cam rose gently to reveal the child's friends running happily towards the girl and the autoid, and the scene faded away to be replaced by the initial view over the beautiful raw planet in the warmth of the sun.

'What you are looking at right now is a real recorded image, but remember, what we just showed you was only a simulation. It may not have been real, but it may be the future.' The cam moved with the soft voice over the restless grass of the plains. And then the cam drew away, up, accelerated hard until the plains were distant, and continued still to rise into the sky, and on into the atmosphere, and space. And stopped there, the planet Dirangesept a glowing bauble to be stretched out for and touched. And reached.

Yes, Auger thought. Yes.

The voice deepened reassuringly. 'Things have changed. You can enrol here.' And now firmly, authoritatively, it said, 'Dirangesept. Be there. Be on Three.'

Auger felt the program release him. He rubbed his eyes and tried to shake off the feeling of a fading headache. He had a burning sense of anger at the outrage he had been shown, the innocent girl, the beast, her saviour, and a sense of justice done, of wrong made right.

He rubbed his eyes again and shook his head to clear it, barely noticing the blood that was still oozing from his fist.

It was crazy to feel like this. The autoids were portrayed as godlike redeemers, which they weren't. They were just the tools of frail men and women, bLinkered, who were flawed at best. At worst they were like Sweet.

He pressed hard with his knuckles until his eyeballs hurt, letting the pain override the anger that he still felt against the beast.

The autoids weren't like that, and the girl was just a Simage, so why should the beast have been like the real beasts of Dirangesept? Auger couldn't believe they were like that. He remembered hearing stories of their beauty as well as their deadliness, years ago, but now it seemed they were merely hideous.

The headache was still there, a dull throb in his temples. He noticed the people around him, their faces pulled tight into anger. He wanted to say something to someone about it, and caught the eye of a young woman with water-effect hair that twisted into a frothy vortex over her shoulders.

'Those beasts can't treat us like that,' the woman began. Auger noticed her fist clenching spasmodically at her side. 'Those animals need to be taught a lesson. That little girl was someone's daughter. She could have been my daughter.' Her voice rose hysterically, breaking as she continued. 'My daughter! They can't do that to my daughter.' A few other people around her murmured agreement. Somewhere a few metres away a child began to wail.

She's right, Auger thought, and nodded reflexively. His head felt vaguely woolly now, his anger an unfocused thing. He felt unable to pull his thoughts together, overwhelmed by a sense of justice betrayed.

Around him the crowd began to disperse, and his thoughts seemed to coalesce as he found himself free to move, and then in time almost alone.

Hours must have passed, he realised. Dirangesept was in his head, still. The D3 project. There were queues at enrolment booths all around the square, now, and he felt a brief pang of failure and resentment that he was too old himself. Above each booth was a holo of the great countdown clock in Parliament Square, the yellow letters telling him that departure was imminent. And they were still recruiting. Auger wanted to go, to do something, to avenge the failure of the first two projects, to help create a new Earth far away.

He shook his head, his thoughts fuzzy and confused. No, he didn't want that at all. He didn't know what he wanted any more, but something still nagged at him.

Dirangesept? No. It was something to do with Dirangesept, though. What was it?

Fly. Fly had died in Fury's Dirangesept zone.

Auger left Trafalgar Square at a run.

It was Fly.

Fly had left the jungle zone running before leaving for the Church of Final Hope. Auger tried looking around the room but the green shadows spooked him and the sounds of the deep forest made him itch. The place seemed different without Fly.

He went through the cries and shadows into the kitchen. There was a mug of coffee made and not drunk on the counter. He realised his fist was still bleeding, and he found a cloth, wrapping it tightly around his hand to staunch the flow. Then he sniffed the coffee and set it to reheat while he checked the surfaces and cupboards, then anywhere else Fly might have hidden something.

There was nothing. No food except the remains of a jar of coffee powder. Auger emptied the jar carefully into the sink and sifted through the dregs before washing them down the drain in a slow brown vortex. The kitchen was perfectly neat and tidy apart from the mug of coffee. Fly had probably left it for Auger. The cook unit was scrubbed, the refrigerator was clean and empty, its freezer compartment containing only an old bag of frozen soyspheres on a hard uneven mound of greying condensation ice. Auger emptied the bag into the sink, half expecting to find something there, but the soy just subsided into mush and gurgled away. He picked up the mug and stood in the doorway, at the edge of the jungle, staring into the wildness. The cries seemed mournful, as if the zone was aware of Fly's absence and wouldn't run properly without him.

'Zone off,' Auger said, but the jungle ignored him. Fly must have customised the Exit, and Auger didn't have the words. He tried, 'Remember what's important, Auger,' but that wasn't it. All that did was bring back Auger's guilt.

He stepped through the greenery to the front door and disabled Fly's power supply at the wallbox in the corridor. The whole place went totally dark, and Auger had the feeling as he stepped back inside that the zone was somehow still in play, some dark beast in there lurking in ambush.

He flicked on his torch, the central disk of brightness on the far wall making him squint, too blinding to see by and throwing everything else into faraway black. He tuned the beam down, making for the window but then changing his mind. He left the window opaque and closed the front door. It was getting hot already without the aircon.

Everything important was here, Fly had said. Twice. There was something here for Auger, something Fly didn't want anybody else to know about, and something he hadn't even wanted Auger to know about unless he was dead.

There was nothing in this room, though. Just the bare walls, table and hard seats, and the boxes for the zone in every corner of the room. Auger took them apart and found nothing but silicon. Nothing in the walls either. He was sweating in the heat, uninterested in the coffee still in his hand. He went back to the kitchen to pour it away and get cold water instead, and stopped there, staring at what the torch beam had caught.

Water was dripping steadily onto the floor from the refrigerator. Auger knelt and pulled the door fully open to peer at the freezer unit. In the kitchen Fly had been obsessively neat. He'd kept everything in the kitchen bleach-bright. And yet despite their age the soyspheres hadn't been embedded in the ice, they had been lying on it. The ice hadn't been allowed by neglect to form around the forgotten bag. It was meant to be there.

Auger went back to the sink and sifted through the soysphere mush once more, but there was still nothing. It wasn't that.

He looked from the sink to the freezer unit again and shone his torch on the shrinking crystalline mound. Just ice. He knelt down and put the torch to the ice, and caught a glimmer of blue buried within it.

He stretched out his arm, pouring what was left of the lukewarm coffee onto the ice. The mound melted a little more and the blue brightened enough to show him the edge of something solid. Auger straightened to find a knife and began chipping at the ice.

It was half an hour before he was able to lever out the sealed blue plastic package Fly had hidden there.

He mopped up the spreading pool of coffee and water on the floor, then rinsed the mug and the slim soft pack that was all that remained on the Earth of Fly.

Auger dug a small folding knife from his pocket, unclasped the blade and laid it on the counter beside the pack. He wasn't sure why he was hesitating about opening the pack. What did he expect? He knew hardly a thing about Fly. How much could Fly have had in his life for a stranger like Auger to be so important to him?

There was a film of sweat on his palms, and a low murmur of street noise outside. His hand was throbbing hard now. Auger wiped away the sweat and tried to block out the noise. He pulled Fly to the front of his mind. It seemed wrong that Auger could be responsible for his death and be rewarded with a gift.

He ran a finger over the soft sheath. The plastic had been weakened by its time in Fly's freezer, and his fingernail left a fine weal on the surface. The ice hadn't penetrated it, but as soon as Auger slid the tip of the knife into the shiny blue wrapping it ripped and gave all the way.

There were two things in the package. One was a fading letter which was addressed to Fly and began *To My Son*. It made Auger think of Jay and the child they would never have. He felt uncomfortable reading the letter. After rambling for a page of love and regret, it ended,

Before I go, I want you to to promise that you will keep this doorway safe. But you must never, ever go there. It leads only to madness and death.

I will always love you.

Your dad.

Auger folded the letter carefully and put it down, and then took out the pair of bLinkers. He set them carefully on the table beside the letter and looked at them. He wondered how old they were. A doorway?

He put the letter and the bLinkers back in the blue pack, went through the drawers again until he found a roll of tape, and carefully resealed the thing. Then he tossed the blood-sodden rag from his fist down the waste chute and took another from a drawer. His hand was throbbing almost unbearably now. The wound was worse than he'd thought. He must have really swung at that table. The blood wasn't going to stop.

He picked up the blue pack, weighing it in his hand. It was small enough to slip into his jacket pocket without even creasing the fabric.

Auger recognised her immediately. She didn't react at all, though. He wondered whether she had recognised him, too. He squinted at her name tag. Astrid Remarque. Registrar.

'That's deep,' she said, looking quickly at his hand. 'Can I check your datasink?' She took her scanner and flashed it over his upper arm. 'I see you have no medical preference, Mr Auger. We can offer you conventional medicine, aromatherapy, homeopathy—'

He cut her off. 'What works is fine with me. Bat's piss and a Hail Mary's hunkydory if it's going to stop the bleeding. Otherwise sew it up or something. I'm not a medic. Just get on with it.'

She frowned at him, then simply shrugged. 'In that case, it's a broad-spectrum antibiotic jab to start with. What were you doing, trying to punch out a trig?' She checked the scan again. He didn't answer her. 'Your rabies is about due, and your hepatitis F and G – you might as well have them, too. You should look after yourself.' She swabbed the cut and said, 'I did some work on nanotherapy in my preclinical year, Mr Auger. I read some papers by—'

'My wife. She's my wife.' He shouldn't have brought his injury to GenMed. He wondered why he had, but not for long. A moth to a flame.

'I guessed that. It must have been very hard for you.' The wound was spread wide now and she was pasting something over the exposed flesh. It didn't hurt, but it didn't smell too good either. 'You were out in the open for some time after you got this, weren't you? The atmosphere on a bad

79

day has the effect of slow cautery on this type of injury. It's an interesting phenomenon.' She touched the wound's edge with a swab. 'But on the other hand there's airborne infection. No point in taking risks. Some of those Indonesian bugs can survive all those miles, swaddled in ash.'

She was working methodically at the wound, and he watched the movement of her hands. She had delicate fingers. The gloves made them seamless, like synthetic digits, like she was a machine. But Auger didn't think she was any machine. He didn't need to be giving her such a hard time.

'I'm going to accelerate this, Mr Auger, if that's all right with you.' She was holding a cloudy plastic 2-ml cartridge up to the light, peering into it. She flicked it twice with a latexed fingernail. A slow bubble rose to the meniscus and vanished. 'Did your wife tell you much about her research?'

'Something,' he said as she finally shook the cartridge and punched it into the barrel of a delivery gun.

'It came pretty much to a halt when—' She broke off as if concentrating on the gun, but that wasn't it.

'Maybe she wouldn't have been able to take it any further anyway,' he said, surprising himself. 'Maybe she took it as far it it could go.' He looked at the gun. 'Nanoagents in there?'

'You said what works is fine. What your wife pioneered is better than fine. That's a bad wound and you've left it open for hours in a bad environment. If that site scars it won't look good, but more importantly it'll contract and leave you with permanently limited mobility. You wouldn't make a very good fist again. No pun intended.' She raised the gun. 'You know how the process works?'

'It randomises collagen laydown.' He remembered that. He'd had to listen to it enough. 'And I'm not a 'fist.'

She began to inject the clear fluid into the periphery of the wound. 'Yes, but it's *how* it does that. Your fibroblasts create a web of collagen, starting at the wound's edge. But as they move into the wound they pull the bundles of collagen fibres predominantly in one direction, and that's what causes the scar and the lack of elasticity. That unidirectional pull. What your wife created was a nangine that makes the fibroblasts replicate to fill the wound *before* they begin to lay down their collagen.'

Auger watched the enthusiasm on her face as she ejected the used cartridge and needle into a bright yellow sharps bin. Jay had had that same enthusiasm. He could almost hear the words coming from her. 'So the collagen laydown is generated at random from within the wound site,' he said, echoing the voice in his head. 'Scarless healing.'

She looked at him, catching the slight flatness in his tone. She glanced across at his notes. 'You weren't injured at all? Your datasink shows nothing.'

It took him a moment to realise she wasn't talking about now. 'I was lucky.' He tried to control his voice. 'We were in the air when it happened. I just saw it, that's all. I just sat up there and watched the whole thing. With Jay beside me. The two of us.'

She looked at him curiously, but said nothing. No blame, no sympathy.

He let her begin to seal the site with PlaSkin, painting it on from a jar with a cotton swab, coat by coat. She glanced up from the wound at him, then back down again. 'Are you okay?' she said, dabbing. 'I'm not hurting you?'

Auger looked around the emergency room. The smell of herbs, flowers, burnt flesh, maggoty flesh, the chanting, the crying, the praying. And this girl daintily painting his skin like a child playing doctor and patient. It seemed insane to him.

'I'm okay,' he said.

She looked at him again, saying nothing again, and he wondered why he'd said that to her. He repeated it in his mind, listening to how he'd said it. I'm okay. I'm okay now you've closed the cut, or I'm okay after what happened on my wedding day? Or maybe he'd been saying I'm not okay at all but I don't want to talk about it any more.

As he held up his arm for her to scan in the treatment record, she said, 'I'm sorry, we don't have your skin shade.'

'What?' He felt suddenly displaced. He looked around at the damaged people and for an instant he clearly saw his arrival at this same place those few years back with Jay screaming and holding on to him. The time between was like a hard, anaesthetised scar.

'The PlaSkin. It's too yellow.'

He looked down at the rectangle of jaundiced skin over his knuckles and touched it, leaving a brief fingerprint on the glassy surface.

She was saying, 'The nangines take an hour or two to penetrate and reprogramme the fibroblast RNA. Then they'll speed everything up exponentially, but you can expect a rapid slowdown again prior to total healing, as the nangines burn out and the fibroblast RNA reverts. The PlaSkin will wear away as the wound heals, and your own epidermis will grow through it. It'll take a week or so, though. Like I said, that was a full-thickness injury.' She stood up, reaching out to him with a tentativeness that surprised him, and added, 'I'm so sorry. If only she hadn't—'

'If only she hadn't married me. If she hadn't—' He turned and walked away. If Jay hadn't got caught up in Fury's attempt to murder me. If, if if. Auger curled his fingers in sudden anger, notching his nails at the edge of the alien skin, ready to rip at it, but then he made himself relax, stroking the barrier that safeguarded Jay's work, Jay's healing.

Behind him he heard the girl shouting down the corridor, 'I didn't mean that. Auger. Auger! Oh, god*damn* it.'

He didn't even realise he was heading for the neuro wards until the outer doors opened for him in a brilliant mercury splash. He hesitated, then thought, What the hell, and plunged through. He tossed a glance back at the doors. Of course they weren't metal at all, they didn't even exist in any real sense. They were an indicator that he was passing into the sterile veil of the wards.

Within the veil he set off towards the second set of doors at the steady pace prescribed by the floorlights, deepbreathing in time with the chimes and hating the sensation of hot and cold that wasn't even necessary, he was sure. The knot that tightened in his gut as he approached the inner doors might have been something to do with the veil, but he doubted it. He couldn't remember the last time, but it was the same every time. It was the anticipation of seeing Jay that twisted in the core of him.

Ten steps into the veil he came towards his reflection again, walking towards himself walking towards himself, the floorlights meeting and meeting, until at the last moment the inner doors shimmered away. He rubbed his eyes and stood for a moment before heading towards Jay's room, walking quickly past all the closed doors along the way. Jay was housed at the end of the last corridor in the wing. In all the time he been visiting her, he had never seen anybody else in the wards. There must be scanners, but Auger had never spotted them. There were pictures of isolated flowers on the walls, and his footsteps made no sound on the soft, pale green floor.

Outside her door he stopped and breathed a few times, then thumbed the door monitor to look at her before going in. On the screen Jay was sitting on her bed, her face hidden in her hands. Her body was shaking convulsively. Watching her, he wondered what it might be like to be wherever she was. He imagined her world as a yo-yo, hurled down at the ground on its length of string that day and now spinning there eternally, a finger's breadth from fracture, its traction abruptly and without warning lost, never ever to regather and surge back up again.

Auger pressed the nurse's alert and watched her smooth her dress as she stood up from her chair beside Jay. He swiped his ID and watched her check it on the internal monitor before opening the door to let him in.

For a second it surprised him that he didn't recognise the woman. For a long time at the beginning Jay had had the same nurse, day in, day out. Not that it made any difference to Jay. Whoever it was, they'd always be a stranger to her. But for Auger it had added to the unreality of it, the unchanging scene on the monitor, the eternal immediacy of the disaster.

'Hello, Jay,' Auger said.

She raised her head and Auger wondered how he could have imagined forgetting what she looked like. The high cheekbones, the perfect shape of her jaw. She was beautiful. Then he saw the swollen redness around her eyes, and realised he could hardly remember her without the tears any more. On the arc of screens behind her the displays fizzed into action, the bright colours of her neural activity announced and recorded.

'Cy?' She rose with his name, stumbling towards Auger as her arms stretched out to him. Her voice fractured. 'Oh, God, Cy, for a moment I thought you were dead too.' She was grabbing desperately at him, hugging him tight and sobbing. Auger stared over her shoulder at the radiant displays.

She was mumbling into his jacket now. 'Where were you, Cy? I didn't know where you were.'

'How are you, Jay?' he said.

She fell back to look at him, trying to collect herself, to control her breathing a little. 'I'm fine. I'm not hurt. But the others . . . Is everyone dead?'

Auger nodded. He felt as helpless as he always did. He had no reaction left any more. There was nothing left in him. 'It looks like it.'

'My parents? Your brother?'

'Everyone. There's just, there's just us.'

Jay pressed her hands to her throat and then drew them hard down over her breasts, across the flat of her stomach, parting them to follow and squeeze her thighs. Her knuckles and the joints of her fingers were white. Her yellow wedding dress – Auger wondered how many of them there had to be for her to wear it fresh every day – stretched and pulled taut, then bounced loose as she took her hands away. 'My dress,' she murmured sadly. 'My wedding dress.' She took a shuddering breath. 'I never want to see it again.' She put a hand to its neckline and made as if to wrench it off, then looked at Auger as if for the first time and said, puzzled, 'Where's your suit, Cy?'

The nurse stood up and came to take Jay's arm. 'Mrs Auger—'

'Who are you? Who are you?' Her voice rising in panic, Jay shook the nurse off with sudden strength and fell against Auger, pulling at him wildly. Auger tried to prise her hands away. He felt sick.

'I have to go, Jay,' he said. The nurse was nodding at him, stroking Jay's hair in a gentle rhythm with one hand while working firmly at her grip on Auger's jacket with the other. Jay was determined but the nurse was stronger and practised, and Jay's hand dropped away, her fist clutching air.

Auger said, 'Will you be okay, Jay? I have to go. Just . . .' He took a breath, hating himself for the lie, even though for Jay it was the truth. 'Just for a few minutes.'

Jay subsided into the nurse's arms. The nurse sat gently on the bed, Jay beside her. The nurse stroked her hands and said, 'It's all right. Settle yourself now. He'll just be gone a few minutes. He'll be back before you know it. Promise.'

Jay took a shuddering breath, looked at Auger and then back at the nurse to say, 'I'm sorry. I'm sorry. You don't understand. We were married only an hour ago and now everyone's dead. Everyone. My family is dead, our friends are all dead.' She turned her face to Auger and it was all he could do not to look away. She whispered, new tears following the worn tracks down her cheeks, 'All we have now is each other.'

And I have even less than that, Auger thought. He bent down and kissed her, salt on his lips. 'I'll be back very soon, Jay.'

Walking back down the corridor, Auger played the scene back in his mind, as he still did almost every day, the same scene. Five minutes, he thought. Relief, anxiety, fear, hysteria and grief. How can it carry on like this? How can it not change?

He walked into the veil again, the chimes tolling him from the wards.

NINE

An old, defunct cinema, its name an unanticipated irony, was where
Lisele and Jocar had lived. There were steel bars on the doors now and no
sign that anyone might be in occupation. But somehow Auger was sure
Lisele would still be there. He stood at the familiar mock-bronze doors
with their patterns of scrolling film, his memory stirring painfully, and he
bruised his knuckles on the solid metal to block out those thoughts. His
knock made little sound. The door shivered and a brief ghost of itself in
ash bounced out at him and collapsed at his feet. The thoughts stayed
with him, though. Jocar would have walked out and been there within
two minutes, Cherry Tree Wood being just around the corner from the
disused cinema. He would have kissed Lisele as he left, and she would
have told him she wished she was well enough to go along too. And a
wave from the door, and never to see him again. A few hours later, she
would have heard and felt the explosion.

There was still no answer to his third rap on the door. Maybe she had
given the place up and moved elsewhere after all. Auger stepped back and
looked up at the crumbling façade. No windows, of course, not in a
cinema. There was no way of telling if there was anyone inside. Just the
ancient sign, silver deco letters greening in the bitter atmosphere. THE
PHOENIX.

He knocked again. She would be there. He waited until, above the
door, the monitor's iris finally unfurled, turned its lens to him, and then
swirled shut again. Auger stood back. A moment more, and the bars
raised themselves and the door opened to him.

'Lisele?' he said, though he didn't need to. She had hardly changed at
all. The strawberry tangle of her hair, the high, sharp bones of her cheeks.
She'd grown thinner, but it was her. He just wanted to give her a chance
to react, maybe to close the door in his face. He wouldn't have blamed her

85

for that. Instead she stood for a moment under the soft light of the ticket booth and then coughed, raising a quick hand to her mouth and glancing into her cupped palm before bringing a handkerchief from a pocket to wipe her hand dry.

'I had an idea it would be you, Cy,' she said, her voice low as she turned around to walk through the entrance hall and carry on up towards the auditorium. He stood for a moment, suddenly uncertain, then followed her, closing the door behind him. He heard the outer bars engage. There was no going back now.

The slope of the auditorium drew them towards the great glittering screen that Auger remembered so well. Jocar had framed it to be a vast, false window, and set it to spring up random vids from the past, current HoloNews footage, anything at all. Sometimes there were old films, sometimes satellite and surveillance footage. The perspective was constantly shifting. Nothing lasted more than a few minutes. You might be looking down from space at the smoking wreck of the world, and a moment later there was just a man and a woman in soft-brimmed hats and sad, soft talk of love and Paris. Auger hoped there wouldn't be that today. Being here was hard enough.

Lisele settled herself into a chair beneath a grinning, blind-eyed golden mask on the wall. The ranks of seating were no longer there, and the auditorium was divided into furnished sections, the stuff of a bedroom here, the machinery of a kitchen there. Where Lisele had led Auger, it was arranged as a living space with a few armchairs and a table. It might have been peaceful, even intimate, if there had been walls. But the screen shadowed and overshadowed everything. There was no peace.

She gestured him to sit too. Light from the screen played on her face. Auger couldn't resist turning to the screen to see an airport runway, its track a long, luminescent glare of visgel. A freightflite was rumbling in to land, hooking into the gel and dragging to a halt. A different time zone where it was dusk, or dawn, and there were palm trees in the distance. No, just archive footage, Auger guessed, easing himself into the ancient stuffing of the chair. HoloNews was always showing film like that, but everyone knew how rarely the freighters actually made such trips these days.

'How have you been?' Lisele said, not waiting for him to answer. She nodded towards the screen, where the image had already changed. A volcano somewhere, its flux of steaming magma pouring to the edges of the window frame. And then a travelling view of the vast foundries and spaceship production facilities of mainland Europe that operated night and day and consumed, it seemed to Auger, more raw material than the collapsing world could spare.

He pulled his eyes away. 'Working, mainly,' he said. 'I've been working. Trying to lose myself in it, I suppose. And you?'

'Not much. I'm fine, really. Where I get my food, the guy there sometimes needs stuff delivered to people like me, stay-at-homes. I do that for him when I'm up to it. It gets me out, I've made a few friends that way. You'd be surprised how many people just don't go out now, Cy. Never. Block it all out. Work in their rooms, live in their rooms, get everything delivered. Food in, shit out. You know, someone told me these days twenty per cent of deaths are lone home deaths, and forty per cent of those aren't discovered for at least a week. People like me find them. Who'll find me, I wonder?' She stretched out and touched Auger's hand. 'I'm sorry, Cy. That wasn't aimed at you. I simply wonder, that's all. When I die, I'm dead, doesn't matter if I'm alone or the centre of millions. What's next is what matters then. But for now, I'm fine. I have my routine, my contentment. And I have fine memories.' Her tone sharpened fractionally for his benefit. 'I make sure to keep them. The *good* things of the past.'

She looked at Auger, and he sensed her consideration of his memories, of how he dealt with them. He felt obscurely ashamed by her.

She glanced towards the screen, seeing his discomfort and changing the subject. 'I saw Fury's church go down. That was you?'

'It wasn't what I intended.' Auger felt suddenly tired, as if what he wanted to say had already been said. 'Just before it happened, Fury looked straight at me,' he told her. 'He looked at me and he turned it around. I thought I had him, but it wasn't that way at all.'

Lisele just shrugged. 'But it's over, isn't it? At last. He's dead. Isn't that why you're here?'

'I thought it would feel better than this, Lisele. Different, anyway.' He rubbed his face. 'I went to see Jay again. The first time in a long time.'

'And now you've come to see me.' She leaned forward. 'Look, I let it all go a long time ago, Cy. Maybe it was Father Fury that day, and maybe it wasn't. It doesn't matter to me now. It's the past. You could have come before now.' Absently, she picked up a book lying on the arm of her chair and clutched it in both hands, her grip hard enough to blanch her knuckles. A moment, and then she sighed and let the book drop into her lap.

'It had to be him, Lisele. There was no one else. But I wanted him to say it.'

Lisele looked steadily at Auger. 'If he'd confessed, been tried for it, darktimed or even executed, it still would have made no difference. It's up to you to look away.'

'Jay can't look away, Lisele.'

'You aren't responsible for her.' Her voice softened, and she seemed to change, touching the cover of the book and returning it to the arm of her chair. 'Any more than you're responsible for me, Cy. Is that what you thought?'

He felt the tears come then, felt and tasted their salt. It was one of the few tastes you could still trust, it struck him. The pure taste of sorrow and grief. He licked his lips dry. Lisele pulled herself awkwardly from her chair and came over to him, accepting him into the warmth of her arms and letting her body absorb everything. She waited patiently until he was still, then held him by the shoulders and looked at him. 'That's a good thing, Auger. That's the first good thing.'

'I'm sorry. I'm so sorry.'

'Don't be. You're the one suffered more than anyone else.'

'But you—'

'I lost my husband, Cy. I felt guilty for a long, long time, for missing the wedding, for missing being killed. Like you, no different.' She coughed, stayed coughing for a minute, eventually bringing the hand-kerchief to her face to stifle herself. 'They say I'm cured, they say I can breathe fine now. But it was my lungs that kept me away that day, that saved my life, and my brain won't let me reclaim them now. Psycho-somatic. It doesn't exist, but it's real enough. It's killing me.' She wadded up the handkerchief and tucked it away again.

'I wanted to come and see you before, Lisele. I tried, but I couldn't do it. I couldn't even call you.'

Lisele nodded. 'You and me, we're all that's left, Cy. I'm glad you came. I would have been sorry if you hadn't.' She stepped through a gap between chairs to the kitchen area and began to make tea for them, moving slowly, breathing long and slow, taking her time. Steam rose from the kettle, the vapour a rising bright aura. She swilled boiling water into a plump blue pot and swirled the pot in her hands, filling it first with warmth. Then she poured the water away and spooned tea into the pot, followed by another pan of boiling water. She set the pot down on the counter and stood waiting patiently. Light from the screen stroked over her, and Auger turned to see a great, boundless ocean. Vast, slow waves burst and rebuilt, surged and broke again. For a moment he thought he glimpsed a flat pale rock at the deep base of the swell. Maybe a rock, maybe the roof of a building. Maybe nothing at all.

Lisele spoke, and he twisted round again, away from the endless sea. She smiled at him as she said, 'It's a ritual, tea, isn't it? Just like for the Japanese, only they know it while we English pretend it isn't, just as we pretend everything isn't.'

He cleared his throat, realising he was thirsty for the tea. 'It's a good ritual, though,' he said. 'A comforting one. It gives us pause.'

She was pouring the tea into two slender porcelain cups now, as if it was real tea she had used instead of synthetically impregnated leaves. Auger picked up the book she'd been reading. *Grasping Heaven – The Experience of your Life.* It unsettled him, the idea of Lisele reading this stuff. But he had no right to judge her. It seemed everyone was reading them these days.

She brought the cups back, spires of steam rising. She said, 'Will you tell me about it? About that day? All I ever heard were the HoloNews reports.'

He replaced the book and said, after a moment, 'Yes, all right. Are you sure you want to hear it, though?'

'I've been ready for a long time, Cy.' She gave him his tea and sat down with hers, holding the cup up to her mouth between her palms and blowing ripples gently across the surface. Her eyes were on him. He could see the sea reflected there.

Auger ran his tongue around his suddenly dry mouth, and started to talk. It was like a speech that he rehearsed every day, he knew the words so well. Telling it out loud was a strange relief.

'The ceremony was over and we were coming away from the party. It was late evening, about eleven. Jocar . . .' Auger watched Lisele's face at the sound of her husband's name. A small smile of remembrance, and then a brief nod, telling Auger it really was okay. 'Jocar had told us how sorry you were that you couldn't make it yourself, and how he'd tell you all about it later.'

'Thank you, Auger.' She patted the book. Auger remembered the two of them, Lisele and Jocar, sitting side by side, the way she would pat his hand in that same way.

He took a sip of the tea and went on. 'So, we'd climbed into the 'flite and I was just lifting it away. I looked back, I was starting to wave, and I noticed the ground looking a bit shaky. Heat distortion through the burners, I thought, but I was banking round at the time and looking out the side, so it couldn't have been that. Then, as I was thinking it was a tremor, there was a low, extended boom.' He closed his eyes, hearing it again. 'I still didn't get it, though. I thought it was the engine misfiring. Jay was right beside me, Lisele. I was thinking, This is the woman I love and have just married, and these are the people who are the most important to us in all the world. I have everything.' His breath caught. 'That's what I was thinking. I have everything.'

He cradled the tea. There were tears in Lisele's eyes, but he knew it was all right. 'You don't think that very often any more, Lisele, do you? Not when the world may end next month, a year ahead.' He took a shuddering breath and went on. 'The explosion was like a solid thing sprouting into the night, a dome of fire, lit and lifted from beneath.' He stopped. 'For what it's worth, Lisele, Jocar must have died instantly, along with everyone else on the ground. I don't know how long the explosion lasted, but it seemed for ever. Probably a couple of seconds. When it had done the light was still there, just duller. What remained of the tent was burning, there were patches of flame all over, all around the park, trees on fire—' He stopped again, abruptly.

'Go on,' Lisele said. She was holding her teacup in both hands. 'It's really okay. Tell me about you and Jay.'

Auger licked his lips, rubbed his eyes, started again. 'Jay was screaming and screaming. She took it in more quickly than me. She already knew everything. That's what did it to her, I think. It overloaded her. I had the 'flite to think about. I took us up clear of it all and then banked round to see what I could do. I was thinking it was a rift, it had taken out power lines or something. But then I thought, if it was a rift, it had no course. It didn't go north or south, east or west. It was just there, the whole world in flames. Still, I thought, it was dark and maybe the explosion and flames had lightblinded me.'

He picked up his tea again, then put it down, shaking too much to hold it. Lisele waited patiently. She'd waited long enough, he thought. He went on. 'I couldn't think clearly with Jay screaming in my ears, so I took auditory override and nilled cockpit and engine noise. I reset the screen to night and tuned down the HighLights.' Auger saw it now, was up there in the silence again. No sound penetrating his cocoon, not even Jay's screams. Everything cut off but the controls in his hands.

'It was as if I was suddenly alone up there, almost disembodied, except that I could feel Jay's hands clawing at me. I shook her off.' He let out a long, long breath. 'Christ, Lisele, I shook her off. There was smoke and dust and those scattered fires like enormous windblown yellow flowers, but there was no noise at all except for a sort of fizzing and the occasional pop. I still couldn't make out the rift's course. I was starting to realise it had been an explosion, and to know it hadn't been any accident either. There shouldn't have been anything down there to blow up like that. It was a wedding. Anyway, smoke was gusting around more strongly now, and the dust was crawling in the air. I kept resetting the screen to improve the view, but it was no good, so I tried to take us down blind, but that was impossible too. I'd borrowed the 'flite from someone I knew, it was a vintage model and they'd tied streamers to it. Jarman and Grouch had done that.' He paused. 'Remember them?'

Lisele nodded.

'They were somewhere down there now, dead too, though I didn't know it. Their streamers screwed up the blindflight systems, so I couldn't try and swing down into the park to do anything. Of course there was nothing I could have done anyway, but I wanted to try. I wanted to try.'

He took another breath. 'So I brought us up and around again. I sent out an alert over the comms and headed for GenMed, thinking any survivors would be taken there. I thought Jay and I were okay. But when I nilled the auditory override she was still screaming and screaming.' He stopped to watch his fist clench and open again. 'You'd think the immediate shock, the adrenalin would have worn off a bit, but it was like it had just happened, that instant. Of course, this is looking back at it, but I think I already had an idea even then that something terrible had happened to her.'

Auger drained his cup. There were a few thin leaves in the bottom of the cup. He swirled them around in the last drops of tea and squinted at them. He couldn't make it out, though. It was an image of nothing. Of chaos.

He stood up. 'That's it. I'm sorry, Lisele. I should have come before.'

'You came when it was the time to come, Cy,' Lisele said. 'At least it's over for you, too, now.' She came and drew him in, holding him tight. He felt forgiveness, and heard the faint crackling of her lungs crushed against his. She coughed as she released him, and then she took his hand and was walking him up the slope of the auditorium and away from the shifting screen and its shadows and lies.

'I'll be seeing you,' he said to her at the street doors. The daylight seemed strange after the glimmering twilight of the Phoenix, scratching at his eyes and making him squint.

'Yes,' she told him, standing with the light behind her, a picked-out silhouette. She added, 'You have to look back at the past, Cy, if only to be sure the doors are closed behind you. But once they're closed, move on.'

He searched her face for a moment, wondering whether she'd read those words in her book, and then said, 'Goodbye, Lisele,' and she repeated it with sadness.

'Goodbye, Cy.'

She would never see him again, he realised. Forgiveness was one thing, but pain was another thing entirely.

Walking away into the street, Auger felt that something inside him had changed. Maybe it really was over for Lisele, but for him it wasn't yet. There was more. He knew there was. Perhaps since the wedding he had been just as trapped as Jay, but more subtly.

For Lisele, moving on meant leaving the badness of the past behind. For Auger, it would mean resolving it, if he had the strength.

He was thinking this as his tasker beeped. He flipped it open and took in the single line.

GET HERE NOW. WISCH.

Auger knew he recognised the man sitting next to Wisch, but with Jay in his mind he couldn't immediately remember where he knew him from. Something about his expression made Auger salute and hold it there, though. And Wisch's expression didn't change when Auger saluted, which was worrying. Normally Wisch would have chuckled, waved the gesture away and told Auger to sit the hell down. Now he let Auger stand there like a flagpole.

The other man's expression didn't change either. He was used to being saluted. And he wasn't 'fist or military, so he had to be Administration, which was really not good at all. Not if he'd come to see Auger.

Wisch cleared his throat. 'Auger, this is Minister Keph Maxenham. Minister, this is Captain Cy Auger, CMS.'

Shit. Auger snapped off the salute. TeeVee, that's where Auger had seen him. Except that on the screen Maxenham's face was chiselled and wise, his hooded eyes were deep blue, and his brow was firm as a flickbook hero's. This was Maxenham, but you'd look twice to know it for sure. He looked hard and sly. His eyes were blue, but the blue of them was pale and empty.

It didn't surprise Auger. The Administration kept their true faces to themselves. Maxenham was Minister for Faith. As far as CMS was concerned, Maxenham was God.

The Minister looked idly at Wisch, and said, 'Carry on,' in a smooth, low voice. Auger noticed a file lying on the table in front of Wisch. A thick, scuffed file.

'Auger,' Wisch said wearily, then stopped and changed it, making the matter formal. 'Captain Auger.'

Auger decided to speed the thing up. He had an idea where this was going. 'Sir, is this about the Fury operation?'

Maxenham lifted a delicate hand and held it there, limp-fingered, as if waiting for the hand to be touched. 'Father Fury,' he said softly. 'Yes. Do you have any idea, Captain Auger, do you have even the faintest idea how seriously, how absolutely you have fucked this up?' He swore delicately and distastefully, looking at Auger as if blaming him for the word. 'Let me make it quite clear to you. We have been plagued by Father Fury for a long time. A very long time. Some years ago, thanks to another fuckup, a fuckup by your predecessor, Fury was responsible for a major setback to the third Dirangesept project. Since then the Administration has worked hard to overcome the delays caused by this setback, and finally we have done so. We are now very close to being in a position to proceed with the third project. It won't have escaped even you, Captain Auger, that we are actively recruiting for the project. And this time we shall be successful. This time we shall know our enemy.'

Maxenham pushed out a hand and looked at the watch on his wrist, an antique golden timepiece crusted with gems. The face was cloudy and pitted from exposure to an environment that the watch's makers hadn't dreamed of, and Maxenham was forced to squint at it. He held the watch there for a few moments longer, so that Wisch and Auger had to notice the opulence of it. Auger glanced at the clock on the wall and said to Maxenham, deliberately, 'It's ten fifty-three.'

Maxenham dropped his hand to the table and flushed for just an instant as Wisch caught Auger's eye and gave him a swift little shake of the head. The hell with it, Auger thought.

'You don't read the signs, do you, Captain Auger? Or maybe you do, and you simply have a death wish. Well, let me tell you that the Administration has no time and no place for failure. Tell me, did you see the news last night?'

Auger shook his head.

'Well, let me tell you something. The media were in Hyde Park setting up their cams in anticipation of next week's ceremony to mark the sealing of the rift. They were on site to record your entire operation, Captain Auger. Everything. The whole fiasco was transmitted live to the whole world, what's left of it. It will take a great deal of effort and re-information to correct the impression presented by that, if indeed we can. Are you with me?'

Auger felt his face redden with anger. 'If the Administration was so keen to deal with Fury, why was the CMS request to arrest him prior to the operation rejected? Tell me that. Why did you block me?'

'You were not blocked. The law was observed. Your evidence was insufficient at that point. Your information was inadequate.'

'My informant—'

Wisch was shaking his head sharply now, trying to close Auger down. Maxenham raised his hand once more.

'Captain Auger, would you oblige me with the time again? Remind me that you can do something right.'

Auger took a breath. 'Ten fifty-six.'

'Then I have four minutes. Do not interrupt me again.' Maxenham sighed heavily. 'But since you bring him up, let us talk about your informant, shall we? Your informant seems to have diverted you from proper control of the operation. He was certainly not your priority and not even your responsibility, and yet you allowed yourself to be distracted from the operation and your duty to such a degree that the operation failed utterly, and did so publicly and in a manner that has seriously embarrassed the Administration.' Maxenham made a gesture to silence Auger, and went on. 'Moreover, the ceremony to seal the rift has had to be postponed, which has further embarrassed the Administration.'

The Minister glanced at Wisch before saying, 'Captain Auger, you are as of this moment indefinitely suspended from investigative duties. You will relinquish all your files to Lieutenant Wisch for reallocation to the officer from the Ministry of Faith who is waiting in your office. You will transfer immediately to Passive CMS. Your duties will henceforth be restricted to dealing with Understands and authorising Leavings. Do you understand me?'

'I understand that I'm your scapegoat, Mr Maxenham. I understand that.'

Maxenham took a breath. 'Now, Captain Auger, the time?'

'Ten fifty-nine.'

'Good.' Maxenham stood up, turning to Wisch. He put out a hand, leaving it hanging there for Wisch to take. It was a tableau by Michelangelo, man permitted to brush the fingertips of the Lord. Auger was in no doubt which of the two hands Maxenham's was.

'A good meeting, Lieutenant,' Maxenham murmured. 'Vinz Szolty, my man taking over Auger's cases, will keep you informed of his progress. He will be reporting directly to me. Publicly he will defer to you, of course. Give him every support. I'm sure you will.'

Maxenham turned on his heel and left before Wisch could answer him. On the wall the clock hit the hour.

Passive, Auger thought. After all this time, Passive. He tried to swallow the bile that rose in his throat with that word, tried to block that memory. Auger wiped the salt from his eyes with the back of a hand. Seeing Jay again at GenMed, and now this.

'Auger,' Wisch was saying, but Auger wasn't listening.

The door to his office didn't give at his push. Observing that the nameplate hadn't been changed yet, Auger knocked. He didn't want to try his doorcode and have it fail. That was what he'd be expected to do. After the knock, he walked down the corridor a few metres and leaned against the opposite wall, not to be seen waiting outside his own office by any of Sweet's crew and not to give that small victory to Maxenham's man either.

After about a minute, a shadow swelled behind the frosted glass and the door opened. Auger pushed himself off the wall.

'Auger? Come in. I thought I'd make a start. I've been trawling your files, getting up on your cases.' Maxenham's man looked like he slept well and long every night. He was just under Auger's height, and his eyes were the colour of dirty water going to ice. He sat down in Auger's chair and nodded at the screen. Then he grinned at Auger and said, pointing back at the defaced door, 'You got any friends? Pissing people off, it's, what, a hobby with you?' The grin stayed, though, and now the man had his skinny hand out.

Auger ignored the gesture. 'It's a gift. Look how I pissed off your boss, and I never even met him before.'

'Yeah, well, the Max doesn't count. If he isn't pissed off with you, one of you's dead.' He snapped the fingers of both hands, leaving his fists thumbs up at Auger. 'I'm Vinz Szolty. Be happy, I'm your friend. I do my job right, the Max'll forget you ever existed.'

'Which means what? I just go out the door and fade to black?'

Vinz Szolty spread his arms. 'Hey, what's with you? You're gonna do that anyway, Auger. This way you get to keep paying your rent and choosing your food. You understand me?'

'Well, whoop-de-doo.'

Szolty wrapped up his smile and put it away. 'You want it that way, it's fine with me. Okay, Auger.' Vinz pointed at the screen. 'Now, I've got a lost file here. Can't access it. You know anything about that?'

Auger shrugged. It was the file Wisch had failed to access.

Vinz pushed the chair back, slapping his hand on the armrest. The last trace of geniality left his voice. 'Look, you don't seem to understand the situation. You're fucked, but at this point you still have a choice. You can spend the rest of your life ticking Understands, or you can spend it in the cold and dark, sucking the water out of stones.' He paused, eyeing Auger. 'Got it yet? I don't need your help. Perhaps I don't like Maxenham any more than you do, but he scares the shit out of me, and that makes me very good at what I do. When I've sorted this out, I get to write the Max a report on you.'

He grinned again and raised his eyebrows conspiratorially at Auger. 'So, you gonna tell me what's on the hidden file? Porn? Little kiddies?'

Auger gestured for Vinz to stand up, then took his place at the console. He pulled the chair in, pushed a key, then looked up at Vinz. 'I can't get in. You've changed the password.'

Vinz's smile was like a spill of oil. 'That's right, Auger. Only way you ever get into this machine now's with me looking over your shoulder.' He leant over Auger, hiding his dancing fingers, Auger getting a blast of shave lotion, of musky wood bark and coriander.

'Okay, Auger, you're on.'

Auger pressed keys, and the screen jerked on and stabilised. Vinz edged him aside and pulled up the file. An error message still blinked over it.

'This comes up as a corrupted file, Auger, no matter what I do. Clever boy, aren't you? But not clever enough. It isn't corrupted at all. You've protected it, haven't you?'

Auger looked at him, saying nothing.

'Jesus, Auger, you got a deathwish? I can shred this wall inside an hour, I promise you. Less than that. You really want me to do that, want that on my report?'

'Okay.' Auger settled at the keyboard and said, 'This'll take a few minutes.' He started his protocols. 'Tell me, Vinz, how long have you been working for Maxenham?'

Vinz let out a little gasp. The screen was suddenly shining with numbers, the whole display alive and moving, racks and rows of digits sliding against each other, merging and slipping, numbers and codes reforming, changing size and colour.

'Three years,' Vinz said slowly, staring at the glittering screen over Auger's shoulder. 'What is this? Are you fucking with me?'

'No, Vinz. I'm accessing the file, just like you asked. This is the entry code. Takes a while to clear. It's encrypted. You were right. Just wait. Watch the screen.' Auger stood up and let Vinz take his place again. Standing beside the desk, Auger followed the numbers in Vinz's eyes. The man was impatient, staring at the patterns, waiting for the screen to clear. He had relaxed at the mention of encryption, though. He must have set the console to record whatever Auger did. Vinz was taking no chances.

'Three years, eh? I've been five with CMS,' Auger told him. The program was still running, numbers swirling in Vinz's eyes, filling the sclera, tracking over the irises. 'Five years in Active. I know cults like you know keyboards. I've seen pretty well everything you can imagine. Indoctrination by drug, by food deprivation, by torture, you name it.' Auger pulled his shoulders back, feeling the bones crack. 'What do you do in Faith, you and Maxenham? You write the rules. Rules? Jesus, Vinz. I'm the one who deals with the shit that drops when your neat little paragraphs and sub-clauses get broken. I deal with the shit when they get followed, too. You ever think of that? You think of the people?'

Vinz shrugged, not taking his eyes away from the screen. 'There's always people. The Administration is by the people, for the people, of the people, all that shit. Likewise the laws. Shit is just what people do. So?'

The numbers squirming in Vinz's eyes were like calculations, every thought in his head seemingly reduced to this, nothing there being of any other value. The idea of it gave Auger a brief, savage pleasure.

'Four years ago, Vinz, there was a cult called The Blinding Light of God. You remember anything about them?'

'I think I heard of them,' Vinz muttered. 'Just get on with it, Auger. Don't think you can try anything here. Everything you do's recorded, backed up.' Vinz rubbed his eyes and stared at the screen, impatient for it to clear. The numbers rolled on, backtracked, swirled.

'The preacher called herself Maya Pyrean,' Auger said. 'Her adherents got bLinkered into the cult's heaven and claimed they had visions there. Wonderful, incontrovertible, almost physical visions, and they wanted to go to this heaven of visions. These visions, Vinz, were not like anything possible in a bLinkered state. It was simply not possible. There was no explanation for it. None. The cult spread like wildfire. About a thousand people had signed their Understands. They were all ready to leave for this heaven. They were set for Leaving. But I didn't buy it. I caught her, Vinz.'

Auger looked at him. The room around them was flickering, the screen brightness increasing and the numbers flashing rapidly.

'Why did you bother?' Vinz said, his voice sour. 'Sounds like a mass fucking delusion to me. Should've just let 'em go, you ask me. Keep the numbers down.' He glanced quickly at Auger, then back at the display. 'Christ, Auger. How long's this take?'

'Nearly there, Vinz.' Auger looked at the door, the glass in which the screen was reflected, flashing. 'It wasn't mass delusion. They all passed their psych tests. They *were* all sane. I didn't know what was going on. Passive wasn't interested. They'd set up the Leaving. I'd run through the cult's program, of course, and it was like they all are, nothing special. I was sure Pyrean had given me a neutered set, but I had nothing to go on, no grounds for suspicion.' Auger paused, watching the numbers flowing in Vinz's eyes. 'I could have just let them all go, just like Passive. You know what I did?'

Vinz didn't answer immediately. Slowly, as if reluctantly, he muttered, 'What?'

'The night before the Leaving, I broke into Maya Pyrean's church.'

Auger waited. It took about ten seconds for Vinz to react this time. 'Oh, yeah?' he eventually drawled.

'I was going to go there alone, but my girlfriend wouldn't let me. She was a research medic. She came with me and saved my life. Are you listening, Vinz?'

Vinz nodded, the briefest twitch of his head. The numbers in his eyes were slowing, the program completing itself. Another minute, Auger reckoned, before the file would be released.

'I found the hardware and the program, and I bLinked. I was right, Vinz. Pyrean had given CMS a neutered program.'

Auger studied Vinz. He was fixed and silent, still looking at the screen. The numbers were virtually static.

'I bLinked, and I was just seeing God, Vinz. It was beautiful. I couldn't speak, couldn't move, didn't care about it. It went right through me. Every cell, every synapse. I knew I had to bLink out, but I couldn't. It was like an instant addiction. Then, when the visions ceased, I found I still couldn't move. If Jay hadn't been there, Maya Pyrean would have come into her church next day and found me there, illegally, and she'd have been within her rights to shoot me dead. But Jay was there and she brought me out, and Wisch backed me up.' Auger put a hand on Vinz's shoulder. 'But that was before Maxenham's time. And before yours. Of course, that case had a clean end, and the Fury case didn't. But I haven't told you everything about Maya Pyrean's visions. You want to know how she did that, Vinz?'

The man from Faith said nothing, just sat there, staring at the screen. The numbers in his eyes weren't moving at all.

'Vinz?'

Nothing. Auger let out a breath, leant across him and and punched the keyboard. The screen cleared of all the numbers, soft green words slowly coalescing in their place to flicker against the pale blue background. FILE RELEASED. Vinz didn't react at all.

'This was it, Vinz. Once she had them bLinkered, she used illegal direct visual images to freeze them physically. Pulses to induce a form of epileptic fit. They couldn't speak to use their Exitline, so they couldn't bLink out. You with me so far? I think so. Then, while they were bLinkered and frozen, the next set of images kicked in. This time it was to induce another type of fit. Not just any old fit, Vinz. Are you listening to me? She induced a temporal lobe epilepsy, something normally very rare. That's what gave them those fabulous visions. And once it was over, they had to rely on Maya Pyrean to release them. Of course they thought she was God. She was taking them up to heaven and then raising them like they were Lazarus.'

A disk slid from the machine and Auger pocketed it, then pressed more keys. On the screen and in Vinz's eyes, there was nothing. 'I'm just carrying out a deep wash and wipe, Vinz, then I'll leave you to it. Your backup'll show all this happening, and of course you doing nothing at all about it. And it'll show an unidentified file removed. But that's all. When I'm done there'll be no record at all of Maya Pyrean's program.'

Auger tried to take the smile out of his voice, but couldn't, saying, 'This ought to put you in solid with your boss, Vinz, if you tell him. On the other hand, you can take my word that the file's nothing to do with you or him, which is true, and you can stay off my back. Don't trouble me, and I won't trouble you.'

He bent down until he was in Vinz's field of view. 'Now, I'm going to reverse this little program, free you up again, and if you want me I'll be in Passive, doing my new job.'

Patting him on the shoulder as he left, Auger added, 'Don't bother to see me out.' And at the door, 'Oh, and still friends, eh, Vinz?'

TEN

Auger hadn't intended to watch the holocast, but he was curious as to how the Administration would handle the Regeneration Ceremony after the images of the fiasco with Father Fury. And it was something to take his mind off Vinz Szolty.

He was only half watching the screen, though, cleaning up after his meal of the previous night. He didn't usually leave the chore so long. Food remnants degraded rapidly and he preferred not to be reminded of the reality of what he'd eaten. He picked the plate up and glanced at the fibrous mush, trying to remember what it had been. There was no clue in its appearance. Lasagna, maybe.

The News Holohead's brightest smile seemed to come into focus on the screen almost before the rest of him crystallised.

'And now we go live to the rescheduled Great Rift Ceremony in Hyde Park, where we are joined by not one, but two Ministers of the Administration.' The Holohead's studio background grid of screens lit up as he spoke. He pointed a long and elegant finger at one of them, and the selected monitor image swelled until it engulfed the Holohead and the whole of Auger's screen. Only a single disembodied finger remained of the Holohead, but his digit swiftly sketched the rest of his outline over the view of Hyde Park, until he was again complete. He shivered violently and leaned towards the cam, towards Auger. 'Phew, you want to know something, guys? No matter how many times I do that, it always gives me the creeps. Like, pop, you don't exist. Brrr. What do you think? Why don't you buzz the station, get them to change the link?' He paused and directed his finger steadily at Auger, holding the pose and saying, 'Remember, You Count!'

The station's number slid in purple digits along the floor of the screen, followed by its slogan again. REMEMBER, YOU COUNT.

The Holohead shook his head and smoothed his quiff. 'And now I have great pleasure in introducing to you the Minister of Stability. Minister Joshu Herald!' He smiled broadly and looked to his side. 'Minister.'

Herald smiled. It was not a smile to compete with the Holohead's, but it was nevertheless a wide and perfect grin. 'Good afternoon, NH. A very good afternoon, and, for all of us, a fresh and glorious dawn, too.'

The Holohead tilted his head. 'Indeed. Perhaps you'd like to take this opportunity to tell us something about the ceremony and the significance of Nugel to us all.'

'Thank you, yes.' Herald faced the cam. A square jaw mellowed by the faintest of dimples, a blunt, slightly flattened and pugnacious nose, and the same thoroughly researched, open yet piercing gaze with which every Minister was endowed by the cam. 'But, first, let me say something about visgel. Visgel, as we all know, is the material that has, ever since shortly after we were shaken by the first of the rifts, enabled us to struggle on.'

He paused at a nod from the Holohead. Across the top of the screen, an illustrative graphic appeared. A cross-section of emerald green land parted in a neat V of a rift.

'With a supporting rigging of cables slung across a rift some metres down, visgel could be laid over sheeting and provide a new surface.' The Minister waited. On the graphic above his head, down a bit from the green surface, rugged black cables sewed themselves tidily to and fro, and a pale green sheet floated gently on to the webbing and settled there, and after another moment a stream of orange visgel poured from an invisible spout to fill the resulting bowl to the brim. A group of matchstick children walked from the rift's edge on to the visgel and began to play there with a ball.

Herald went on. 'Visgel, however, had its limitations. While it was fine as a fill-in for most rifts, adequate as a foundation for roads and small structures, and an excellent injected underpinning to stabilise larger structures against small and even distant medium tremors, it was not a long-term solution. Visgel is insufficiently elastic to be used to restore the larger rifts that we are seeing today.' The graphic blinked off, to be replaced by another of a broader rift. As before, visgel was laid over the sheeting here, but this time as the children played, small splits and fissures opened in the overstretched visgel. The children's ball rolled into one of the cracks and the children scrambled for the safety of the edge. One of them didn't quite make it and tumbled down after the ball, a swirl of tiny arms and legs.

'A serious problem, Minister,' the Holohead agreed, nodding sagely.

'Yes. For some time, then, we in Stability have been directing our efforts urgently towards a solution.' The Minister allowed himself an expression of broad satisfaction. 'And finally we have one. Nugel.'

'Tell us something about that?'

'With pleasure. Unlike visgel, Nugel is a full-depth rift-fill material. It is ultralight and like visgel it is initially delivered in the form of a fluid. But here the comparison ends. Upon dispersal in air, the molecular structure of Nugel changes into what I might describe as a series of exponentially replicating and expanding honeycombs. It rapidly expands a hundredfold, a thousandfold, more.'

Creases rippled across the Holohead's broad brow. 'It sounds very complicated to me, Minister.'

'Science is complicated, NH, until you understand it. And then it is very beautiful.' The Minister smiled. 'Nugel is extremely beautiful.'

'As we already know, Joshu.'

Herald turned sharply round and the cam drew back to bring Maxenham into the frame.

Auger left the crockery sitting in water and sat down before the screen to give it his full attention. Maxenham was a fraction taller than Herald, he noticed, a sign that Herald was currently less in favour within the Administration.

The Holohead was beaming. 'Minister Maxenham, welcome. It is a great pleasure to see you here for the ceremony. One might expect it to be an event more fitting for the presence of Stability. Might I ask what brings you here?'

Auger registered Herald looking as if he'd also like to know that. Something was going on here, and Herald had no idea what it was.

'Certainly,' Maxenham said. 'I'm sure we all saw the troubling earlier holocast images of the misfiring of the Nugel deliverers and the tragic destruction of the Final Church. We were all of us puzzled and extremely anxious about that.' Maxenham glanced easily at Herald. 'My fellow Minister here more than most, certainly, with his direct responsibility for Nugel. Well, I am able to announce, as part of today's ceremony, that there was a great deal more to what we witnessed than was at the time apparent.'

Auger wondered what Maxenham was up to.

The News Holohead nodded and drew down his eyebrows in concentration. Herald looked, as far as the holo-moulding of his features could betray his expression, both startled and furious. He hadn't been briefed on any of this. This was not how the Administration ordinarily managed things. Certainly not how it managed internal power struggles. They were sanitised. They happened off stage, off air. Ministers resigned at the peak of their powers and their loss was mourned.

The cam pulled in and dropped a fraction until it held only Minister Maxenham, who seemed taller yet. The Administration fanfare sounded, and Maxenham waited for the last echoes to die away.

Maxenham held up a hand and brandished a sheet of paper. 'I have here a letter received by my office and addressed personally to me, Minister of Faith. It arrived on the day that Father Fury's church descended into the Great Rift. It is a brave letter, a letter that almost brought me to tears.' Maxenham's blue, blue eyes were shining. Even the dots of his pupils were burnished pips. '*This* is the truth.' He held the paper up. It quivered as he said, 'This is the truth of what happened, and it is a lesson to all of us who might sit in false judgment over others.'

The cam cut briefly to the Holohead, who was wiping an eye with his sleeve, and returned to Maxenham. It ignored Herald.

Maxenham pursed his lips as if considering his words. Bullshit, Auger thought, watching him. It was all rehearsed.

'Father Fury was well aware of the importance of the Ceremony, and of Nugel, to the world, to all of us. He knew how hard the Administration had worked to produce Nugel and safeguard the lives of its community, its family, its . . .' A pause, a long, shivering, heartfelt breath. 'Well, as Minister of Faith, I feel I can go further still and say, its flock.' He stopped dead and nodded before sombrely adding, 'Father Fury felt like that, I know.'

He looked for a moment reflective, sad. His hero's brow creased. His voice deepened and slowed. 'How do I know that? I know it because I know what led Father Fury and his congregation to do what they did.' He sighed heavily, shifted his shoulders as though adjusting a burden there.

'There is an ancient tradition on Earth of sanctifying an important new building by burying an innocent soul in its foundations. Father Fury quoted me that tradition in his final letter. It was in that awesome, selfless and heroic spirit that he and all his brave people acted when they deliberately hurled themselves into the Great Rift.'

Maxenham pursed his lips and held up the paper as if in quiet salute.

'We never knew,' the Holohead murmured.

'No,' said Herald. 'We didn't.'

'Sadly, the letter only came to light an hour ago,' Maxenham said. 'We have so much correspondence at Faith, and much of it addressed to myself personally, that this one was temporarily overlooked. I have, as a result of this, asked the Administrator for an increase in my staff, and I am pleased to say that he has granted it me. On a more solemn note, he asked me also to say a blessing in memory of Father Fury and his congregation, as Minister Herald fires the first official burst of Nugel into the rift. The Administrator felt that such a thing would be more appropriate, under the circumstances, than a triumphalist speech.'

Maxenham glanced at Herald, who smiled tightly. 'Of course, Minister. I shall be more than happy for an excuse not to give my speech.'

'Thank you, Minister. You are as always very gracious. When you are ready.' He gestured Herald to take up the golden nozzle of the ceremonial Nugel gun. Gripping it with two hands, Herald raised it from its forked mount, directed it into the rift and tried as best he could to turn his head at the same time towards the cam which was focused on Maxenham again. It was impossible, and he gave up, his shoulders slumped in the realisation that Maxenham had completely outmanoeuvred him.

Maxenham bowed his head a fraction and put the tips of his fingers together, making a temple of his hands. 'May the deities in which we believe reward Father Fury and all his congregation for their magnificent self-sacrifice by granting them that for which they gave their lives. May the Great Rift be healed, and may all rifts be so healed until the Earth itself is healed and restored once more to its perfect state of innocence and youth. Amen.'

The Holohead closed his eyes and dipped his head. 'Amen.'

The cam cut to Herald, who echoed, 'Amen,' and tightened his grip on the nozzle. The cam rose swiftly to hang directly above the Minister of Stability as he let the Nugel loose. The tube stiffened and jerked, and he struggled to control it as the jet of orange at first choked and spurted, and then spewed a sharp and continuing burst of gel that shot down into the rift, its colour darkening in the shadowed depths. Smoke and dust rose, swirling. The cam drew back a fraction further and panned across to show more and more men delivering Nugel into the rift from both sides along its length. Herald passed his nozzle to an assistant and withdrew, returning to Maxenham and the Holohead. He looked flushed. It was impossible to tell whether it was exertion or anger that coloured him.

Maxenham pushed out a hand and shook Herald's. 'I'll leave now, Joshu. This is your day. Your responsibility, your glory. Well done, Minister. The congratulations of the Administration go out to you.' He clapped Herald on the shoulder, squeezing gently.

'Thank you, Minister.' Herald wasn't sure how to deal with this abruptly entirely magnanimous behaviour. He wiped his brow. He was if anything slightly shorter still than Maxenham, Auger noticed. Perhaps he was simply bent with exhaustion from holding the nozzle firm, but Auger didn't think it was that. Something very strange was going on here, and it was quite clear that Herald was aware of it. This was unquestionably more than the usual Ministerial jockeying for position. Faith, for some reason, was in the ascendant.

The Administration fanfare sounded again as Maxenham stalked magisterially away.

'Would you take us through the rest of the day's events, Minister Herald?' said the Holohead.

'Certainly.' Herald tried to collect himself. 'Well, it should take a few hours to fill the rift. The Nugel is designed to maintain lateral pressure on the sides of the fault, and automatically rebulk there if further slippage occurs. The surface layer will be stabilised, obviously, to prevent undesired ongoing vertical bulking. Later we shall lay soil, plant trees, and the park will be restored. Elsewhere all over London, all over the country, Nugel is as we speak being pumped into rifts. It is also being transported to wherever else in the world remains accessible and where it can be effective.' Herald smiled and breathed a huge sigh, his composure returned.

Fool, Auger thought.

The Holohead made a grand gesture meant to encompass the entire Great Rift. 'All in all, then, a magnificent success, Minister Herald. A tribute to you and all in Stability. And, let us not forget in our gratitude, Father Fury who is buried for ever down there, hurled there by his own hand in selfless hope for all of us.' The Holohead turned directly to the cam. 'We exalt him for it. The world is renewed.'

Auger nilled the screen on Herald's complacent smile. And the past is reinvented, he thought. But not for Fly. There was only Auger to remember Fly.

Astrid looked at the desk, then back at the door. This wasn't Auger. A toad of a man, this, with his scowl at being disturbed.

He lifted his head and took Astrid in, incuriously at first, then curiously. His expression eased. He said, 'Can I help you?'

'Yes. I'm looking for Auger.'

The scowl tightened again. 'And why would that be?'

'It's about a case.'

'Well, if it's Auger you're looking for, I'm the one you want.'

Astrid looked at the man, at his narrow, dull brown eyes, his flabby fingers. 'No, you're not.' Not a toad, she thought. A carrion bird.

Vinz jerked his neck and pushed his chair forward. 'I'm afraid Auger's been transferred from this department. I'm Vinz Szolty. Talk to me. You only want Auger if you want a ticket to kill yourself, and I don't think you want to do that, Ms . . . ?'

Astrid made to turn on her heel.

'Tell me which case,' Vinz called after her. 'Let me help you.'

She stopped. 'Okay. GenMed. Two deaths. The second was Rudd Merchant.'

Vinz leaned back comfortably in the chair and cradled his head in a mesh of his fingers. 'Oh, that. False alarm, you might say. That was an unfortunate thing. There was a thing between two colleagues, your friend Auger and Detective Sweet.'

'What do you mean, false alarm? And Auger isn't my friend.'

'I'm glad to hear that. Let me explain. The GenMed case should have been Sweet's. It was a Pacifist case by rights, but Sweet didn't want it, so he passed it over to Auger. Auger shouldn't have taken it, but he has a personal thing, a problem with GenMed.' Vinz shrugged his shoulders. 'A mistake. Auger made a number of mistakes.' He rocked in the chair and showed his teeth in a stained smile. 'Perhaps you'd like to make a complaint. I'd be happy to register it.' He cocked his head and waited. 'Ms . . . ?'

'You're saying it was murder then. A Pacifist case. So I go to Sweet, do I?'

Vinz sprang his hands apart. 'No. No. I'm not being clear. This whole thing is an embarrassment to the department. It's not going back to Sweet. They were both suicides, slit wrists. Some stupid moron found the second body, that's all, and put it on the bed, and then was too scared to admit to it.'

'But two like that? And no one's even curious?'

His expression was losing shape, his face twisting. 'Look, Ms . . . ?'

'I'd still like to speak to Auger.'

Vinz stood up and saw himself shorter than Astrid. He sat down again. 'I'm afraid that won't be possible. Departmental policy. But if you'd like to leave your name, I can convey a message to him. Ms . . . ? Ms . . . ?' He waited some more. 'Ms . . . ?'

'I think maybe you need a stomach pump, Mr Szolty. You sound like you swallowed a fly,' Astrid said, walking out of the office and letting the frosted glass door slam behind her.

She stopped in the corridor and thought about Auger. She hadn't liked him that much, but that had been before she'd met Vinz Szolty.

Vinz had said he could get a message to him. Not that it would have got there, Astrid was sure, but she thought Vinz had meant that it might have. So Auger was probably nearby. Still in the building, maybe. And what else had Vinz said? You want him if you want a ticket to kill yourself, that was it.

Which means he's in Passive.

Astrid went back to the front desk. The reception officer made her wait, though she could see he had nothing better to do. He was making as if looking at his cambered bank of monitors but his eyes were shifted sideways to examine her. She tapped the desk and he swivelled his head slowly, centring her in his gaze.

'Can you tell me where I go for Passive?'

The desk officer shook his head. 'Passive? You sure about that? You don't look the type. You look more the active type.' He pumped his hips, his mouth open, stroking the tips of his teeth with his tongue. There was fur on his tongue. 'I can give you that. You interested in action?'

'I'm interested in a Leaving.'

He pouted at her. 'Hell, pretty girl like you? What is it, your ass is too big? Looks fine to me.' Slowly, licking his lips, he looked her up and down. 'Life can be a fucker, huh? Sure you don't just need showing the best of it?' He leered at her. 'Look, I'm off in an hour. Maybe you just need a good Samaritan. Maybe we can go some place, you and me, work it through, just the two of us?'

She gave him her best smile. 'Actually I wasn't quite sure. But thanks, you've convinced me. So where do I go to kill myself?'

He shrugged and gave up. 'Uh, out the door here, go left, you'll see it. Can't miss it. Uh, hey—'

'Really, thanks. You made up my mind. I love you for it.'

She walked out the door, feeling his eyes on her back like grime.

It was mid-afternoon, and the street was almost miraculously clear. She could see all the way down the road as far as the tilted traffic lights that still flicked aimlessly through their sequences, despite the fact that there was no traffic to govern across the disrupted asphalt. And Astrid found herself waiting at the crossing for the light to usher her across. The security of rules, she thought, picking her way across the road. She looked left and right. There were termite mounds as tall as men on the streets, swarming with activity and growing randomly on pavement and road. A few years ago they had started to erupt, and now they were everywhere. They made Astrid shiver. When there was fog they loomed like ghosts, and when the air was clear, as it was now, they were like vast urban warts.

They fed off something in the visgel, and in certain lights they seemed almost to glow dull orange or even red.

The desk 'fist was right, you couldn't miss it. After a few hundred metres a blanket of mist gathered ahead of her. Phony mist, she realised, and the holo came at her through it as she approached the building. The mist withdrew. Nightingales twittered tinnily around the curlicues of graceful silver lettering above the building's portico. Nightingales were extinct, she was pretty certain, but maybe that was fitting.

Leavings. An Enterprise of Faith.

It was probably only a couple of storeys tall, but the holo made it seem to rise infinitely high into a sky blue and clear for hundreds of metres before wispy clouds gathered at last to stroke the building's delicate white marble walls. It was like a tombstone.

As she walked into the lobby, a few birds detached themselves from the sign to accompany her, fluttering back as she approached the desk.

'I'm looking for Auger,' she said.

The receptionist gave her a smile of deep sympathy. Astrid wondered if that was part of her job description or a reaction to Auger's name. 'Certainly,' she murmured. 'And your temple is?'

Astrid frowned. 'Well, the thing is, I'm not sure I've got the right day. Who's he seeing today?'

The receptionist ran her finger down a list. 'The High Window.'

'That's me. Where do I find him?'

She looked at Astrid, her head tilted in uncertainty. 'Are you sure? It's just—'

'I'm the Opener of the Window. Where do I go?'

The receptionist leant over her counter and pointed, her fingernails glittering silver in the atrium's muted light. 'Mr Auger is in The Room Before. It's straight down that corridor, after The Room of Wishes and before the male conveniences.' She still looked doubtful.

'Thanks. And bless you.'

The corridors were wide, green and peaceful. They reminded Astrid vaguely of the neuro wards at GenMed, and she wondered whether Auger had thought that, and how he might feel about it. The sense of woolly tranquillity, of dulled minds. Only here he was shepherding them to oblivion.

She knocked once at the door of The Room Before, and went in without waiting.

The receptionist must have told him she was coming. Auger's face was a storm as he stood up. 'Who the hell do you think you are, mocking these people? They at least deserve some dignity.' He slowed down abruptly. She saw recognition bloom in his eyes, and as it did, contempt replaced the thunder on his face. 'You. The medic.' He said the word with a dismissive flick of his head, and for a moment it was just the memory of Vinz's contempt for Auger that kept her from walking straight back out again into the filthy air. He was flexing his fist too, and she noticed the PlaSkin over his knuckle like a patch of jaundice.

'I'm sorry. I needed to see you. It was just to get in.' She frowned at his overreaction. 'I just had to get past her. What did I do? Why are you so mad?'

'Why am I mad?' Auger shook his head and went to a door at the rear of his office and opened it enough for her to look through. 'The adherents of the High Window,' he said, keeping his voice low. 'Look at them. They're waiting for me to sign their Understands. They're sightless. I mean, they were once. They've all had successful corrective surgery, and they can see as well as you and I can. But they don't believe what they can see any more. Their deacon has told them they're in the wrong world. They shouldn't be here at all. Their Window is to a paradise of sight, and they want to jump right through it. And that's what they're all going to do, run down a long red carpet at the top of the cliff at Dover and soar away into paradise.'

And they were all wearing goggles with lenses of deep, deep blue, Astrid saw. No wonder the receptionist had questioned her. Astrid looked from face to face, each one throwing back at her two tiny turquoise images of herself standing beside Auger.

'Five minutes,' Auger said into the room. 'We'll start in five minutes.'

One of the men nodded patiently. 'The true world is eternal.'

'Okay, I'm sorry. I didn't know,' Astrid said as Auger closed the door on them. 'But don't take your job out on me. And don't take mine out on me either.'

He didn't react. She tried again. 'How's the hand?'

'It's healing.' He sat down heavily. 'Well, Opener of the Window? You've got five minutes.'

'I came to talk about Rudd Merchant.'

'Not to me,' he said. 'Not any more.'

Astrid felt herself beginning to boil. She was always in the wrong with Auger. 'Funny, I just heard that from someone sitting in an office that had your name on the glass. Look, Auger, I came here with a proposition.

I don't think you can keep your end of it, but here it is anyway. I've got no one else to tell it to. No one's interested in Rudd's death, and I know he wouldn't have killed himself. I also know he belonged to no cult. I want your help. Frankly, I can't think of anyone else.'

'That's a proposition?'

'You have a problem with medics, Auger. That's a statement, by the way, not a proposition. Shut up and listen to me. After you left Emergency, I went over to Archive and read about what happened to Jay Auger. I didn't realise it was quite so . . .' She waited, but he didn't react. 'The case was never solved to your satisfaction, was it? And she's in the long-term neuro unit at GenMed. She's never recovered or even improved, though, and I guess you blame the medics there for that. You blame all medics, in fact.'

'That still isn't a proposition.'

She shook her head. 'You must really work hard on your asshole quotient, Auger. *This* is the proposition. Help me with Rudd's murder, and I'll help you with Jay. I can probably get to see her notes, see if GenMed's been negligent.'

'It still isn't much of a proposition. I can get her notes any time. She's my wife.'

Astrid sat back. Now she had time. He wasn't going to throw her out. 'No, you can't. She isn't your wife, Auger, is she? Her assigned lawyer got her a decree nisi a year after the accident. Non-consummation.'

That stopped him. She thought it with a satisfaction that immediately melted away. There was something in his eyes that for a brief moment revealed a cache of deep and constant pain. The anger was a mask for that. The pain was still raw. After all this time, it was still raw.

He said, his voice suddenly muted, 'How did you know that?'

'When I pulled her name up on the system, she came up unmarried, which I wasn't expecting. I wondered if it was an error, so I followed it up. It wasn't hard.'

She tried to read Auger's face further, but there was nothing. The storm had passed, and there was nothing left.

'The assigned lawyer did it for your sake, Auger, on GenMed's advice. They knew she was never going to recover. They thought they were giving you the chance of a life.' She shook her head, looking at him. 'They let you visit her, they still call her Jay Auger, but you have no next-of-kin rights. You're looking at a sealed vault. I work there, Auger. I can talk to the people and they'll talk back to me. All you'll get is an echo.'

'You're offering to help me? It sounds like you've made up your mind already.'

He was impossible. 'I'm just saying you need me, Auger. If you don't like that, I actually don't give a damn.'

'You do give a damn, though. Not about Jay, of course. You just need someone to investigate your friend's death.'

'Well, look at who I've asked for help. A guy with a job writing suicide chits.'

Astrid leant forward into the monitor. She hadn't been into the neuro wards for a long time. She didn't like the silence of her footsteps in the corridors, the locked doors with their muffled cries and concealed mutterings. But this was different. A monitor instead of a window. This wasn't security. This was paranoia.

She leaned into the comms grille. 'Excuse me, but they're paging for a neuro nurse. There's a brainstem trauma patient in Emergency and no one's responding.'

She waited as the nurse in the room turned to the cam to say, 'I'm sorry. I can't leave this patient unattended. You'll have to find someone else.'

'That's okay, I'll cover here for you.'

The nurse still hesitated, and Astrid wondered why. She should have been grateful for the chance to get out for a few minutes. Her patient was weeping on the bed, face in the pillow, body heaving like a pump.

'They said it was an emergency,' Astrid told her again, putting urgency in her tone. 'Brain injury. They need a specialist nurse. I told you I'd cover here.'

The nurse still hesitated, but finally she conceded, saying, 'Okay,' and thumbing the buzzer to let Astrid in.

The crying, no more than a background fuzz through the monitor's comms, ripped at her ears as the door opened. The woman on the bed sat up at her entrance and wiped her eyes, still sobbing desperately, her body pitching with it. She pushed herself on to the floor and stood there. She stared for a moment at Astrid, as if expecting to recognise her, then took enough breath to gasp, 'Is there any news?'

If there had been an answer to that, Astrid wouldn't have been able to say it. She simply stared. The yellow wedding dress looked as if the last stitch had just been sewn and she had shimmied herself into it for the first time a few moments ago. Real silk, the harsh clinical halogens hitting it like spotlights on pooled oil, throwing out gleaming whirls and coils of saffron, jasmine, flax and topaz. It was a magnificent dress, the taut bodice coming down from a low V at her breasts to cinch tight at Jay Auger's waist, and from there the silk ruched over her hips and then flared to the ground. Despite her tear-blotched complexion, the lips curled in hysteria, Jay Auger, with the high bones of her cheeks, her pale grey eyes and her swirl of blonde hair, was beautiful. What she might have looked like on her wedding day, in love, a few years younger, in this same dress or its original, made Astrid think of Auger and feel she could understand how he had become what he was now. For an instant she wondered also what she herself might look like in that dress, what she might feel with Auger at her side. Stupid thought. Auger, of all people.

'Just soothe her,' the nurse said, ignoring Jay and telling Astrid as she went through the door, 'You can't do anything else, anyway. This is how she is. Don't get caught up in it. I'll be back as soon as I can.'

The door closed behind her, and Astrid took her eyes from Jay and looked around, curious. The room was strange. It was quite characterless, which was odd for the environment of a long-term in-patient. Jay had been here for years, but there was nothing personal to be seen. There were none of the trinkets of normality, no pretence at the room being a home, a domicile of choice. No ornaments, still-pics, souvenirs. But it wasn't like any other room on the neuro wards either. It didn't even resemble a vacant neuro room.

It was teasingly familiar, though. It took Astrid a moment to work out why it was quite so familiar.

Jay Auger's room had been carefully and perfectly made into a precise duplicate of one of the presentation and diagnosis cubicles over in Emergency. Jay Auger was being housed in a clone of a five-minute holding chamber.

Of course it was. Jay Auger was – had been – a medic. Her room was designed to fit her perception of the situation. Of where she would feel she should be in her perpetual present. A window on to the corridor would have compromised that. It had to be a windowless room with a monitor. It wasn't paranoia at all. Or else it was Astrid's. Astrid looked around again. The only odd thing about the room was a high shelf beside the monitor cam. On the shelf was a socket for vids and a line of vids. Astrid stood up and took a disk out. There was nothing on it but a date. She examined another. Every disk was dated, and they seemed to cover a period of a few months, the first period of Jay's incarceration here. Odd, she thought.

Then she thought, I'm being taped, and went cold for a moment. She reached for the machine, but there was no tape in the unit. It wasn't in use. She shook her head at herself. Paranoia.

She picked up the folder of notes at the end of the bed. It was as thick as her wrist.

Jay was sitting at the edge of the bed, still sobbing. 'Is there any news? What about Cy? How is he? Is he all right?'

'We're doing what we can,' Astrid told her, trying to keep her voice level, to hold herself at a distance from the woman's terror. She felt like she had felt the first time she'd watched a patient die and known that there was nothing to be done but to be there. 'We have to wait for some news,' she said, opening the notes. 'The situation isn't clear yet. I think it's going to be all right, though.' She began to leaf through the papers, trying to block out Jay's wailing.

It was quickly apparent that the file was incomplete. Jay's history was impossible to follow, to make any sense of. She flicked forward and back. Referrals to consultants were not accompanied by their reports, and yet there was subsequent oblique reference to those reports. Treatments were referred to by code and date, and when she went to the front of the folder to find the list of codes, she saw them all tagged 'Confidential. See separate file.'

There was no other file, though, and, frustrated, she went back in the folder to the immediate post-trauma period. Again, there was dated reference to consultants' names, but the pages of specific notes were missing. She carried on flicking through, and began to see the same consultant's name recurring. Dr Saffer.

The name was vaguely familiar, but she didn't know many of the neuro staff at GenMed, and according to the records Saffer had been seeing Jay only for the first year or so. He'd been out of the picture now for over a year. And Astrid had been at GenMed for about two and a half years. Saffer had probably moved on, whoever he was.

Jay was tugging at her arm. Astrid let the notes drop into their case at the end of the bed. She took out her reader. 'Jay, I just need to check your datasink.'

Jay rolled her sleeve up for Astrid, calming down instantly. Trauma victims always reacted like this. It was the reassurance of the procedure. The jerkiness of her sobbing even slackened. Astrid shifted herself slightly until she was sure her body was shielding the monitor's cam, then she thumbed Record on her reader and just held Jay's arm. She was suddenly aware of her own breathing beginning to settle, that she herself was feeling more calm. Jay's hysteria was contagious, the stress passing from her like a current. After half a minute, a light on the reader told Astrid that the data had passed, but she held on to Jay's arm, letting peace flow between them, letting silence suffuse the room.

A moment later Jay began quietly to sob again, and Astrid realised that the cycle had completed itself. Jay's memory had reverted to the explosion again, and the last few moments of tranquillity had been wiped clean away. She'd read about it in the note summary that had told her of the divorce, but the reality of Jay Auger was hard to take in. She thought again of Auger having to cope with it, and understood him needing someone to blame, just as she understood GenMed's reasons for advising the divorce.

'Where's Cy? Is he all right? Where is he?' The sobbing was building again in Jay like an accelerating motor.

'It's okay,' Astrid told her, taking her arm again and making as if to perform another data-access. It wouldn't matter. It was just giving her a few minutes of calm that would anyway be forgotten. 'Your husband is fine. He's helping the rescue operation.'

'But everyone was killed. I saw it. They're all dead.'

'It wasn't as terrible as it seemed. A lot of them were hurt badly, but it seemed worse.'

'Really? You're telling me the truth?'

Jay looked at her, a long, full gaze that went so deep that Astrid had to look away, at her hand on the woman's arm, on the tiny serpent-and-staff tattoo that marked the datasink. Lies were neither better nor worse than the truth to Jay. Nothing meant anything, and everything meant nothing at all.

And then Jay was shuddering more, and the tears were starting to run down their old reddened tracks again. The fugue had resumed. She looked round in sudden panic. 'Where's Cy? Where is he?'

Behind them the door opened. Half expecting to see Auger, Astrid turned round to see the nurse standing there.

'There was no neuro case. I wasted my time,' she said. And then, sharply, coming swiftly to the bed, 'What do you think you're doing?'

She jerked Jay's arm from Astrid and rolled the thin cotton sleeve down, covering the tattoo. 'You aren't authorised to access her data. You should know that.'

'I wasn't,' Astrid said. She showed the nurse her reader with its function display set to nil. 'I was making like it, and it was calming her down. I don't know what her problem is, but I can see she presents as an immediate trauma victim. I was simply treating her like one. It worked.'

The nurse stared at Astrid, then at Jay, who was crying hysterically, releasing a tidal wave of tears. Astrid wanted to put her arms around her, somehow to ease her pain. All the nurse seemed to want to do was stare Astrid out.

'Fine. If you don't believe me, ask her,' Astrid said, before standing up and walking out of the room.

The apartment door still had a CMS ACTIVE – DO NOT ENTER alert across the lock, as well as black-and-yellow SOCtape over the nameplate and hinges. Auger nilled the alert and then ripped it off. It seemed to come away too easily and he paused to check the LuSeal. It was intact. He held the 'Seal's translucent edging up to the hall's neon light and squinted at it. Someone who knew a little bit about them had been tampering with it. It must have been a pretty half-hearted attempt, though. They hadn't known as much as they'd thought. He bent down and rubbed the lock with his finger, then rubbed his fingers together. Or else they'd known a great deal more than that. He wiped the film of grease on his trousers, then went in and closed the door behind him, resetting the LuSeal with his remote before flicking on the light. He turned to survey Rudd Merchant's room, then went to the window and looked out. He could see the entrance to the neuro wards from here, and the colonnade that led to Ferec's office, too. He thought briefly of the bell jar there.

There wasn't anything else to see out there. Medics wandering around in white coats, their pockets stuffed with stethoscopes or dowsing rods or whatever else it was they carried round with them. 'Fist trigs hunched on the corners, though as far as Auger was concerned the main crime you got in a hospital was carried out inside the wards. All the trigs were there for was to protect the medics. The hell with that, Auger thought sourly. The hell with it.

He nilled the window and turned back into the room, and pulled a copy of Gray's *Anatomy* from a bookshelf. He riffed his finger down the disk's index ribbon, watching chapter headings flare up and fade again on the screen. He punched the notebook function and found nothing there, put the disk back.

Auger let his eyes wander over the shelf again. Nothing caught his eye. He went into the bathroom and knelt by the bath. There was a faint tide mark near the rim, which he ignored. He pulled a swab-tube from his pocket, unsealed the stopper and reached down to ease the swab tip carefully down the plug-hole. He wiped it around the pipe as low as he could, then pulled the swab out again, carefully sinking it back into the tube which he resealed and slipped into his pocket. He didn't expect anything from it. It was just to be able to tell that medic he'd done something, carried out his part of the deal. Medics wanted to kill themselves, it was fine by him. If they wanted to kill each other, that was no loss either.

He was starting to his feet when he heard the single soft rap at the door.

He dropped his arm and listened, his heart racing. He shouldn't be here. If he was caught in here, that would be the end of Astrid's assistance.

But there shouldn't be anyone to knock on Rudd Merchant's door. Even if you didn't notice the alert on the door, you couldn't miss the SOCtape. Anyone who had a right to enter would have just nilled the alert and come straight in. Anyone else ought to stay clear. No one should be knocking at a scene-of-crime door.

At the second, louder knock, Auger pushed the bathroom door, leaving it just ajar. He switched the light off in the room. The extractor kept on humming above him, but it was low enough to be just a bad aircon system. He moved to the door and crouched down by the hinge so that he could squint through the vertical slit low down. By scanning with his head he could get a pretty good view of most of the main room.

He barely caught the suck-scrape of the alert being disabled, and Rudd Merchant's door opened quickly and closed again as a man slipped inside, immediately swivelling round to reset the alert. He was wearing a full-face respirator.

He took a while over the alert, and Auger realised he was reprogramming it, too. Clever. Anyone else coming along would think it was faulty. They'd go off to find a techie and this guy would be able to slip back out again unnoticed.

Auger cautiously adjusted his position on the hard floor, leaning on his knuckles rather than his palms to avoid his sweat sticking him to the plastic and making a sound if he pulled up to shift again. He waited for the man to turn around, into the room. There had been something familiar about the man, despite the respirator. His ears, or the curve of his neck. There was no conscious recognition, nothing certain, but Auger's heart had started to race at that swift turning glimpse of the man as he came in, and Auger trusted his heart.

The man didn't turn into the room, though. He went away to the side, glancing along the walls, scanning the shelves. By leaning carefully, Auger could still see him, but his angle of view was so narrowed that he could make out no further detail.

The man stopped, riffing his fingers along the spines of books on a shelf, and Auger saw by the colour of his hands that he was wearing surgical gloves. Auger ran his eye along the wall and noted the upper edge of a framed Magritte print level with the man's eyes.

He came forward now, heading for the desk, but that didn't help Auger, whose angle of vision was made more acute still. The man was standing by the desk and seemed to be taking stock, touching his lower lip with an index finger. He tapped his finger a few times on the desktop, then began to pull drawers out and search through them, working swiftly and without panic.

Auger waited. That was fine by him. Everything there had been copied. The whole room was duped. He shifted slightly again, trying to get a closer look at the tapping man's face, but his vision was blurring from squinting one-eyed through the slit, and his left knee was beginning to ache. His knuckles were throbbing, too. He adjusted his position carefully, lifting his feet so that they didn't squeak on the plastic flooring.

The man was standing up from the desk now, closing a drawer, smoothing his pocket. He tapped his finger once more on the desk, decisively.

Auger tried to come smoothly to his feet but found his left leg cramped and had to put out a hand to the side of the shower to stabilise himself. As he started to settle again the extractor fan above him clicked and shut itself down.

The abrupt silence bounced around the walls like a solid thing. Damn, Auger thought. Timer linked to the light switch. He put his eye quickly back to the slit.

The man was tipping his head up and standing in the middle of the room, peering towards the bathroom.

You weren't expecting company, were you? Auger thought with satisfaction, his hand on the bathroom door and swinging it wide. The man was fast, though. He had already turned and was almost at the door.

Auger was up and out of the bathroom, stumbling with his tingling leg but in no hurry. It would take the man a few moments to nil the alert. Auger had him. He pulled the sharplight from its holster.

The intruder had forgotten about the alert. He had his hand on the doorhandle as Auger said quietly, 'Okay, mister, it's locked. You locked it. Why don't you just come back and sit down?'

The man half turned, then abruptly ducked, yanked the door open and was gone.

Auger lowered his weapon, cursing. The man hadn't reset the alert at all. He'd just attempted to and failed.

Rubbing life into his leg, Auger made for the door, thinking, Unless he knew I was inside all along and wanted to make me think we were locked in together.

Auger looked down the corridor. There, at the far end, the man jinked to the left and was gone.

'Shit,' said Auger again, but louder. Something in there so important that he'd watched Auger go in and had to chance it anyway. Auger slid the sharplight into its holster under his arm and made after the man, who was already at the top of the stairs, end of the next corridor. Auger yelled, 'Stop there,' as the man took the flight in two leaps, disappearing to his waist with the first, then vanishing altogether.

Auger was hard behind him. From the top of the stairs he saw the man's feet beyond the inner glass doors, hesitating at the outers. Auger took the stairs in two and just saw him go left as the outer doors swung shut.

Or maybe he'd known Auger was off the case, and had known it wasn't quite that much of a risk, that Auger would be slow and cautious. Ferec?

Auger brought his filter to his face, shouldering the inner doors. They held. An LED display flashed up in front of him. ATMOSLOCK NOT YET CLEARED. PLEASE WAIT. Auger smashed the heel of his hand into the red glass blister of the emergency override unit and both doors instantly retracted. The alarms started to sound. Auger fixed his mask as he headed after the man, out of the main gates of GenMed.

It wasn't hard to see him. The streets were full of wind, and everyone but the running man was hunched down against the gusts of ash and blown fragments of the world. Auger was about twenty metres behind him, and content to remain there. He was fit, and he was confident he could outlast him. He'd let his quarry tire himself out.

The man was heading up the access ramp to London Bridge railway station. Auger followed, breathing easily with the filter. Under the station's great canopy the wind was dead and the man lengthened his stride and picked up speed. The concourse was deserted, the station closed since a rift had devoured the track two stops down the line a week back, taking a packed train along a down curve to oblivion.

Auger stayed behind his quarry across the concourse, his feet slapping the ground as he ran. He watched the dusting of ash splash up at the feet of the man in front, rising into the air and settling again so slowly that Auger kicked through the sinking blur.

Out of the concourse and into the keening wind again, and Auger almost lost him as he went left, not over the bridge but down towards the river bank. Vaulting a wall, the man was for an instant silhouetted against the grey sky, and the image was fixed in Auger's mind of him glancing back to see if Auger was still there. His filtered profile puncturing the air, a fist raised in triumph or threat. Definitely something familiar in that profile.

He vanished over the wall. Auger reached it a moment later, scrambling up and hesitating on the wall's fine edge, using the height to see where the man had gone.

But he saw nothing. It was a maze of buildings here, warehouses gone to rats and rot. Something moved high to his right and Auger caught it, but it was just an old CCTV stiltcam panning towards him, still for some reason functioning. And another movement, and this time it was a settling twist of raised ash at ground level, by the corner of a building.

Auger hit the ground again at a run. But he noticed the rasping of his breath, and had to turn his oxygen intake up. The mask magnified his breathing. They were close to the water, the smell of decay strong and rank. But the man was in sight, and Auger saw that his stride was shorter now. He was tiring. Who was he?

Down an alley and through a narrow arch, the man swinging aside a hank of chain that was still rattling as Auger ducked past it to round a corner.

And as he ducked, something caught him across the head and he fell back against a wall. A weight fell on his chest, the man's knees jabbing into his ribs and taking his breath away, and he was unable to resist as the filter was ripped from his face. The foul waterside air hit his cheeks like a slap. He caught a glimpse of the man's face again, frustratingly obscured by the mask. No help at all. He could hear the man's breathing, fast and laboured despite the filter. He was tired. He held Auger for a moment, staring at him for a longer moment than Auger was expecting, not just laying into him. The shadows of his eyes were there behind the bLinkers, wide eyes looking at Auger as if for the first time.

Starting to gasp in the harshness of the air, Auger wondered again whether there was something familiar about him. Did he know Auger? Was there a glance of recognition or acknowledgment in those covert eyes?

The man pushed himself off Auger, turned and began to run again. He ran through a brief lance of sunlight that caught the surgical gloves on his hands and made them seem to glow, to stand out a moment longer than the rest of him, fading back into the dust and gloom. Auger stumbled groggily to his feet and set off after him, but after a few metres his eyes were streaming and his throat starting to burn. He forced himself on, telling himself the man was almost spent, trying not to think of his own exhaustion and the growing fire in his lungs.

He was slowing, though, feeling nauseous with the burning and the stench of the water, and knew he couldn't carry on running much longer without a filter. After another minute he had lost sight of the man altogether, connected to him now only by a diminishing wake of ash, and had almost given up.

And then around a corner he almost tripped over something that the man's wake of ash hadn't quite settled enough to bury. Auger's vision was blurring, and he nearly stepped over it and carried on. But he knelt and picked it up, brushing the ash from it.

It was his discarded filter. He jammed it back on his face, and with the sweet oxygen he felt a rush of elation. His quarry had made a mistake. He'd underestimated Auger.

Auger picked up speed again, the fire in his chest quenching. The ash trail was still there for him, and rising as Auger made up lost ground, but the man must have realised it was giving him away in these lifeless alleys. He was cutting out of the maze and heading towards the main street again.

But Auger was closing hard on him, only ten metres behind him as he vanished around a final corner to be back on a populated road.

The street wasn't that busy, though, and the man was easy to see. He was clearly tiring, finding it hard to lift his feet, and Auger was gaining fast. His own strength was fading, but he knew he had his quarry now.

And then the man stopped dead on the pavement, almost as if hit by something. A mist seemed suddenly to envelop him for a few moments before swiftly dispersing. He gathered himself and took off again.

Auger didn't have time to think why the man had stopped. He was too close now, just a few paces from having him, little more than a stretch of the arm away. He ran on, giving the chase his last dregs of strength. His legs were aching now and he needed it to be over. But the man was having to accelerate again from standing and Auger was already at full speed. A few more metres . . .

. . . and suddenly there was a stone wall immediately in front of him. A solid wall out of thin air.

Auger felt his ankle twist as he skidded on the cracked pavement, stopping hard and instinctively pushing his hands at the wall of brickwork to stabilise himself.

'Shit,' he yelled, bracing himself, and yelled it again as his hands plunged straight through the wall, and he fell forward on to his face. The wall burst around him and words congealed out of the brick dust to shiver in the air.

BREAK THE BARRIER. THE NEW DIRANGESEPT PROJECT NEEDS YOU!

The holovert and its message dissipated, but it was too late. The man had gone.

'Shit,' he shouted again. He sank to his knees in the street, feeling drained and lost. The holovert flashed again.

BREAK THE BARRIER — BE ON THREE!

BREAK THE BARRIER — BE ON THREE!

Auger didn't even have the strength to crawl out of its trigger field.

ELEVEN

A month after the wedding Auger had moved out of the house he shared with Jay. The vast, sprawling mansion block where he lived now had been punched sideways by a rift that had taken out most of East Finchley a few years back. After the dust had settled a troupe of squatters had moved in with a couple of thousand tons of reject qualcrete and visgel and cobbled the whole thing back together. They had added their own touches, too. Where floors wouldn't meet they built ramps, stairs, whatever they felt like at the time. They left corridors dead-ended or gaping over the street in open-mouthed bewilderment. They filled in windows at random and meaninglessly rerouted stairs. Parts of the building they blocked off entirely, sealing whole floors like tombs.

And when they were done, they plugged the remaining defects with more visgel, this time embedded with receivers tuned into the satellites that beamed down gameware.

Now the building was awash day and night with character echoes and random gamezone fragments. Wagon trains rumbled down the halls, aliens fired plasma guns from the shadows, terrorists parachuted down the stairwells screaming all the clichés of war. And all the time crashings and scrapings came from the entombed areas, and everyone pretended that that too was just the games.

Auger didn't mind. None of it bothered him. He liked the privacy. No one was going to come here after him. And he liked the people there, most of them, most of the time. They knew what he was, but they also knew what the 'fists thought of him, which as far as they were concerned outweighed anything else.

When he'd first moved into the block Auger had brought along a tech to look at his room, a bug specialist. It wasn't the holos that Auger minded, or the noises – they were a kindness in comparison with the memory of Jay's screams that came from inside his own head. It was just the unpredictability.

The tech had pointed his instruments around the room, prodded nervously at the extrusions of visgel and said, 'I ain't touchin' this. This place is worse than a goddamn nightmare. Receptors and transmitters everywhere. I try and take out any of this, the whole building's likely to come down with it.' The man screamed, ducking a scimitar. Auger just let the blade sweep through his neck and waited for the barbarian to fade away. Maybe he was already used to it. Maybe he just didn't care.

'Thanks,' he said. 'You want me to show you out?'

The man looked at him. 'You're really staying?' He shook his head, stuffing instruments into his belt, swearing and trying to bat away something that had a scrawny hand in his pocket. He made for the door. 'Don't worry. I'll find my own way out. You wouldn't keep up with me.'

So Auger got used to it, the uncertainty of the place. He accepted everything it threw at him. Most of the time now, he hardly even noticed it. The world was awash with games anyway. Screen games, hologames, bLinker games. You could play in arcades, on the street, anywhere. You could live your whole life in a game if you wanted to. It was probably an easier option than reality – game logic was more consistent than reality these days, Auger thought. The visuals were certainly clearer. There might be justice and the chance of a happy end.

Tonight some program was making Auger's place a reef. His cupboards housed moray eels, his kitchen table was a barnacled treasure chest. The walls were ramparts of coral, undulating purples and greens. Auger ate his dinner underwater, observed by clownfish that nibbled at the food and then vanished back into the reef, unimpressed by his cooking. He didn't blame them. He was pleased when the whole thing faded away, leaving him slightly faint from hyper-ventilation after minutes of subconsciously restricting his breath.

He cleaned up after the meal, a sour metal taste in his mouth. It was always the same. The food looked fine when you bought it, but the only taste you ever seemed to get from it was the aftertaste.

Still stiff from the afternoon's chase and angry with himself for losing his quarry at the end of it, he pulled out his bed and sat down at the edge of it and rubbed his eyes. At least the room was almost his own again. All that remained was the tiny gecko, splay-footed and motionless on the ceiling tonight, looking like it had been stamped on to the grimy plaster. Auger used to think it was a piece of renegade software slipped free of its program, but it had maintained its sentry duty and its prissy paddling around his walls and ceiling ever since he had arrived, and he'd grown accustomed to it. Now that Fly had gone, it was the only company he had.

'So, what's happening at GenMed?' he said aloud to the gecko, wondering who he'd been chasing out of Rudd Merchant's room. Could it have been Ferec? It had to have been a man, Auger was sure. And whoever it was, if they hadn't already known him, they'd be able to identify Auger now. Not good.

He slept in his clothes, badly, dreaming of walls surrounding him, of wasps stinging him, and woke early to a room in the centre of a spectral moonlit savannah, the gecko squatting on a full silver moon. Not a dream, at least. Auger yawned and rolled himself out of bed, and under the shower he ran his fingers over his scratched palms, thinking what a mess he was making of this. But there was something very strange happening at GenMed, no question any more of that. He wondered if Astrid was in any danger. For some reason the thought of her made him conscious of his heartbeat, racing slightly.

'Okay,' he told the gecko, draining a mug of coffee in one acidic swallow and settling himself at his screen console, bringing it to life. 'Let's take a little control here.'

He keyed Sherry's number from memory – she'd made him promise he'd never enter it anywhere or write it down, and even if it was just her paranoia, he respected it. He figured she had a right to her paranoia.

He opened his systems and waited while hers did their trawl, checking he was who he'd said he was, and that he wasn't subwired or counter-trawling. Auger was happy to wait for that, it was a service anyway. His own systems and comms bugpoisons were a long way less deep and lethal than hers.

A face came up on the screen. Not hers, of course, she'd never do that. It was something she'd customised from a holobank. The image almost made him chuckle. It was the nearest thing to a joke she'd ever made.

'You've had your hair done,' he said. 'The colours suit you.' The holo's swirling hair was green and mauve, highlit with streaked crimson. His screen couldn't quite cope with it, the hues separating and merging.

The holo twisted its lips, smiled fractionally. He tried to imagine Sherry doing that, but couldn't. It had been a long time, though, and maybe she'd changed.

'Can I see you, Sherry?' Keeping it short, knowing she'd want to be offline as soon as she could, and needing to be back at her sleep screen, checking her night.

A blink of thought, then, 'Two hours,' she said, and abruptly the screen cleared and shifted to Administration Green, and with it the triumphal trumpet tones of the Administration's theme came hard into the room.

In the centre of the screen, in darker green, words bloomed.

DIRANGESEPT UPDATE.

'With the departure of the third Dirangesept Project imminent, this is an Administration progress announcement.' It was the News Holohead's voice, slowed and lowered a fraction.

The words faded and a pinprick of black opened in the heart of the green, and swelled until the green remained just a thick frame. Space, Auger realised. The cam was somewhere in space. From the left of the frame a shining silver curve drifted into view, and the cam pulled steadily back to haul slowly across the whole of the ship with all its curves and vaulted arches. The arrowed head of it like a spire, the vast columns, solar-shadowed aisles and sweeping buttresses of its architecture.

The cam swept along the glorious silver curves. Auger's vision was thrown out by the lack of perspective and he was unable to tell if the curves were concave or convex, flexing in or out. The words fixed it for him, the words on the flank of the hull in gothic script, the ship's name. The cam rested on them. 𝕿𝖍𝖊 𝕯𝖊𝖑𝖎𝖇𝖊𝖗𝖊𝖗.

The cam continued on, revolving around the ship as if in its orbit, then pulling slowly away until the craft could be seen in its entirety. It was immense.

As if in answer to the thought in Auger's head, the Holohead's voice murmured, reverently, 'One thousand men and women will embark on this ship, bound for Dirangesept. Fifty thousand autoids will travel with them, armed with plasma and shortlife nuclear weapons, weapons of light and fire, weapons of certain victory.'

The cam panned back, and another ship came into view, the Holohead remarking, 'And here, another thousand Far Warriors. Another fifty thousand autoids.'

And the cam moved on, to show beyond that ship, another, and beside that another, and the Holohead's voice fell to silence as the cam withdrew through the ranks of the armada, the awesome multitude becoming clear until the ships seemed, if not to fill the whole immensity of space, at least to be the grid that defined it. It was a compressed image, Auger knew, marshalling so many far-separated ships into the frame, but still, it was astonishing.

'One thousand ships,' the Holohead told Auger in a hushed voice. 'One million Warriors. Fifty million autoids. We cannot fail. We shall not fail.'

The Administration theme sounded again, and the green frame came in to swallow the ships before Auger's screen nilled itself once more.

He checked the time. Two hours, Sherry had said. She was easing up on herself. Or else she wasn't sleeping.

Standing in the corridor, waiting for her to unlock for him, Auger wondered how long it had been since Sherry had been out of her room. She said nothing as she opened the door just wide enough for him to slip through, and she reset the locks again immediately.

Waiting for her to be done with the door, he glanced around. The cams were mounted high in the ceiling, masquerading as light fittings. He guessed she'd be watching his visit as soon as he left her.

Sherry went back to the monitor on her desk and sat down. She back-tracked the image, peering intently at the screen. Auger knew what he was going to see there as he walked over to stand beside her.

It had been like this for three years now. On the screen was a view of her bed from directly above, framed by the floor around it and then the four walls, their lines barrelled by the wide lens. The only illumination came from the LoGlo of the window to the screen's left, washing the room with thick, honeyed light. On the bed, Sherry, a sheet over her, the sheet transparent, and Sherry naked beneath it and gilded by the glow, asleep. Nothing of her was hidden. At the bottom right of the screen, a time record glimmered: hours, minutes, seconds, divisions of seconds. A clock was the only thing on the small table beside her bed, too, the face angled to be visible from the cam as well as the bed. Their times were synchronised perfectly. There was nothing else in the room. Bed, table, clock, Sherry. And the cam, of course. The room was arranged purely to provide filmed, recorded sleep.

Auger settled himself to watch with her. Sherry on the monitor was shifting in her sleep, agitated, throwing her arms out and then hunching them into her body, pushing out her legs and curling them up again, not settling, never at rest. The recorded time was spinning on at twice actual, according to the display, magnifying Sherry's disturbance.

'How are you?' he said eventually. On the screen he read two forty-three a.m. and a flurry of seconds.

'Fine, Auger. I'm fine.' Her attention never left the screen. 'What's it like out there?'

'He hasn't been caught,' he told her, which was what she'd been asking him. She asked him every time he visited her. He never would be caught, Auger knew, and she probably did, too. And even if he was, it wouldn't help her now.

A movement more sudden under the sheet passed on the screen, and Sherry tensed, stopped the vid and reversed it, unfolding herself on the mattress until just before the abrupt shift in position. She paused it there. She was lying on her side, legs stretched out, knees together, fists clenched and arms splayed, rigid in sleep. The edge of the sheet had caught in her toes and stretched taut, making the sheet a film glazing her body as if she were a player in a porn vid. Sherry ran the picture again, slowing it to realtime, and as she did, the sound abruptly came on too, startling Auger. A long dreaming moan from Sherry on the monitor, a quick rustle of the sheet as she pulled sharply into herself, an oddly eroticised foetus, and turned her face to the mattress, drawing her knees into her chest. The sheet slackened over her, its translucent folds scoring her body with luminous fuzz in the light-augmented picture. Sherry let it run on for ten seconds, her body slowly stilling and relaxing, and froze it again. Not looking at Auger, she said, 'Do you think that jumped? Did I lose something there? Did something happen?' She leaned into the monitor, squinting at the faintly trembling image. 'Was there something else under the sheet?'

'No. Just you, Sherry. It's just a sleep movement. Check the clocks. Nothing happened. You were probably having a nightmare.'

She nodded. 'I thought so.' And sent the vid forward, double speed again.

And this was how she spent every day, he knew, checking her night's sleep, checking every second of unconsciousness. As she had checked herself every night since she had been drug-raped three years back. The guy who had picked her up somewhere had spiked her drink and taken her back to some place she didn't remember, a place with a mirrored room set with cams, and there he had raped her four times over a period of five hours and twenty-seven minutes, timed, and she remembered none of it. She had been conscious for every moment of it, though, turning as he asked her, raising herself and lowering herself, answering his questions – 'Do you like this?' – truthfully. 'No, it hurts, please will you stop now?' she had said, but never resisted him, never once disobeyed. He had worn a mask all the way through, as well as gloves and condom, though she didn't actually remember any of it, anything about him, or it, even when the copy of the vid had arrived, correctly addressed to Sherry, a week after it had happened.

Auger had authorised surveillance over her for a month, and when that had drawn nothing and he'd been forced to pull it he had spent all his spare time doing it himself. And then Sherry had had the cams installed in her room and started to spend her nights sleeping and her days checking her nights.

He looked at her in profile now, the sag of her eyelids, the deep lines of her forehead. At least she was watching the tapes accelerated. Last time he'd visited her she'd been watching them all the way through at real time, sometimes even half speed, and if something drew her away from the monitor she'd have to restart the whole night again.

The doorchime went off in the silence of the screen, and Auger jerked even more than Sherry.

'My food delivery,' she said. 'Will you go on watching the screen if I get the door?'

'Fine,' Auger said, feeling warm with the fact that she was prepared to trust him with this. She went to the door and activated the monitor and its cams. A timer started on the doorscreen, sudden seconds leaping onward in purple italic. Out of the corner of his eye, Auger saw the delivery guy leave a sack of cartons and cans at her door and retreat. Fourteen seconds, a few tenths, a riff of hundredths, a blur of thousandths. The cams trailed him along the corridor, watching him away, ticking him off. Sherry waited for him to be gone and the corridor clear before opening the door and bringing the sack inside. She bolted the door and stood by the monitor, rewinding it and then running through it until it was done and she was back with herself again.

She'd come to the 'fists the following morning, after waking up in her own bed, beaten and sore and with no idea why. No hysteria when he'd interviewed her, but her speech and reactions damped, dull and slow. He'd accompanied her back here, to her place. There was nothing to suggest anyone else had been here, her clothes were laid out by her as she always set them out before going to bed. Maybe she'd done it to herself, she thought, had a fall in the street, an accident, come home dazed and put herself to bed, though that didn't explain the soreness of her vagina, her anus, her cut lips, the weals and bruises elsewhere.

Still, she had managed to persuade herself of an accident, until the next day when the vid arrived at her door, carefully wrapped in blond aquasilk and tied with a bow of fine red ribbon like a lover's gift. That was when the hysteria had started. She had watched it all the way through, five hours and twenty-seven minutes of it, before bringing it to Auger. He had escorted her back to her room, and she had never left it since. She had rejected his advice to move away, refused his help to do so. Why should she? What good would it do? Her rapist would know. After all, he had made no mistakes, washing and air-drying her thoroughly at the end of it (it was on the vid), and leaving her a forensic dead end.

So only the cams made Sherry feel safe, and only Auger could visit her.

He had wondered why she trusted him, what there was about him, but it was only his height, his mouth, the shape of his hands. That it couldn't have been Auger in the mask. There was more between them now, of course. Not quite trust, perhaps, but the closest Sherry would ever come to it any more.

The clock on the screen was reading six fifty a.m. Ten minutes later it hit seven and her alarm jerked her awake. She swung herself out of bed and immediately looked straight up at the cam, into her own eyes and Auger's. He felt for a moment like the rapist, not knowing why, and not liking it. Her breasts were there for him to see, her nipples with a morning's slight hardness.

'Conscious,' she said into the cam, and Sherry beside him froze the image. The recorded night was over and proved safe.

He looked at her, knowing she could have nilled the screen at that point instead of leaving herself there for him to see. It was different watching her awake and naked on the screen somehow. While she was asleep, she was in some way not Sherry. That was it. This made him a voyeur. He knew what was in her mind. It made him uncomfortable.

It was an effort not to look at the screen again, if only because she was waiting for him to do so. But he knew Sherry was testing him now. Her fragile trust needed constant renewing. He remembered what she had said to him a year after it, when he had momentarily misjudged her state of mind and asked her if she wanted to go out for a walk or something, sit in a café somewhere, that he'd be with her and it would be okay, he'd make sure of it.

'Men,' she had said, not looking at him but making it plain anyway. 'Present company excepted. You know what men are, Auger? What a man really is?'

He'd shaken his head, silenced by the sudden venom in her voice.

'Two slugs joined at the balls. The smaller one controlling the larger. That's all a man is.'

He'd never forgotten that, and he'd never suggested anything like it again to her. She felt secure in here. And even here, she felt only guardedly safe with Auger.

Now she sighed. She seemed to transform as she took a long inward breath after the sigh, and she looked at Auger as if he'd only just now come through the door.

Maybe that's what it was, he thought. She'd just woken up, her day was starting. Everything before this had been a part of sleep. She nilled the screen at her side without glancing at it.

'So, what have you been up to, Auger?' she said, nodding pointedly.

Even her voice was slightly different. Auger glanced at his scratched palms. 'I was chasing someone. I lost them.' He gave her a wry smile. 'I was stopped by a holovert for the D3 project. The power of advertising.'

'I hear they're pushing it everywhere,' Sherry said. She seemed to relax. 'The last project, they say people were lining up to go. I guess it's not like that any more. They can't be recruiting very easily. Not long to go, either, is there? I lose track these days.'

'Didn't you see the Administration Flash—?' he began, then realised that, of course, she hadn't. Her security would have blocked it. She watched everything, sitting here in her room, but only as long as it was her choice to watch it. 'They say they have a million Far Warriors set to go. And fifty autoids each.'

'A million?' She smiled at the idea of it.

'If you believe the Administration. They showed the ships, but who knows, since they're still recruiting? You don't see queues at the signing booths. The ships could have been holos, or at least their numbers holo-augmented.'

Sherry sighed. 'I wonder if it's really worth it. If the project has a chance. Quite apart from the moral aspect of it. We call them beasts, demonise them, but what do we really know? Maybe they have a right to their own planet, whatever they are. Perhaps that's why people aren't signing up for the project.'

'You think so? The survival imperative will always stampede over the moral one. If D3 is undermanned, it's just because no one really believes it has a hope in hell. Look at the past projects. The beasts knocked us back the first time, we could say it was just bad luck. Not the second time.' He shrugged, gave her the edge of a smile. 'They fucked us in the head, Sherry.' He glanced at the window, up into the sky, and said, thinking of Maxenham and Vinz Szolty, of Passive, 'And anyway, we have another choice now. We can kill ourselves and go to heaven.'

Sherry chuckled, then stopped that, mock-serious. 'And there's Nugel, and the Cultivation Nets. A reparable planet, and food for all. So maybe staying's an option again.' She shook her head at the idea of it. 'Sure it is.'

At that she stretched out her hand and took his, looking at it, turning it over, a medic now. Which was what Sherry had been, before the rape. A pathologist. Her rapist had probably been a patient, but there were too many to investigate. Even Auger had had to accept that.

'So, what brings you here?' she asked him at last. 'Not a plaster for your scratches.' She inspected his hand more closely. 'Have you been fighting in the playground too, Auger? They didn't fix you up too good. That's a terrible colour match. Where was that done?'

'GenMed. Your old place. They were out of my shade. It's a good job, though.' As he said it, he wondered why he was being so defensive of the girl.

'Yes. Neatly done,' Sherry said, letting his hand go. 'Nanos, eh?' She paused before uncomfortably following her own lead-in to the question. 'How is Jay?'

'No change. No change at all.'

'I'm sorry. You want to talk about it?'

He never understood how Sherry could be so screwed up about herself and then be able to cut away like that, chat to him about Dirangesept, be supportive of him over Jay. 'It's not why I'm here,' he said.

'That's not what I asked.'

'No.' He could never talk to her about Jay, though, however easy she tried to make it. What had happened to Jay was in some odd way too close to what had happened to Sherry. But both events were inexplicable, ever-present. So how could he cry about Jay on Sherry's shoulder?

'No,' he said again, firmly. He wondered if he could sense relief from her. Maybe she didn't cut away completely after all, just made an effort for his sake.

'What, then?'

'A case. I've been pushed off it, but I need your help. Did you hear about a suicide at GenMed a while back? A medic, Rudd Merchant?'

She nodded. 'Yes. Slightly unusual case, wasn't it? What I heard, it sounded straightforward enough, except for where the body was found, and that there'd been another one just before it, almost identical. But copycat suicides aren't so unusual, are they?'

'No. Well, I didn't think it was for me at all, but when I got bumped off it, I started to wonder.' He fished in his pocket and gave her the swab from Rudd Merchant's bath. 'Can you do anything with this?'

She took it from him and listened while he gave her its story, and then she held up the swab in its plastic container. 'That's no problem. I'll get hold of the post-mortems too. They were too embarrassed to take away my laboratory pass when I left GenMed, so I can access the files easily enough.'

She went into what she called her kitchen. Auger didn't know what she could ever cook in it. As far as he had seen, it was full of pathology equipment. Sherry tested herself daily for drugs. Tested her blood, her piss, her shit, tested her food before she ate it. Tested her sweat too, it wouldn't have surprised Auger.

He waited until she called through to him, 'The swab's going to take a while. I'm running a number of tests on it. Come in.'

It was a professional laboratory in there. Flasks, test tubes, beakers and crucibles. A centrifuge was running a dull hum, shivering the makeshift stand it was bolted to. Spectrometer results spilled from another table stained with chemicals. A professional mess.

'You're still freelancing, then,' he said.

'From time to time. Long as they deliver and collect on my terms. It pays some of the bills.' Sherry peeled off a pair of gloves and tossed them into a burnbox, then sat back down at a screen and punched herself in. Auger watched the GenMed logo appear, the pumping heart in a gloved hand, then watched her work the board until it began to murmur and a printout started to unfurl from the machine. He reached out and let it ripple into his hand.

'The swab results still aren't ready,' she said. 'You want to wait for them, or do this another time?'

'I'll wait.'

'Okay.' She took the fan of printouts from him. 'Meantime I'll just have a skim through these. It looks like they did a thorough job, anyway. Should be some answers here.'

He followed her back into the main room and watched her read the post-mortem notes. She scanned through them casually to start off with, then slowed down and began checking back, picking up a pencil and marking the notes, becoming more involved in the papers. Eventually she stood up, frowning, and wandered back to the kitchen without saying a word. She came out again ten minutes later, still wearing the same frown.

'What is it, Sherry?'

'I'm not quite sure yet.'

'Tell me anyway.'

'Okay.' She unscrolled the notes and riffed her thumb through them for Auger's benefit. 'This is the first one, Neffer Haenson, and this is a big PM, Auger. A real job. I'd expect half this much.' She thumbed the opening paragraphs. 'So, the first death. It looked like suicide, in the bath, his blood drained away with the water. Like we said before, straight-forward enough. But at that stage, you think, why carry out so comprehensive a PM? Hmm?' She held up the notes again, emphasising it. 'They *really* did a job on him, Auger. Turned him inside out, pretty well.'

A small chime rang in the kitchen. Sherry stood up and disappeared there, then returned, studying a scrap of paper. Auger waited.

Still holding the paper, she said, 'Rudd Merchant. Same method of suicide apparently, but this time the body's found on the bed.'

'You can discount that factor, Sherry. I know who did that. A friend of his found the body. She didn't believe it was suicide, it or the first one. So she lifted the corpse from the bath, moved it to the bed. He wasn't a big man, and no blood in it, the body would have been just about light enough for her to lift alone. She's stronger than she looks.' He wondered why he'd said that. But she was. She was strong. 'She wanted to be sure the death was investigated. That's why she did it.'

Sherry nodded. 'So you think it's murder too.'

'I didn't. I'm changing my mind.'

'I'm inclined to agree.' She brandished the paper. 'Your swab, that was a good thought, Auger.'

'Let me guess,' he said. 'No blood products.'

'That's right. None at all. If it had been suicide, or even if someone had found Merchant, or been with him when he died, and washed out the bath after moving him – your strong friend, say, or else a killer – there still would have been traces of blood products in the drain beyond the plug-hole. But there were none. So Rudd Merchant didn't die in the bath, and I think it's not crazy to assume that Neffer Haenson died the same way. Which means they were taken there after death to make their deaths seem to be suicide.'

'Go on,' he said, impatient. He'd got this far already, and she knew that. But she'd got further, and that was what he was interested in.

'Okay, the next piece of the puzzle turns out to be the post-mortem notes themselves. Now, this is strange. They took brain sections in both cases. Exactly the same. What's the question you're asking yourself at this point, Auger?'

He thought about it. 'Why for Haenson? Taken in isolation, that was just a straightforward suicide. The second one raises questions about the first, so you go back, recheck the first, check everything again, go further. But before Merchant's death there would have been no reason to do it for Haenson.'

'Exactly. None at all. But they analysed the brains to death, excuse me. Everything else was just picked at and stitched up by comparison. Internal organs, tissues, the rest. But the brains—'

'They were interested in the brains, Sherry. I got it. Go on, will you?'

'Hold it, Auger. You haven't got it. They weren't just *interested*. It goes even further than that. I don't think they were even *concerned* with the cause of death.' She sat back, then leant forward again immediately, unable to conceal her excitement. 'My guess is they knew that. These weren't post-mortems they were carrying out. These were something else. I've seen notes like this before. These were the dissections of laboratory animals. This wasn't pathological examination. This was vivisection, Auger.'

Auger opened his mouth, but nothing came out. He'd had a couple of theories, expected Sherry to give him one of them. But this hadn't featured at all.

He tried again. 'You mean they were killing them in the first place?'

'Not necessarily. Not directly. It could be that they were carrying out research and something went wrong, and they just wanted to find out what.' Sherry sat back and rubbed her chin. 'Look, you're really going to have to leave this with me. There's something about it that I still haven't quite got.'

Auger stood up, still stiff from chasing the man from Rudd Merchant's room. His shoulder was aching again, too. 'Okay. I'll speak to you, Sherry. Thanks.'

'No problem, Auger. It's good to have something real to do. It's been a while.'

For a few minutes he played with the two bLinker packs on the table. He glanced up at the gecko, but the gecko was no help.

He kept pushing them around. One was the pack from Fly, the other he'd picked up at Passive after finding that the adherents of the High Window could not go ahead with their Leaving, on the basis that if they didn't believe this world was real, then they didn't believe anything in it, including their Understands. So their declarations were invalid. He'd sent his decision to Vinz Szolty and taken the rest of the day off before Szolty could get back to him with a reversal.

He pushed Fly's pack to one side and picked up the other bLinker case, stroking the curved letters chased into its ovoid casing.

A GLIMPSE OF YOUR PERSONAL HEAVEN.

Heaven. It was what they all promised, one way or another. Death was all they delivered, though.

He clicked the case open and tipped the bLinkers into the palm of his hand where they sat warming, their neural tendrils wriggling. The bridge-piece was unusually thick and heavy, which was odd, because the exensors were as fine as he'd ever seen.

There were a few words of embossed script on the inside of the case. *Courtesy of Dr McCrae. Envoy.* And contact details. Auger had them at the office, ready for tomorrow. He snapped the case closed and let it drop to the table.

McCrae was offering a tailored heaven here. That was something different at least. It had to be a good offer for the preacher to be taking so many with him. Rolling the bLinkers in his hand, Auger wondered what the program might tailor for himself.

Okay, let's find out, he thought. He set the bLinkers over the bridge of his nose, then settled back on to his bed. The eyeLids had turned everything to black, and he could just make out a few odd motes darting across his eyeballs, bright specks and trails. He tried to follow them, but all he could do was chase them harder until his eyes ached. The weight of the bridge-piece irritated him briefly.

Over a minute, and the program still hadn't kicked in. Auger wasn't impressed. He let the motes dance for him to pass the time, moving his eyeballs, managing to guide the particles in the wake of his eye movement, and then he noticed the background of his vision lightening. There were more scattered motes now, and a general pattern to their motion. They were no longer dependent on him. He seemed to be moving through them, and with an abrupt surge of dizziness he realised they were stars and their background was space, the universe.

He took in a sharp rush of air. This was striking. Auger hadn't seen it done quite like this before. He'd been carried unharmed through fire, seen choirs of angels and been shown the depths of hell, but this was actually almost subtle. Well, it was another angle.

He continued to glide passively forward, and what seemed to be a galaxy ahead became a drift of smoke into which he gently passed.

There was some more clever stuff with the background that took a few minutes, comets, a distant nova, and then a human form started to coalesce from a mist of silver haze. Auger couldn't quite focus on it. It could have been a man or a woman, and it could have been the same size as Auger just a few metres away, or thousands of miles away and un-imaginably vast.

In another stirring of smoke, it raised a hand, and Auger looked in the direction it was indicating. There was a voice in his head, a soft, sexually ambiguous voice with a slight lilt to it.

'Welcome to the afterworlds, Auger. Well come, and be welcome here.'

Auger felt the smoke surrounding him, both cloaking him and binding him to the speaker. *God the all-knowing, knowing my name.* The bLinkers were smart, memory sifters. That had to explain the unusual weight of the bridge-piece. McCrae had built himself an expensive hook.

The voice was continuing. 'In the afterworlds, there are as many heavens as there are hells. So why leave it to chance? Your future can be what you want it to be. Here, it can be something unique, but more than that, it can be unique to *you*. It can be your very own past made good.'

Looking at the godhead, Auger was able to make out vague features. It was perhaps more male than female, with soft blue eyes and a high, creased forehead. The lips of its mouth were thin and almost bloodless, moving not quite in synchrony with the words that Auger was not hearing through his ears.

'Let me show you something, Auger, something to illustrate that you might believe me, and that this world beyond might be the world of—' the smoke behind the figure was moving, parting '—your dreams.'

Auger watched it unfold for him.

He should have guessed. Jay was there, standing in the long yellow dress, staring at him with the strength of her love, her eyes bright and happy. Her cheeks flushed. The priest in his purple and silver cloak, all their friends, happy and alive. There was Jocar. Beside him, Tomasz was taking pictures with that old camera of his, the flash clicking away so intensely that it lit up the godhead's smoky form as he watched with Auger. Auger had forgotten Tomasz with his camera.

The godhead made a subtle gesture and the scene moved on. They were leaving now, himself and Jay, lifting away in the microflite, spinning round the park in a great rising curve, taking it all in. Everyone below them was waving. There was a small explosion on the ground and Auger almost looked away, his heart suddenly leaping and pounding, but it was just a firework fizzing up into the air to burst beside the cockpit of the microflite in a fading spray of electric blue glitter.

'This is enough,' Auger said, glancing at the godhead. 'Don't show me this.'

'But it can be like this,' the godhead replied in that gentle lilt. 'It can be like this for ever. Or it can be different in another way. It can be what *you* want, Auger. Only come with me. Come soon. Come.'

The microflite was over the trees and the wedding guests were out of sight. More fireworks rose in the microflite's wake, and Jay was looking back at the swathes of charged colour and hugging his arm, saying, 'Oh,

Cy, do you know this is the best day of my life? I wish it could last for ever. I'm so very, very happy. I'll never forget it. All of this for you and me.' She touched his cheek with the palm of her hand, and Auger almost felt that touch again. He wanted to lean his head into that soft touch as she murmured, 'I never even dreamt it would be so wonderful. I love you so much, Cy.'

'And I, I . . .' He couldn't say it. He couldn't say a thing. The fireworks in their wake, the stars above, and Jay here at his side.

She looked at him with sudden concern. 'Why are you crying? Is something wrong?'

'Yes,' he said, as if to Jay herself. It was too much for him. He'd had enough.

'Exit now,' he said.

In the blackness of exit, he gently bLinked out. He touched his cheeks with the tips of his fingers. After his glimpse of heaven, only the tears were real.

PART TWO

PASSIVE

TWELVE

'Okay, that's it. Just sign it and you can go.'

The man could hardly sign his name. Auger watched his tongue work as he set down the spiky letters. Eight seconds a letter, it took him. Auger could see him getting by for all of his twenty-two years on skin-print confirmation and the text reader he'd had to use as a prompt to utter the Understand. Not that it mattered any more. Not where he was going tomorrow. Auger wondered what McCrae's heaven held for him. It wouldn't have to be much to be an improvement on what he had now, though. Auger pointed him out through the door and called another one in, peeling the next consent form off the pile. The signed pile was taller than the unsigned now, and Auger's voice was going. But at least so was the memory of McCrae's heaven with its vision of what might have been for Auger.

There was nothing he could do with any of these to stop them. The Leaving would go ahead for all of them, the thousand or more processed through his office and all the other offices in the building. Even what he'd done yesterday with the High Window had already been reversed by Szolty. They would all die.

Passive, he thought. Two days, and it was already beginning to erode him. All he had to take his mind away were his true memories of Jay, and the thought of the medic who said she'd help him. And of course Astrid's own problem, which was starting to seem interesting. Maybe she wasn't like the rest of them. Auger wondered about the man in Rudd's room, the man he'd almost caught. He could have just been a looter, after a dead man's possessions, but Auger was sure there was more to it than that.

The door opened again, bringing him back to his desk.

Bringing him back to where he was. Passive. But he'd be damned if he

141

was going to accept that. Damned if he was going to sit there and do Maxenham's work.

This one was a girl. She looked very young, too young. Auger looked at her form, squinting, and said, 'I can't quite read your writing. What's your date of birth?'

She told him, snapping the numbers out in a high, fractured voice. She had bleach-streaked short brown hair, and her cheeks were freckled. 'So you're how old?' he asked her as she sat down. She put her hands on her knees, palm down. Her nails were bitten short, the palps of her fingers swollen.

'I'm fourteen.'

'Ah, yes.' He rubbed the stubble on his chin. She was looking at him with big eyes, and he knocked his hand against the stem of the desk light, letting its bright cone flare over her face. She didn't flinch or look away, and Auger watched her pupils diminish and swell quite naturally.

He looked back down to the form with her details and said her name aloud. 'Lethe LeCantho. I'm sorry, Lethe, it's been a long day.' He blinked hard and yawned. 'Your date of birth again? Your writing really isn't clear.' It was, of course. It could have been machine-inked, that careful rounded script, no letter's edge leaking from its box. No confidence. Writing was new to her. He imagined her licking her lips in concentration, making certain, making no mistake as she signed away her life.

She repeated it, and it was still there in the way she answered him. It was not like she was saying something she knew incontrovertibly to be true. She was telling him something she'd been told was the right answer. She had the wrong sort of certainty.

'You have your passport?'

The girl fished in her pocket, bringing the document out and setting it on the desk in front of him. Auger noticed the difficulty she had flexing her hand. He flicked through the passport. It was perfect, as he'd expected, like her lettering, and he gave it back to her. He wasn't going to break the story or her documents. Not in the time he had. It was all going to hold together, he knew that. 'Okay,' he said wearily. 'You've read the form? You know what's going to happen?'

'Yes,' she said, and her eyes lit up like stars, her face opening in a smile that almost broke Auger's heart.

There was nothing else to do, so he passed the Understand over the desk to her. The palm of her hand was dark, callused and pitted, and as she reached out for the form, her sleeve rode up her skinny arm. Auger hesitated, pulling back a fraction to let the Understand fall on the desk just in front of him, making her stretch further, riding the sleeve up towards her elbow. She was about to snatch the form when he took her wrist in his hand and held it gently. She started to pull away, then realised from his instant release of his grip that Auger wasn't trying to do anything to her. She let her hand lie there, exposed to him.

He smiled at her, then looked at her palm again and turned her arm over and back. A pattern of purpling tattoos spiralled around her forearms. They were too old and blurred for him to make out their detail. They should have meant something to him, he knew.

'What are these?'

She took her thin arm back. It was like a scribbled stick. She rolled the sleeve quickly back down to her wrist as if embarrassed, smoothing the rough material with her hand. 'I had them done a few years ago. I saw the design in the studio. That's all. They don't mean anything.' She looked at him again with that same earlier confidence, and picked up the Understand from the desk.

Auger sighed. 'Okay. Read it to me,' he told her.

She read it aloud like a prayer, her face pale and radiant. It must have been the fiftieth time he'd heard it today, but this time he seemed to be hearing it for the first time.

' "I understand that I shall be terminating my own life with no guarantee of any subsequent existence, despite what I may have been promised, and that I am of sound mind as certified by Dr Karl Teiler." Okay? Can I sign it now?'

He nodded, and she signed awkwardly, having trouble holding the pen in stiff fingers. But handing the form back to Auger, she looked at him as if he had just blessed her. He couldn't meet her eyes. He checked her name against Teiler's list. Teiler hadn't questioned her sanity any more than he had queried her age. But, then, it wasn't Teiler's job to confirm her age. He wondered how much the psych got paid for this. There was no way she was fourteen. Auger nodded again at the girl and wondered exactly how Teiler defined sanity.

He glanced at the next form. 'Okay, Lethe,' he said. 'You can go now.'

She hesitated then, and Auger knew she'd been prepared for more, been expecting more. He wondered about the tattoos on her arms. To have faded so much, they must have been done at least eight years ago. Even if she was as old as she claimed, she couldn't have been more than six years old.

He looked again at the name on the next consent form. 'Go on, then, Lethe,' he said once more, and watched her out of the room.

He could see the resemblance as soon as the next one pushed through the door. The woman had the same open smile as her daughter, the same features. And the same faded tattoos, but these freely displayed.

She had the same confidence, too. Auger didn't challenge it. He checked a few details on her form, then leaned back in the chair. 'Tell me why,' he said. He was looking at her and seeing the child. 'I've spent half a day here going through your Understands, and I don't understand at all.'

'Because there's a better place. It's as simple as that.'

'You're so sure? There's no doubt?' Despite himself, he could feel the small yearning in his own voice, and he could see her react to it.

'What is there here?' she said gently. 'What is there any more? We know what exists beyond. Why wait? Why waste more time?' She was so serene. If the smile that went with the words hadn't been the same as her daughter's smile, Auger thought he might almost have reached out to her.

'I don't want eternity,' he told her. 'I just want a day's peace, a night's sleep.'

'You can have that. You can have anything. Why not come with us? There's room in heaven.'

Auger shook his head. 'I can't change now. I'm set.' He sat straight in his chair for her. 'How old do you think I am?' he asked her.

She tilted her head, looked at him closely. 'Thirty-three? Thirty-four?'

He let himself smile. 'You mean at least forty, don't you? You don't have to be polite. I'm almost grey. My muscles are turning to fat. I'm thirty.'

Her laugh was a cool breeze in the air-conditioned room. 'You aren't so bad. I've seen more worse than better. Come with us. We need more men. There will be work, Dr McCrae says. Hard work, but good work. Not like this soulless gate-keeping.' She made a gesture that took in his office with its piles of forms and papers, its dismal, provisional air. 'And there will be rewards, too. I might take you under my wing.' She smiled at him again, this time an adult smile of promise and complicity. 'Nor will you age.'

'Age shall not wither me, eh?' Auger said, meeting her smile, and then, 'But look at you,' letting her see him looking at her. He let his eyes move down her body, seeing the gentle inward curve of her neck become the firm brace of her shoulders, taking in the defined rounds of her breasts, the tautness of her waist. She did look good, Auger thought. Very good. Her daughter might have looked this good one day. He picked up her form and glanced at it. 'You're thirty-two, you look twenty-five. You've aged better than me,' he told her. 'It's a tempting offer.'

She leaned forward a fraction. 'I could be yours. I could be yours for ever.'

He sighed. 'I'm too old for eternity. But you . . .' He shook his head, smiling ruefully at her. 'And you've had a child, too? I'd never believe it. How old were you when you had her?'

'Twenty,' she said, smiling.

Auger nodded slowly, waiting for her to catch up. He sat back in the chair, giving her time, still nodding. Her smile turned to ice as she abruptly connected with the situation. Auger picked up her form again. It was suddenly as if something in the room had been switched off.

'I mean eighteen,' she said. She tried to thaw the smile again, but it cracked and failed. She pulled out another one. Auger didn't respond. She leaned towards him, the light on the desk throwing her cleavage into bright curve and hard shadow. 'Let me show you what could be yours in the beyond. Let me just show you.' She touched the top button of her dress, the shining button at the valley of her breasts, and began to rise to her feet.

'Are you trying to bribe me, Ms LeCantho?'

She was immediately back in the chair. The cone of light slid away from her and settled faintly on the interview monitor unit across the room, throwing its proclamation into relief. Auger glanced at it, drawing it to her attention. PROPERTY OF PASSIVE. PERMANENTLY RECORDING. DO NOT DISCONNECT. DO NOT REMOVE. She took it in, then looked back at Auger.

'I made a mistake,' she said crisply. 'That's all. I meant I was eighteen.'

'She hardly looks ten, let alone twelve.'

'She signed her Understand, didn't she? Her ID's solid.' The woman smiled, yet another breed of smile. This time she looked nothing like her daughter. 'It's too late. There's nothing you can do.'

Auger shook his head. 'You just gave me sufficient doubt, Ms LeCantho. On that basis I can hold her for a ChronDNA test. I believe it will take a minimum of a week.' He took the daughter's Understand from its pile, folded it neatly and put it aside, then held out the woman's own form. 'I don't suppose you'll be wanting this now?'

She snatched it from him, snapped out the verbal declaration without even glancing at the text, and signed it, the pen scratching and stabbing into the paper. She slapped the form on to the pile and stood up. 'You aren't stopping me. This isn't what you're here for. You don't know what you're doing. You have no idea.'

When the woman had gone, Auger sat for a few minutes with his hands flat on the table, palms down. Then he picked them up again and examined his sweat prints on the greasy plastic veneer until they faded away. He pulled the last form from the bottom of the pile and walked over to the door.

'Dr McCrae?'

The man was sitting with the mother and daughter. The young girl was in tears and her mother broke off hugging her, the two of them rocking gently together, to flash a look of pure hatred at Auger.

Standing up, McCrae rested his hands on the shoulders of the women and whispered something to them before moving easily through the waiting room's packed chairs towards Auger. He smiled at Auger and Auger closed the door, making a gesture for McCrae to sit.

'It isn't my turn,' the preacher said. His voice was low and melodious. 'This is about the LeCanthos, isn't it?'

McCrae looked vaguely familiar to Auger, and there was something about him that made him want to listen to what the man had to say. He saw McCrae immediately to be different from the others. There was an authority to him, a true sense of dignity.

'Let me tell you about the LeCanthos,' McCrae said. 'The father died a while ago, and the mother and her child want him back. They want to be with him, their family to be together, to be made whole again.'

The preacher had an air of sad, deep understanding about him. Auger felt bad about what he had to tell McCrae and wasn't sure why. Perhaps it was that McCrae just seemed a truly good, decent man. 'That wasn't exactly the impression I got from the mother,' Auger told him. He wanted to mention the child's age, but somehow that seemed irrelevant now.

'If Ms Lecantho said or did anything inappropriate, she apologises. She is desperate. Her daughter, too. I'm sure you can appreciate that, Mr Auger. These are desperate times. Be charitable, Mr Auger. All we have left here in this hard world is our humanity. It behoves us not to forget that.'

His voice was soft and certain, and Auger was starting to nod, agreeing, grateful that the matter had been resolved. And then it struck him. The Godhead. Its features were McCrae's. Not perfectly, but the resemblance was unmistakable.

Auger straightened. 'Dr McCrae, do you know that it is an offence to pass yourself off as a deity?'

McCrae bowed his head. 'You mean The Glimpse? Our images have been examined by my lawyers. The points of similarity per second fully comply with your regulations.'

Auger took a long breath. Faith was letting everything slide away, it seemed. But he wasn't going to let Lethe go so easily. 'The girl isn't fourteen.'

'My understanding is that she is,' McCrae said evenly. 'She looks younger, I know. But Ms LeCantho, her mother, also looks younger than her age. As I'm sure you noticed.'

'Dr McCrae, your, your—'

'Our Leaving, Mr Auger.' McCrae's tone was setting harder. 'That is the word. It is a respectable word. Please use it.'

'Your Leaving is scheduled for tomorrow.' Auger noticed the man registering the derision he had hung on the word. He wondered what sort of a doctor McCrae was. Probably the same sort as Teiler. He wished Teiler was going with McCrae.

McCrae said, 'Yes?'

'I'm going to withdraw Lethe LeCantho from the schedule of Leaving, pending a ChronDNA test. I think she's too young to give independent consent. Obviously I have no grounds to withdraw consent from her mother, but perhaps you could have a word with her and ask her to delay her Leaving for her daughter's sake.'

McCrae sighed. 'The time has been set. We are expected. If we delay . . .' he shrugged.

Auger held back the urge to ask what the hell difference it would make. He'd learnt that lesson a long time ago. Planetary conjunctions, premonitions. They had all the answers and none at all.

'Okay,' he said wearily. 'I'll need details of the girl's closest other relative.'

'She hasn't any. As I told you. There is only her mother. Everyone else is dead.' McCrae leaned forward, sugaring his voice, the Godhead once more. 'Let her come, Mr Auger. Show her some mercy. Let her be with her mother. Believe me, she will be in a far better place.'

'I'm not arguing with you, McCrae. Not about mercy. Take the mother, then. You're not having the girl.' Auger suddenly placed the tattoos, the spirals down the girl's arms. He'd seen the pattern before. He'd seen them on the street. They'd been a scorpion cult, walking the streets, carrying dagger-tailed scorpions in the bare palms of their hands. The scorpions symbols of the imminence of death, as if living in this guttering world wasn't that.

'Just take the mother,' Auger said again. The mother's hands were perfect. She would have used the child as her carrier. The child barely old enough to be walking.

'Tell me, Auger,' the preacher said. 'Where will you go when you die?'

'Death isn't a journey, McCrae. Death is a fact. Now, are you done?'

McCrae didn't immediately stand up. 'You can't do this to the child,' he said.

'I said leave,' Auger told him.

McCrae left the room. Auger went on with the Understands. There were fifty-two more. He could challenge none of them, but every time the door opened he could hear the girl screaming for her mother.

The screams of Lethe Lecantho were still in his mind when he got home and closed the door behind him. He went to the hole in the floor where he kept everything of value to him, and slid out the disk he had taken from under Vinz Szolty's nose. Right now he just wanted something to remind him of Jay.

He took the disk to the screen and opened it. The file meant nothing to him, as it had always meant nothing. He was sure it would have meant nothing to Vinz Szolty, had he found it, but the gesture had mattered to Auger.

All Jay's notes were on that file, all the details of her research. When he had been asked, after the wedding, if any of her notes had been kept at home, he had told them no, believing it to be true. They had returned a few times, her colleagues, taking tea and giving sympathy and asking, as they left, in afterthought, if he'd come across anything since the last time.

He hadn't discovered it until he had moved to this holo-haunted block. It had been concealed in a book of photographs, slid into a neat slit in the cover and sewn up. It was the stiffness of it that had finally alerted Auger. Not the stiffness of the disk, but of the housing of electronic shielding that had made it effectively undetectable. An odd thing to do, he thought. But wise, perhaps, in retrospect. The apartment he had shared with her had twice been broken into in the weeks after the wedding, professional computer thieves taking everything the first time, and probably kids the second time, ransacking and taking apart everything in the place, destroying all, taking nothing.

And then, all that time later, when he had found the disk hidden away, he had taken it to his office and stored the file there, where it would be safe. He didn't know why he had kept it. It had been an impulse, no more than that, to retain a part of Jay. And by then, the time to give it back to her team seemed to have passed. It would be out of date by now, her research. And this was just a copy.

He scanned the text of the disk without seeing any of it, the words and numbers that were her world; thinking just of her entering it all, sitting then as he was now sitting. He thought of his scar now, and flexed his fist smoothly. The PlaSkin was fading, his own skin colour starting to replace the synthetic shade. Her work remained. Perhaps, at least in his head, so did Jay.

The screen went to grey, and Auger knelt to replace the disk. He had put the blue package with Fly's bLinkers in the cavity alongside Jay's disk, and now he brought the package out, feeling as he did so a twinge in that shoulder again. Perhaps it was just guilt.

He stood up, still with the package in his hand, thinking for a moment what to do.

It came to him. He had once come across a game hacker who had been used in a practical joke that he'd discovered to actually be a sanity-scam. A will-buster. What was the hacker's name? He'd come to Auger with it, and Auger had managed to keep him out of the notes, out of darktime. He owed Auger.

Tatoro. That was his name.

THIRTEEN

'See this nodule above the bridge here,' Tatoro said, 'it's a long-range transceiver. You can bLink into the zone from anywhere at all. That's standard these days, but this unit's very old. Five, six years maybe.'

'Can we find out what it is without bLinking?' Auger asked.

'Easy enough.' Tatoro flipped the bLinkers over, pointing out a tiny line of ridged script that meant nothing to Auger. Letters and numbers, some kind of manufacturing code. 'But this is unusual. See this thing?' Tatoro flipped the bLinkers again and, as if it might prick him, touched a tiny black blister on the side of the transceiver. Auger had assumed it was a fault in the plastic. Tatoro squinted hard, and Auger saw his pupils swell briefly and retract again, the irises fade and deepen.

Tatoro put the bLinker unit down on the table and rested his cheek-bones on the heels of his hands, elbows on the table to either side of the bLinkers. He moved his elbows apart, carefully lowering his head a few centimetres, and held it there, rock still. Without looking up, he muttered, 'Sorry, it's just I get a limited depth of field at this mag. Ah. Ah. Yes, this *is* honey.' He whistled, low and long. 'This is very *much* honey.' He sat up, squinted again and rubbed his eyes. 'That's a passport. Out of date, but effective. Guaranteed the user safe access, so you didn't get your skull fried. That's what happens to wetbacks – zonehackers, to you. This has to be a *very* exclusive zone.'

'What zone?' Auger said.

'Sorry. Hang on.' Tatoro slid across to the lightbook down the desk and flicked the screen on. 'Passported bLinkers are all security logged. Let's just . . .' Auger watched the numbers roll down the screen and lock one by one into solid pillars. The final one clicked like the last tumbler of a safe, and a small textbox opened onscreen. Auger couldn't make it out.

'Well, hey, blast from the past,' Tatoro said, leaning back into his chair until the backrest squeaked.

'Tell me,' Auger said.

'May not mean anything to you. Zone by the name Cathar?' Tatoro picked up the bLinkers and stared curiously at them for a moment before throwing them down on the table where the tendrils squirmed. 'Never mind,' he said. 'Worthless. Can't even recycle the bLinkers.' He sighed. 'You know anything about Cathar? It's back a few years now.' When Auger seemed not to have heard, he said it again. 'You know anything about—?'

'I know a bit about it,' Auger said quietly. Cathar was legend. It was the game that finally sank Maze, the biggest game company of them all. 'What do you know, Tatoro?'

'Truth and rumour, that's what I know, but I don't know where they meet. Story goes, Maze was working on bLinker technology. Perfect bLinker technology, the perfect zone. Cathar was the zone. It was in a late stage of development, the guinea pigs all Far Warriors, Vets of the Dirangesept projects.'

'I've heard that,' Auger said. 'Most of them died, didn't they?'

Auger didn't need Tatoro's nod. He knew it. That was Madsen, that was the legendary CMS fuckup. Madsen had completely missed the Maze/Fury connection. The Vets at Maze had all belonged to Father Fury's first congregation, and the preacher had either killed them or had them kill themselves, so it was said. The director of Maze amongst them. The company never recovered from it. Shortly afterwards Maze sank like a stone, and Cathar was left dead in the water.

And Madsen had never even seen the connection. He'd had nothing. So there was nothing to stick Fury to it, and he too had submerged.

But unlike Maze, Fury had resurfaced again. He had screwed Madsen, and now he'd come back and done Auger too. Twice.

Auger looked at the fist he had made, and opened his hand. At least this time Fury was dead. At least there was that.

He looked at the bLinkers lying on the table. Fly's father must have been one of the guinea pigs at Maze. Madness and death, he'd told his son. No wonder.

Tatoro stared hard at him. 'Yeah, that's right, most of them died. Well, you'll know Maze ran the zone pre-release for just a few months after that. It became something of a cult even so, but it was shut down when Maze bellied up.'

'Anything else?' Auger asked.

'Not much. Just wilder rumours.'

He hesitated, and Auger prompted him. 'Like?'

Tatoro scratched his chin. 'Well, you know the zone testers were Far Warriors, and the Warriors came back to Earth with beasts in their heads?'

Auger thought of the research wing at GenMed, that glimpse of a face at the high window there. Maybe a Vet with a beast in his skull. 'Go on.'

'Well, one of the crazier stories about Cathar was that there were beasts running wild in the zone. Like, for real.'

Auger reached towards the bLinkers on the table between them, and drew his hand back again.

'Yeah,' Tatoro said. 'Anyway, it doesn't matter. There's no Cathar any more.' There was a faintly wistful look in Tatoro's eyes as he said it. It reminded Auger of a preacher's look, discussing heaven. Players believed in their games the way preachers preached their heavens. They lost games and killed themselves over them. They even signed responsibility-disclaimers when they bought games, and it abruptly struck Auger that this was no different from the Understands that the heaven-bound signed in Passive.

With a regretful sigh, Tatoro said, 'They say even Dreamtide 3 isn't as real as Cathar was. It was the perfect game.' He smiled, for a moment far away, then returned to Auger. 'These bLinkers?' He pushed at them with a finger, watching them react. He looked surprised for a moment, then relaxed again. 'They look live, but that's probably just a proximity reaction. Try and bLink and one of two things'll happen. If they're genuine bLinkers, zone'll be a pirate cut with some sloozy game that's even older than chess.' He gave them another jab. They twitched again.

'And if they aren't genuine?' Auger said.

'Then you'll be in a black zone with no Exitline. End of story.'

Astrid stepped off the walkway and through the columns. The air hit her sharply, making her draw breath. The glass walls of the research wing had a viridescent patina, and she saw herself approaching from the colonnade as if she were walking among drowned ruins. She was only out of the net's protection for a few metres, but her face was itching as she reached the doors to the wing. The doors almost sucked her in. They closed behind her with a hiss.

She went across to the reception desk, wiping her eyes. 'My name's Astrid Remarque. I'm here to register for a research project. Troy Gordo told me to mention his name.'

The receptionist hardly looked up, pressing a white buzzer on her desk. There were three buzzers on the desk and a tarnished fineweave silver comms grille, and nothing else. One of the other buzzers was also white, the other red. 'You can see the door. By the lift. It's marked Dr Carroll. Go straight in.'

Three buttons, Astrid thought, nearing the door. Research, white button. Dirangesept Vets, also a white button. And a panic button. What are they afraid of? What might happen here?

The lift doors were closed. The indicator lights were set in a slack curve above, a bright dot blinking at the far right. Fourth floor. One of the Dirangesept floors.

'The door, I said. You don't need the lift.'

Astrid turned and nodded to the receptionist, calling back, 'Thanks.' She opened Dr Carroll's door and went inside.

A woman stood up behind a long desk, reaching her hand over it as if to reel Astrid in with it.

'Hi, Astrid. My name's Rox. Rox Carroll. I'm head of the research team here.' She shook Astrid's hand perfunctorily. 'If you don't mind, I'm going to put you straight into my side office. There's a psychometric test set up which I'd like you to complete first.' She stood up and opened a door for Astrid, ushering her through into a tiny room with a table and screen. 'I'll collect you in an hour.'

The screen was already on when Astrid sat down, and the first question vanished before she had punched an answer, and a screen message flashed up.

PLEASE RESPOND TO EACH QUESTION WITHIN FIVE SECONDS

After an hour, Astrid's eyes were burning, but the screen was clear and Rox was at the door. 'All done? Would you like to come back into my office?'

She waited for Astrid to sit down before taking her own seat. 'I hope you didn't mind the test. I know it took a long time, but it's hard to create a test that a medic can't spin. Not that you'd try to, but you know how it is. It's automatic, isn't it?' Rox smiled, an all-the-girls-together smile that Astrid matched, playing the game. 'You waste time trying to work it out, don't you, and you screw the test without intending to.'

Rox was right. Astrid had tried to analyse the test, without success. There had been a tranche of behavioural questions, the usual repeats, rephrases and reapproached questions, a ton of family history, but very little for Astrid to make anything of.

'I'm sure you're curious but, of course, I can't tell you anything about the project. I'd be happy to tell you anything about most of the specific procedures we'll be using with you, though. If at any stage you want to ask anything, please do. If I can't tell you, at least I'll tell you that. But there's one thing I can tell you, and I expect it's the thing you most want to know.'

She waited. Astrid wondered what she was expected to ask.

Rox laughed. 'You needn't be shy about it. It's why you're here, after all.'

Astrid gave her a thin, frozen smile, wondering what she'd let slip in the psych test. Or maybe she really knew why Astrid was here. Maybe Troy had told her she'd been questioning him about Rudd and she had something to hide.

'A hundred a week.' Rox sat back.

Astrid's smile unfroze. 'Great,' she said.

Money. That was all Rox had meant. 'That's great. It'll help a lot. Clear the rent and then some.' She felt something more needed to be said. Rox was looking strangely at her, and she wanted to put her at ease again, wanted that fake complicitous girly smile flashed at her again. 'Actually, I was thinking about the wing here just a few days ago. I was on Emergency and a guy came in, name of Auger. Had a cut hand, and I gave him nanos for the scar. I remembered the name and made the connection. His wife used to work at GenMed, here in this wing, in nano research, of all things.'

Rox seemed to stiffen and colour slightly. 'Before my time.' She picked up a sheaf of papers from the desk and snapped them down again, closing the point. Astrid wondered what had done that. Was it the mention of Auger? Did Rox know about the investigation Ferec had cut short? Or was it the reference to Jay?

For no reason at all, Astrid was quite sure it was Jay. But why would she react like that?

Rox was moving on, though. She put the papers to one side and rested a hand on them, pushing down. 'Now, procedures. Neurological exercises, on the whole, bLinkered visualisations. Later they'll be mediated by a bLinkered zone. We'll be monitoring your responses. And that's just about all there is to it.'

She obviously couldn't quite bring herself to smile, but Astrid could see that that was her usual procedure at this point in the induction. Astrid had really hit a nerve with Jay Auger. For the first time, she wondered whether Auger was something more than just paranoid about his wife. His ex-wife.

'Not bad for a hundred a week,' Rox was telling her. The words were clearly rehearsed, but Rox had been thrown and wasn't managing the expression to go along with them, and they came out sour and resentful. She seemed to realise it, and made an effort to smooth the moment away. 'We'll set up a credit transfer today. But I'd just like to carry out one last test before you go.'

She reached beneath the desk and gave Astrid a set of bLinkers. They resembled those of Troy's, but these were lighter, and the eyeLids were opaque. When Astrid bLinked, all she saw were complex plots of her brain. She felt slightly dizzy, too, and was aware of her chair sinking back. Her arms felt heavy. She felt a tiny sensation elsewhere. 'What's that?'

Rox's voice came to her as if from another room. 'I'm just taking a blood sample at this point. Don't worry.'

Astrid found that she could selectively focus through her own brain. After a moment she lost that control.

'Okay, I'm overriding you,' Rox told her. Her voice was a strange booming whisper. 'What you can see now is the activity of your temporal lobes. I want you to see if you can change their colour at all for me.'

Astrid saw the maroon transform slowly to a deeper purple. It seemed to take for ever.

'Good. Now, what I'm about to do is heighten your proprioceptor response to your right cheek.'

Astrid felt suddenly aware of the right side of her face. It wasn't warmth or pain, just an awareness of the area.

'Excellent.' There was a faint hiss to the word, as if Rox had gained a slight lisp. 'You can feel it, can't you?'

'Yes, it's, it's like it's slightly warm. It's along the distribution of my right facial nerve, isn't it?' The sensation was so precisely defined that she could almost visualise it, the cutoff at the bridge of her nose and down the centre line as sharp as if she were following it on an anatomy diagram.

'That's good.' The lisp was gone. 'Okay, now I want you to concentrate on the feeling, and keep watching the lobe in your head.' It sounded as if Rox was directly above her now, whispering. Her hearing. They were playing with her hearing, too.

The colour in her mind began to deepen, and then it reversed, went pale and vanished. The warmth in her cheek receded.

'Okay, that's it for the day. Thank you very much, Astrid.' Rox's voice had returned to its normal clipped delivery.

Astrid let the bLinkers drop into her hand. She rubbed her cheek and then her ears, and looked around.

Rox had turned away. Astrid glanced at the table and saw a cartridge lying there, and a used hypodermic on a square of gauze.

'I thought you were taking blood,' she said.

Rox raised her eyebrows. Her face was empty, and Astrid realised she was no longer a colleague to Rox. She was a subject now. A guinea pig. The dead glance on Rox's face was something Astrid was familiar with, but never before as a recipient. She saw it daily throughout GenMed in jaded medics who stared straight through the people they treated, all care drained, all empathy long lost.

She thought of Auger again, the man trying to get help for his wife when no help was possible. He'd have had sympathy at first, counselling if he'd wanted it – though she thought he wouldn't – and then when he persisted, he'd have got nothing but that dead look.

Astrid nodded towards the cartridge. 'That's not for taking blood. That's a delivery system.'

Rox held the dead look as she showed Astrid an ampoule of blood in a sterile pouch. 'This was yours. The delivery cartridge wasn't. Now, if you have no more questions, the banking desk is in the lobby. Please come tomorrow. Goodbye.'

But the delivery cartridge hadn't been there before, Astrid was sure of it. She stood up. 'What time tomorrow?'

'After your duty. I believe your rota is the same all week?'

Astrid could see that Rox was waiting to be asked how she knew that, but it would be easy enough. The rotas were all posted, and Rox would only have needed to access Astrid's. She would have done it while Astrid was bLinkered. 'Fine,' Astrid said.

The banking counter was behind a tall arc of heavy glass across the lobby from the reception desk. Astrid gave her details to the clerk to set up the transfer to her account. The screen distorted him faintly and exaggerated his movement. 'That'll see off a few bills,' she told him, smiling.

His smile in return was perfunctory, the man not even bothering to meet her eyes. 'Let's see,' he said, 'a hundred a week, starting tomorrow.' As he checked the screen and turned it towards Astrid, the glass barrier parted centrally and tracked aside for her. The clerk looked thinner now. 'Please would you validate that?'

He looked pointedly away as she punched her code in and then nilled the screen. As if there was any privacy any more.

She swung the screen back to him. 'Done. Oh, and by the way, maybe you could help me? A friend of mine was due to transfer some credit to me, but the transfer was frozen when he died unexpectedly. My bank won't tell me if the credit's likely to be honoured when his account's freed after the post-mortem. It's been a while now, and I'm a bit anxious about it. I know he was a subject on the same project as me, and I wondered if you could possibly check his account.' She smiled apologetically. 'Just to see if the transfer's logged, that's all. To set my mind at ease. His name was Neffer Haenson.'

The clerk gave her a tight smile, tilting his head. 'I'm very sorry, but I can't do that. His details are confidential.'

She shrugged. 'Oh well. I'll just have to wait. Never mind.' She felt her heart thud as the arc of glass closed the clerk away again.

They had his details, then. Which meant that both Rudd and Neffer Haenson had been guinea pigs here.

About to leave, she glanced back towards Rox's office to see the researcher stepping into the lift. The doors closed behind her, and the indicator light above flicked a few times and stopped at the extreme right.

Fourth floor. Where the Vets were. And Rox had been holding the red glass ampoule of Astrid's blood.

FOURTEEN

The first problem was finding her way in. Auger had given her instructions, telling her it was going to be harder at night, the darkness colluding with the satellites spinning up there among the stars, casting down their webs of illusion. He hadn't been exaggerating.

The building itself was easy enough to locate, a great four-storey block shimmering darkly at the side of the High Street as if a blaze had been partially extinguished and was starting to flare again. Everything else in the vicinity rippled with shadows and dust. There were no carrion dogs, no animals at all prowling around. And as Astrid walked closer she saw that what had seemed dull flames were actually the stretched and melting forms of golden men and women in the throes of passion or pain, and closer yet she heard them screaming and groaning as they twined, rose away and disappeared like bright smoke into the night sky.

She passed through them, ignoring their stroking hands – she seemed to feel the touch, pricking her skin to gooseflesh – and their beseeching cries to rescue or perhaps to join them. After her shift, she wanted nothing of them. She didn't really want to see Auger right now, another damaged man, but she had agreed to it and wasn't going to break the deal. She probably didn't need his help, she knew that now. She was on the track. And if she wasn't careful, she was going to become his crutch like she had almost become Rudd's.

The golden creatures rose all around her, swirled away and faded into the sky. Auger was probably a lost cause, too. She'd rejected Rudd, and she was going to find out why he had died so that she wouldn't have to live with the remote chance that he had killed himself over her, and if she had to help Auger, it would be only as far as Rudd's case required it. Beyond that, Auger was on his own. He ought to just let his wife go. Not even his wife. He should just face it.

There was the door, twenty paces from the corner, exactly as he'd told her, adding that he didn't know how it might appear to her. It was a hellmouth pouring with fleeing souls. Great. She walked through the flames of them and in.

Dark, suddenly, and she waited for her eyes to adapt. No one sane could live here, she thought, climbing the tilting stairs. There was no sense to the place, neither the crazy fact of it nor the illusions that haunted it.

Then his door opened and he was standing there. He almost welcomed her inside, and she had a sense not just of surprise that she'd made it, but of gratefulness. That jolted her, and she wondered if this was why he lived here, for the company of the place.

'You look tired,' he told her, unexpectedly taking her coat from her and hanging it by the door, then absently running a hand down it to straighten the creases.

'It's been a long night,' she told him. 'It's hard when they want to be saved but won't let you use what will save them. They don't want truth, they want incense and myth.'

A golden couple oozed through the floor, screaming, tearing at each other, and slowly rose away through the ceiling. 'A pain/porn channel,' Auger said shortly. 'Sorry. Nothing I can do.'

Astrid shrugged. She looked past him at the table, where there was bread and cheese. Auger caught her glance. 'I thought you might be hungry.'

For a moment she didn't quite know why that touched her. 'I am,' she said. But sitting down to it, she knew why. She had just been readying herself for him as he had been before, bitter and furious. This was what she wanted him to be, though. Human. Breaking a stick of bread, she glanced up and caught him looking at her.

No. Not this, she thought, trying to harden herself. This is just my guilt reformed, she told herself. I don't want him. I can't want him. If I do, it's simply to redeem myself with Rudd. I have just to give him what I brought here, and leave.

He said, 'Jay never stopped to eat while she was working, and I guessed you'd be the same, never with the time, the thought of it.' He was breaking a wedge of cheese and passing it to her, blue-veined crumbs littering the table.

'Don't you sleep?' she asked him. 'This time of night. I'm just off duty, but you—'

'I sleep enough,' he said shortly, then seemed to catch himself. 'The bread tastes a little better than it looks. The cheese is good, though. From Albania. The time it takes to get here doesn't seem to harm it. One of the few things.'

She copied him, following a mouthful of the bread with the cheese, and found that the pungency of the cheese masked the bread's aftertaste. And she found herself relaxing with him, heard the thought in her mind slipping into the air. 'You know something, a glass of wine would go with this.' Forgetting for a moment in the taste of the bread and cheese that it was Auger she was with. She felt herself colour.

But he said, surprising her, 'I have some wine somewhere,' and he had opened a bottle and poured two glasses before she could think of a way to reverse the moment.

She held her glass up to the high opal light. The wine was red, and the colour returned her vividly to GenMed a few hours back, to the woman coming in with a bottle of blood she wanted blessed by a qualified medic.

'Yes, blessed,' she had repeated calmly to Astrid, nodding. A plump, sensible-seeming woman in her fifties, sensibly dressed, a nondescript filter dangling at her neck, a dull brown coat pulled closed against the cold night, darker brown leather gloves stretched tight over her plump fingers. Nothing unusual about her except the blood and the blessing. Astrid had made an excuse and notified the 'fists, shaking as she punched the emergency code, but the operator had all but laughed at her. There was no crime, it could have been wine in her bottle. The 'fists had better things.

But Astrid knew it was fresh blood, at least a litre, and the woman wouldn't tell her where it had come from, and she had panicked and vanished again before Astrid could do anything else. Back to someone, somewhere, dying or dead. And probably murdered.

Auger was staring at his glass too, as frozen as Astrid was, and she wondered what thoughts were in his head. Thoughts of Jay, she expected, and whispered, 'Is it Jay?'

There was a movement on the wall, catching her eye. A tiny lizard, its feet plucking at the plasterwork as it moved a few centimetres and halted again.

'Jay,' Auger murmured, far away.

Astrid set her glass back on the table. Bring him back, she thought. This was going nowhere, the dead of night, the two of them morose and sinking helplessly.

'How's your hand, Auger? The PlaSkin?'

He reached his hand across the table to her, and she took it, turning it

160

under the poor light. It was healing well now, the periphery of the PlaSkin blurring evenly. She noticed the scratches on his palms, too, and ran her fingers over them, and looked at him, raising her eyebrows in a question that he didn't answer.

'It's fine, thanks,' he said. 'It's good.' He left his hand there, leaving it to her to let it go. A warm hand. She closed it gently into a fist, as if testing its mobility, but just holding it. She thought, Am I this desperate?

'Okay.' She released the hand, pulled her reader from her pocket and held it out towards him until he focused on it and pointed her to the monitor across the room. Sitting down to synch the reader with his machine, she said, 'I saw her, Auger. I have her datasink details here. I haven't reviewed them myself yet. I thought I'd wait until I saw you.'

It seemed to lift him out of his reverie. She wasn't sure if she liked that, what it said about Auger and herself, but at least he was easier to understand now. He had a case to deal with. She waited for him to sweep the table quickly clear of food and sit down again beside her.

Fine, she thought. The night's niceties, such as they were, were now over. 'Okay, what do you know about medical datasinks, Auger?' She began downloading her reader, and watched Auger observe the words and numbers starting to form on the screen. He was different now. The parameters had shifted. He was his job.

Jay Luz. DOB 20/02/55 Female. Blood group A Rh neg.

'It's a no-wipe slate,' he said. 'It keeps your basic medical details.'

'That's right. The bare minimum. Essential notes, that's all. Critical instructions for emergency personnel who might need to treat you. Stuff the medics absolutely have to know immediately, and nothing more. Normally all you get is blood type, any relevant genetic information, allergies and medications.'

The screen shifted as she moved the record forward and back, then headed for the top. A list of childhood vaccinations made itself apparent. Booster doses, then she scrolled down, leaning forward at a couple of brief courses of drugs. Their dates of commencement and discontinuation were noted, a few days apart. Astrid frowned at those, wondering why a healthy woman would be on such medication, then smiled to herself and murmured, 'Of course. Immunosuppressants.'

'What?'

'Jay was working on nangines, wasn't she? She would have been self-experimenting.' Astrid nodded at the screen. 'She wouldn't have wanted to risk rejection, so she was suppressing her immune system. Not necessary, but she was a good researcher being careful. You don't need immunosuppressants for most nano-procedures. Nangines don't act chemically, so they don't trigger an immune response.'

The screen moved on. There were the usual respiratory problems, chronic low-grade viral and bacterial infections, the usual combination of pollutant- and aircon-related stuff. Astrid ran briefly through it all. Allergies, none. Serious illnesses, none. She went on.

'Ah. Now we're at your wedding,' she said, low. 'This is it.'

15/10/80 Acute psych trauma. Phys NAD. Consult GenMed Neuro. Ref 472389265.

She glanced at Auger, explaining, 'Acute psychological trauma, no apparent physical dysfunction.' She stopped a moment, contemplating the screen, before going on. 'If anything happens to her, emergency personnel are to contact GenMed Neuro as soon as possible. That's standard. She'd be considered an acute patient. There would be information that emergency staff have to be aware of.' She paused and shifted in her chair, thinking back.

'Go on,' Auger told her. 'That's all plain enough. She was psychologically traumatised, but physically okay. What about the next date?'

'Hang on,' Astrid said, remembering. 'She was seeing a Dr Saffer at this point, it was in her notes. But the notes were incomplete. And there was no one by that name in the neurology department at that time. I checked that.'

'It wouldn't necessarily appear on the datasink, though, would it?'

'No. Still.' She pointed at the screen, frowning. 'They're being very coy, Auger. They're saying there's a problem, but they're not saying what. Just "Consult". That contravenes the datasink protocol.'

'Move on,' Auger told her. 'We can come back to that.'

'Okay.'

10/11/80 Consult GenMed. Blood only. No medication. Ref 173364438.

'I don't get this at all,' Astrid muttered.

'What's wrong with that? It looks plain enough.'

'Look at what it says. "Consult GenMed" first, and *then*, "Blood only. No medication." In that order.'

'So she's not on anything. What's surprising about that?'

Astrid shook her head. 'It doesn't mean that, Auger. It means she's to be *given* nothing by emergency staff. Nothing but blood. But more important, the GenMed reference comes first. It's saying, contact us before you do *anything*. She might be bleeding to death, but tell us before you even touch her. GenMed's really hyperventilating over her, for some reason.' She played her lip between her teeth. 'And it's a different case number. That means sealed notes. Why sealed notes?'

Auger's forehead bunched into lines. 'I don't understand. Why? Nothing's changed since the previous entry. It's just a month later.'

'We can't be sure of that. Remember, this datasink only contains emergency information.'

'But nothing happened in that time. She was just in that room. They were just watching her. They told me there was nothing they could do.' His voice was rising. 'I was there all the goddamn time. All she was doing was crying.'

'Are you okay?' Astrid said. 'Do you want to stop?'

'No.' He wiped his cheeks. 'I'm done, now. Thanks.'

'Okay.' Astrid scrolled all the way back to the immunosuppressants. 'Now, look. Here she's on medication that affects emergency treatment, and the medication is specified. As it should be. But . . .' She scrolled forward again. 'But not here. Which has to mean that something relevant is not being disclosed. And that, like I said, is illegal.' She glanced at Auger. 'Let's move on.

05/10/81 Discontinue previous protocol. No medication contraindicated. Consult GenMed.

Astrid sat back. 'Just over a year later, and the situation is reversed. She can be given anything again. But the "Consult GenMed" remains, although it's been relegated. They're still being really careful here.'

She scrolled down the datasink, but the rest of the screen was blank. 'And that's it.'

She sat back and stared at the list. 'The thing is, why would they have wanted her off all medication for that year? Are you sure she wasn't on something they prescribed during that time? Did they ever tell you they wanted to medicate her? She's a psych patient, remember. You were still her husband back then. You'd have had to authorise anything. They would have had to consent you in her place. Auger? Auger?'

He shook his head. 'After the accident, I went to see her every day. I took it for a few months, going in to see her, and it became obvious that it was doing her no good. They thought – and I hoped – that she would come out of it in time. But she didn't. Then they said maybe it would be a good idea for me not to be in there with her. Maybe somehow I was reinforcing the amnesia, the fugue.' His eyes half closed. 'I think they knew I was irrelevant to her, though. They were just being kind to me. They could see the effect she was having on me. They said it would be better if I just watched her through the monitor. So I did that. She never changed. They were talking to her, trying to guide her out of that circle. But I was beginning to see it was a whirlpool, and it was sucking me down with her. I kept up seeing her on this monitor. Then after eighteen months they said maybe I could start visiting again, in her room, that it wasn't going to do any harm – though they might just as well have said it wasn't going to do any good – and I did.' He took a shuddering breath. 'By then I'd made her into something that only really existed on the monitor, in that little box beside the door of the room, and suddenly being with her again, having her claw at me like that . . .' He stopped.

'They knew what would happen,' Astrid said gently, wanting to stretch her hand and touch him. 'They knew it was time you moved on. Maybe that was the only way. You were both arrested there, one each side of that door. You were the only one who could walk away, though. If that's how it's going to be for Jay, you have to accept it. I know it's hard, Auger.' She remembered Jay referring to him as Cy, but it was impossible for her to think of him with a first name, a familiar name. Auger held himself away like that, like it was all taking place on a monitor and he could always just walk away. Even if he couldn't.

'I consented,' he said softly. 'I signed the consents for her. I signed a general medication consent. One of those proxy forms.'

'Informed Consent?'

'Informed Consent? What's informed?' Auger looked at her and smiled. It was a hard smile, and she remembered how he had been at first. What he thought of medics.

'Well, then, she shouldn't have been on a drug trial.' She licked her lip, staring at the data display. Auger said, 'What do you mean?'

'Due to the placebo effect, a drug trial is one of the situations in which it is permitted to withhold information from a datasink. But you signed an IC, so she wasn't on a trial. They'd have needed your consent.'

'So what else is there?'

'There's only one possibility we need consider. If they were using nanomedicine.'

'That's an exception?'

'In legal terms, it isn't clear whether nangines are drugs or surgical instruments, so the law doesn't apply. They say it's too new to draft law, but really they don't want the law to be involved. Gives them free rein. There are no drug interactions with nangines, remember.' She felt strange talking to Auger about nanomedicine, about his wife who had been one of its pioneers. It felt intimate and wrong somehow, as if she were intruding on their private life.

Auger nodded. It didn't seem to bother him. 'So if they were using nanomedicine on Jay, they didn't have to register it on the datasink. And if the procedures were minor, they wouldn't have needed immuno-suppressants, so, again, the datasink would stay clear.'

'That's right. But it still doesn't explain why they were so adamant about no medication during that year.'

'Astrid—'

'Wait a moment, Auger. Let me think.' She went back to the first date, the wedding, and sat back, staring at it, a finger to her lips. 'There's something else that's very odd here.'

'What?'

She was bolt upright in the chair now, and struggling against a tautness in her voice. 'Jay's amnesia.'

'I know all about that. I don't want to hear it again.'

'No, Auger. It's important. It's very important.'

He shrugged and gestured for her to go on.

'Okay, listen. There are basically two causes of amnesia – organic and psychogenic. Sorry. I mean caused by physical or psychological trauma. I'd just assumed your wife's was organic. That she suffered physical trauma.'

'Why did you assume that? We didn't crash. I told you that. We were caught in the shockwave of the blast, but we didn't crash. We weren't injured. Neither of us.'

She shook her head impatiently, wanting him to see how crazy this was. 'It's the *type* of memory loss she has. If, like you said, neither of you was physically injured, your wife's amnesia has to be psychogenic.' She slowed down for him. '*Without* physical cause. Are you with me?'

'You've said that. And I've told you she wasn't physically injured. I don't see the point of this.'

'Think about it. Psychological trauma classically results in amnesia

165

relating to the event. You forget what happened. It's called retrograde amnesia. In simple terms, Auger, amnesia caused by emotional shock alone is *protective*.'

She waited for Auger. He nodded slowly, and she went on. 'But Jay's *locked into* the event, the moment of the crash and its immediate aftermath. She remembers it all, Auger. Her amnesia is not retrograde, it's anterograde. It's *from* the moment of the accident.' She looked at him, waiting for a reaction.

'So?' he said stubbornly. But he was seeing it, dimly.

'Jay can't lay down *new* memory. Her amnesia is not what you'd expect. It seems to be psychological, but it's not protective at all.'

Astrid waited, watching him comprehend it. She helped him along. 'Jay received an emotional insult but she's suffering from an amnesia associated with a physical cause. Don't you see? That makes no sense at all. It's the precise opposite of what you'd expect.' She thought for a moment, trying to make it plainer for him. 'It's like you nick your finger with a knife and instead of closing, the wound just carries on opening up.'

Auger took a moment, then leaned forward and nilled the screen. He sat and stared at the grey rectangle, then said, 'Let's stop and have some coffee.'

She watched him make it in silence, wondering how he was reacting inside to what she'd just told him. He brought her over a mug and sat down.

'Okay. That's for us to think about,' he said. 'It's my turn now.'

She hadn't expected that. She'd anticipated the evening to be hers, her helping him, but there was a decisiveness in his tone that surprised her, especially after what she had just told him. But maybe that was just his way of dealing with it.

He took a sip of the drink. 'I spoke to a friend of mine who used to work at GenMed. She says the autopsies they carried out on Merchant and Haenson were more detailed than you'd expect. And neither of them was exsanguinated in the bath.'

'No surprise,' Astrid said, but his face stopped her from going on.

'I'm talking about the autopsies, not the cause of death. They were both pretty much dissected. It was like they were vivisection experiments.'

Experiments, Astrid thought. She murmured, 'They were both involved in projects in the research wing before they died. As paid guinea pigs.' Her own voice sounded suddenly small to her as she said, 'I am, too.'

Auger looked at her and then at the wall, at the unmoving lizard there.

166

He turned his coffee mug in his hand, and then said, to her surprise, 'Be careful, Astrid.'

'I will.'

And he moved on, as if such a tiny thing between the two of them as that had been a step too far. She hardly listened. The exchange replayed in her head. The tone of their words. Be careful, Astrid. I will. As if it was a contract between them.

He was sitting, waiting for her, and she realised he must have said something more. 'What was that?' she asked.

'I said, when you moved Rudd to the bed, was there anything else you did?'

'Oh,' was all she could say for the instant. She tried to say something else, but another 'Oh,' was all that came. He knew she'd done that. He'd guessed it, worked it out. Of course he had. But just saying it like that, not blaming her, not making her know he'd caught her out, just asking the question.

Now he was just waiting patiently. She liked that. She said, 'Nothing else. I was careful. I wore gloves to lift him. I had them in my pocket. One of the things about the job, you're always carrying a set of gloves. My prints would have been everywhere else in the room anyway. We were very close.' She remembered lifting him up in her arms, cradling him gently, so light he was, without his life.

'Close?'

The question caught her out. An odd question, coming from him. She felt like hugging herself, like having someone hug her. Like having Auger hug her. 'He was a close friend. He wanted more. I didn't.'

He left it there, just looking at her for a moment longer, as if to evaluate that in his mind. She wondered what part of him was asking her that. She also wondered what part of herself was answering.

'I have to go,' she said eventually.

He stood up. 'One last thing. You know something about nanomedicine.' He was on his knees on the floor, edging away a section of board. Bringing out a disk.

'Look at this,' he said, loading it and watching the script form on the screen. 'Does it mean anything to you?'

She shrugged. 'It's an experimental data record. Anything meaningful is coded, though. Look, it's just a record of dosages, measurements, celltypes . . . Wait.' She tailed off. 'Where did you get this?'

'It was Jay's.'

'Well.' She pointed. 'Look at these techniques. Some of it is mainstream now. But some of it . . .' Astrid shook her head. 'She must have been years ahead of anyone.' She touched the information bar. 'This is just a copy. So the information exists elsewhere. And the original will have recorded the act of copying.' She sighed and sat back. 'It's useless, anyway. There's no context. What is it?'

'They were looking for it.' Auger let out a deep breath. 'After she died. Her colleagues. They were asking. And then we were – I was burgled.'

'Competitors wanting it? Or GenMed wanting it kept secret?' She immediately answered her own question. 'GenMed has no competitors.'

'Does any of it mean anything to you?'

Astrid was still scrolling carefully down the file. 'Not much—' She stopped. 'Look.'

Auger whispered the word, making it sound like a distant quake. 'Dirangesept. I never noticed it before.'

'Jay was working on the Dirangesept project, Auger. And actively, too. They weren't just using her research. She was part of it.'

Auger shook his head. 'She never told me.'

'And they didn't want you to know. That's why they wanted the disk. That was all.'

'Why wouldn't they have wanted me to know?'

She shrugged. 'You would have started an investigation, Auger, and an investigation would have shut down their research. I'm just guessing.'

'You think—' Auger stopped, hit by the thought as if by lightning. 'The explosion. Whoever did it, they were after her, not me, weren't they?'

He fell silent. Astrid reached past him and closed the program down. She could see Auger was far away now. With Jay. She got up and murmured, 'It's late, Auger. I'm going to get some sleep. There's nothing else we can do tonight.' She waited for him to say something, anything, but he just nodded, not even looking at her.

Guilt. That was what he was feeling. She knew about that, with her guilt over Rudd. His was more complex, though. The guilt he'd had over what had happened to Jay and had been meant for him was now guilt over not having known the truth and not saving her. He'd probably never get over it.

She closed the door behind her softly, and started down the corridor. She looked back as she turned the corner to go down the rickety stairs. Framed by a vast, shining moon, a wolf was silently howling at Auger's door. As she watched, the scene faded and his was just another door again, along a lonely passage.

After Astrid had gone, Auger sat in the dark, or in what approximated for it. The night passed. Echoes and shadows surrounded him. And as the dawn came, he found himself remembering a conversation between himself and Jay, the two of them walking away from the wing at the time the Dirangesept floors had started to go up, the ancient foundations pumped so full of visgel that it had started to ooze out of the ground all around the wing in fat orange fingers.

Walking through the colonnade, she had asked him, 'What do you think about Dirangesept, Cy?'

'The project?'

'Yes. And the beasts.'

He had glanced at her and said, 'Why, have you been talking to the team working on the Vets?'

'Yes.' Down the steps from the colonnade now, approaching the tall, arched iron gates. They had put their filters on. Jay's voice changed. 'What do you think?'

'I heard they're intelligent. Are they?'

'Apparently. But there's no real communication with them. Do you think we should be going back there?'

'It's our only hope.' He had paused in the dust and ash, and looked at her.

Our only hope. That was how the Administration described it. Jay had taken his hand and squeezed it.

'But not if it means eliminating the beasts,' he had added. 'Genocide.'

'Wouldn't it be suicide to have that chance and not take it, though? Could we knowingly do that?' As if it was a theory she was testing on him. Not serious but more than curious.

'That isn't an argument, Jay. They aren't two sides of a coin.'

'No.' She had smiled and blown him a kiss through the filter, and they had walked on, hand in hand.

He had loved her.

She had already been working on the D3 project.

FIFTEEN

Too numbed to nil the screen, Auger sat and watched McCrae's Leaving on the evening's HoloNews. It was nearly the last item, less important than the latest D3 enrolment figures, less momentous even than a small advance in food technology and the evening's games status reports.

'And now,' the News Holohead was saying, his face wreathed in a smile, 'a mass suicide. Why should this even appear on the holocast, you may be thinking. And normally you would be right. Current estimates run at an average of over a thousand authorised Leavings a month, most of them matters of dozens or a few hundred. But today saw the largest Leaving yet, and with it, the state of things may be about to change. Here is my report.'

The animat shrank back, away from the image burgeoning on Auger's screen. A caption ebbed and flowed in slender, lavender lettering. RECORDED EARLIER.

They were all seated, the whole of the stadium filled with McCrae's keen suicides. The cam began directly above, the stadium an oval with its strike of muted orange where visgel had patched last year's rift. Eighty thousand of them, each carrying the small black box they were issued as they entered the stadium.

Eighty thousand, Auger thought, watching them sitting placidly in their seats. Eighty thousand, and he had saved one kid out of the few hundred he'd processed. He'd thought he'd got one over Vinz Szolty, but he'd just caught the tail end of it. Vinz Szolty had just been showing him what a fool he was, letting him believe he could throw a spanner in the works when Faith had been setting up offices for the processing of McCrae's Understands all over the place without Auger even knowing it.

'A phenomenal late surge of applicants for this Leaving resulted in the

170

stadium being, as you can see, filled to bursting point. This was the scene earlier today from the National Stadium.'

The cam zoomed down to float before the pulpit. 'Each man is an island,' McCrae was saying. His voice was deep and solemn. 'Each of us is alone from birth unto death, and all that connects us in the end is memory.' He leant forward on his hands. His brow furrowed. 'What is heaven? I'll tell you what heaven is. Heaven is our joyous memories made eternal present, and so each heaven must be our very own.'

The cam was directly on McCrae now, and Auger frowned. It was as if McCrae were his own Godhead, lecturing not to his flock, but to the audience of the holocast. The cam was on him as reverently as it had been on Maxenham.

'We shall be alone in heaven, and yet we shall be together at last, as we have never been together before.'

Auger let the words go past him as the cam rose to track along the terraces of McCrae's acolytes, views of their faces fading and merging, all the bright-eyed multitude.

The cam drew back as they opened their boxes. The entire stadium seemed to ripple as the multitude of black boxes turned on opening to display the white of their inner lining. Auger couldn't watch them swallow their capsules. He closed his eyes, remembering that first Leaving, Jay at his side. When he opened them again to the silence of the screen and saw the slumped stillness of the congregation, he was shaking.

The image faded, and the Holohead returned to the studio. McCrae was at his side, the preacher smiling at the News Holohead.

It had to be a pre-recording, the interview made before the event. Auger wasn't interested in McCrae's last words. He was about to nil the screen when he noticed the italics drifting across the screen. *LIVE*.

He wasn't dead. McCrae wasn't dead. He hadn't taken his own capsule.

Auger felt the bile rise in his gut, stinging his throat.

The Holohead said, 'Tell me, Dr McCrae, how does it feel, as a preacher, to have shepherded your flock into the next world, and yet remain yourself this side, as it were, of the pearly gates?'

McCrae steepled his hands. 'I am delighted to take advantage of today's edict from Faith. My work here is far from done. While I am delighted that my congregation have attained their happiness beyond, it is right that I should be permitted to continue my work here on this Earth, spreading the word of the Kingdom of Heaven. The Kingdom of Heaven, after all, is never full. How do I feel? I am proud.'

That made no sense. What had McCrae just said? What edict?

The Holohead nodded as if processing thought, lips pursed with muted empathy, the animat's high signature quiff of greying hair bouncing vigorously. 'You don't feel there's any danger in allowing Leavings to take place without the preacher departing with their congregation?'

'Not at all. Why should there be? We'll all of us get there eventually – you excepted, of course, NH.'

The Holohead acknowledged McCrae's joke, its quiff leaping higher than ever, as McCrae went on. 'There remain the psych tests and checks for those choosing to Leave. Nothing slips past those tests, it seems. Perhaps Minister Maxenham might feel there's room for a relaxation there, too. And might I also take the opportunity to suggest that the high Leaving Tax—'

'That's to cover the cost of Earthly disposal, isn't it, Doctor?'

'Yes, NH, but my point is that it's excessive and discriminates against the poor. It's a regressive tax. The Administration might consider . . .'

Auger left the holocast and accessed the Leavings Listings, running a search and finding her name among the Departed. There she was. LeCantho, Ilorna. Lethe's mother.

And Lethe, wherever she was, was all alone now. Auger tried to imagine her, a street-conditioned kid, her only softness the love she had had for the mother who had used her so. And the mother too, so lost, so desperate and determined to die. And now, thanks to Dr McCrae, dead.

Auger wondered what would become of Lethe. He knew about the orphans' hostels. Most of the kids in those places were orphans to the rifts, but plenty more were orphaned by the toxic atmosphere or had been simply abandoned, gene-scarred children bequeathed some chromosomal plague by their runaway parents.

He let the Listing fade and returned to the News. The interview with McCrae was finished. The Holohead's expression shifted, slipping with a compressing of his eyebrows and a falling of the corners of his lips into the face he used for sombre news. He paused too, and turned his head to one side to be framed by another cam. The frivolity had withdrawn from his quiff. The studio fell away to be replaced by a vista of grass and trees.

'We're now in Hyde Park, where only days ago we were witness to the ceremony of regeneration, in which the Great Rift was repaired with Nugel.' The Holohead was standing close to the site of the Final Church. He made a gesture towards the remains of it, a few struts and shards of blackened metal, and said, 'Father Fury's sacrifice may prove after all to have been in vain.' He began to walk towards where the rift's edge had been.

The animat pointed to the ground and, yes, there was the bright orange surface of the Nugel, faintly convex, faintly gleaming. By now, Auger seemed to recall, it should be set hard enough for the 'dozers and carvers to cut and roll to a smooth sub-surface a few metres down, to be overlaid with new earth, smooth-textured and rich with nutrients ready for Minister Herald's scheduled tree planting. What was the Holohead talking about?

'It looks perfect, doesn't it?' The Holohead began to stroll along the rift, saying, 'This is how it should look after a day, after a week, after a hundred years. But this patch was relaid only yesterday. As we move on . . .' The gel level began to fall away until it was fifty metres below the rim's level, and the cam rose to the Holohead's shoulder to show the depressed orange floor looking burnt and puckered. '. . . It is clear that there has been a catastrophic failure of the material. I have with me Minister Herald of Stability. Minister, this is a sad sight. Can you explain it? What went wrong?'

Herald came into the frame, his face more rounded than it had been on the last Holocast. Blemishes were apparent, too, blotches of eczema. His hairline was receding. The Minister stared down into the rift, shaking his head. The cam lifted to show scraps of charred orange still clinging to the higher, bare sides of the rift, and a movement away towards the margin of the screen drew the cam to display a frond of pale blue flame on the Nugel floor squeezing into the air. After a few moments the fire winked out, and where it had been the Nugel surface was further depressed. The cam moved to reveal more such spontaneous fires rising and blowing themselves out over the gel's shrinking surface.

The Minister pulled himself together. 'Ah, at present, we don't know why this should be happening. We've checked all the equations, ah, and the only thing we can come up with is that pi must be behaving as a variable.' His lips stripped back briefly in a crazy smile. There was sweat on his cheeks. His collar was damp. 'That is, the coefficient of thermal expansion we've proposed here, the expansion rates of the gel under the sort of unexpected pressures we're encountering at the base of the rift, ah—'

'Minister,' the Holohead said sharply.

Herald's voice rose. 'I have no explanation for this. Pi is not a variable. I know that. There must be some error in our calculations, but I simply don't understand how that could be. Every step was checked by computer. Every single step. Our computers, Administration computers . . .' He shrugged and faltered, unable to go on.

The Holohead nodded gravely. 'A serious setback for Stability, Minister.'

Herald wasn't listening. He had lurched to one side, an arm flailing for balance. The cam slewed back to be directed at the ground where a crack had appeared, snaking from the rim's edge and branching as it went. The ground was shaking, and Herald dropped to his hands and knees before managing awkwardly to rise again to his feet. His voice was a squeak. Eyes wide, he looked around. 'What?'

Small cracks and fissures were spreading out from the rift's edge all along its length now, the cam panned to reveal.

There was plain terror on Herald's face. He turned from the Holohead and started to run. The tributary of a huge crack shot across his path through the grass. He leapt wildly and made it across the fissure, sprawling at the feet of the Holohead who had soared easily clear. Herald stumbled on, groaning and coughing, and came to a halt at another lateral crack of a metre's width. He stared around himself again. The rift was propagating jagged cracks more rapidly still, orange smoke rising from them in feathery plumes. Herald put a hand to his mouth and coughed. Ministers didn't wear filters for interviews, even in the open. It showed frailty. Herald was looking very frail.

'Come on, Minister. We have to hurry.'

Herald jumped the crack, but landed badly and stumbled forward towards another. He shrieked and threw himself to the side to avoid tumbling down. As he lay on a tiny islet of safety, gasping for breath, another fissure swept past him and gathered his legs into it. He screamed, desperately holding on to a clump of long grass, lost in the ground to his waist.

'For God's sake, help me. Get me out.' His voice was stretched and breaking.

The Holohead held out a hand towards Herald. 'But I can't, Minister. I don't exist.'

Herald screamed again, the hank of grass sliding through his fingers. Auger caught a swift glimpse of the pink palms of his hands stained green, and Herald was gone.

'And neither do you, Minister, I'm afraid,' said the Holohead dolefully. 'And now, with that tragic sight, I'm informed we have to return to the studio for an Administration Newsflash.'

After the fanfare, it was Maxenham. Somehow, Auger knew it would be.

'A dreadful accident,' Maxenham said. 'Minister Herald will be greatly mourned by the Administration as well as by all of the community for whom he worked so tirelessly.' Maxenham paused for a few seconds, his head lowered in remembrance, then raised it and went on. 'At the urgent request of the Administrator, Stability's calculations have been checked by our computers here at Faith. It appears that there is a basic and serious flaw in the molecular structure of Nugel.' Maxenham was looking grave, far more so than when he was momentarily mourning Herald. 'The flaw, unfortunately, is not one that can be corrected. Nugel is as a consequence being withdrawn as a matter of extreme urgency. Rifts to which it has been applied are being closed off as we speak, along with an outer safety zone of a kilometre. Export has been halted.'

'Minister.' It was the Holohead.

With a jut of his jaw, Maxenham indicated him to go on.

'Minister, the cracks—'

'Fortunately, they are self-limiting. If you would now go to Hyde Park?'

The animat nodded, and the cam roved over the damaged area. The cracks had ceased propagating, and Nugel was welling gently and steadily from them, its lines easing gradually forward from the rift's edge, its progress following the faults. Where the Nugel hit the surface and slowed, blue flames rose, tasted the bad air and expired, leaving the gel like a tracery of cauterised lichen.

The Holohead walked over the cracked ground, hurdling fissures, searching, then made a gesture and stopped. The cam drifted to display the area he was indicating. Auger could see the knot of ripped grass beside the fissure. The thick tide of Nugel arrived slowly from the direction of the rift and rose, bearing upon it the corpse of the Minister of Stability. Herald's neck was twisted and his eyes bulged. After a moment, flames from the gel caught his clothes and began to consume him.

The image began to diminish and fall behind the Holohead, until the holocaster was standing before the screens back in the studio. 'This is the News Holohead delinking from this sad and sombre holocast. The world this evening is not such a safe place as we were hoping it was going to be with the advent of Nugel. At this fragile moment in time it looks like our best hope is once again the third Dirangesept project.'

The animat's tone changed. 'Have you enlisted? Do you know someone who might? It isn't too late.' He tipped his head. 'Or for those of you with an eye not to another world but to the next, maybe the future lies instead with Dr McCrae. Heaven, or the stars. Goodnight, and vivid dreams.'

The Holohead winked, pointed at the cam and said, 'Oh. One more thing. Remember, You Count!'

SIXTEEN

'You're late,' Dr Carroll said shortly.

'Five minutes,' Astrid said. 'Is that a problem for you?'

'We're paying you well. We expect punctuality.'

'You're already getting my time and my blood. What else do you want?'

Rox sniffed and ushered Astrid straight out of her office, escorting her to the elevator.

'Where are we going?'

'The top floor.'

'Isn't that where the Vets are?'

'They're up there too, some of them. But don't worry.' She tipped her head. 'You've heard stories?'

'Everybody's heard them.'

'More rumour than truth, I'm sure.' Rox waited for the elevator to murmur to a stop. 'Our facilities are up here, mainly for reasons of security. Our work is very sensitive. Industrial espionage is a real risk. But you needn't be concerned. The Vets are under high-level security. They have no more access to us than we do to them. They're sealed off.' Rox began to walk briskly down the corridor. 'But we get to hide under the coat-tails of their security. It means we save money, and you know how hard money is to find for research.'

Rox opened the door, and Astrid thought, when she caught her breath, But not that hard to find. The room had to extend the entire length of the wing. It looked even longer. On the wall to her left was a bank of screens, and at each a researcher sat working.

Rox laughed at Astrid's reaction. 'It isn't quite as it seems. Most of our researchers are only here in holo. They're sealed away, and their work's lead-lined. They each have their own cel to deal with. Some of them are in London, the others anywhere you can think of.'

There was something insubstantial about them, Astrid saw. The sharp overhead light had concealed it at first, but the long row of workers was disjointed and quivering slightly, a line of pennants fluttering independently in the same faint breeze. No one in the row acknowledged the presence of a neighbour. As Astrid watched, one of the men stood up and turned around, walked toward the middle of the room in a preoccupied manner and abruptly disappeared.

'So, what's my role?'

'Like I told you, we'll be bLinkering you and monitoring your reactions to certain stimuli. You don't have to do anything at all, except react, be yourself.'

'What sort of stimuli?'

Rox waved a hand. 'Neurological. Visual. Situational. A variety. Did you sign your disclaimer?'

'No. You never said there was one.'

Rox glanced away and back, and there was a form in her hand. She waved it at Astrid, the stiff paper crackling in the air. 'Sorry. It's standard procedure. You ought to know that. Do you want to stop and read it before we go on?'

'If you don't mind.'

'Sure,' Rox said. 'I'll give you a few minutes.'

The form was standard, as Rox had said. Astrid scanned the wording.

THE PROCEDURES

I understand that all necessary medical precautions will at all times be taken during the procedures, and that to the best of the operators' knowledge no part of the procedures to be carried out carries any risk, but I do understand and accept that nevertheless I may suffer unanticipated physical or psychological effects as a direct or indirect result of the procedures.

It was like an Informed Consent, she thought, and thought of Auger signing one for his wife, signing her away. Astrid wondered whether she was signing herself away here.

'Like I said, a standard disclaimer, more or less.' Rox was at her shoulder with a fat-barrelled pen, holding it like she might have held a hypodermic syringe.

'It doesn't quite read like one when it's yourself signing it,' Astrid said, forcing a smile. She took the pen and signed it.

Rox handed the form to someone at her side. At the corner of her vision Astrid noticed the researcher who had slipped from his holofield snap back into sight to sit at his desk again.

'Fine. Let's get you bLinkered, then.' She took Astrid's arm and walked her to a small bay at the edge of the chamber where a chrome cocoon squatted on a low plinth. 'It's a CrySis pod,' she said.

'I know. I've seen them before.'

'Good. It's what we use for convenience. The monitoring equipment has been adjusted for our purposes. We're not freezing you, of course. The pod provides basic life support as well as the software for our project, so we can keep everything under total control.' Rox lifted the lid, then turned and pulled a screen from its wall mount. The liquid matrix in the pod was dark green, thick and smooth, meeting the pod's inner wall with no meniscus, as if slicing deep into the dull metal sidewall. 'Would you disrobe and enter the pod now?' She smiled at Astrid. 'Everyone assumes it's going to be cold when they get in for the first time. It isn't at all. The matrix is set to body temperature.'

Astrid took off her clothes and slipped them into a small grey locker beside the pod. The silver of the curved screen was like a skewed recording of herself doing it and then slipping herself with just the same neatness into the pod. Rox was right. She could hardly feel the matrix, just the initial pressure of her heels breaking the surface, and then her body being swallowed. Otherwise it was like a vague tightness all around her. She reached up and took the mouthpiece, chewing on the rubbery bite-block until it was comfortable, then took a short breath of slightly rancid air and pulled the lid down over herself.

'Feeling okay?'

It took Astrid a moment to realise it was Rox. There was an ebbing memory of something else, sunlight and the shadow of something – an animal, maybe – and then it was all gone like a forgotten dream.

'Astrid?'

She felt dizzy, and then that too was gone. 'I'm okay. What happened?' She remembered bLinking, and nothing else. 'Didn't it work?'

'It worked fine, Astrid. Here, let me help you out.'

Rox's hand was under Astrid's arm, lifting her, steadying her. The green matrix rolled down her arms, her belly, her thighs, leaving no trace of itself on her skin. It was emptying from the pod at her feet. She felt momentarily weightless. Her movements were excessive. 'There. Are you steady now? It sometimes does that, the first time. Knocks out your balance. We're fixing it, though.'

'I don't remember anything.' She took a towel from Rox, touched a hand to her hair. Even that was dry and untangled. The towel was just to cover herself.

'Don't worry. A lot of these tests are repetitive, and your memory of them would screw things up. We just use a back-end wipe.'

Astrid nodded, thinking, And I won't be walking out the door and talking to anyone about the tests either, will I, Rox?

'And that's it for today. Why don't you dress yourself and come out?' Rox disappeared behind the screen.

Astrid clothed herself and then slid the screen back into its mount.

Rox was examining a sheet of paper, waiting for her. Seeing Astrid, she folded the paper and walked Astrid towards the lift, preoccupied. She pressed the down arrow and waited for the door to open, ushered Astrid inside and said, leaning in to select the ground floor, 'It wasn't so bad, was it?'

The doors began to pull closed. Rox swung clear and gave a brisk wave. She had turned away before the doors met in a soft kiss and sigh. Astrid leant against the wall of the elevator, irritated by the abrupt dismissal, and on impulse pressed three as the light was shifting between the two floors.

The cushioned floor pushed at her soles as the lift stopped. The doors opened and she stepped quickly out, ready to shake her head and step back again as if she'd made a mistake. But there was no one in sight.

The third floor was as calm and silent as the fourth had been active. Taking up the entire floor was a great bank of identical pods like the one she'd just climbed out of. There had to be at least fifty of them. She went up to the nearest pod and looked at its monitor, then peered down through the dark glass cupola. There was a face inside, blurred by the glass and distorted by the gel. Short hair fanned out like weed. The bite-block pushed out the crimson lips. The cheeks were bloated. The eyes were staring straight at her.

She pulled back, wondering whether she had let out a sound, and quickly examined the readings. The gel temperature flickered between two numerals. Two, three degrees.

These had to be the Vets. And they were in CrySis pods, and they were being kept in cryonic stasis.

About to go, she noticed a small screen set into the pod's wall. On impulse she activated it. An image flowed into sharpness. A dark image, and she bent close to make it out. It was a shadowy face of rock. No sunlight. So, either night or inside a cave. The image was trembling and shifting slightly with near rhythm, and she realised the rhythm was the breathing of the viewer.

She stood up again quickly and looked at the pod's occupant, but he was quite still.

On the screen the view tilted in restless sleep, and there was something more visible, but hard to make out in the gloom. She hooded her eyes and saw it to be a rough cage on a wheeled cart. Animals inside the cage, maybe. And tall, hard-muscled men, and a shorter robed and cowled figure leaning over another body in the cave.

The cave was filled with bodies on small beds, and the viewpoint of this image was at the same level.

As she closed down the screen, she noticed a short line of text at the image's base. Date and time, some name and a string of numbers that meant nothing to her, but had to identify the Vet, and then the word Cathar.

Back in the lift, she slumped against the wall and closed her eyes. All she was seeing was the cowled head in darkness bending toward her face, and a hand reaching out to touch her cheek. She felt herself flinching.

A long beep sounded. The doors opened on the ground floor.

Auger headed through the building towards the property vault. The vault was two floors down, and after the first flight the stairs took him hard left and the lighting began to dim and fail. The steps were increasingly cracked and split underfoot. Here and there visgel bulged through the fissures, fluorescent under the spitting neon. It felt to Auger as though he was entering the past, each step some measure of time. The stairs turned again and again, dislocating him until at the bottom of the stairs, at the mouth of the vault, he saw Harry.

Harry peered at him across the vault's counter, then smacked the worn and cracked plastic with the palm of his hand and said, 'Auger? Is that really you?'

'Walking and breathing.'

Harry showed him a smile that creased up his whole face. 'Good to see you. It's been a while.' He shook Auger's hand hard, then let it fall, a frown forming on his brow. 'I heard you've been moved from Active. I didn't believe it. What's going on up there?' He jerked his eyes up.

'Politics, Harry.'

Harry nodded. 'I guessed. You should stay out of it, Auger. Politicians . . .' he shrugged them away.

'Easy for you, Harry. Down here.'

'I know. I know.'

There was silence between them. Harry had always been down here. Daylight would probably turn him to dust. His skin was pale as moonlight and his flesh looked soft as ash. He was at home with the things of the dead, collating and cataloguing them, protecting them from the clutch of the living. It wouldn't have surprised Auger to find that Harry slept down here at night.

'So what brings you down to these old boxes?'

Auger sighed. 'That day, Harry. Memories. And you know how long it's been. I figured it was just about time now. I thought I'd take a look, if it's okay with you.'

The life went out of Harry's smile. 'I shouldn't let you. Out of Active, you've got no rights now. Only claimants past this gate. And immediate relatives. And there's nothing of Jay's in that box.'

'Just a look, Harry. They were my friends. And you know they had no one else, that's why the boxes are still there.'

'Well . . .' Harry's hand shifted a fraction on the counter and the gate drew back. It started to slide into a recess in the wall, and stopped halfacross. Harry gave the gate a kick and it jumped the rest of the way. He pointed a finger into the vault and hit a button on the desk. Away down the vault, a sequence of lights came on, slow at first and then arrowing into the distance, throwing up a vision of endless storage. Tiered shelves banked away, tilting with boxes, the air teeming with dust. The far distance was grey and tiny.

Harry cut the most distant lights, and Auger felt a little more comfortable. The vault was like eternity made manifest.

'You want the third block,' Harry told him. 'It's date filed.' He started to give Auger the date, then realised what he was doing and stopped again, and in a different tone he said, 'The inventory's correct, Auger. Just make sure you leave it as you found it. I have to check it, but I'll do it after you've gone. Don't embarrass me, okay?'

Auger nodded. Harry raised his eyes a moment, then looked back at Auger, steadily. 'Look, there's people upstairs going to be doing darktime one day, and I'm not aiming to join them. You understand me? I shouldn't even be doing this.'

'I know that. Thanks, Harry.' He looked at the old man stationed here, protecting the possessions of the forgotten dead. Auger wondered what he did all day. It would have driven Auger crazy, sitting for ever at the mouth of this endless shaft.

Harry shrugged and looked away. 'Hell. Look, Cy, I don't know why I said that. Time was, I never needed to say it to anyone. Now I'm even telling Cy Auger. Times . . .' His voice faltered and fell away, and he swept his hand over the corner of the desk, brushing a small rill of dust into the air.

'Times change, Harry.'

'Christ, I'm sorry. I didn't mean to, I wasn't saying—'

'I know what you were saying, Harry. Don't worry.'

'I've been down here too long, I guess. That's all. I forget things. How to talk to people. I should get out. Ask for a transfer.'

'Good idea, Harry.' Auger smiled. Harry chuckled.

Beyond Harry's desk, the vault grew rapidly cold until after a few hundred metres Auger was shivering. He drew his jacket tighter and hurried along the aisles, jinking until he found the right row, the shelf he needed.

He flicked the shelf light on, and just looked at the closed box for a minute. Dust was thick on it. These were the unclaimed possessions, the detritus that remained after any relatives had claimed what could be matched to an owner, and after Sweet's team had filched what they wanted. It was a standard archive box. Auger brushed the dust away with his sleeve, and gently lifted the lid from the box.

There wasn't much inside for him to look at. A few dozen objects, no more, each one touched by fire and sadness, and everything stroked with a patina of ash or dust. He reached in and found himself holding a shard of fractured jewellery. He rubbed the ball of his thumb over it, and a blue stone suddenly shone bright. Auger replaced it gently, then on an impulse bent down in the vault's freezing atmosphere and sniffed at the box. Somehow it all reeked faintly of smoke, even now. But maybe that was just his brain linking the box with his memory.

He went on sifting through the box, thinking of all their names, the names of his parents and Jay's, of their friends. He picked up a metal pendant, smoothed by fire into a teardrop, and the image of a face drifted into his mind, a young girl, soft-skinned, her hair tied back and the ponytail swinging with glitter. Jojo's and Diffach's child, Auger thought. But he found that he couldn't recall her name, and this made him stop. Jojo and Diffach had had no relations alive, and the only one to bear their memory was Auger, and Auger couldn't even remember the name of their child.

He returned the pendant and went on searching until he found a piece of paper screwed up and crushed among the bits of metal. He smoothed it out on the shelf with the flat of his hand. It was a copy of Harry's inventory, the list of evidential material. Harry had written it out by hand, with his ancient pen, in his neat and careful handwriting. Harry always did that. It was his small gift to the anonymous dead, his gesture of dignity. Auger scanned the list until he found what he was looking for.

ONE OLD CAM(?), BROKEN. MARKED: LEICA.

That was all it said, but Auger's heart thudded. He went back to the box, sifting right to the bottom, dust or ash rising, the past parting for him.

And there it was, the cam, battered but still whole. Auger picked it up and held it, wondering what it held for him. Sweet must have looked at it and thrown it into the box with everything else that he hadn't bothered to examine. He hadn't even thought of it. He must have just glanced at it and thrown it aside, not even curious about it. And by the time Auger had recovered enough to question Sweet's total failure to come up with a single suspect from CMS files, the case had been declared closed.

Tomasz's cam. Tomasz had had no relatives, no lover to take his possessions from here. He'd been obsessed by old technology, taking pictures constantly with that ancient thing. It was his memory, he always said. Auger had forgotten about it until he'd bLinked into McCrae's Glimpse of Heaven and had seen the flash going off again.

He stroked the battered cam's curves and edges, thinking of Tomasz grinning and saying, 'That was a good one, Cy. Wait till I get it developed.'

And Auger and Jay teasing him for the work it would involve. Why didn't he just get a holocam like everyone else?

Holding it, turning it over, Auger remembered Tomasz having to load some sort of cassette into the back of it, but he couldn't see how. He tried to visualise Tomasz doing it, but all that came back to him was Tomasz playing with the cam, the flash burning like a flare in Auger's eyes.

But all of that was gone now, remaindered in a past so distant that it was another life. No one from that time still existed except himself and Jay, and Jay's existence was just a stutter of time, an everyday tinnitus that most of the time he could ignore.

Auger turned it over, the past, the cam, trying to remember what to do. The back of it opened, he knew that, and he had just found the lever that would flick it when he saw Tomasz, heard him once swear, 'Shit, I forgot to rewind the film,' and stare forlornly at the crackling black plastic ribbon with its lost information.

And there, Auger almost shaking as he rewound it, the mutilated casing groaning but the mechanism still apparently sound, grinding away until the lever was abruptly free, its grip relinquished in a harsh sigh of metal. Auger thought he'd screwed up, then realised he'd finished rewinding. He opened the back, carefully, and a small black and yellow cylinder fell to the floor. Auger bent to pick it up. Kodak.

He slipped the cassette into his pocket, closed the Leica again and replaced it in the box. Then he slid the top back and held the palms of both hands there for a few minutes, thinking, remembering and mourning.

And after that he made the long walk back to Harry's desk. He felt the lights extinguishing themselves behind him, hurrying him from the vault.

'Done?' Harry asked him.

'Thanks, Harry. I appreciate that. Listen, one more thing. Do you remember the guy before me at CMS, name of Madsen?'

'Sure I do.' Harry pointed back down the vault, and Auger turned sharply, half expecting to see a pale figure stalking him out of the darkness. But the dark was blank.

'Not too far down there,' Harry said. 'Madsen's things. Papers, mainly.'

'Oh,' Auger said flatly, feeling more disappointment than he'd expected. 'He's dead. I wasn't sure.'

Harry nodded. 'Declared dead, Auger. Madsen was good. Like you, maybe better. He had enemies, I think. He disappeared, and they eventually declared him dead on probability. But as I said, he was good. I like to think he's still out there. But, then, I like to think the sky's still blue up there.' Harry grinned at Auger. 'Maybe that's why I stay down here, because as long as I'm here, everywhere else can be just how I imagine it to be.'

'Not so crazy after all, Harry, are you?'

Harry smiled. 'I liked Madsen, and I like you, Auger. I don't ever want to see your possessions in a carton down here. Politics did for him, remember.' He turned away, waving Auger back up the stairs. 'I'm going to check the inventory now, Auger. Good thing it isn't done by weight, eh?'

Auger started up the steps. 'If you say so, Harry.'

SEVENTEEN

The road out of London was stacked back wheel to wheel, and the trip punctuated three times by rifts in various degrees of correction. The first delayed them most, three carriageways compressed to a single lane suspension crossing that swept the car a hundred metres above the rupture. Astrid rolled the window down as they climbed, and the vent system roared, compensating. Great flakes of ash flowed and eddied at the periphery of the car's microNet, and she stared out through the interference over the blighted countryside, and then looked down into the rift. She could see the spiders down there, working in the heat and smoke, knitting cable from side to side, and wondered how people could do such a job. The thumpthump of the machinery on the banks seemed to hollow out the air.

She kept the window closed the rest of the way. Talking to Troy was fine and easy, as easy as talking to herself. After an hour of the journey she guessed where he was taking her, but she didn't say it, enjoying the pleasure on his face each time he asked if she had. He was good company. Not like Auger, and she wondered why she was thinking of Auger, why she was making the comparison.

Out of relief, she told herself. To be with someone undamaged for a change. Someone straightforward. She looked across at Troy, the ragged, strong profile of his face. Okay, damaged, but just physically. Openly. She touched the hand he'd left resting on the control stick. An outer harm that had given him strength and empathy.

He said it again, glancing across at her with those eyes. 'Guessed yet?'

It would have sounded stupid to keep denying it now. The signs were every few kilometres, at every junction. 'The Net. The Cultivation Net.' She didn't need to feign her pleasure, saying it. 'But I thought we were just going for something to eat.'

At the Net he manoeuvred the car into the space he must have called ahead to reserve. She had heard of unbooked people queuing outside the Net's vast park zone for days.

She climbed out of the vehicle, slipping on her filter, and he took her arm. 'We'll get something to eat,' he said, squeezing her hand.

The long glow was ahead of them, and she could see the crowds of visitors clutching at the wire. The hum of the high pylons expanded in her ears as they approached.

'It's quite something.' She'd seen it on holo, but never before visited it. The Cultivation Net was almost a site of pilgrimage. The fence itself was ten metres tall, the weave of its thick silvered wire open enough to poke a few fingers through, but not quite a hand, and topped by a great steel cable stretched taut enough to seem a rigid bar. There were steel palings at intervals of fifteen metres, and from a distance the Net seemed to be formed of an endless series of immense, brilliant screens, each linked to the next. On each paling, at head height, was a sign. DO NOT CROSS. DANGER OF DEATH. At the base of the fence stood the viewers of the Net.

Troy and Astrid eventually found a few free metres of fence-space and stood there to take it all in. Beyond the fence the fields shimmered, illuminated by the constant gentle glow of the Sunlights on their high spires. The vast and endless fields of corn here, and elsewhere within the Net of other crops, of vegetables, fruit, of herbs and spices, all bursting with life, almost exploding with their adjusted, accelerated magneto- and photosynthesis. And great herds of cattle in the distance, their coats glossy, their size surely larger than was natural. And sheep, bison, ostriches and more, fading brightly into the distance.

It was another time, another country, almost another world, it seemed to Astrid. Unconsciously she tightened her grip on the wire. Out here, the skies were like stirred ash, but in there it was spring and summer, it was eternal harvest-time. All that spoiled the image were the tenders of the land, the tillers who wore sealed suits and goggles instead of smocks and jerkins, and who drove squat silver combines instead of carts and horses.

'Tell me about you and Rudd,' Gordo said, after a while. 'I didn't know him well.'

She adjusted her grip on the wire. 'There isn't much. I'd known him since we were kids. I'd always wanted to be a medic, and I think he'd always wanted to be like me. He was searching for something, and he saw that I'd found what I was looking for, and he thought that would work for him, too. But he didn't just want what I wanted. He wanted me, too. I didn't want him in that way. He kept trying, and he kept searching. Poor Rudd.'

The mesh was warm and trembling, and comforting in a strange way. She let it go, looking down the long, straight fence. Others down the line were desperately clutching at it, bright-eyed and white-knuckled. She murmured, 'We're all searching, aren't we?'

Troy grinned at her. 'Is that a dig at me and TNM?'

She smiled, liking him for that. 'No. I meant, well, the world. I suppose it's within us to search, to want more than there is. It's in our DNA, isn't it? Like a genetic adrenalin. When you trace it down, it's just Darwin, all the endless striving.' The fence before them hummed with life, and she said, 'When the world's fine and easy, we search for the spiritual, the material better, and when the world's not well, we search even harder. To survive. To save this world, to seek the next. Whether the next is in this universe or . . .' She made an onward gesture with her hand. Leavings, she thought. Auger. Auger again.

'And the world isn't fine,' Troy observed. 'A coffin in a vault of dusty stars.'

Astrid smiled in recognition of the line. 'End Without End', she remembered. By Jon Sciler, the poet. It could have been about himself, that poem whose lines were graffiti everywhere. The Dirangesept poet, dead and quoted everywhere. He'd killed himself, as poets sometimes do, and lived on, as they sometimes also do.

'He followed me everywhere, Rudd. To become a medic. To GenMed. Joining TNM was the first thing Rudd ever did without me,' she said.

'Don't feel responsible, Astrid. I don't.'

'He didn't kill himself.'

She stared again along the fence, at the people who stood there and drank in this promise of salvation, this false promise, as in London they gazed at holoverts for the D3 project. And now as they seemed to be signing up for Doctor McCrae's personal heaven in their thousands. Since the Leaving at which he alone had remained standing, McCrae was everywhere. He was a celebrity.

'Rudd didn't kill himself,' she repeated.

Troy said nothing, and she felt bad about the implied criticism. 'Sorry.' She pointed at the fabulous land beyond the humming wire. 'This is very strange.'

'Yes. You think it'll provide enough food, though?'

It was a safe subject. Troy was making conversational peace. It was what people talked about – food, its production, its taste, its future. And the rifts, and D3. Not religion, because religion was personal and intimate with death, or had been until McCrae, and not politics, because there was nothing there to discuss, with no party except the Administration and no political issues but food, the rifts and Dirangesept.

She accepted his peace and said, 'Maybe. Food production's rising, they say, and the population's dropping.' That stopped her, though, making her think of Auger again. He'd told her the frequency of Leavings had been rising even before McCrae, and she wondered how many were killing themselves every day now. Still, more food for the rest, it crossed her mind. She felt guilty for the thought.

Gordo misunderstood her silence. 'Yes, and if D3's successful, there'll be colonists going. Who knows, maybe the rifts'll be totally under control by then. Maybe we'll have a real choice. Stay or go.'

That pulled her up. 'Stay? Would you stay here?' It was the first time she'd heard anyone even suggest that. Surely the Cultivation Nets were only intended to make it tolerable, make it possible to hang on here until Dirangesept was made safe.

'Maybe,' he said. 'It's our heritage, after all. Our Earth.'

She thought about that. Would it still be ours? We couldn't live under those lights. We'd always be on the wrong side of the fence, caged out, living in the cinders. But maybe that is our heritage, maybe it's all we deserve. And this small inhabitable edge of the Earth would be patched with gel, its wounds bandaged and packed, unrecognisable any longer as Earth.

'Shall we go?' he said. 'I think it's time to eat.' And they retreated from the fence to find his car.

The light was going now, dusk advancing, and as they drove along the side of the fence, she had a further sense of warmth and comfort from the Net. The harvesting machines were glowing under the Sunlights as they pulled up their clouds of bright ripe corn, and the sowing machines followed close behind them, churning the ground and spreading the new seed and fertiliser. And the Sunlights constantly renewed the land. It was hypnotic and never-ending.

The vehicle bounced along, and they seemed to be making no progress. Distance was impossible to gauge beneath the Net. Time seemed to have no meaning, no effect. There was no day beyond the fence, no dawn or dusk or night.

An abrupt last flare of sun fell on the road, making even the Net dull in comparison, and the fence a sudden mesh of glitter. And in the blaze of light Astrid looked to the other side of the road. They were passing a real field, blighted by the climate. A lone farmer was bent there, working with some sort of angular digging machine, and in that instant Astrid had a real sense of connection with him, a sense of his land, his crop. There was a tree in the corner of his field, knotted and wind-bowed, and she realised that there had been no trees beneath the Net, as there had been no hedges, no buildings, no contours even of the land. But in that hand-tilled, desperate field, she saw the rich colour, the crisp light, the dense shadows and the fine curves of the hillside. And the man alone, struggling with his land. But with it, she realised, and not against it.

'It's beautiful,' she murmured.

'Isn't it? I'm glad I brought you.'

She glanced at Troy. He was flicking his eyes between the Net and the road. 'Nearly there, he said. 'Are you hungry?'

'Yes.' She was thirsty, too. The vehicle's aircon had dried her throat, and she hadn't eaten since they'd set off before noon.

Kafkafé. The restaurant sign glimmered at the very edge of the Net, where the fence changed direction and suddenly shot north towards the sea.

'This place gets the best of everything,' Troy told her. 'It all comes fresh from the Net. On the plate within the hour. The only real atmosphere the food sees is the ten metres between the Net and the kitchen door here.'

Astrid was impressed. Kafkafé was famous. They said that to eat there was to be transported fifty years back in time. And they said that to get a table there, you had to have booked it back then, too.

'I have an Administration contact,' Troy said, reacting to her glance, grinning. 'We'll drink a toast to his wart.'

She laughed, touching his warm hand. 'But we won't think of it while we eat.'

The restaurant was lit by candles. The walls seemed to be stucco. They were hung with paintings of better times. Astrid ordered from the French section of the menu, a steak with sauce à l'ancienne. The steak rare. He ordered alligator from the Pacific list.

Her food looked perfect. A caramelled puddle of onions rippling the glistening sauce. She cut into the seared meat and it yielded perfectly, pink and tender. The aroma rose to her like a sweet memory, and she felt as if she might swoon. She knew how it should taste, how it always tasted, but this had to be different. Troy was looking at her in expectation, and she felt the saliva gathering in her mouth.

The texture was wonderful, like she'd never tasted before. But after the first few bites, it was still mush in her mouth, although the aftertaste came late and was slightly less pronounced than usual.

She swallowed. 'I haven't had anything this good for years,' she told him. Which at least was true. It wasn't his fault that she remembered better and that it mattered to her. 'How's yours?'

'Fine,' he said. He forked a mouthful of noodles into his mouth and they ate in silence for a while. Astrid wondered where in Norfolk the alligators were farmed.

'How are you getting on with Rox?' Gordo said eventually, setting his silver cutlery neatly back on the plate. He had eaten everything while she was halfway through her steak and slowing down.

'Okay. I think. Do you think her project's to do with D3?'

He chuckled. 'She's secretive, isn't she? But it has to be, up on those floors. I didn't want to say anything before you signed up, because I thought it might put you off. You don't mind, do you?'

'No.' She relaxed. She hadn't been sure how he'd react to that question. 'Do they wipe your memory, too?'

He nodded. 'I get flashes sometimes. Something'll trigger something. Do you get that?'

'Yes.' She remembered the screen on the Vet's CrySis pod, the cowled figure leaning. 'Yes,' she said.

Troy nodded. He didn't take it further, and she wondered why. What he'd experienced. She was about to ask him when he changed the subject.

'What about the meditation? Is that going well? I haven't seen you at the meetings.'

'I haven't had much time. I've been on nights.' She'd had the bLinkers for a month now and hadn't tried them yet.

'That's okay. I just wondered.'

He didn't seem to want to take that any further either. She put her fork down, her appetite gone. 'Troy, you've been in GenMed how long?'

'Three years. Nearly four, I suppose. Why?'

'I was talking to someone recently, and they mentioned a Dr Saffer. I haven't heard of him. I wondered whether you had.'

Gordo touched his napkin to the corners of his mouth. The napkins were starched linen. He said, 'Who was that?'

'Dr Saffer.'

'No, I meant who were you talking to?'

She shrugged, wondering why he'd asked her that. 'I don't remember.'

'Well, it doesn't ring any bells,' he said.

'He was a neurologist, I think.' She'd looked Saffer up in the neurology register and had come up empty, but she suddenly didn't want to tell Troy that. She was ready to let the subject drop. It seemed to have triggered something in Troy.

But Troy smiled. 'Neurology, eh? Well, there's no neurologist in GenMed by that name. Never was, I'm pretty sure. What made you think that?'

'Why are you so certain?'

'I was in neurology myself. I had a house job there a couple of years back. Didn't I tell you?'

'No.'

'Well, If this Saffer was ever here, I'd have seen his name in notes, even if I didn't come across him personally. The only Saffer at GenMed's an obstetrician. But there is a neurologist called Saffer over at NerveCentre.'

Astrid tidied her cutlery on the plate. NerveCentre. The sauce was starting to separate into a glutinous emulsion. Eat quickly and eat it all, that was usually the best way. That way you avoided the worst of the taste and you didn't get to see what you'd consumed. Even at Kafkafé.

She wiped her mouth, rubbing her lips hard with the fine cloth. Maybe Saffer had come over from NerveCentre to see Jay Auger.

Troy was obviously waiting for her to say something, but there was a look in his eyes that drew her into herself. If he'd been in neurology, he'd know about Jay, but she wasn't going to ask him. Not yet, anyway.

'That must be it, then,' she said. 'I remember what it was. There were a few of us talking about referrals. I think someone said he was good for neuro problems. That's all.'

Gordo nodded. 'He is good. So they say. You feel like dessert?'

She shook her head. He ordered durian. When it arrived, the fruit was entirely odourless. If they couldn't provide the delirious taste, Astrid wondered what the point was of genetically removing the fruit's notoriously foul stench. She wondered whether he expected her to sleep with him, back at GenMed. She wondered whether she was that interested in him. His face was no longer any problem to her. She still didn't quite trust him, but that was a matter of time, she thought. She did like him.

As they drove back, she thought of the meal. It was already fading from her memory. It was nutrition without substance. And the Cultivation Net would be extended. It would become like the food it bore, a veneer that would become rooted over the real world, in time to replace it entirely.

He dropped her at the door of her building. There was a kiss on her cheek, his lips softer than she'd imagined, and nothing more. As he left, she felt faintly cheated, just as she had been by the meal.

Auger pulled the notched ribbon of film straight and stared at it. Twenty-eight images, the tail of the film dark and blank. He cut the length carefully into five sections of six frames each and slid them into the pockets of a clear filing sheet, then held the sheet up to the light.

In negative, the images were hard to examine. He could identify Jay clearly, though, in the wedding dress that had been her mother's. The dress flaring at the shoulders, low across her breasts and coming tight into her waist – Auger's breath caught as he remembered holding her around her waist that day. And then the dress spreading out from her hips in a style so out of date, so wonderful, so beautiful on her. He picked her out by the shape of the dress, but on the negative it was as dead black as it had been shining bright, as yellow as a fairy-tale sun. Like the day itself had reversed, a few moments later, life to its opposite, and happiness too.

The images. Concentrate on the images. He searched for someone he wouldn't recognise, hoping to bypass the need to print them all, to see everything again, but it was impossible. The negatives held their secrets like a code. He couldn't translate that reversed world.

He went into the darkroom and began the long, awkward process of printing. He'd practised with some of Tomasz's old negatives, and knew he could do it, just as he had processed the film.

The first one he was nervous about, though, prodding the paper in the bath of developer until shapes began to form. The blacks came up first, the shadows in the trees at the edge of the frame, details of clothes. And there was his own face. He looked young, he realised with a shock. Time had scratched away at him, etched and lined him, weighted his shoulders.

And there was Jay, her dress blooming on the paper. Her glorious smile.

He stared at her as she came up, kept staring until he saw he'd left her too long, she was greying and the image's afternoon had darkened into night. He pulled the dripping paper out, crumpled it up and threw it into the bin.

After that, he printed them without looking more closely than for the contrast to be right, without searching for detail. All twenty-eight of them, one after the other, until they were all lying in the bath of fixer. The chemicals stank. The room smelt like a morgue.

Tomasz was the only one not represented on the film. There were a few people Auger could no longer fit names to, though he had memories for them all. Not to be able to name them, he thought. He went through them once to bring back the day, and again to search for anyone he didn't know, anyone who might have been trying to kill Auger or Jay.

The pyrotechnician was there in some of the exterior shots, always working alone with his bright cones and cylinders, his powders and fuses. Auger knew nothing about fireworks but a little about explosives, and nothing on Tomasz's images of the pyrotechnician looked at all odd. No unusual casings, nothing that might be or conceal a timer, nothing handled with special care.

He went back to the beginning of the sequence. Five frames of their arrival at Cherry Tree Wood, followed by thirteen of people in groups on the grass, talking, laughing, drinking. The net had been rented for three hours, so three hours of this, and no sign of an alien in their midst, Auger was sure.

On to a few shots of the ceremony, and finally some of the preparations for them leaving. Jay being helped into the microflite with her dress, Auger waving, carrying out his preflight checks.

And then taking off. Auger closed his eyes, remembering that, Jay laughing and waving, bursting with joy. Then the next frame that had to be the last Tomasz had taken before the explosion, but only half the frame was visible, the rest bright white, washed out by light leaking from the following frame. The one after that half white, half black; half flooded with light, half unexposed.

So the flare of the explosion had cleared half a frame in each direction. And that had to mean that Tomasz had been taking a picture in the instant that the explosion had occurred.

Auger looked at the frame before. The half frame. He blew it up and reprinted it, until the grain on the image was like sand. The microflite moving across the frame, into the darkness of the explosion. And in the cabin Jay with the look of total happiness that he remembered. He felt water in his eyes. That incredible happiness.

And then nothing.

He put the image down. And now also, nothing, he thought. Had Tomasz seen something at that last instant and tried to photograph it? Or was that just a coincidence? Was there nothing to be seen?

He retrieved the negative of the subsequent split image and held it up to the light. Was there something there? He put the negative in the holder and set the developing light to its lowest, closed the shutter down. The rectangle of almost darkness settled on the table. He made a print of it. All he could see was the texture of the paper and the faults in the lens. Shapes wandered across the blankness, shapes from his mind. Like a Ouija board, a planchette, unconsciously driven. He looked again. There was nothing there.

EIGHTEEN

'Oswell, I've got a favour to ask.'

Oswell looked at him and then away, walking on into the ashes of the day. 'Auger. How are you? We had a shit-eating session with some guy from Faith the other day, and you were part of the main course.'

Oswell hadn't changed his easy pace, and Auger dropped back half a step. 'His name was Vinz Szolty, Oswell. He's Maxenham's man. When Maxenham takes a piss, Vinz'll be there to tell him how good it tasted and hold out a cup for more. What did he want with you?'

'He seemed to think that you'd screwed up just ever so slightly.'

Auger could only see the back of Oswell's head, but he imagined a slight smile on the 'fist's face as he said it. Auger grunted.

'He said it reflected on Sweet's crew,' Oswell went on, 'and he seemed to think you may not leave the GenMed case alone. He was saying you might just try and creep back into the frame, even though you'd been warned off. He told us you were a useless fuck and that contact with you was contagious.' Oswell half turned for a moment, letting Auger see a faint grin. 'Vinz Szolty makes Sweet seem like an angel of light. I don't think he likes you, Auger. What did you do to trigger that? If he's Maxenham's playbunny, you must be ringing alarms all the way up to God. Because what I hear, Maxenham's his right hand.'

Oswell still hadn't changed pace, strolling steadily along the ashen road, the fine powder clouding his ankles. He didn't seem too anxious to escape Auger, but maybe he was just concerned about drawing attention.

'You want me to walk away, Oswell?' Auger asked.

'The GenMed case has been given to Jacko. Wisch sits in his office and throws paper into a bin all day, except when Mr Szolty calls out for more coffee. No, I don't want you to walk away. I want something to do.'

Auger let out a long breath. 'I was hoping you'd say that. Jacko, huh? I didn't expect that. How's Jacko doing with it?'

'What do you think? Vinz told Sweet to give him the case, which pissed Sweet off alpha plus. Sweet's too stupid to realise that Vinz just wants it screwed up, so he thinks it means Vinz doesn't trust him. And Jacko's even more stupid than Sweet, so he thinks Vinz is all his Christmases in one slimy little parcel. He thinks it's his big chance. And Sweet sees Jacko licking someone else's ass instead of his own. If it weren't that you'd gone and there's two dead guys and not a rat's chance in a cathouse of a closure to the case, I'd be laughing.'

Auger thought about it. Up ahead, he noticed a 'fist trig stationed on the corner of the street. Oswell had spotted it too, by the slight acceleration in his pace, the ash rising higher at his feet. Auger slowed and turned into the doorway of a shop selling food-aids and began to inspect a display of aerosol texture stabilisers and aftertaste diminishers. As Oswell receded into the ash, he called softly after him, 'You know, maybe Jacko could do with a hand, Oswell.'

Astrid waved to the desk clerk as she passed him, pushed the door and came out of the research wing feeling tired, as if she'd spent a busy night in Emergency. Her head felt light and somehow puffy.

It was like this for a few minutes every time now, after her bouts with Rox. Her thoughts were hard to gather, and disjointed memories came and went like lost leaves in a storm. She put an arm out and rested it against the cold stone of a pillar. But the storm subsided every time.

She didn't feel like what passed for coffee, and stood in the colonnade for a moment in indecision. She wanted Troy Gordo to happen upon her and take her off somewhere, but he wasn't going to do that, and then she thought of Auger, and of Jay. Without thinking, she crossed over to the neuro wards and made her way to Jay Auger's room. The door was locked, and she knocked. There was no answer. She pressed the entry code and still couldn't get in. As she wandered back, she saw Jay's nurse coming towards her.

'Hi.'

The nurse gave her a sour glance and made to walk by.

Astrid stopped, half blocking her way, and the nurse waited.

'Look, I just came to say I was sorry about that misunderstanding. You didn't get into any trouble, did you?'

'I didn't tell anyone. Did you?'

Astrid shook her head. 'Odd case you've got. I mean, dressed up like that.'

The nurse made a face. 'This is neuro. What do you expect?'

Astrid smiled and turned as if to let the nurse pass, then picked up her pace and walked along with her. 'Who's minding her now? You take shifts with someone?'

'I did. Not any more. It's just me now. There's a specialist treating her. He comes in with his own team. That's when I get my breaks. They don't need me there.'

'Treating her? How are they doing that? What can they do?'

The nurse shot Astrid a curious look. 'They're still trying to locate the problem. They don't tell me too much. I don't think they've seen anything quite like her before. They spend more and more time with her. It's fine with me. I get my full pay and I'm with her just a few hours a day now.'

They were at the door. Astrid waited for the nurse to go in, and the nurse waited, too.

'You're not going to say anything, are you?'

Astrid shook her head. 'Of course not. Like I said, I just came to say sorry.'

'You'd better go, then. They're a bit paranoid about her.'

Jacko rose to his feet as Oswell went in.

'You don't need to stand up, Jacko. It's your office. Sit down.'

Jacko sat.

'Listen, Jacko, I wondered how the GenMed case was going. You making progress?'

Jacko looked away. 'Sure I am. Did Sweet send you?'

Oswell shook his head. 'I was just thinking about you. Sweet isn't too happy right now. Truth is, I don't think he wants you to solve this one. I think he's a little bit jealous.'

Jacko looked so miserable that Oswell almost felt sorry for him.

'You know, Oswell, you're the first person's come to see me. Except Vinz, of course.'

A small light went on behind Jacko's eyes as he said that. A very small one. Any brighter and it would overload his system, Oswell thought. 'Well, you need to know who your friends are, don't you?' he told Jacko.

'Yeah. He said I should take as much time as I wanted. It's an important case.'

'Looks like that's true,' Oswell said. Sure it was. Too important to ever be solved.

'Yeah, but he said because of that I can't have anyone to help me. It's confidential. And while I'm doing really well . . .' His face slid, his eyes pleading with Oswell.

Oswell took his time, wanting it to look good. 'Jacko, I haven't got too much on right now, so I thought maybe I could give you a hand. If you like. Check out a few things for you. Vinz doesn't need to know.'

Jacko's face set at this, and Oswell backtracked quickly. 'I mean, Sweet's pissed off with you, and you know how he and I are. I'm isolated, right? And Vinz trusts you, you're going to be jumping over Sweet's head soon, the way you're going, so I figured you could be helping me before long. And while you're doing really well, Vinz isn't going to be waiting for ever. So you need results. I was thinking, maybe I could just help you speed things up. Do the footwork. In the background. What do you think? Do us both good.'

'It'd have to be secret,' Jacko muttered. Oswell could see his thoughts like they were printing themselves slowly in the air above his head in big, misspelt words. Oswell read them out for him, thinking that otherwise they'd be here all day. Vinz had chosen Jacko perfectly.

'Of course,' Oswell prompted him. 'Vinz said no help. And at the end of it you'd still get the credit all to yourself.'

Jacko nodded. 'Yeah, I would, wouldn't I? You couldn't say anything.'

'That's right. Just give me a copy of your case disk, and I'll get on with it. No one knows I've got it, we both carry on independently, compare notes later. How about it?'

'Yeah.' Jacko looked like he might hug Oswell. 'Yeah, let's do it.'

Auger ignored it the first time, and the second too, though he listened more carefully and even said, 'You hear that, Larry? Do we have a visitor?'

The gecko just flicked its tail, though. A tiny spaceship completed a docking procedure against Auger's kitchen door handle with a hiss of retrothrusters, and Auger went back into the music.

But the third time, Auger opened his eyes. The spaceship took off and evaporated. And the knock rang out again.

He went to the door and checked the security monitor. He wasn't expecting Astrid. And not even the craziest itinerant wandered uninvited into this block and didn't run straight back out again, and no one who lived here ever troubled the neighbours for a cup of sugar. Auger thought he was probably the only sane one in the place, though he was pretty sure everyone else thought exactly the same thing about themselves. No one knew where he lived either, except Astrid. There was no one else to know.

The picture came up on the screen behind a storm of static. The only sharp images in the block were the holos. Everything else swam with interference. But he recognised her instantly. It was the girl. Lethe LeCantho.

Auger froze the screen, not knowing what to do. He couldn't leave her out there, though. She must have followed him back to the building. This was ridiculous. She ought to be in a hostel somewhere by now. Hell, if McCrae was still alive, he ought to have done something for her.

Auger brought the screen back to live, and she was gone. Shit, he thought, and jerked the door open.

She was down on the floor, hugging her knees, staring up at him. He pulled her to her feet and brought her inside, and sat her at the table.

She said nothing, so he asked her, keeping his voice as calm and reasonable as he could, 'What are you doing here?'

'I'm not staying in that place. You fix it. It's your fault.'

Auger swore under his breath.

Her look made him back off. He had to remember she was only twelve. She looked more today. She'd hit puberty, or it had hit her. 'Okay,' he said at the end of a long silence. 'Okay. Tonight. You can stay here one night. Tomorrow I'll see if there's somewhere else they take kids like you. All right?'

She just kept on looking at him, kept looking until he stood up and went to the kitchen. He pressed his hands hard down on the counter, took a breath and called through to her, 'All right. You want something to eat?' He poured a few handfuls of dried pasta into a pan and sluiced water over it, setting it to heat. When she didn't answer, he called out again, 'When did you last eat?'

'Two days ago,' she yelled back.

Auger picked up the bag again and cascaded the whole thing into the pan. 'You eat chilli sauce?'

'As hot as you've got. I don't get the aftertaste so bad if my buds are fried.'

He grunted at that, and then looked around. She was standing in the doorway, staring at him. He stirred the pan, irritated. She was relaxing, and he didn't like it. She'd be thinking he was an easy touch now. He offers me food, he'll let me stay.

She stuffed the food down her throat and was finished before he was halfway there. He told her to go and make herself more, keeping his voice flat and featureless. The spectral tigers barring her path were no match for her hunger. She accepted the holos without question. But, then, a few days ago she had accepted death without question.

When they were both done, Auger pushed the plate away. 'Bedroom's through there. I'll sleep here. You can wash in the bathroom. I'll knock on your door at seven in the morning. I want you dressed and ready by seven-fifteeen.'

She stood up, but didn't move from the table. Her stance was street-tough, but there was a child's anxiety on her face. 'Why are you being like this? Why can't I stay here? Just for a while.'

'No, Lethe.'

'It's your fault I'm here. You're responsible for me. I wanted to go with my mother.'

'Your mother had no right—'

'I'm not talking about *her* right. I have a right too.'

'Your right is to be given the chance to reach an age when you can exert your right.'

'I know what I want.'

'You want to die?'

She looked down. 'No.'

'So go to bed.'

'Fuck you.' She marched into his bedroom and slammed the door. Larry slid along the wall to rest like an etched plaque beside the hinge. Auger cleared the table and thought about Lethe and her mother. He wondered what it took to put yourself in the hands of a man like McCrae.

When Oswell's call came, he was still thinking about Lethe. It took him a moment to register the machine's chime in the other room. He flicked the screen on at the third repeat, and raised his palm quickly at Oswell to silence him, turning his head to the bedroom door.

The shower was still sluicing. It seemed to be interrupted for a moment, and then the tone changed again and he relaxed. She was just moving around under the jets. Playing with the water. She was twelve. Still, he kept his voice low.

'How's it going, Oswell?'

Oswell was on the street somewhere. He was using a portable, and Auger's tracer system was having problems with it, which was good. It meant Oswell was taking no chances. The image kept fading and returning.

'I have a disk for you,' Oswell said. His voice was filtered, reedy. It sounded nervous. It should do, Auger thought. Oswell was taking a big risk.

'Okay, I'll pick it up. Tomorrow?'

Oswell nodded, then squinted and said, 'Are you alone there, Auger? What the hell's that?'

Auger turned around, ready to shout at Lethe, but it was just a grizzly bear, teeth and claws bared, rearing up at his shoulder. Auger waved a hand through its gut, and the bear faded away. Its snarl was the last thing to disappear, hanging over him like the memory of a threat. The shower was still driving its white noise through the wall.

'Don't worry. It's just where I live,' Auger told Oswell. 'It's just the reception here.' He gave Oswell a place and time, then hung up and watched the screen grey.

In the morning, he knocked on his bedroom door at seven, and pushed it open five minutes later when there was no response.

Lethe had gone.

NINETEEN

Maybe it was the scrambled contact with Auger, maybe it was talking to Jacko, and maybe it was just the way Vinz Szolty stared past him whenever they passed in the corridor. And probably it was nothing more than the contamination of the streets seeping through the pores of his clothes, but Oswell's back was itching like crazy. He kept glancing over his shoulder, but there was never anyone there. He wasn't being followed, he was sure of it. He couldn't be, in this depth of ash. It had been building up for weeks, and today the air was no clearer than stirred mud. Oswell was using his best lenses, but at their highest setting they gave him little more than two metres of murky penetration. Once or twice, turning sharply, he thought something receded swiftly from the periphery of his vision, and once he had dashed back in the direction of what he thought he had seen, but there was nothing, and a few paces at speed had turned the curdled air thick enough to pull his vision down to a bare metre and give him a filter-failure alert, leaving him hunched up and gasping.

No, there was nothing. It was just the contagion of Auger's paranoia.

Oswell checked the street once more before he stopped at the glowing double doors of the Wire Bar. A gaggle of beggars sat slumped in creased survival bags within the faint protection of the bar's weak Net. They were young, and even with filters and bags they wouldn't survive long on the streets. The dust would silt up their lungs and seed them with cancers. The young, Oswell thought, pausing for a moment to look at them. The young who are our future.

The rosy glimmer of the bar's doors lent their faces a florid, healthy glow, but their eyes were puffy and dark. Feeling bad, as he always did, Oswell tossed a few coins among them, causing a flurry of activity, and noticed that one of them failed to compete for the scattering of small money. A girl, hard and scrawny, flashing him a look that went somehow to the heart of his guilt. He pulled out another coin and threw it straight to her, that she could simply open a hand and catch, and walked quickly into the bar. Out of the corner of his eyes he saw her allow the coin to bounce from her jacket and fall to the ground where another child scavenged for it.

The doors closed behind him and he took a shuddering breath, feeling unaccountably bruised by the experience.

Inside the bar, an overhead grid of failing halogens pricked the smoky air. Oswell chose a table beneath a dead bulb and sat down to wait for Auger. The place was half-empty, and he ordered *citron pressé* and a jug of water, drinking the sour juice straight down and then swallowing the water in swift, long mouthfuls before the aftertaste could kick in and sabotage the harsh flavour.

The Wire Bar had been Auger's choice. It was full of junkies of one sort or another. Oswell wiped his mouth and took a look around. A man slumped at a table across the room sat up abruptly, shrieking, and flailed his arm, knocking a thick brown shot-glass clattering to the floor. No one except Oswell even glanced in his direction, but Oswell unintentionally caught his eye for a moment. The man looked away before Oswell did, and Oswell knew he himself had drawn more attention from the bar in that moment than the man had, by showing curiosity.

This was a crazy place to meet. Anyone coming here was going to stand out like a snake in a sugar bowl.

He tried to relax. That was the point. But it was okay, no one had followed him. The dust that had blinded him on the streets had also swaddled him and kept him safe. He'd checked his clothes for bugs, and he'd spent two hours walking the half-mile from Pacifism to the bar.

After ten minutes he changed his table to watch the door more easily. He drummed his fingers on the table, then stopped and looked at them, and cleaned the yellowing smear of grease off them, and put his hands down on his lap. Give it half an hour, Auger had told him. Then give it up and go. If Auger hadn't turned up by then, the transfer was off.

After a quarter of an hour, he noticed that the barman was slipping tabs to a few of the customers. Oswell watched one of them throw an off-white disk down his throat and slump awkwardly down again, then after a few minutes take a couple of long breaths and start staring around the room with a new intentness.

Oswell watched the man, curious, wondering what the barman was dealing. Nothing in the bar had changed, but the guy was examining the place as if it was a new world.

Not a plain hallucinogen. Oswell ticked that off. The guy wasn't interested in his own body, wasn't turning his hands over, wasn't freaked by a changed self. And the drug wasn't a metabolic enhancer, the guy wasn't testing his strength or reactions. He was just sitting there, staring, watching, quite passive.

Oswell pushed his chair back, making himself more comfortable. The bar was ignoring him now. He patted his pocket, checking the disk for Auger was there.

Searching. That's what the guy was doing. Turning his eyes over the whole bar, peering. Looking for something. Oswell glanced idly away for a few moments as the man's eyes covered him, but he was still staring as Oswell came back again. Oswell smiled easily, and the roving stare moved on.

It was a consciousness thing, had to be. Oswell reviewed what he knew about C-ware. X-ray eyes? Maybe that was it. Maybe he was seeing through everything, his unconscious selling him images of aliens beyond the walls, of revealed sex, of the 'fists on his tail – Oswell arrested that projection of his own and checked the time. He'd give Auger five more minutes, then go. Auger must have had a tail, hadn't been as thorough as Oswell. But at least he'd spotted it, hadn't endangered Oswell.

The guy over at the table suddenly stopped rigid, staring off to Oswell's left. He clenched his fists on the table and dropped his shoulders and slowly began to sob. Oswell twisted round to see what the guy was staring at, but as far as he could make out, the man was fixed on no more than a splash of muddy yellow paint on a patch of wall.

Oswell gave up on it. He couldn't work it out. It had to be something new. There was always something new to fuck you up.

Then across the bar, he noticed a woman who had swallowed one of the barman's tabs and was simply turning a coin over and over in her hand, smiling to herself.

It was the look on her face that gave it to Oswell. That look of total absorption. Not the contentment that it told him of. The guy had taken the same tab, and he wasn't at all contented, sobbing now as if to shuck his skin. But head up and absorbed in the stain, not daring to look away from it even as he fell apart. And her, not drifting into her joy so much that she could turn her eyes from the coin.

Oswell suddenly knew the whole thing. He knew he could have walked up to the guy and taken his money, taken everything he owned as long as he didn't pass between him and the wall and break the spell. Someone could have led the woman away and raped her as long as they didn't try to take away the coin in her palm. She wouldn't even remember it, caught there in the web of some memory that the coin had triggered and brought up high and close.

Prousts, they were called. Neural managers, sophisticated visual memory effectors. Oswell had once taken one, and a chair in the corner of the room, an ordinary plastic chair that he'd had for years, had suddenly become the chair his mother had sat in when he had been nine or ten years old. The only similarity had been in the curve of the backrest, but time became that time, and she was sitting there, seeming so content that it had made him start to cry. Usually he remembered her very dimly, but now he was able to examine her face within that captured memory, the fine lines of care and age, the tears of affection swimming from her eyes and down her cheeks. A hand rising, the fingers wiping away the water and going on to brush wisps of greying hair from her forehead. He couldn't precisely place the memory, but it had comforted him for weeks after he'd taken the proust.

The trouble was, you couldn't predict what sort of memory was going be dredged up. And these clear-as-crystal memories were untrustworthy, too. They surfaced impure, tainted, cut with the unconscious. The proust let slip the unconscious, which welled up to blur into the conscious, and then the brain colluded with the drug, suppressing and altering all linked information to make the changeling memory fit. The new past fractured the present, and the brain mis-set those fractures and made mis-sense of them.

But the new world it made would not fit reality. The forgotten memory of his mother had cheered and comforted Oswell for months, and it was only a year later, when he happened across an old picture of himself at the age of that proust-dredged recollection, that he had started to shake. His mother had been dead for years by the time of that memory. There were documents that proved it, other pictures. Of course there were. She had never been as old as his most perfect memory of her. She had died young. And over the next days other memories resurfaced to accompany the documents and pictures, less vivid but consistent, and yet that fermented image of his mother in the chair was now how he remembered her. That, that was his crystallisation of her.

Oswell had been lucky. He had come to terms with it. His new memory of his mother had become a lasting comfort, a tolerable dislocation. But people killed themselves after taking prousts. Days later, hours perhaps, if the memories were unbearable. Oswell glanced at the sobbing man with his crippling, mis-remembered pain. It might take years even, if the memories were good but impossible to harmonise with everything else around them and had no core of certainty. If their worlds were irreconcilable.

Love flowed from that image of his mother. Maybe that was what had enabled Oswell to accept his experience. The emotion stronger than the vision. Emotion can't be false, it struck him. Perhaps emotion, in the end, was the only reality.

Oswell sighed, remembering, then checked the time again.

Shit, he'd been drifting. It was too late for Auger, and Oswell stood up. If he had been followed, the drug was a fine reason to be here. He could say he'd been tipped off about proust-dealing at the Wire Bar. And if he left without reacting, it wouldn't look good.

He strolled up to the bar and beckoned the barman over, flicking his ID at the man. Even in the murk of the place, the Pacifist badge glittered, but the barman didn't look impressed by it. Oswell put an elbow on the counter, leant up close to him and whispered, 'Listen to me. If I come back and find you're still dealing, I'll close this place so fast and tight no one'll remember it ever existed. You hear me?'

The barman shrugged Oswell away and began to slouch off towards the till. Ringing it open, he said, 'Yeah? Which means how much not to come back?'

Oswell pocketed his badge. 'It doesn't mean anything. It's what'll happen.'

He walked to the door, past the sobbing man, wondering what memory the poor guy had that could be linked to that patch of wall. The man's shoulders were heaving as if he was struggling not to crack wide open. Oswell was pleased to come out of the bar again and into the filthy air.

The beggars were still there, and the kid he'd failed to give money to was the first to approach him. She obviously didn't remember him, or didn't care, or else she thought he wouldn't remember her. He wondered what state the bar's clientele were in when they emerged. Maybe they were ready to give away everything. The coin he thrown hadn't been enough for her, that was all. She wanted more.

She was standing directly in Oswell's path, her long coat flapping at her ankles, and he had to push past her. She scowled and pushed him back with surprising force, and he staggered a few steps before regaining his balance. As he walked away and through the Net's smudged veil, he pulled his jacket straight.

And unbearable pain was instantly in his chest. His ribs caved and cracked so sharply that he heard the toneless chord of the rack of them snapping in unison. The agonising pain blinded him and threw him into dark, airless space as his breath was gone from him in the same rush and he was being slammed against the wall by what felt like a boulder thudding into his chest.

As he instinctively bent over to take a hard, rib-stabbing pull of air, the filter was jerked from his face. He felt a nostril rip. Sourness flooded his lungs and the smooth lines of a 'fist trig swelled from the fog. His filter rattled to the ground, and he heard a brief crunch as the trig's metal foot crushed it flat. There was a thudding of feet as the crowd of beggars fled. Behind Oswell the glowing doors of the bar went dark, and he heard the dull sound of a lock engaging.

Sliding down the wall, fighting panic, he tried to slide a hand into his pocket, but the 'fist's cuffclaw was already around his wrist, braceleting it before easily lifting and spinning him round to catch the other wrist behind his back. Oswell had no chance to get to the disk.

Out of the ash a figure materialised to stand beside the trig. A short man, his hands jammed into the pockets of a long coat. A slim black filter was moulded to his face, a slender black unit, semi-opaque, flush with his cheeks, his brow, the bridge of his nose. He stared for a moment at Oswell, then turned to the trig and said, 'You'd better fit him with some more jewellery, I think. A full set. Just for safety.'

'Vinz,' Oswell got out eventually. Every breath was pain. There was nothing he could do. The trig worked him quickly until he was bent over with a restraining collar dragging at his neck and Magnacles at his wrists and ankles. Only the wrist units were activated, the tight bands as good as welded together behind his back, but the pure weight of the rest was enough to hold him still.

Vinz's head barely came up to the equator of the trig's abdomen. Oswell tried to ignore the pain and steady himself, leaning his forehead against the trig's cold belly. He tried to think. He had done nothing. Remember that. 'Where am I going to run to, Vinz? And what the fuck is this?' He wondered who the trig was, but not for long.

'Jacko isn't a great keeper of secrets, Oz.'

Sweet.

It wasn't so bad as long as he kept his breathing shallow. 'You two kissed and made up, then,' he managed.

Vinz put a hand on the casing of Sweet's trig. 'Take his jacket off, would you, Sweet? Lighten his load a little.'

Sweet notched the cuffclaw under the collar of Oswell's jacket, beneath the thick metal circlet, so that Oswell could feel the cold metal scratch at his throat. Oswell swallowed, knowing enough to hold as still as he could.

The claw tensed and swept down Oswell's chest. His jacket ripped down, parting without resistance, and Oswell felt blood warm on his skin before the cauterising cold of the air. He drew a hard involuntary breath and his ribs made him scream. The pain of the scream was even worse. The trig passed the jacket to Vinz, who began fastidiously to root through the pockets.

'Not here. Shame. We'll have to check his trousers. Sweet, would you?'

Sweet slid a cuffclaw back under Oswell's necklet again, jerking his head up until the trig's domed head was aimed straight at Oswell's. Another claw dug into Oswell's midriff and moved down to engage with his belt, opening a fold of flesh as it began to yank down. Oswell bit his lip, bit right through it and hardly noticed. Now there was real pain. Nerve-shredding pain washing through him.

'Oops. Need to work on my fine control,' Sweet said. 'Here we go, now. Gently does it.'

Oswell felt his cock shrink in. He couldn't help pulling back, away from the ripping claw.

'You know, Sweet, I think he's attempting to escape,' Vinz said brightly. 'Would you lock his ankles, please?'

Oswell's feet snapped together as the Magnacles engaged, and he lost balance and toppled back against the wall. His trousers ripped away and were a snatch of cloth dangling from the trig's claw. Sweet giggled and passed them to Vinz. Oswell tried half-consciously to push himself upright, but couldn't make it. He wasn't even sure where upright was. Vinz was throwing down the rags of trousers and looking suddenly tense and unhappy.

'It isn't here. Shit and shit. Hitch the fucker's wrists to his neck, Sweet. It must be on the ground here somewhere. Christ, you're a careless bastard.'

Oswell's wrists rose smoothly up towards the back of his head which was simultaneously snapped back by the collar, cutting off his breath. This was way over the Magnacles' legal limit, he thought faintly, drowning in pain. His shoulders were popping out with the pressure on his arms, and his ribs were cracking outwards now. His lungs were flooding with blood and he could feel himself going under. All he could see was the filthy sky and it was darkening. He started to slide down the wall, his vision closing in from the edges. The pressure was growing. He was at the bottom of a deep well, sinking, drowning.

But Vinz was at his face, holding his chin in the palm of a hand. He turned away, glancing at something out of Oswell's line of sight. 'Sweet, loosen this, you moron. If he can't breathe, he can't talk.'

The pressure at his neck relented a fraction, and his arms eased slightly towards his waist. He started to float back up the well. The blunt knives of his ribs drew in again, sawing into his lungs.

'Where is it, Oswell? Where's the disk? We know you took it. Jacko told us.'

Oswell let a thin foam of blood slip from his mouth. Vinz bent closer, relaxing his grip on Oswell's chin. His voice softened fractionally. 'We'll get you to the medics, Oswell. We're not interested in you. Just as soon as you give us the disk.'

Oswell looked down at the ground, which was a mess of blood-smeared ash. It must be there somewhere. Sift through that, he thought. See what state it's in when you find it.

Vinz let Oswell slide all the way to the ground, then stood up and hissed at the trig, the words coming down to Oswell like bubbles, like tiny word bubbles bursting in his ear. 'Sweet, you damn moron, you've killed him.' He sighed and knelt by Oswell again. 'Can you hear me, Oswell? This is all Auger's doing, isn't it? Not your fault. He was blackmailing you. I know that. I just want you to say you were going to give the disk to Auger. That's all you need to do.' Vinz's face blurred and receded briefly. 'You better be recording this, Sweet, or you're fucking dust.' And back to Oswell, his voice soft and smooth. 'The medics are on their way now. It's going to be okay. You just have to say something for me. Listen to me. I want you to say, "Auger asked me for the disk." That's all. Can you do that?'

Oswell nodded. Medics. He couldn't hear medics. Just blood rumbling in his ears like a slowing, receding tide. He formed the words in his head, knowing they had to be clear. He nodded again.

'Ready?' Vinz looked at Oswell, then glanced at Sweet. 'Okay, Oswell. Then we'll let the medics at you. They're right here.'

Oswell cleared his mouth of bubbles and started. The breath that carried the words was a rattle. Every word was agony. 'Proust. Dealing proust in the bar. Came out, was assaulted outside without warning. Killed. Killed by Szolty and Sweet.'

'Fuck it, that's it.' Vinz stood up sharply and turned away. 'Sweet, max the Magnacles. He's had his chance.'

'They won't go to max, sir. There's an override.'

'Then disable it. Don't you have any goddamn initiative?'

'Yes, sir.'

Oswell felt his neck pull back again and his hands rise up his back to meet the collar, hesitating as they reached the limit of extension of his shoulders, then continuing again as the joints cracked and released. The circlets hummed and shivered as they pulled and drew together. Oswell felt a final blinding pain and saw a blinding light, and in the light a vision of his mother in her chair, welcoming him.

And then nothing. His legs bent as his feet rose up his back, and there was a brief whine as the magnets strained to overcome the resistance and then succeeded. Oswell's neck snapped just before his hips dislocated and he folded awkwardly in two.

'I never seen that before,' Sweet said.

'Well, you've seen it now. Listen hard to me, Sweet. Erase that recording. Oswell was dealing drugs. We arrested him and he tried to escape. Your Magnacles developed a fault. Report and file it. You got that?'

'Yeah.'

'And don't think you've got anything on me, Sweet. That would be a big mistake. No one does that to me.'

'I got it.'

'Okay. Now I'm going to call in some backup, and I want you to find that disk. It's here somewhere.'

Auger watched from across the street, his shoulder itching vaguely. He had been outside Pacifism to watch Oswell emerge, and he had waited long enough to see Vinz come out after him. Vinz was good, too, although the smog helped him. Auger kept Vinz in sight, in the hope that Oswell might lose him before getting to the Wire Bar, but it didn't happen.

And then Auger watched Oswell into the bar, watched on anxiously as a couple more trigs arrived and stationed themselves at the front and rear doors of the bar.

There was nothing at all he could do about it. Not a thing. He stood and watched Vinz talk into his comms, knowing Vinz would be arranging a patch into the bar's security cams.

Auger guessed three minutes for that, but Vinz had stopped talking and was scrutinising the screen inside a minute. Fast. Vinz must have high clearance to let him do that. Not asking but telling.

Outside the bar, Vinz made a big, slow turn, smiling, a smile clearly meant for Auger to see. If Oswell hadn't passed the disk, he still had it on him. And Vinz was going to get Oswell, even if he wasn't going to get Auger.

When Vinz had sent Sweet up to Oswell coming out of the bar, Auger had almost walked away. He figured Oswell would decide on his best option and either play dumb or play stupid. They might not have proof he was linked with Auger, and if they did, it wasn't likely to get him much more than demotion.

So he waited, dropping back down the street, exchanging one doorway for another. The smog thickened, cutting Auger away from the scene, but he could hear them giving Oswell a beating through the dust.

And then silence. They must have beaten him unconscious, Auger thought.

The smog cleared fractionally, and Auger saw, as if it was frozen, Oswell down, dead without any question, and Vinz with a look of fury on his face, talking into his comms again.

Auger started to back away down the street, then turned and ran, knowing Vinz was bringing in a net right now to catch him.

'Maybe you shouldn't be here, Astrid,' Auger said across the table when they had finished eating. He had given her bread and cheese again, and in her company he hadn't even noticed the taste. He had spent hours on the streets searching for the wine they had drunk, and he had looked forward to her arrival. Even the building had almost behaved itself, limiting its intrusions to a murmuring sandstorm that billowed through the room for half an hour and then quietly blew itself out.

'Why not?'

'Because I'm losing everybody who helps me. Everyone I'm close to. Jay's gone, and Fly, and now Oswell. I saved none of them. Maybe I even killed them, Oswell and Fly.'

There was an odd look on her face, as if she was making something out of that in her head. She said, 'Are you worried about me, Auger?'

'I don't know,' he said, and didn't know why he couldn't just say, Yes. 'But they're gone, and it's my fault.'

She reached her hand halfway across the table towards him and left it there, saying, 'Listen to me, Auger. There was nothing you could have done to help Jay, and the other two, they knew the risks they were taking. I know the risks, too. You need to worry about yourself. Not me.' Looking at him, she picked up the bLinkers he'd left on the table, McCrae's Glimpse of Heaven. As if daring him to stop her, she raised them to her eyes and bLinked. Her head jerked, steadied.

He watched her face and felt better for that. With the eyeshades over her eyes he could observe her more closely, take in the beauty that he hadn't really noticed before, or maybe just hadn't wanted to see. The high arches of her cheeks, the perfect curves and reverse curves of her lips, the fine inward sweep of her neck.

Her lips moved as if blowing a word, then set firm, then trembled. After a few minutes she came out. Her cheeks flushed, and he wondered what her heaven had held.

As she rested the bLinkers again, he said, 'It's all right, I'm not taking that route. I was processing his Understands. I thought I'd done a tiny bit of good, but I seemed to have screwed that up, too. McCrae, he's just crazy. It's the people who give him rein who are dangerous.'

She shook her head. 'You're wrong. I've seen McCrae on the HoloNews. Be careful of him, Auger.'

'McCrae?' Auger laughed, thinking of the man. 'I knew a preacher. Father Fury. He was dangerous. McCrae's a fool. I don't know what they're doing, but they're using him.'

'You really think so?' She dropped the bLinkers back on to the table, settled back into her chair and said, 'Do you know anything about schizotypy, Auger?'

He shrugged. 'I know a little about schizophrenia, it's one of the reasons we get psych tests done on our cultists before they take everyone with them. To weed out the schizos. McCrae was clear. Whatever he is, he's not that. Is that what you mean?'

'Schizophrenia, then. What do you know?'

'They're crazies. They hear voices, they get God confused with a lightshade, they think the lightshade's telling them to kill everyone.'

She gave him a weary smile. 'They hear voices. Okay. Do you ever hear voices, Auger?'

Auger chuckled, shook his head.

'You talk to yourself, in your head? Ever do that?'

'Of course I do. Everyone does.'

'That's right. It's part of what makes us what we are, human. That reflexiveness, that ability to question ourselves. Yes?'

'That's not psychotic schizophrenic behaviour, is it? Otherwise we'd all be crazy.'

Astrid frowned at him. 'You think the difference between you and a schizophrenic is that they live somewhere way up in the sky?' She gestured with her hand, a descriptive, fluid movement that took his gaze through the ceiling and into some high blue heaven.

She brought her hand down again, earthing him. 'You think you're down here and they're way up there, impossibly removed, in cloud-cuckoo-land? You're wrong, Auger. They're just standing a few steps away. Maybe it's a few steps you'll never take, but that's all it is, just a few steps. Not any great leap into the sky.'

Auger watched her face, wondering what she was trying to read in him. He felt his expression locked, but the lock giving, as if she was trying to urge tears from him, a scream even. He knew she was right, knew it in himself.

'Go on,' he said.

'Schizotypy. It's a continuum, schizophrenia. Not something you've either got or you haven't, like a cold or a cancer. It's a long, smooth range, from talking to yourself at one extreme, as every one of us does, to paranoid psychotic behaviour at the other. Of course we all talk to ourselves, and most of us sometimes feel that little voice, the *I and Thou*, raise its volume, hear it momentarily become like something heard externally. On the edge of sleep, maybe it's what occasionally jerks you from half asleep to half awake.'

'Okay. I get you. Go on from there,' Auger said, motioning with his hand.

Astrid nodded, acknowledging his attention. 'Then a bit further along from us, you've got the visionaries. The people who know things, are told things by a higher authority. By God, an avatar, by dead souls. They are the channellers, the prophets. Most of the time, they're under control, they can use it at will, more or less. It can be mediated by trance, by drugs. The seance, the voodoo ceremony.' She cut her hand flat through the air. 'And that's the point about schizotypy. You're not necessarily pegged at your point along this continuum. You can slip forward and back. Stressors can nudge you along, temporarily or otherwise.'

'Drugs are a form of stressor, aren't they? And seances?'

'Yes.' She stopped and waited.

'Our psych tests at CMS,' Auger said. 'Like I said. They're designed to check all this, take out these people.'

'Come on, you don't believe that any more than I do, Auger. They're looking at people *before* the stressor. And the cultists know what the answers should be. They can beat the tests. The tests are shit.' She sighed. 'The Administration knows that, though. You don't have a society that sanctions mass suicide unless that society is prepared, and happy, to permit it. The overwhelming majority of these people are not clinically sane when they kill themselves, and we all know it. The tests are just to comfort us.'

He didn't bother to argue with that. He just went on to say, 'What about the cult leaders? McCrae?'

'They're charismatic, which helps build a following. They're a few steps along the continuum from their congregation, of course. But their congregation provides them with reassurance, stabilises them at their point on the continuum. They hold out a promise of eternity or whatever, and as long as the congregation accepts it, and they keep building slowly, the leaders could probably carry on like that until they die of old age.'

'But that's not how it works,' Auger said slowly, realising she was giving him a variation on his own briefing to the 'fist team before the Father Fury fiasco. 'They make promises and they have to keep them. And when small things don't happen as they should, it worries them.' He lapsed into silence.

'Yes. Stressors. And in such a charisma-dependent environment the small failures provoke dissent. Which is a major stressor. Which may hurry them a few clicks on, maybe trigger a full-blown psychotic episode.'

She looked at him.

'It becomes all-or-nothing,' he said. 'They set up the mass suicide. Major, major stressor. So when they're all set and ready to kill themselves, and a number of them have cold feet, the psychosis kicks in, and they kill everyone. Mass suicide becomes mass murder.'

She carried on looking at him. 'That's right. How many did Father Fury take with him? A few hundred? McCrae's building himself a congregation of thousands.'

Auger whispered, 'Bang.'

'Big bang, Auger.'

TWENTY

'Tired, Auger? You look tired. Been getting enough sleep?'

Auger looked up from his desk and pushed away a pile of Understands. He tried to put Oswell from his mind. He felt his heart racing. He'd had to come in today. Not coming in would have told Vinz for sure that he had been working with Oswell. He levered his mouth into a small smile and said, surprised as he could make it, 'Vinz. What are you doing here? I thought we had an agreement.'

'That disk on your computer?' Szolty raised his eyes. 'I'm not interested in your little secrets. Keep them. Like you said, we're friends. I came like a friend to offer my condolences over your friend Oswell.' He held Auger's gaze, waiting for a reaction, but Auger gave him nothing. 'I assume you know he's dead.'

'I know he's dead.'

'Of course you do.' Vinz smiled, but Auger could see the question in his mind. So Oswell hadn't given anything away. Thanks, Oswell, he thought.

'So I came to offer my condolences,' Vinz said. 'I'm sure he's in a better place.'

'You should know. I heard you sent him there, you and Sweet.' He couldn't hold that back, but it was the rumour anyway.

'He was moonlighting, Auger. It was a misunderstanding compounded by an equipment malfunction.' Vinz inspected his nails and said, not looking at Auger, 'You wouldn't be moonlighting, would you, Auger?'

'Where would I get the time for that?'

'Too busy here, eh? Not what I heard. Your productivity hasn't been what I expected.' He walked around the desk and looked at the screen. 'You've been here two weeks now, Auger, and you're getting behind.' He flicked the screen off and straightened his spine. 'I'm getting complaints about you.'

'I thought you had your own work to do, Vinz,' Auger said.

'Not much to do, these days. I'm efficient. Cases get solved.'

'Or shelved.'

'And there are the new regulations, too.'

'I've seen them, Vinz. I see McCrae's been authorised to conduct Leavings without needing to die himself. What's that about?'

'He made representations to Faith. The Minister saw how it made sense. McCrae's a fine preacher, so why should further congregations be deprived of his ministry? He was very convincing. The Max agreed with him and saw to the change in regs.' Vinz smiled. 'Should be making your job a lot smoother, anyway. Which gets us back to your getting behind here.'

'I'm going through the new regulations, like you said. They take time. I don't see why—'

Vinz's voice hardened. 'You don't listen to me, Auger. You don't *need* to see why. You need to get on with it, that's all.'

Auger sat back. 'So you're running Passive too, now? Is that it?'

'No. I'm not running Passive *too*. I'm just running Passive. There's been a change. Active's closed down, Auger. Active's redundant. All your cases are closed. Wisch has been transferred across. CMS is an administrative arm of Faith now.'

Auger slumped in his chair. It was like a circle, he thought. It had started with that first sanctioned Leaving all those years ago, Auger monitoring it, and Jay at his side, and now it had come all the way round. He should have seen it coming. Splitting CMS into Active and Passive. It was insane to start with, but he should have realised it wouldn't end there. It was as if the 'fists had been split down the middle, one half committed to fighting crime and the other set to allocating it, and now the paradox was resolved by way of madness.

Vinz scraped a fingernail along the desk. 'Think of it like working in a passport office. Your job's just to stamp the visas.' He grinned at Auger, and Auger had the feeling that there was more to come, that even this wasn't all.

'Why do you keep me here, Vinz?'

'I like my rats under glass.' He stood up, staring around Auger's office. 'Go home, Auger,' he said. 'Take the afternoon off. Watch the News this evening. I think you'll be interested. I think you'll find your job a lot easier, come tomorrow.'

Lethe was sitting at the table, waiting for him. He wasn't in the mood for her after Oswell and Vinz Szolty. He was going to ask her how she'd got in, but didn't bother when he saw what she was playing with, tossing it ostentatiously into the air and catching it again.

'You've got a message,' she told him, pointing to the comms console. An orange pinlight flickered there.

He ignored it, looking at the red disk in her hand. Red for Evidence Record. He tried to keep his voice level. 'How did you get that?'

'It's what I do with it that you should be asking. I made some coffee. You want some?'

He pursed his lips. 'You're really something, Lethe, aren't you?'

'I'm not going to any home. I want to stay here. I can take this to the 'fists and tell them where I got it.'

'You won't be staying here if you do that.'

She shrugged. 'I go, you go.' She held the disk up, turning it in her hand. It flashed light on the gecko, prompting a small flick of its tail.

'Why me?'

'I told you. You're responsible. My mother said. I think your friend owes me, too. You owe him.' She paused. 'So?'

Auger took the disk from her. 'If I could get you into a place with other kids your age, wouldn't you like that?'

She tried to grab the disk back, and he held her away.

'No, maybe not,' he said. 'The thing about those places is, you go there, you learn all sorts of shit from everyone else. You go in bad, you come out worse.' He tossed the disk up, and she caught it before him.

'Not a good idea, where you're concerned.' he said. 'I wouldn't want any of the kids there exposed to what you might decide to teach them.'

'So?'

'You can stay. For now.'

She threw him the disk, and he watched her trot towards the bathroom. There was a new bounce to her gait. After a moment the shower came on, its noise seeming to soak into Auger's skull. He wished it could wash away the vision he had of Oswell's body snapped backwards and broken.

He opened the disk and bLinked into it while Lethe cleaned herself up. He hoped it was going to be worth it. Oswell had died for what was on here.

The disk bloomed into his head. He scrolled down the index and went straight to the record of Rudd Merchant's room. He looked around for a moment, remembering where the intruder had been standing, then took a height measurement at the Magritte's top border, then stretched a line there along the angle of vision he had had from his crouched viewpoint in the bathroom, and fed the geometry into the disk's calculator.

Allowing for heels, the man had been one-eighty centimetres tall.

Not much, but it was a start.

Auger then went to the desk, his feet cycling him forward in the simmed room. He pulled open the top drawer. Whatever the man had removed from there had still been there when the record had been taken.

There were just two things in the drawer. One was a stethoscope. Too awkwardly bulky to have been so swiftly stuffed into the man's pocket, and why take such a thing anyway? And the other thing was a metal bLinker case.

Auger picked it up. His fingers slipped on the slim clasp, but it wouldn't open for him. For a moment he thought it was just locked, but it wasn't locked. Jacko simply hadn't opened it to record its contents. Auger swore. He wouldn't have been able to bLink into it anyway, inside the record, but shit! He threw the case at the wall in frustration, and when it vanished, he picked it up again from the drawer. He looked at the case, turning it over in his hand. Just above the clasp, there were three black letters chased into the aluminium casing. TNM.

Why take that? It wasn't a secret that Rudd had belonged to TNM. Were the bLinkers themselves the target? Why go to such risk? Every member was issued with a set. No need to steal a set from a sealed and SOC-taped room.

Unless it was simply to suck Auger along. Unless the thief had known Auger was in there all the time.

And Oswell had died for it.

He came out of the record to find Lethe cooking something on the gas stove. He wasn't sure it was her at first, maybe what he was seeing was something the block had dreamed up and dropped into his room. She was clean and tidy, her hair gathered back and caught in a ponytail. She was wearing a shirt of his, the sleeves rolled up fat, right up to the shoulders, but the shoulders of his shirt were at her elbows. She had looked young when she had tried to sign her Understand, but now, trying a different way to be older, she only looked even younger.

'You need some clothes,' he said.

'So do you. Is this the only other shirt you've got?'

'Not any more, it seems.'

She pulled the pan off the heat and started towards the sink with it. Auger could see it was too heavy for her, and went to take it from her. She fell against him, and he felt the roughness of his own hands against the surprising roughness of hers. She was young, and she was not so young. He wondered about that life of hers, what she had learned, what she had been taught. He remembered her mother leaning into him, letting the light fall on the cleft between her breasts.

His spare shirt fell open at the top, and Lethe caught it together late in her hands, staring up at him, eyes wide. Not so young, he thought.

He took the pan to the sink and drained the vegetables. They sat down, Auger and Lethe.

'Okay, Lethe, listen to me. There are rules here, and they don't get broken. I don't know what you used to do when you were with your mother, but you keep yourself covered up, like I keep myself covered up. Nothing is ever going to happen between us. Nothing. Do you understand that?'

She shrugged, unconcerned, and he realised that that whole act had been to test him. She was just checking him over, making sure she was safe here with him. Lethe wasn't as fragile as she made out. It struck him that her behaviour at Passive with the Understand could have been an act, too. She might not have wanted to go with her mother in the first place. Lethe could easily have made herself look older that day for Auger, signed her Understand and departed with her mother.

'Okay,' he said when she was finished eating. 'I want some peace. I've got things to do.'

'So have I,' she said. 'Thanks for the meal. See you later, then.' She shrugged on her coat and said, 'We're clear, Auger. No debts now.'

Debts, he thought. Everything was negotiation with her. Pay and payback.

He waited until he was sure she was out of the building before going to the comms unit and calling Sherry back. Her message was timed one-fifteen p.m. And it had to be important, he knew. She never checked her sleep that fast, to be done just after mid-day.

Her face came up frowning. 'Listen, Auger. I've been thinking about your suicides. I went back to GenMed, had another little riffle through their pathology files. The brain section analysis still bothers me. And the exsanguination doesn't make any sense at all. I've had a thought. Do you know anything about the victims? They weren't by any chance phobic, were they?'

'What do you mean?'

She shook her head. 'No, forget it. Crazy. They weren't Vets of the Dirangesept projects, were they? No, of course not. They were too young.'

'Hold on. They were both involved in a research project at GenMed, in the same building as the D3 project. There is a connection. Sherry? What is this?'

Sherry's gaze moved offscreen. Auger heard a disk whirr, and for a moment he was staring at her through a film of dense mirror writing. Sherry's eyes scanned the screen, and then it cleared again.

'No,' Sherry said finally. 'Both your deaths were the same. Those were impossible, your two are just a puzzle.'

'Sherry, what the hell are you talking about?'

She sat back in her chair and said, 'Okay. You remember Maze, don't you?'

Maze again. 'Madsen,' he sighed. 'You're going to tell me about Madsen, aren't you?' He wasn't sure he wanted to know.

'If you like.'

She held his stare for a second, waiting, but he didn't stop her.

'I knew Madsen, Auger. He came to me when he was investigating a case at Maze. I did some reports for him on a series of strange deaths that made no sense. Impossible suicides. Maze was the connection. It wasn't just another games company. Maze was controlled by the Administration. They were searching for a reliable way to deal with the beasts on Dirangesept. To kill them. They never quite succeeded, but what they do seem to have managed is to find out roughly how the beasts operated. They developed a gamezone in which the beasts would manifest themselves.'

'Cathar,' Auger murmured.

'That's right,' Sherry said, nodding at him. 'That was the zone. The beasts brought back in the Vets' brains manifested themselves in Cathar. But Maze failed, Auger.' She paused for a moment. 'It's possible that research is still going on, though, trying to find a way of killing the beasts. That may be what they're doing at GenMed now.'

'It has to be,' Auger said. 'It's D3. The third project. That has to be based on some advance, doesn't it? Otherwise it'll be the same thing all over again, just like D1 and D2.'

Sherry gave him a mirthless smile. 'Not necessarily. How much time is there? Have you seen the global quake stats?'

'No. They're restricted.' He narrowed his eyes. 'Have you seen them?'

'Of course not, but why do you think they're restricted? Rift reports have increased just five per cent in the last year, but the Administration budget for Stability is up twenty-five per cent. The only way that makes sense is if reports are being suppressed.'

'But we're okay here, aren't we? The food—'

'All I'm saying, Auger, is that D3 has to go, and the Administration is probably praying for something to be successfully developed before the ships reach 'Sept. But regardless of anything else, the Administration needs some external point of focus. Some hope for the people.'

'Other than the hope of heaven,' Auger murmured.

'Exactly. If they won't be pointed at life, you point them at death. But what's in between, this disintegrating hulk of a world, you simply make as palatable as possible, and you hide the facts.'

She made a gesture of dismissal. 'Look, this is just apocalypse chatter. Let's go back to your bodies. They were exsanguinated. Why do that? It's not easy to drain the blood out of a corpse. If you've got a corpse and you want it to look like suicide, there are ways, but it isn't easy. Whatever way you want to use, bloodletting is one of the hardest to give the appearance of. Draining a corpse without leaving marks isn't easy.'

'Meaning?'

'I don't think they did that. I don't think the victims were dead when they were drained, Auger. But they weren't conscious, and they weren't sedated either. There would have been drug traces.'

'So?'

'I'm guessing they were in comas. Easier to exsanguinate, because the patient's still alive. And a coma fits the post-mortems, too. Why they were so interested in the brains.'

Another thought struck Auger. 'The whole of GenMed's involved in this, isn't it? Not just the research wing. It isn't simply a rogue researcher or a maverick team.'

She nodded. 'Has to be GenMed all the way through. The pathology department had to give limited information to the 'fists for Haensen, then to CMS for Merchant. And GenMed will be conducting the PMs for this project, too.' She glanced down, frowned, then looked up again. 'Okay, why exsanguinate them? It's an odd thing to do. Any ideas?'

'Well, if GenMed wasn't bothered to conceal anything from its own pathologists . . .' He shrugged, not seeing where to go from there. 'I give up.'

'Was there something in the blood? Something they wanted back? Part of the experiment? Maybe something they wanted or needed to reuse?'

'Or something they didn't want accidentally found by the 'fists. Or CMS.'

Sherry nodded. 'Or that.'

They fell silent. Auger's screen hummed. Only one thing was left, he knew, and Sherry wasn't going to be the one to say it.

'Nangines,' he said, finally. Oh, Jay, he thought.

'Maybe,' she said. 'Yes, maybe nangines.'

Auger sighed, then took a breath and said, 'Okay. I need to know about Madsen.'

'There's not much I can tell you. I told him to get out of CMS while he could, that he'd be blamed for the whole thing, but Madsen would never listen to me.'

Her face softened. Auger could see there had been something between them, which surprised him.

'Whatever Madsen knew, he took with him. Looking back, I think he was protecting me. We were in touch for a while, but when I was . . .' Her voice faltered, and she took a shuddering breath and went on, 'Well, after that, I didn't answer his calls. I cut him off. Then I heard he'd vanished. I think he's dead, Auger. He was a good man. That's all there is.'

Her face changed again, and before Auger could say anything else Sherry cut the contact and the screen greyed.

Auger sat in front of the dead screen and let his room surround him with its fantasies and illusions until it was time for the holocast.

It was the lead item. McCrae was with the Holohead, one to one. Only Ministers of the Administration usually got that tightness of focus. The preacher was speaking slowly and carefully, and Auger, watching him, found himself unable to shake away the image of Jay and himself swinging away from their wedding in the microflite, the fireworks behind them and the future once more ahead.

McCrae was holding up the bLinkers now, his Glimpse of Heaven, and the cam was closing in on the angelic lettering with its impossible promise.

The preacher's voice was soft as warm butter. 'I understand that for many of you the leaving of this world is a hard choice to make. Many of you who yearn for heaven have hesitated, and understandably. But there is now an alternative.' McCrae's arm swept back, and the cam went with it, moving to fix upon a sleek, low chrome pod behind him.

'Many of you will be familiar with CrySis pods. Cryonic stasis is a well-established procedure used for interstellar travel, as well as in the facilitation of many medical and surgical techniques.' He reached down to trace his fingers along the curves of the pod, the cam registering his hand's distorted reflection.

'You may wonder what interest I, a preacher of the word of the Lord, a bringer of heaven, might have in such a machine.' He walked slowly around the pod, his hand still trailing over it. 'This machine is at the same time a more basic and a more complex development of the conventional CrySis pod. It is designed to be stable and self-maintaining at temperatures at the lowest extremes of God's universe, and it is built to last as long as God's universe lasts.'

McCrae came around to the front of the pod again, the Holohead bobbing eagerly in his wake. 'Your heaven is infinite and it is eternal,' the preacher said, raising the bLinkers before him like a sacrament and gazing straight into the cam. 'The Lord places no limits on the rewards He offers you, His servants. Thanks to the blessings of the Lord, your imagination also is infinite, and it is your imagination that bounds your heaven. And God's universe too is infinite, and thus to travel through God's universe is to travel eternally.' He waved an arm in a slow, broad gesture. 'Imagine it, space and time without bounds, without limit. Imagine your heaven in space and time without end.' He touched the pod again, reverentially, making a pair of small movements on the breastplate of the machine that were, Auger realised, a benediction, a sign of the cross.

His voice dropped to a whisper. 'You who were tempted by the heaven that the Lord has gifted me with to offer you, but feared too much the final leaving of this life; to you . . .' he raised the bLinkers again '. . . to you I offer heaven eternal without the passage of death. I offer life eternal without affliction of the body or anguish of the soul.'

'Hold your horses a minute, there,' the Holohead said, chuckling. He trotted around the pod. 'Can you give us some detail, here, Minister? This sounds too good to be true.'

'Is God himself too good to be true?'

The Holohead looked appropriately chagrined, and McCrae went on. 'Energy requirements in the bitterness of space will be minimal, and after all, the pods, and their cargo, demand that very bitterness.'

'And how much room is there in heaven, may I ask? After all, you're talking about a lot of hardware here.' The Holohead patted the CrySis pod and chuckled again, irrepressible. 'This isn't just a pair of bLinkers and a poison pill, is it? What is the cost of paradise? What is the bottom line?'

'That's a very fair question,' McCrae conceded. 'But the Mission is prepared to accept contributions of every kind. After all, you're leaving the world behind when you enter the life eternal.' His voice became solemn as he stared into the cam's wide eye. 'You shall cast off your possessions like an anchor, and, lo, they will become the fuel that lifts you away.'

'A fine image.' The Holohead drifted back to McCrae's side again. 'And I imagine the heaven-bound avoid paying Leaving Tax this way.'

'Yes. But there will be a new Departure Tax.'

The Holohead grinned. 'Like the old saying goes, the only certain things in life are death and taxes. Well, it looks like you can now cheat death, but taxes are still another matter. This is the News Holohead reporting from the ministry of Dr McCrae, signing off and wishing there was a place for animats on the heaven-bound ships.'

TWENTY-ONE

Vinz came in first thing, as Auger knew he would. He spent a moment fingering Auger's paperwork, as if he had wandered in for that, and then said, 'You saw McCrae, then, Auger? Happy now? Are your poor little morals assuaged at last?'

'Where are the ships coming from, Vinz? And the pods? And this eternal power? It's bullshit, isn't it?'

'Not at all, Auger. The ships and the pods exist. The ships are what's left of the D2 project, stripped down, re-engined and re-equipped, and the pods are not so very different from conventional CrySis pods.'

'And the power? What about that?'

'We harness the stars, Mr Auger.'

A new voice from behind him, sly and familiar. Auger twisted round, knowing it already. 'McCrae,' he said flatly.

'Dr McCrae, yes,' Vinz said. 'I invited the minister to come in to Passive today. To build some bridges, heal a few wounds.'

Auger let a spit of breath from his lips. He looked hard at Vinz, murmuring, 'And bring the dead back to life? Can he do that, too?'

McCrae didn't hear that, or affected not to. He came forward smiling, his hand open and stretched out towards Auger, assuming a handshake. When he realised Auger wasn't playing, he let the hand fall, but held the smile a moment longer. 'You still don't trust me, Mr Auger. I'm sorry for that.'

'Don't be. Tell me, McCrae, what's the difference between what you do and what a mass murderer does?'

McCrae glanced at Vinz before responding, and Auger wondered which of them was using the other. Had Vinz engineered this meeting, or was it McCrae? The preacher smiled at Auger again, a deliberate, empty smile this time. 'You think you're insulting me with that question,

226

don't you? But why should I be insulted? Choice is the answer, Mr Auger. All that I have ever done is offer an opportunity that was offered in turn to me by the Lord.'

'You haven't taken that opportunity yourself.'

'Not yet, no.' McCrae shrugged away Auger's expression. 'But that isn't my answer to your question. My answer is that that is my choice. The Lord gave me that choice, just as I give it to others.'

'You mislead them. What you give them isn't any sort of a choice.'

'A matter of interpretation. Is your form of control really any better?' He shook his head mildly. 'You can't control people,' he said. 'No one can. You can't be the shepherd for others. The Lord is thy shepherd, remember, and only the Lord. Not the law. Not anything of man's creating.'

'But if they're brainwashed—'

McCrae laughed, a descending peal of easy chuckles. 'Brainwashed? What does that mean? Really, Mr Auger. Brainwashing. Education. Information. They are all words, and all words can lie. But belief, that is a different matter altogether. Words are irrelevant to it.'

He touched his chest, pressing his finger there until the tip blanched. 'Belief is of the heart, Mr Auger. If people truly believe in something, and – to be *technical*, if you like – nothing has been done to manipulate the function of their brains, then they must be permitted to act as they wish. That is a definition of freedom. The freedom to exercise free will. By licensing their freedom, as is your job, Mr Auger, you ensure that they may achieve what they desire without pain, and you ensure furthermore that no one is coerced into suicide.'

He smiled easily. 'And suicide is legal after all. It used not to be. So if it's permissible for one person to kill themselves, why not two, or ten, or fifty thousand?' He waved a hand, releasing the figures into the air. 'But that isn't any longer an issue, Mr Auger. Is it? Our argument is redundant. CrySis, not death. None of my congregation will die.'

'Really? An eternal voyage through space?'

'God willing, yes. And if not, if a ship burns up, fails for whatever reason, whatever act of God, in a hundred years, a thousand, will they not have had more years of conscious, joyous life than you have had, Mr Auger, and still go on to stand at God's right hand?'

'And if the ship fails in a year, if the pods fail and they regain consciousness in that limbo? What then?'

'My congregation place themselves in my hands, and in the arms of the Lord. The Lord will not fail them.'

He glanced at Vinz, then back at Auger again, and chuckled. 'Let me give you an example of the perfection of my heaven, Mr Auger. You have had a Glimpse of it? I can see you have. My heaven is pan-congregational.' He touched a finger to his chin, thinking. 'Here is a scenario for you. If you were in heaven and Mr Szolty here was also in heaven, I would guess that your roles in each other's would not exactly synchronise. Which would contradict the premise of heaven for one of you. But in my heaven, in God's heaven, there is no conflict. There is an infinite number of heavens, and each of you could have your own ideal relationship with the other.' He clapped Vinz on the shoulder, chuckling again. 'And it would be no sin either.'

Auger looked from the preacher to Szolty. There were like old friends.

Vinz Szolty smiled. 'We're looking at true multi-denominationalism, Auger. Not to mention a massive increase in applications for Leavings, and an easing of the Understand protocols as the heaven-bound are not dying. It's a win-win situation, Auger. Everybody's happy. No one dies, no one loses.'

'And the Administration takes more money in taxes than ever.'

'Spaceship production's expensive at the best of times, and these aren't the best of times. We need all the funds we can get. D3 is close to embarkation, and we have as much of a responsibility to this world as Dr McCrae has to the next. No one's complaining about the taxes, Auger. Neither the heaven-bound nor the Earthbound.'

The staff café was nearly empty. It was three in the morning, and the few medics in there were grouped under the few functioning striplights close to the service counter. A few waitresses were clearing tables away in the shadows, readying the canteen for early breakfasts. In the farthest of the shadows, Astrid sat yawning with Troy, winding down after her shift as he readied himself for his. It was good to be with him after Auger, she thought, though it struck her that when she was with Troy Gordo, she often had Auger in her mind, but she never thought about Troy when she was with Auger.

Stupid thought. She swallowed coffee, hardly noticing the heat of it blistering her palate, and said, 'Troy, have you seen any of the other floors in the research wing?'

'One of them, yes. Where they're carrying out CrySis research. I think they use the Vets for it. Why?'

'I saw it the other day. It was creepy, all those pods. I thought they were empty at first.'

'You should ask Rox about it. She'll probably tell you'

'I got the impression she wasn't too keen to tell me anything.'

He laughed. 'Rox is just paranoid. She thinks everyone's an industrial spy. You remember you asked me why I said you were so good for the research project? I'd already given her your name as a possible subject, after the first time you came to TNM. She had you vetted, you came up glittering. No industrial contamination, as she calls it. That's what made you suitable.'

Astrid felt suddenly cold. She tipped her head and said slowly, 'You had me vetted?'

He raised a hand as if to fend her off. 'Hey, slow down. Not me, Astrid. Rox did. And you came through okay, didn't you?'

'That isn't the point, Troy. You effectively instigated it. You didn't tell me that was going to happen.'

'What's the problem here?'

She drew a breath. 'People have lost jobs, lost everything, after vettings. Random ones, irrelevant ones. You know that, Troy.'

He shrugged, his cheeks coloured a fraction. 'I'm sorry. Maybe I took a small risk.'

'You took a risk? *You* did? You didn't even ask me?'

'You'd have said no.'

'Damn right I would. Jesus.'

There was silence between them, a long silence that Astrid didn't feel like breaking. She stared through the window at the darkness, wondering whether Rox knew about her and Auger, about him looking into Rudd's death. But she couldn't have, Auger wasn't officially on the case even. Ash swirled under the walkway lamps, sulphurous ash with a jaundice tinge.

She stood up, and he looked alarmed, coming to his feet, too.

'I'm going to bed,' she told him.

'I'll walk you.'

'You'll be late.'

'I'll say I overslept. Don't just go, Astrid. I'm sorry. I didn't think.'

He held the door for her, followed her out. She calmed a little. Maybe it was okay. If Rox had suspected anything at all, she'd simply have told Troy that, no, Astrid wasn't a suitable subject for the project. And maybe she'd have leaked the report to Ferec, and Astrid would have lost her job for some invented reason. But none of that had happened.

'Okay, Troy,' she said. 'At least you told me now, I suppose.'

And anyway, she liked him.

He grinned at her. She could almost see his relief. 'I've been wanting to tell you. I've felt bad about it for a long time.'

'Okay, it's done.'

They walked in a comfortable silence. He came with her all the way to her door and stopped as she opened it. Astrid paused, then said, plunging into it, 'Troy, you couldn't do something for me, could you?'

'If I can. What is it?'

'You used to work in neuro, didn't you?'

'Sure. My research doctorate was in neuro. Why?'

They were inside her room now, the door closed. 'How would I go about accessing confidential vidfiles from patient records?'

'How would you? *Why* would you?'

She hesitated. There wasn't really a lie that would sound even remotely convincing. Either she trusted him or she didn't. Or rather, either she had a choice or she didn't.

A little lie, then. 'There's a neuro patient I'm curious about. It's Jay Auger. Anterograde amnesia. She's one of the only cases alive, and I'm wondering how she presents. There must be vidfilm of her, but obviously it's confidential. You couldn't access it, could you?'

He shook his head. 'Not officially, no. But I still have a research priority code. I remember Jay Auger, she was a researcher here, too, wasn't she? Nanomedicine?'

'Yes.' Had she said too much, the way he was looking at her?

'I was curious, too,' he said. 'We all were. But she was given total privacy, no peeking.' He was at her console now, raising colours on the screen, coding himself in.

'Okay, her vids should be available for research, but anonymised. The idea is you can't find her if you're looking, but you can use her case if you don't know who she is. We'll just do a reverse search.' He grinned again, happy to be helping her. 'Give me a research title, then.'

Astrid thought. 'Anterograde amnesia.'

'No. Too close. Anyone like us could do that, looking for her. She'd be one of a few dozen, that's all, and GenMed would definitely bar her notes from that. They'll only release it if the parameters are wide enough that she'd be one of a few hundred, minimum. We can't make it too easy for ourselves.'

'Okay, what about psychogenic amnesia?'

Troy took his hands from the console. 'Psychogenic? I thought you said it was anterograde?'

230

'Yes,' she said shortly. She hadn't considered him picking up on that but, of course, he was going to. Well, no going back now.

He said, 'This isn't just curiosity, is it? What's going on?'

'I don't know. That's what I'm trying to find out.'

'Is that why you were so pissed off about the vetting?'

'I was pissed off about the vetting because I thought I could trust you.'

He nodded. 'You can trust me, Astrid.' He keyed it in.

2539 VIDFILM SEQUENCES ACCESSED.

'I think that's anonymous enough for them to have let her through,' he said dryly. 'That's a lot of amnesia.'

'There's a lot of trauma,' she answered.

'Still, two and a half thousand. It's a lot to trawl through.'

'Can you do a colour search?'

'Yes.'

'Her dress is pale yellow.'

He keyed the colour in.

3 VIDFILM SEQUENCES SELECTED.

Troy ran the first. A man sitting in a chair, blood staining his yellow shirt. He was slumped there, shaking his head, touching the blood in clear disbelief. A voice was caught mid-sentence, an interviewer saying neutrally, '. . . did with the blade, or anything . . . ?'

Astrid stopped him, not wanting to know the rest. 'It's not that one.'

It was the next one. The yellow wedding dress. Jay was lying on the bed, the dress bunched up, sobbing into the pillow. The nurse sat, tidied the room, made a few notes. Troy let it run on for a while, then fastforwarded it. The nurse speeded up, and Jay became a staccato frenzy of tears. Troy stopped, rewound to the start, then selected another clip. This time the nurse was comforting her. He ran it for a while again, then changed to another clip. 'Odd,' he murmured.

'What?'

'There's no time or date recorded on the vid.'

'So? It's at the head of each segment.'

'Yes, but it should be on the vid, too. On every frame. Like the other one. This makes no sense. The vid just runs on. Time of day noted only at the beginning of the segment.'

He clicked on another tape, forwarding, slowing, forwarding and slowing it. This time the tape ran for several weeks, continuous. He kept going. Run and stop, run and stop. It was unvarying. There was nothing except Jay in tears, or asleep. The same nurse was with her all the time, moving around, helping dress her or prepare her for bed.

'What were they doing, recording it like this? What was the point? If it's undated, it's clinically invalid. There are no interviews here, no investigations.'

Astrid agreed. 'And, look, it's shot from above. As if it was surveillance film.'

'No, that might make sense. Jay wouldn't be likely to accept cams in plain sight. She'd question their presence, no matter how hysterical she was.'

'Maybe the nurse would know. It's the same nurse every time.' Astrid waited for her to be facing the cam, froze the image and peered at the name clip on her uniform. 'Nurse Haroun. We could ask her.'

Troy sighed and shook his head. 'I don't think so. I remember Teyma Haroun. She died a few years back in a rift accident.'

'Pity,' Astrid said. And then said, not immediately sure why that sounded wrong, 'When was that? When did she die?'

'Two years back. Anyway, why would that matter?'

What had Auger said? He'd visited Jay every day for nearly two years, and nothing had changed. Not even the nurse.

'Oh, God,' Astrid whispered. She felt suddenly cold to her bones. The sense of it came to her like tumblers in a lock. Everything fitted.

Jay's datasink had banned medication for that year. And most of that time Auger had had to watch her on the monitor. He hadn't physically been with her at all, supposedly not to further traumatise her.

Astrid closed her eyes, seeing it clearly in her mind. On the monitor screen Jay unchanging, the nurse unchanging. Not because it was always the same nurse and because Jay was in her endless fugue, but because Auger had just been watching recordings of her. That's why the tapes were undated frame by frame.

And she knew why it had been done, too. 'You said Saffer was an obstetrician, Troy, didn't you?'

'Yes. Why, Astrid? What is it?'

'All that time, she wasn't in the room at all. She was somewhere else altogether. Maybe in the research wing.'

'What?' He looked at her. 'Why would they have done that?'

No medication. Of course not.

'Because Jay was pregnant.'

And as soon as they had discovered she was pregnant, they started to record her every second. They made sure they had enough film never to have to risk Auger realising he was seeing the same scene twice, even if it was always the same. That was why the same nurse was always there. They always showed him images of Jay recorded before her pregnancy began to show, and he never even knew it.

Astrid wondered what Jay might have made of it, growing bigger, locked in that fugue, going into labour, locked in that fugue, giving birth still locked in that fugue, and then having the child taken away, and herself still locked in that fugue.

At least the confusion would have faded as her body recovered. But what of the child? Had it been adopted? And why keep its existence from Auger in the first place?

Troy said it. 'But why not tell him?'

She shrugged. 'I don't know.' She stood up. 'I've got to go and tell him. He has to know about this.'

Troy closed down the monitor. The room darkened. 'At this time of night? And aren't you supposed to be with Rox in a few hours?'

'How did you know that?'

'Hey, calm down. I asked her when you were next on.' He smiled at her. 'So I could accidentally bump into you as you came out. I told you, she's not as bad as she seems. But she won't be happy if you miss your session. You can tell Auger afterwards.'

'I'm not sure. She could have something to do with this, Troy.'

'Rox? It's hardly likely. Anyway, you've been vetted and cleared.' He made an apologetic face. 'Even if she is involved, she doesn't know we know a thing.'

It was his 'we' that clinched it. 'Okay,' she said.

He reacted with a big grin. 'Look, I'll tell you something else, then. I shouldn't, but the hell with it.' He pulled his TNM bLinkers from a pocket and settled them over his eyes. And slowly the skin of his cheeks and forehead seemed to smooth itself until the knots in his face relaxed, the craters filled in and his complexion became perfectly smooth. His acne was quite gone. He was as beautiful as an angel.

Astrid couldn't speak.

'And look, Astrid,' he said. His hand rose to the bLinkers and he let them fall into his palm. 'I can even hold it for a short while.'

She watched as the effect gradually faded, the knots drawing in, the pits and scars returning. He leaned forward, slowly, the corners of his eyes lined, showing his uncertainty as he offered her his lips. She let him kiss her, then held him, and then, when she felt soft enough to hold him skin against skin, she let him go, smiling, touching his cheek with the back of her hand.

'You'd better go,' she said. 'Remember? Your shift.'

TWENTY-TWO

The commslink alarm woke Auger some time in the night, fetching him from a dream he couldn't recall to the gecko sitting on the ceiling above his head. For a moment he thought the alarm was the lizard calling him with a clicking of its tongue, but then it flicked its tail and was gone, leaving Auger to swing himself out of bed and stumble to the screen on his desk and thump its alarm with the heel of his hand. The silence hummed.

He sat down heavily as the screen began to rouse itself, the matt grey of the glass colouring up as Auger rolled his shoulders and tried to stretch himself awake. His joints cracked. The gecko glanced opaquely at him from the wall. He rubbed at his stinging eyes, attempting to impose order on his thoughts. Not Wisch, not Vinz Szolty, so who? Who at this hour?

And he knew, was wide-eye awake in the instant.

Sherry. It was Sherry's night-time system patched into his. Her alarms were rigged to wake her and Auger together. Anyone breaking into her apartment would wake them both as surely as if they'd been sleeping side by side.

Auger punched the keyboard, his fingers fluently repatterning the board to her security configuration, and then he had to wait, drumming his fingers on the table and muttering to the console, 'Come on, come on,' as if it would make a difference.

Her main room screen flashed up first, and he scanned the scene quickly. No movement there. The lights were down, the image scudding with grain. They weren't even in yet. Auger took a lung-scraping breath and forced himself to relax. No panic. They wouldn't get through that door anyway, the alarm had been triggered when they'd simply touched it. That was how paranoid Sherry was.

Auger heard his own nervous laugh bounce into the room, almost startling him, and he cursed Sherry half-heartedly for her paranoia. Drunks probably, their hooch spinning them free of gravity, leaving them to stagger against her door in the night. He chuckled. That screeching alarm bounding through the corridor would have given them a hell of a shock.

So, he told himself, nothing to fuss about. Just night worry. Summoning calm and settling down, he pressed keys to jump him to the corridor view, double-checking it was a false alarm.

The image jolted. Whiteout.

'Christ,' he muttered, sitting back and raising his fingers from the board. The cams must have malfed.

He began to lean forward again. No, it was smoke crawling over the screen. The cloudy white of it slowly dispersed, and he watched, puzzled, as the corridor swayed into sharpness.

There was no one in the corridor. He swiftly arced the cam up and down the strip of walkway with its recessed and shadow-edged ranks of closed doors. No one coming or going. No one reacting to the alarm screaming in the narrow space by risking putting a head out in misplaced curiosity either.

Auger pulled his chair forward and his heart thudded. Beneath the cam's housing where Sherry's door should have been, there was nothing. Just the remains of the smoke sucking into the dark of Sherry's apartment.

He punched the keys again, swearing hard. Sherry's paranoia had finally paid off. She'd been right and he'd been wrong. Her rapist was back. He'd burst through the door just as Auger had switched views. He'd missed him. But how had he got in? From what Sherry had told him, you could have walked through the wall more easily than penetrate her locked door.

Back to the main room, and it was still empty except for a few dissipating threads of wispy smoke, but this time it was empty for a different reason, he knew. The man was already through it, probably heading into the short corridor leading to Sherry's bedroom.

The bedroom screen came up before he'd got through the swift key sequence to take him there. Sherry overriding him, he realised. She was staring up at him, at the cam that was now his eye. She was naked, sitting cross-legged on the mattress and cradling a squat grey gun in her arms. And there was a hard grin shining on her face.

'He's here, Auger, isn't he?' Her voice was tiny and distant, but he could almost feel the satisfaction in it. 'At last. He couldn't resist it. I knew he couldn't. I knew he'd come in the end. All this time I've been waiting, and now he's here.'

'Sherry—' That was why he'd got in, he realised. She'd left a chink of light for her rapist. She'd channelled him through to her. All those years of paranoia, of living a dead life, she had not just been hiding away, she'd also been her own bait.

'I've disabled the inbound commslink, Auger,' she went on. 'I can't hear you. I don't want your help. Sorry, but he's mine. I don't want to see him until he's dead. This is for me alone. You can just watch. Keep me a record.' She was running her hands along the gun's flank, checking the powerslide, thumbing the selector. Happy with it, she slung the gun over her shoulder and let it swing by the broad leather strap, leaving her hands free.

He was wondering where the gun had come from as Sherry leant over the bed and reached beneath it to bring out something more, a chubby single-barrelled device with a ribbed nose that flared to a fat lens at its end. It looked like a compressed torch. She unwound a set of slim goggles from the barrel of the device and settled them tight over her eyes. The convex eyeshades were searing white ovals, brilliantly reflective. They flooded the light-craving sensors of the cam. As she moved, her eyes left twin trails burning on Auger's screen.

Under the bed. She'd never told him any of this. She had never really trusted him after all. Even if he wasn't *the* man, it was enough that he was a man. She was only talking to him now, he guessed, out of the cold logic that if he was here, he couldn't be there.

He went to the cam in the corridor outside her bedroom and froze, his fingers locked on the keys.

There were two of them. Two, not the one man she was expecting. And not simple rapists either, from the weaponry they were carrying. In the enhanced dimness of the corridor Auger recognised sharplights and the concertinaed diffuser pump of an oxygen depleter. They were wearing full-face gas masks, and they were uniformed in black.

Auger watched them lay out their equipment methodically on the threadbare brown carpet by her bedroom door. These weren't rapists, and they weren't burglars either. They knew exactly what they were doing. They hadn't gone for the stuff in her living area, they were going straight for her bedroom, for Sherry herself. Auger wanted to shout at her. He stood up, then sat down again. It would take him at least half an hour to get there. There was nothing he could do. He couldn't help her. He wondered whether to call the 'fists, but she'd made him promise never to do that. Never, no matter what. The 'fists were men, like Auger.

One of the intruders was retreating to the kitchen now, and Auger hesitated with the choice before deciding to follow him.

The man went to Sherry's aircon system centre and ran his gloved fingers over the console, punched a few keys, waited until the on-light nilled, nodded to himself and started back to his partner. Then he stopped abruptly and made a detour to Sherry's laboratory. He ignored the technical equipment and instead spent a moment examining the comms unit there.

Auger frowned. Odd thing to do, with everything else there to catch his eye. Why a straightforward comms unit?

GenMed. That was Sherry's dedicated line to GenMed.

Oh, shit, Auger thought, feeling ice in his gut.

The man returned to the main room and inspected the primary comms unit, the unit through which Auger was patched in.

Auger leaned away from the screen and held his breath. The man's masked face filled the screen, his eyes hooded grey shadows beneath the plastic and metal mask. Auger could hear the man's filtered, measured breath. It was almost as though he was staring straight at Auger and past him, taking in Auger's room, the shelves of books around him, the pictures on his wall, the smallness of his life.

Auger wanted to duck down, even though his head told him the man was staring at no more than a blank screen, but he couldn't move. He waited for the man to realise the unit was active and nil it, but instead he patted the top of the screen, pulled himself up sharply, turned away and headed back towards his partner, who was kneeling and fiddling with the lock on Sherry's bedroom door. Auger was left with the uncomfortable feeling that the man knew that someone – maybe Auger – was there, and it didn't matter a jot.

Auger returned to Sherry, trying to shake a feeling of increasing dread. She was standing on the bed, motionless and staring up at her aircon grille. Her burning eyes in the wraparound goggles made something unearthly of her. She jerked her head, leaving twin swirls of white flame on Auger's screen. The hairs began to stiffen on the back of his neck and he rubbed at them with a hand, knowing suddenly what was about to happen.

Outside, one of the men was directing a sharplight at the door's lock. The jet of light punched into the lock, and the man nilled the beam instantly and passed the sharplight to the other man. He set the thin delivery shaft of the depleter against the hole in its place, then paused and glanced at his partner.

Auger switched quickly back inside the bedroom. Sherry was at the door, looking down at the lock. She must have seen the sharplight penetrate it. A faint violet field was seeping through the punctured lock and dispersing into the room. Almost instantly Sherry's head started to drop, but holding the squat-barrelled device in one hand, levelled at the lock, she took a grip on the doorhandle and yanked the door wide.

The kneeling man holding the oxygen depleter involuntarily jerked his head up and looked straight at her, then reflexively stared into the eye of the torch pointed directly at him.

The screen whined, went to bright white and cut out. Auger winced, blinking. A lightning image of his room was imprinted on his retina. It faded slowly. He looked around, almost dazed, at the room in darkness. It seemed unfamiliar with its cupboards, its shelves, the remains of the meal he'd half eaten before falling into bed half a life ago.

His sight began to return. There was nothing on the screen but a faint pink nimbus. Auger could only wait as the picture slowly came back, and the sound. Five seconds, perhaps.

The first man was down and screaming, hands to his goggled face, and Auger guessed that the blinder had cauterised his retinas. His goggles would have been worse than useless. They were light-enhancers, and he had been staring with them directly at the blinder, exactly as Sherry had intended.

But Sherry had not expected a second man. She hadn't even seen him. She was on her knees, gasping for breath in the partially depleted air. The blinded man had dropped the depleter and it was still maxed, its nozzle flailing and spreading its violet blur into the air.

Sherry crawled towards the device and managed to pin it down and nil it. The bloom of colour wilted and failed. The blinded man was still screaming and tearing at his mask, but the webbing of it was holding it in place, and it seemed to Auger as if he was trying to tear his own face away. Sherry got to her knees, swung the grey gun from around her back and used its wide barrel to force the man's head to the floor and held it there for a moment, the barrel at his temple, waiting just long enough for the man to realise what was happening and go abruptly silent.

'I knew you'd come back. Are you going to beg, like I did?' she asked him. Her voice was flat and void.

He made a single sharp movement that may have been a response and may have been an attempt to shrug the gun barrel away, but he made no sound.

'It wouldn't make a difference if you did,' she told him. Her voice was calm and so steady that Auger sensed it was on the edge of disintegration. 'Not to me, not to you.' She leant on the stock of the gun and twisted it, screwing the barrel into his temple. A tiny noise came from him, now. It was not a sound Auger had ever heard come from a man's mouth before. It seemed to come from far, far away. It made Auger shudder.

'I've waited a long time for this,' Sherry said. 'Since we first met, I've spent my life waiting for you. I've wondered what you looked like. Now I don't care.'

She bore down on the gun. Her knuckles were white with the pressure and her fury. Auger could see the gun begin to sink into the man's skull. He made a choking sound now and brought blood from his mouth and nose and the rims of his eyes. He was starting to jerk and seize as Sherry sighed and blew his head through the floor.

And then in the echo and wreckage she laid herself down like a child and began to cry, not even aware of the other man who was kneeling and shaking his head groggily a few yards from her. The man had been shielded from the direct line of the blinder by his partner, Auger realised, but he must still have been secondarily affected by the flare. Sherry was sobbing and still woozy from the effects of the oxygen depleter, and wearing the blinder shield over her eyes, and deafened by her gun, and expecting nothing more.

For a second Auger was unable to look at the screen, and he glanced at his clock, at the elapsed time. Twenty minutes. Maybe he should have run, tried to get there in time. Maybe he still should. Maybe she could hold the other one off that long, if she realised he was there before he recovered.

And then, abruptly, Sherry looked up and saw him. He must have made a sound. She drew in her knees, raised her head and looked at him.

Time started again. Auger stared down at the two of them like God. Like a helpless God. Sherry's goggled eyes were lakes of blazing fire as she pulled up the smoking grey gun and hauled it round to take aim at the man only a metre away from her, but he was lunging forward as she fired and the jolt passed over him and cracked the wall. He knocked her over and landed beyond her, rolling to a crouch. She pulled the gun up again and fired, but he had moved already this time and she was on her back and he had her chin tipped back and from somewhere a knife that he was holding at her throat spread taut as cord.

Her eyes were pointed directly at Auger, and he could hardly look at their searing brightness as the knife moved and Sherry jerked beneath the man in a long, long spasm and finally was still. Only her blood came and came, a scarf, a shawl, a shroud.

The man stood off her and stumbled to the main room, and Auger followed him without knowing any more what he was doing. Call it in now, he was thinking. Call the 'fists like you should have done straight off. Sherry won't mind now.

But he couldn't do it, couldn't move.

There was a movement at the broken doorway, and the man who had killed Sherry glanced up from the comms console where he was standing.

Back-up, Auger thought dully. The job had taken too long and they'd sent back-up.

But the killer didn't react like he was expecting back-up. He crouched and retreated to the shadows of the room's far corner, the glint of a small gun quickly sparkling in his hand and immediately hooded by the palm of the other.

Auger went to the corridor cam and saw a new man there, backed flat against the wall. The man yelled, 'I'm armed and aimed. Drop your weapons. Come out slowly.'

He wasn't a 'fist, Auger saw. Not by what he was wearing, a crumpled and faded blue shirt and trousers and a whole-head filter so old the face rubber was pitted and etched. And the gun he was holding, a bulky old model that looked like it was built of plastic and steel. And the 'fists would have sent metal, not flesh, a pair of duty trigs at least. Auger shook his head in despair at the screen. The man was a vigilante, awoken by the noise, his courage eventually got up enough to come along too late and get himself killed.

But braver than himself, Auger thought. Still, the vigilante would be killed, Auger had no doubt. The man inside Sherry's apartment was a professional.

The vigilante coughed inside his filter. He was breathing as if he'd been running hard, which would explain why he was wearing the filter, if he'd come from outside the building. Maybe he had. Maybe he'd heard the thing from across the street.

Inside the room the killer cupped a hand at his mouth. 'Don't shoot me. I'm coming out. I have no weapon. I live here. They robbed us, they killed my wife and ran.' The man was trying to put terror into his voice, but it was still coming out steady. 'I'm coming out, okay?'

Auger went inside. The killer was on his feet, holding both hands high, but with the backs of his hands forward. Auger could see the tiny gun hugged into the palm of his right hand so that he could still splay his fingers like those of the empty hand. He was staying in shadow and coming slowly out of the dark of the apartment. To the vigilante he would appear unarmed, scared and harmless.

The vigilante stepped back as the killer emerged and stood in the doorway, motionless. He squinted at the vigilante, his knees sagging in a mime of exhaustion.

The vigilante made a gesture with his gun.

'Okay, right. Don't shoot me. I'm dropping my arms now. Dropping them wide, see? Very slowly.' The killer's voice was even and hypnotic. 'See? Very slowly.' He was lowering his arms outwards in two wide arcs, shaking the empty hand now as if in cramp, wincing and smiling, drawing the vigilante's attention to the empty hand as he flicked the gun in his other hand into a shooting grip and pulled it smoothly round to fire at the vigilante an instant too late. The gun's charge dug a chunk out of the ceiling as the killer's head whipped back and took the rest of him down. A thin thread of blood swept through the air and drew a slick red curl on the wall behind him as he fell.

The vigilante stepped over him and went into the room, went through it and made for Sherry's bedroom. He found her body and knelt beside it for a moment, removing the goggles and touching her eyes gently closed.

He knows her, Auger thought.

The vigilante went to the main room again and stopped at the comms console, just as the killer had. He pulled a lighter from his pocket, twisted a scrap of paper from the desk into a taper and threw some more of Sherry's files onto the table around the unit, then went to her laboratory and came out with a flask of liquid. He poured it onto the desk, withdrew to the apartment's doorway and threw the flaming taper on to the table.

Auger cut to the corridor cam as the vigilante moved away down it, but didn't see any more because his screen greyed out as the comms from Sherry's unit burnt out and were obliterated.

He sat there, staring in the darkness at his dead screen. Sherry's comms unit. They'd killed Sherry and they were following through. They'd killed her because she'd been asking about the GenMed deaths, and if the vigilante hadn't done what he'd done, they'd have used her main comms unit to trace back to Auger.

The vigilante had known that. They'd have traced back to him, too, then. He was protecting himself.

That shot, taking out the killer like that.

Not just a vigilante.

And if he knew Sherry, maybe he knew about Auger.

Astrid went to the desk clerk and made an apologetic face at him. 'I'm sorry, but is there a toilet down here? I'm due on the fourth floor and I don't think I can make it.'

The clerk opened his face into a grin and chuckled at her. 'You medics. Running everywhere, got time for nothing. If the world's going to end, why rush even faster?' He shook his head. 'Slow down. People are going to die anyway, we all are. Down the hall, beyond the elevators.' He pointed an arm for her to follow.

'Thanks.' Bending forward a little and moving in a stuttering gait, Astrid followed his directions, glancing back at him at the turn of the corridor. He was twisted round in his chair, grinning and waving her on.

Out of his sight and straightening up again, she passed the toilets and found the emergency stairs, taking them two at a time. Her feet boomed faintly on the metal steps, but the whole building was founded on visgel and the damping effect of it mostly cloaked her ascent.

She skipped the first floor, ducking past the viewing panel of the door, and carried on up. At the next level she looked openly through the glass, filling its frame with her face so that if she was seen, she would not be identified as spying.

There was no one there, only a row of beds and a partition wall beyond them. It was simply a ward. No research equipment, no researchers.

She pushed the door open and let it swing gently closed behind her. An aromatic hospital warmth instantly assaulted her, a warmth scented with sterile soap scrubs and rubber. She stepped forward into it, reassured by the familiarity of it.

The beds were occupied by pregnant women. She almost laughed at the ordinariness. It was a gynaecological ward, nothing more. It made no sense, though. Why such a thing here, hidden away in the research wing? It wasn't as if GenMed was short of space.

Going forward, her feet soft and silent on the rubber floor, she saw that all the women were asleep, in the ward's warmth their swollen bellies exposed and quivering with the easy, peaceful tides of inhalation and expiration.

Astrid stopped beside the nearest woman. She smiled to herself, feeling like putting the palm of a hand to the woman's balloon-taut skin with its cargo of trembling life, and then realised with a shock that the woman wasn't asleep at all. Not breathing like that, so evenly, not slumbering quite so motionlessly. And now she noticed the drip feeding into her wrist, the tube into her other wrist that wasn't a drip, and the rack of monitors and column of steady-feed fluid pumps stationed at the head of the bed.

This was life support. The woman had to be in a coma.

Astrid looked up, looked around.

All the women. But that was ridiculous, unlikely to the point of impossibility, so many of them. Astrid counted the beds, twenty-five of them, each with an unmoving mother-to-be, and each woman identically tubed and wired.

An ultrasound scanner sat on the bedside cabinet. Astrid pulled examination gloves from a box and swiped a finger through a dish of gel, gelled the soft, convex head of the probe and activated the screen, then rested the probe gently on to the woman's belly and looked at the screen. It took her a moment to get her bearings, moving the probe's head over the smooth dune of tight skin with its umbilical dimple. The screen was a wasteland of rutted and stippled grey revealing hints of craters and mounds that Astrid couldn't quite fix upon. It struck her, as she guided the probe over the woman's stomach, that she could have been examining a recon vid from another planet. She knew the stories, knew about all the hopeless missions there had been to find a planet of refuge before Dirangesept was finally discovered. She had seen the vids of barren worlds. She knew what the discovery of Dirangesept had meant, and its two failures of colonisation.

She continued moving the probe, searching the landscape. Something's moving in there, she thought. Where are you?

Everyone knew there was no real hope of taking Dirangesept. Maybe the new generation of autoids were better, but autoids weren't going to take that world from the beasts whose planet it was. It would need something more, but despite all the research, no one had come up with a thing.

The probe swept to and fro on its film of gel, and still there was just a rippling grey desert on the screen. 'You're in there, little one, I know you are,' she murmured aloud. 'Don't be frightened.'

Nevertheless, D3 had to go. There was no alternative. The ship is on fire and sinking, and you're standing at the rail watching the last lifeboat sink. What do you do? You still jump. You jump into the dark, cold sea because it was still a better bet than the sinking, blazing ship.

She stopped the probe, her breath catching at the sight. There. She twisted her wrist a fraction, adjusting the image. A tiny white spine rippled in and out of focus, so bright it was almost luminescent. She tried to chase it down the belly's curve, to follow the spine's flex and locate the head, but the scanner's head was rousing the foetus, and it was moving away from her. She tacked the lubricated reader patiently to and fro across the rise and fall of its mother's stomach, and found herself murmuring, 'Don't worry, little one. I'm not going to hurt you.'

On the screen, cross-sections of tiny limbs shifted like heavy bubbles as the baby stirred. The image resembled an archaeological dig now, the hard tissues reminding her of packed earth. Everything was hard black, moon white or a shade of grey, as if what she saw was as much separated from her by centuries of time as by a few centimetres of tissue.

As she continued to scan, trying to build a solid picture in her head from the bi-dimensional trawl, she realised that the proportions of the baby seemed not quite right. It was a third-trimester foetus, and big, too. It had to be nearly at term.

She flicked on the foetal blood flow monitor, and the accompanying audio came on with whooshings and blowings and rolling thunder. The sudden noise in the silent ward made her start. She nilled the audio quickly and for the first time since she had sat down at the woman's side she glanced around. There was still no one in the ward.

The scrolling readout of the foetal blood flow came up, shark's teeth in a snowstorm. Nothing wrong there. She continued to scan for a few moments, then sat back in the hard chair.

It was the skull. Changing the screen, Astrid froze the picture at the broadest cross-section of the skull and took a head diameter, then checked it against the limb lengths.

The skull was oversize, not only relative to the limbs and the rest of the body, but in absolute terms for a foetus. She stared at the image, thinking. Hydrocephalus? No, the shape of the skull seemed normal, and the texture was like dense earth. No fluid there. It was simply a huge skull. A skull encasing a huge brain.

A nearby sound startled her, and she jerked the probe from the woman's belly. The gel made a small sharp tut of protest at the seal yielding. Astrid quickly nilled the monitor. She tore a length of paper wipe from the wall dispenser, cleaned the gel from the probe and replaced it, and went towards the partition at the end of the ward where the sound had come from. It had been like a whimper, a baby's sleeping sound. She walked rapidly because she knew that she wouldn't make it if she stopped to think.

There were about twenty of them. Twenty babies. Astrid halted in the doorway and whispered to herself, 'No. No,' as if by saying it she could make it not so.

They were in cribs and cots, and some of the older babies on the floor too, playing, sitting, crawling. Every one of the infants out of the cots had a slender metal armature around its baby-bald skull, the armature attached to a complex drawstring of cables in an orthopaedic rig taking the weight of the head. Astrid had never seen anything like it. Each skull-supporting rig was fixed at the apex of a spindly cage rolling on the floor, moving with the baby, remaining just out of reach of its chubby hands.

Astrid put a shaking hand against the wall and stared. The babies could move quite freely, taking their cages with them, but the devices brought them to a halt before they could touch a wall or another child. The restriction, even the presence of the cages, didn't seem to bother them at all. They were apparently quite accustomed to it.

'Oh, hallo. I didn't hear you come in.'

A woman in the corner, a nurse, Astrid saw. She was changing a nappy for one of the babies. It lay there flat on a changing mat, its head so uncomfortably raised that it might have been on a pillow, but that was simply the size of its skull.

'It's a real nuisance, this,' the nurse said. 'The whole thing needs redesigning, but no one takes any notice of what I say. It takes five minutes getting it off and twice as long getting it back on again. And that's without doing the nappy in between.'

Astrid watched her struggling with the rig, reattaching the net to the cage before awkwardly threading her arms between the struts to lift the baby from the mat and setting it back on the floor. Astrid realised the nurse assumed she was on the research staff.

On the floor, one of the babies noticed Astrid and pushed itself to its knees, the rig's legs telescoping, rearing smoothly with it. The baby turned away again, abruptly uninterested in her, and she saw more of the armature, a sculpted vertebral column that traced the child's own all the way down to the sacrum, where it vanished beneath a large white nappy.

She noticed something else now, now that she had taken the most obvious in. To varying degrees, every single infant had poor skin, mottled with sores and scars.

'It's well enough signposted, isn't it, Astrid?'

'What?' Astrid turned round to see Rox smiling at her. It looked an easy smile, but her hands pushed down into her pockets were little fists.

'The toilet. Or did Jasper mishear you at the desk?'

Astrid shook her head. Words wouldn't come.

Rox made a gesture to the nurse, who was looking from Rox to Astrid and realising she'd made a mistake. 'Give us a moment, would you, Maylee?'

The nurse nodded quickly and scuttled from the room as Rox glanced at a clock on the wall. It seemed incongruous to Astrid, up there with its straightforward hands and ordinary numbers, its reminders of the day that existed outside these rooms.

'We have a few minutes before you're due upstairs. All right, then. You're just curious. This is one of my projects. What would you like to know?'

Astrid found she had no questions, or rather no thoughts she could filter down into questions. 'The mothers,' she said, trying to take her mind from the babies who couldn't touch each other, couldn't be hugged, couldn't take milk from the breast. 'The mothers,' she repeated, thinking only how they must feel, or would feel if they could feel anything, to see what had become of their babies.

'Good question. Of course they aren't anaesthetised, we can't risk foetal drug transfer. They're not comatose either, at least not in the conventional sense of that.' Rox half smiled. 'Ironically, it was Jay Auger through whom we developed the technique. She was self-treating with neurologically functioning nangines.'

'Why?' She asked the question numbly into Rox's pause, just to fill the silence, but she was aware that Rox was divulging something to her.

'It was part of the Dirangesept research here. Unfortunately it seems that the shock of the explosion at her wedding disrupted her nangines, and they went somewhat out of control, closing off certain pathways and introducing some rather annoying loops. It set us back considerably.' She shook her head, then brightened again. 'Still, to every cloud a silver lining. As a result of that, we were able to develop a nangine protocol to produce consciousness modification without the need for conventional drugs.' Rox smiled benevolently, steering Astrid to the doorway from which they surveyed the motionless mothers-to-be. 'So our subjects, or more precisely the mothers of our subjects, need not suffer the discomforts of their pregnancies.'

The numbness was beginning to wear off, and Astrid was feeling cold and slightly faint. She touched her forehead and felt a rime of sweat there. 'The babies,' she said.

'Yes. Our subjects.' Rox glanced at the time again, and turned back to the nursery. 'The brain, Astrid. The brain, the human brain.' The children crawled and played, each isolated in its supporting cage.

247

'Brain function. Neurones are important, certainly, but more important are the synapses, the connections between the neurones. We're born with fifteen thousand million neurones. That's a big number, but the number of possible connections between them . . .' She sighed, thinking of it, as Astrid stared in heartache at the infants.

'That number,' Rox went on, 'is greater than the number of atoms that exist in the entire universe. With neuronangines we can start to explore those connections, start to document them as years ago we explored and documented the human genome.'

On the floor a couple of crawling babies approached each other, but their cages fended them apart. Unconcerned, one of the babies stopped and sat up while the other changed direction and manoeuvred the wheels of its cage around a stuffed bear until it was able to pick the bear up and cuddle it. Another baby came towards Rox, who put out a foot against its cage and gently redirected it back into the room.

'We're aiming further than that, though,' she said, her eyes on the baby. 'To get our complement of fifteen thousand million nerve cells requires thirty-three divisions of the first cell.' A new tone entered her voice. 'Here, we're extending that. We've managed to trigger an extra division.' She frowned, nodded her head at the room. 'Skull size increases, as you can see, but not, in fact, by as much as we'd anticipated. To an extent, the cells simply compress further. All the births are Caesarean, naturally.'

Astrid murmured, 'Naturally.'

Rox didn't notice the irony, carried away with her project. 'One tiny problem is that the development of the brain takes place in the first trimester, which is the same time as, for instance, the growth of the skin and the liver. The mothers can't seem to compensate the foetus for its brain's energy requirements at this time, unfortunately.'

Astrid watched one of the babies rub at a weeping sore on its cheek. 'Where do you get your subjects?' She saw puzzlement on Rox's face. 'The mothers, I mean. Where do you get them? Do they have any idea what you're doing?'

'They come in for abortions. There are enough of them wanting that these days, God knows.' She made a moue of delicate distaste. 'They are relinquishing their babies. They sign to that effect.'

'They—' Astrid saw that she was pursuing the wrong approach with Rox. 'They lose months of their lives. A Caesarean scar. How do you explain that to them?'

'No scar, Astrid,' Rox chided. 'You should know that. And the time?

Well, what with the months of treatment for post-operative compli-cations, they should be happy that we waive their charges. It really isn't a problem. And anyway . . .'

She stopped herself there. Astrid wondered what she'd been going to say, but Rox took her arm to guide her towards the elevator, back through the room of pregnant women. Astrid wanted to shout at them, wake them up, yell at them to flee, but it was too late for that, too late for anything. It was probably too late for herself too, it struck her. Rox wasn't one to share her secrets anyway, and this was a secret to be stored deeper than most, even in a world going as sour as this one was.

Astrid made to resist, but Rox took her arm in a grip stronger than she expected, and pulled her on.

'Why?' Astrid asked her. 'You haven't told me why you're doing this. This isn't pure research. This is directed, isn't it? What is it for?'

They were at the lift. Without relaxing her grip on Astrid's arm, Rox pointed at the clock. 'It's for victory, Astrid. We're late for your project now. You've spent too much time in the toilet already.'

She touched the sensor and the door to the lift slid open. Two men stood there waiting for them.

'Chaperones?' Astrid said.

'No. Guards. I'm afraid the time of trust is gone, Astrid.'

TWENTY-THREE

Auger didn't recognise the tall man with skin like a long-ago chemical burn. There was something familiar about him, though. He thought for a moment that the man was looking for a Leaving. There was a look of almost apathetic despair about him.

'Come in,' he said, stacking the morning's pile of Understands. It seemed everyone was after a Leaving now. Since the announcement of the CrySis ships bound for a bLinkered heaven, Doctor McCrae had suddenly gone from being a two-bit preacher to God's second son. There were ninety thousand applications already, and this was less than a week after the announcement. All the other death cults had lost their eager suicides to McCrae.

The man stood beside the chair Auger pointed him towards and said, 'Are you Auger? I've been looking for you.'

He seemed naggingly familiar to Auger, who indicated the chair again, and this time the man sat down heavily and said, 'I've been trying to find you. I didn't want to use the comms.'

'You want to register for a Leaving?' Auger picked up the glossy brochure that looked like a come-on for a weekend holiday. Vinz's idea, or perhaps McCrae's.

Leavings – Your Life In Your Hands.

'No. I'm a friend of Astrid Remarque. My name's Troy Gordo.'

A medic. He was a medic. Auger must have seen him at GenMed. That was it. Maybe somewhere else, too. His eyes were astonishingly piercing.

'What can I do for you?' Auger was thinking, A friend of hers? What sort of friend? He took a breath, identifying the thudding of his heart with surprise as jealousy. Had Gordo come here to confront Auger? This was crazy. How could Auger be jealous?

Gordo wandered across the room and stopped at the cabinet on the wall. He clicked the glass with a fingernail. He was nervous, not wanting to look at Auger.

'They're called vehicles,' Auger said, when Gordo stayed silent. 'Easy ways out.' He watched Gordo realise it, his face reflected in the glass, but his pitted face was impossible to read. A slight narrowing of the eyes perhaps. Sometimes people would sign their Understands and then go to the cabinet and just look for a few minutes. Auger would gently say to them, 'The Understand isn't a contract. You can leave it here and go back out the same door now, if you like.' They hardly ever did, though.

'Vehicles,' Gordo repeated.

'Suicide pills of one form or another. Neurotoxins, whatever.' Vials, cartridges for injection, capsules, PowerBursTrodes, boltguns. Shelves of them. He noticed some joker had scrawled something at the top of the cabinet. *In case of emergency break glass.*

Gordo put his back to the cabinet and faced Auger, though his eyes looked away. 'There was a report posted at GenMed yesterday.' His voice was abruptly muted. 'I wondered if you'd heard.'

'No. What?' Auger's fist opened and closed again. This wasn't a confrontation. It was far worse than that. It was far worse than anything. He knew what Gordo had come here to say.

Gordo still wouldn't look at him. 'The report was just a routine notification of a malfunction of life-support machinery. Just a registration for insurance purposes. No one died. But it was in the research wing.'

'No one died?'

Gordo nodded. 'Astrid.' His face was set in that emotionally leached expression medics used, Auger saw, that offered neither hope nor sympathy. It embraced both survival and death, and cared about none of them. God-damned medics.

But Auger came forward out of his chair and smacked the flat of his hand on the table, taking pleasure in knocking that look from Gordo's face with the sound. It was all right. She wasn't dead. She was alive. The stack of Understands slid to the floor and spread into a muddle of paper. Auger's heart thumped. Astrid hadn't answered the message he'd left for her two days ago. She'd told him her duties were often rotated without warning, and she could be on call for days, so he'd left it, persuading himself not to worry. And now this.

'She isn't dead,' Auger said, making himself relax as he worked it out. She could have been dead, but she wasn't. GenMed was obliged to file a report anyway, though, if the equipment was connected with life support. Like Gordo had said, it was just a legal requirement.

'That's right. But she's in a coma.' Gordo paused. 'Maybe a PVS.' He looked at Auger, waiting to see if Auger needed it interpreted.

Bloody, bloody medics, Auger thought, staring back at Gordo. 'Persistent vegetative state,' he said. 'I know what a PVS is.'

Gordo's expression didn't change. He looked around the room again, searching for something to focus on that wasn't Auger's face of accusation.

Auger followed his gaze. 'The graph shows application rates for Leavings. The recent steep climb reflects active interest in McCrae's heavenbound armada. Fascinating, isn't it?' He waited. Gordo stared stupidly at the curve. 'Well?'

'The research. I didn't tell her the whole thing.'

There *was* something about him that was familiar, Auger knew. He'd seen him before.

'I originally told her the research wing isn't connected to the society I run, the TNM society, but it is. Rox – Dr Carroll – is behind TNM. I get her her guinea pigs.'

'And she gives you?'

Gordo touched a finger to his rutted cheek. 'I have a skin disease. It's untreatable. She said her research could provide a cure.'

'Her research?' Auger felt himself running low on patience. 'What research is that? The same research that put Astrid in a PVS?'

'Calm down, Auger. I'm telling you. Just listen. It's nangine research. Neurological nangines operated in tandem with peripheral nangines.'

Auger didn't trust himself to speak. He sat back, waiting.

Gordo wouldn't look at him. He said, 'Rox injects them intravenously, then guides them to their sites of operation. BLinkers provide control via biofeedback. The neurological nangines control local nangines.'

'Your trick,' Auger said. He remembered Astrid telling him about it. He remembered her voice, the wonder in it. He remembered her mouth, her lips. The memory of her was suddenly an ache in him.

'Yes. Rox wouldn't call it a trick. It was a huge breakthrough at the time.' Gordo rummaged in his pocket and brought out a small vial with a pushJect cap, and laid it on the table. 'This is it,' he said. He put it to his arm, miming. 'I just stab it into my arm, simple as that, just before a meeting. The nangines disperse and get taken up by their receptors. With the bLinkers I can localise it and reverse it. And afterwards, I drain the nangines.'

'Go on.'

'There's a rare, crippling disease called FOP. Fibrodysplasia ossificans progressiva. The connective tissue, the stuff that covers muscle, simply turns into bone. Slowly, progressively, the sufferer seizes up. They might as well be encased in rock. Living statues.'

Auger stared at the little vial on the table. It could have been one of the vehicles in the cabinet on the wall.

'FOP is caused by the inadvertent triggering of a single specific connective tissue protein that creates bone out of soft tissue. The nangines in this vial are specific to that.' He squeezed his arm, as if reassuring himself. 'It's claustrophobic, though, even when it's just your arm.' He closed his eyes, shivered. 'It's risky. Without the central nangines and the bLinkers, everything peripheral would turn to bone.'

'Get on with it.' There was bad coming, Auger knew, and he didn't like Troy Gordo pushing him for sympathy.

'She told me she could reverse this.' He touched his face, fingered the blemishes and flaws of his skin. 'It doesn't last, yet. There's an inertia. But soon it will last.'

'This was the purpose of the research?'

'No. This was a side product.'

Gordo was looking around the room again.

'Vehicles. Graphs. Understands. Me.' Auger tried to control his voice. 'There isn't anything else in the room, Gordo, except the door. That's all there is. It's a place for people to sign their lives away. What was the purpose of the research?'

'The research was to do with Dirangesept. The nangines are designed to patrol the brain and prevent the beasts from infecting it.'

'Astrid didn't know that.'

'It was a research project. Research projects are sensitive. Volunteers don't get to know.'

'She didn't know they were sending nangines into her brain.'

Troy shrugged. 'I'm doing it.'

'Not the same nangines, Gordo.'

'Rox said it was safe.'

'Safe? You must have known about Haenson and Merchant. What did you think about that?'

'She said they were accidents. There was nothing that could be done. The research was too important to be interrupted.'

Auger slumped in his chair. Haenson and Merchant had been exsanguinated to withdraw the nangines from the corpses. GenMed had killed Sherry because she had accessed the pathology reports. They would have got to Auger too, if it hadn't been for the vigilante.

Troy spread his hands and stared at his palms. 'Before she went to the wing, Astrid came to me about Jay. She'd seen Jay.'

Auger nodded. He rolled Gordo's vial under the palm of his hand. The glass grated on the surface of the table. Auger picked it up. So light. The liquid seemed quite clear. The stab-point under the glass blister looked quite innocent. He closed it gently in his hand.

'I helped her access some files. Astrid wanted to go straight to you with what we found, but I persuaded her to see Rox first, to do her guinea pig stuff. But she never came out again.'

'What did you find, Gordo?'

Gordo started to search the walls again. Dirty, pale green walls. 'We found that your wife was pregnant.'

A silence, tiny at first.

Then, 'No,' Auger said flatly. 'She would have told me.'

'She may not have known. It may have been early. Is that possible?'

The night before. The week before. Every night of that week. He remembered, sinking his head into his hands, and said, 'Yes, it is.'

Gordo was staring at the door now, as if wishing himself through it.

'Did she have the child?'

The question seemed to startle Gordo. 'I don't know. We didn't find out.'

The dirty walls of the small room seemed to be closing in on Auger and tilting. A child. He looked at the cabinet of vehicles and felt faintly nauseous. *In case of emergency break glass.* He moved his head, trying to tip everything straight again. Gordo was looking at him strangely, and it was that distantly appraising medic's look on his face that snapped Auger back.

He took a moment, then looked up at the medic. 'Did you go into Rudd Merchant's room when I was there?'

'What?'

Gordo's face told Auger the surprise was real. It hadn't been him.

Auger picked up the bLinkers and put them down again. Cathar. Maybe Astrid was in there, and maybe she wasn't. He'd heard of bLinkered people going into comas, but they'd been fucked up anyway, or used fucked-up software.

And Jay pregnant, maybe a child, too. His child. But try not to think about that now. He tried to think of Jay, but found there was nothing there.

He picked up the bLinkers again, fingering the little bump that was the passport, thinking of Fly. He held the bLinkers towards his eyes and watched the tendrils squirm anxiously. Like worms, he thought. Like graveyard worms.

Madsen would have known if it was safe. Auger thought about him, tried to remember everything he had heard about the man. He had made mistakes, Madsen, but he knew all about Cathar.

But Madsen had to be dead. Everyone said so, said Madsen had to be dead. Auger thought about that. And he thought that no one said Madsen *was* dead.

TWENTY-FOUR

'I'll see you later,' Auger told Lethe, pushing away what was left of his breakfast. He noticed she was wearing a new shirt. It made her look clean and young. Like camouflage, he thought.

She made a little moue of her lips, and said, 'Where are you going?'

'To see someone.' He wasn't sure why he was even telling her that, but it felt good to have someone to tell other than the gecko on the wall.

And somehow the unmoving lizard reminded him of Astrid now. He was pretty sure they wouldn't terminate her, at least not too soon. Not like Haenson and Merchant. They were being cautious, notifying about the supposed malfunction. They weren't taking any more risks right now.

'I'll come with you.'

'No. If anyone comes—' He stopped. Maybe it wasn't such a good idea to leave her here alone. They might make some connections and come for Auger, and find her. 'Okay. But I'm not your father, Lethe.'

'That's good. I'd probably have killed you by now. Or you me.'

He couldn't tell if she was joking.

Renting the copter for the day cost Auger more than he wanted to spend, but in the end he had no choice. He asked for a 'flite but found he couldn't even sit at the controls of the machine. The last time he'd done that had been his wedding day. This time he looked across at the rental guy's wide What-a-deal! grin in the passenger seat and had seen only Jay's hysteria, heard her screams in his ears like yesterday, and pushed the stick away like it was live. Lethe looked at the rental guy and said, 'My dad. Claustrophobia.'

It took him the first half-hour of the flight to get thoroughly used to the big machine's controls. The concentration he needed to fly this thing helped, though, calmed him down, and Lethe was good too, talking constantly, taking his thoughts away.

They took a detour towards East Anglia, Lethe saying she was curious about the Cultivation Net, and headed for its wall of glimmering light rising into the day's grey sky. A few kilometres away from it, the proximity-triggered warning nearly deafened them, beating into the skin of the cockpit.

'This is a secure facility. Anti-terrorist air defence missiles are now locked on to you. Turn around now. There will be no further warning. Missiles set to launch in ten seconds. Nine seconds . . .'

Below and ahead, and closing, the Netted fields gleamed green and rich and stretched away towards the sea. They seemed as if they could feed the world.

'Six seconds. Five . . .'

Lethe was grinning, but abruptly leant forward and said, 'Hey!'

'Two . . .'

Auger rolled the copter away from the Net and headed on, checking and double-checking the charts. It had been a long time since he had seen Arti.

After half an hour of silence, leaning back into her seat, Lethe said, 'Did you see that?'

'The Net? It's quite something.'

'Just as you turned tail. You must have hit an angle. I saw it.'

'What?'

'The Net. It's just a narrow strip. The rest, going back, it's just a holo. It's fake.'

'Uh-huh.' Auger shrugged. 'You're surprised?'

They rose into Cumbria and Auger let the copter's autopilot take over, becoming a passenger and staring down with Lethe through the bubble of glass.

Up here, the ash was thin and the air was almost clear. It was as glorious as Auger remembered. The great sprawling hillsides were still largely cloaked in forest. Black rock blistered the slopes, and the lakes were bright and sinuous. Fires had thinned out the trees since he had last been here, and much of the green had gone to brown, but the upsetting of the environment here seemed an act of benevolent nature.

Watching it pass beneath him, Auger felt almost renewed. Here, it was still magnificent. It was primeval, a place where life was about to begin and not to end. Even the rifts seemed muted, unable to cut their swathes through the thick armour of the mountains. They had no scale. They expended their energy in reaching the surface, then gave up and simply sighed smoke into the air. It was possible, Auger thought just for a moment, as he looked down at all of this, to believe again. Lethe, beside him, was staring too, held by the landscape.

And on they went. Auger nilled the autopilot to take the stick again only as they reached the brimming mountains of Wastwater. On impulse, he cut speed over the lake and stopped, hanging there with no sound in his ears but the comforting, heavy pulse of the rotors above him. Then he settled back in his seat, gazing down.

Deep black and dark-sided, Wastwater was a place of suicides. It wasn't the destination suicides who came to Wastwater, but the despairing enders of it all, the loners.

There was no reflection at all from the water of this lake. It was silt-dark. They came here in their 'flites and set them to circle, and circled till the fuel failed and they tumbled down, moths to this dark flame. Auger rolled his palm over the copter's smooth control stick, the machine juddering, the pulse of the rotors jumping.

'Hey, Auger, let's go.'

'Are you sure? You don't want to—?' He skipped the rotors again.

'I'm sure. Just go, okay?'

'Good.' He took a last look at the black side wall of the lake with its shards of glitter that the scree had not yet carried down below the black surface, and pulled the copter away, on towards his destination.

Ten minutes more, and a 'flite passed in the other direction, and then another, and Auger knew they were close. And over a ridge, and there it was, marked as if by a beacon. A descending spiral of 'flites waiting to land on the floor of the small natural crater.

'What is this, Auger?'

He pushed the copter to the top of the spiral, then nudged the stick gently down and rolled to starboard, falling in behind the last 'flite in the line. He felt like a vulture as he took his position in the aerial whirlpool.

The sedate queue spun them down slowly, and they lost two hundred metres in ten minutes. There was no other way to reach the site. The slopes of the crater were too steep, and its base too compressed. There had to be order above, to reach the chaos below.

'It's a scrapyard. A scrapyard for drones. High-altitude weather sur-veillance craft.'

In a while a couple more 'flites tagged patiently in behind them. The circle tightened as it descended, and eye contact was possible between 'flites, but all the pilots kept their eyes on their screens. It wasn't simply the risk of it. This was a pastime for the solitary. The only acknowledgement of the presence of others was the strict adherence to the protocol of the queue.

The craft before Auger's hit the nadir of the vortex, cut away and drifted towards the western wire to land at the slope's edge, and Auger almost stalled as its pilot flashed him clear to come down.

No road led anywhere near the site. No one was ever intended to come there or to leave. Stripped of everything that might be easily recycled, of all but the basics of flight, the drones were bLinker-guided to the site and crash-landed and forgotten. In London, Bristol, Edinburgh, wherever, the pilots Exited at the last instant, tossed their bLinkers away and sauntered off for a cup of coffee.

Auger dropped low, circled the yard briefly, scanning for somewhere relatively safe to set down, and signalled the next 'flite its clearance as he drew in and touched down. The earth was dry, brown and dusty, rising and enveloping the 'flite as it stilled, and then sinking back down to leave the craft veneered in it.

Auger waited for the engine to reach silence, and sat for a while with just the comms active. The small console screen in front of him wrote and erased the words TRAWLING and WAITING, the one following the other, for five minutes before a message replaced them.

AUGER. WELL, WELL. I'LL BRING YOU IN.

'Stay close,' Auger said, stepping out of the copter and flicking on his pager.

The tall wire fence surrounding the yard had long ago been dragged down, and now it was as flat as a carpet. There was no longer the faintest spring in it as Auger crossed it, following the arrows on his tasker.

In front of them was a micro mountain range of ripped metal and plastic. It seemed small enough from above, but down here it took on a new scale. It was at least twice as high as Auger remembered it. He began cautiously to climb through the wreckage, testing his footing constantly. The yard was a dangerous place. Shattered fuselages and broken wings lay in vast fragile heaps, disturbed only by the next drone to fall from the sky or by careless scrap-hunters. The bodies of scavengers fooled by the deceptive stability of the landscape were scattered across the site, but no one was deterred, and the pockets of the dead were rifled as keenly as were the carcasses of the drones.

Auger scrambled through the wreckage, cursing Arti for living here. He looked behind him. Lethe was skipping over the wreckage like a kid in a playground.

Arti's home was a welded network of drone fuselages set in a lazy cocoon of impact buffers constructed from more fuselages. It was buried deep inside the scrap mountain, safe from tremor or crash or crime. He had piped water from a spring, and a cache of food that would probably outlast the world. Guided by Arti, Auger found the start of the downward route that led there, and began to descend. Lights came on to lead and light them, and extinguished in their wake. Eventually the lights framed an oval doorway that opened smoothly at their approach.

'Who's with you?' Arti filled the doorway and stared incuriously at Lethe.

'Arti, this is Lethe. She's staying with me.'

Everything inside Arti's home was metal, and the lighting was harsh. Everything looked dark or brilliant. Auger squinted. Lethe hooded her eyes with a hand. Neither helped. Arti wore glasses that were a flickering mosaic as his eyes darted behind them. They blended tone into the black and silver for him, gave him greys and hints of colour.

'She's a bit young, isn't she?'

'She's older than you think. And don't jump to conclusions. Not about her age, not about anything else.' Auger's eyes were getting used to the polarised light. It was like seeing everything a little late and off centre. It maintained Arti's advantage.

'He hasn't got a computer,' Lethe said, peering round Arti's room. 'You told me he was a computer neuter.'

She gave Arti a dirty look, which was wasted on him, as Arti's only curiosity beyond screens and boards concerned boys. And curiosity was all he had, Auger knew, his sex hormones having been wrung out of him. Arti was a big flabby virgin. He hadn't touched anyone with sexual intent, ever. But Arti had been born with his paedophile father's genes, and so he'd been chemically castrated at puberty under Sins-of-the-Fathers legislation. He had no desire at all towards boys, just a technical curiosity about whether he might have had such desires.

'No, I don't have a computer,' Arti said mildly, taking no offence. 'There's no point.'

'Arti doesn't need one,' Auger said.

It would be something traceable back to him. And anyway, he couldn't afford the sort of thing he needed, buy or rent. But what Arti did have was clients with computers. He carried out data-collating research for major clients in return for slacktime use of the power. His clients had no problem with that. They knew he could take it any time he wanted, but that way they felt in control. What would someone like Arti want to do, anyway? The work he did was all stuff that needed vast computing power but no real skill. And Arti made sure all his clients came here and had regular face-to-face meetings with him. He knew how he came across to them – any hint of sex leached away, a waddling-into-the-room, big-bellied, broad-breasted not-quite man with a squeak of a voice and the complexion of someone who never ever ventured on to a street. A nervous being entirely devoid of threat. A person to be trusted. And that appealed to Arti. He knew that what had been done to him had focused him on his own, personal work, and he was very happy that that same thing presented him as a safe entity to the fuckheads whose networks he abused.

'I want to try to find someone, Arti. Someone who may or may not still be alive. Here.' Auger passed Madsen's file over to Arti. It wasn't thick. Madsen's life was worth just a few pages. Arti ran his chubby fingers down it, his head nodding like a slow, ponderous metronome.

'Easy enough. Looks like you've got just about everything here,' Arti said. Then he stopped and frowned. 'Oh. I see. There's no credit coding. If he's alive, he's living on cash. Totally.' He slapped the papers on his desk and sat back until the chair squeaked. 'Ah. That makes it hard. How much time you got?'

'I don't know. It might have run out already.'

'Okay.' Arti pulled out a fat black terminal from the desk, grunting with effort as he jacked it home.

'Ah, there's his dick after all,' Lethe said.

Arti ignored her, unrolling a keypad. 'Let's feed the data-eater, then.'

Lethe came round to Arti's side and leaned over his shoulder. 'What are you doing?'

'Nothing special. First, I'm checking him out for tangential credit. We might be lucky. He might be indirectly traceable. He might use only cash, but the people he takes it from or gives it to might declare it. Credit's always the key. Everyone using credit can be traced by electronic means. Credit-card transactions, comms devices, you name it. But not just cards. There's also a requirement to electronically record every cash transaction over twenty ecus. Madsen might not record he's received any cash, but someone giving it to him might have recorded that fact. So we'll try that route first.' He waited, then said, 'Nope. I'd have been surprised, but it was worth a try. Okay, next.'

Arti started punching keys again, his stubby fingers moving at speed. He pushed himself into the desk, his belly enveloping the edge of it as if it were physically plugged into his flesh. 'It's hard even to get hold of unrecorded cash in the first place for black market use, but once it leaves the system, it can't get back again. If you receive undeclared cash, you can't spend it legally due to back-checks. So some people stay permanently out of the system, which, once you develop the habits, is actually easier than doing the odd one-off black market deal. But you're laying yourself open to crime, since declaring a theft triggers an investigation of your finances to check you haven't been dealing on the black market. So if anyone who's ever dealt with Madsen has ever declared a crime, we might get him.' Arti's fingers worked for a while, then stopped. He sat back, extruding the desk's edge. 'Right, I'm still drawing a blank. If Madsen's alive, he's thorough.'

Which works both ways, Auger thought. If Madsen's thorough, maybe he's alive.

'Okay,' Arti said, 'last step's to carry out a void search. It's the only thing left, and it's only going to work if we have a vague hunt area.' He looked up at Auger. 'I need one piece of information to start off with. Can't carry out a void search in a vacuum.' He grinned at his joke, making sure Auger got it. 'So, you got anything?'

He waited, and Auger said, 'What sort of information? What's a void search, Arti?'

Arti sighed. 'Okay. In an economic environment where everything can be traced, undeclared cash transactions leave a void, right? It's like this. You've got a thousand people in a closed environment, nine-ninety of them you can follow their credit trails, and they being good citizens, they declare what they can remember of their cash transactions. That leaves you ten people. They're the people who don't use credit. Most of them, it's obvious, they live by cash because they can't get credit, or they just want to make some stupid protest, make some point. "I am not a number", that sort of crap. We're all numbers, for God's sake. They aren't totally committed to it, the protesters. They're like vegetarians who wear leather. They're on the fringes, and you can generally trace them with just a little effort. Deep down, they want to be seen to be protesting. So that's nine out of those ten.

'So, now you got just one guy left, and he's much more interesting. This tenth guy, this one in your thousand, he lives purely in these voids created by cash transactions. Let's call him Madsen. He *wants* to be concealed, and he's more crafty. He lives at the edges of these credit-starved and protesters' lives, these nine, transacting only with them. So his transactions are one removed. To find him, you have to look at the edges of the edges. You with me?'

Auger nodded.

'Good. So what do we do? We find someone lawful who declares cash transactions, then we find the transactees, and investigate them, and so on. But it can take months, Auger. You need a lot of computing power. And *en route* you turn up a lot of bugs and roaches you're not interested in. But listen to me. Even with this, you need a hook. One thing, one place to start the search. Otherwise you'll get your guy in the thousand, and he'll be the wrong goddamn guy, because you've been searching in the wrong goddamn thousand.'

'So?'

'So I need one piece of solid information. And when I've got it, I need maybe a month. You got a month?'

Auger thought of Astrid. 'No. No. I haven't.'

Across the room a monitor flashed red. 'We've got a drone coming in,' Arti said, taking the screen in. 'Fifteen minutes away. You'd better go. Good luck, Auger.'

He stood filling the doorway for a moment, then closed it, leaving them to the moving capsule of light that ushered them away.

The scrapyard seemed dull and ordinary after Arti's steel cavern. Auger climbed into the copter after Lethe and marked a position in the queue to depart the yard, then lifted away, joining the rising vortex of 'flites. Some of them remained above the site, waiting for the drone to arrive, and Auger sat in the air high above them, chasing his thoughts. Most of the stayers kept low, jockeying to be first to land after the arrival of fresh salvage. The drone came in from the north, its pale, stubby wings scratched, its engine stuttering, and slipped over the crater's rim. One of the 'flites rose sharply to avoid it. The drone seemed to be commencing a victory roll as it plunged. A brief plume of flame rose, but no more than that. No fuel was wasted here. The crunch of metal was louder than the thin explosion. Already a spiral of scavengers was forming above it.

Sherry had said Madsen liked to drink coffee. Good coffee. It wasn't much to go on, but it was something.

Auger turned the copter away and headed back to London.

TWENTY-FIVE

'Well? He there or not?' Fargo demanded.

Jaime peered down the alley, not certain whether there was anything to see. The tramp was usually sitting cross-legged against the far wall, maybe twelve metres away. The few square metres of space that were the old man's home were kept warm and mostly clear of dust and ash by the exhaust streaming from the vent shaft back there. From where he stood with the others at the mouth of the alley, Jaime could feel the mild heat on his cheeks like a flush of embarrassment. The alley stank of garlic and anchovy, courtesy of the pizza place that fed the vent shaft, with an extra topping of urine and stale shit from the old man.

Fargo snorted, the sound exiting through his filters like a belch. 'I don't see him.'

'Maybe he's just asleep,' Jaime said. Jaime wasn't sure why he had said that. It came out without him thinking about it. The old man could easily be hidden under his pile of rags and tatters in the shadows of the shaft's mould-bearded neck.

'You ain't backin' down now,' Fargo said, staring at Jaime. He extended a finger and poked him in the chest, hard. Jaime took a step back, and Zee giggled, making as if to poke Jaime himself. Zee was the only one of them smaller than Jaime, but he acted as tall as Fargo. Fargo never slapped him down. There was no need. He'd never challenge Fargo, and anyone who wanted to would have to go through Zee first.

'Ain't backin',' Zee mimicked.

'I just don't think he's there,' Jaime said, trying to take everything but reason from his voice. He glanced at Riandra, who was gazing up at Fargo. So that was it. Jaime felt stupid for letting her persuade him to tell Fargo about the tramp and his little bundle. Fargo and his gang. Fargo and his stupid fucking game.

'He's there, he's there,' Zee squawked, pointing.

Down the alley the pile of tatters seemed to be shifting.

'Rats,' said Jaime stubbornly.

Fargo looked hard at him. 'We're goin' in. Right?'

'Right,' Zee said.

Riandra looked at Jaime, then at Fargo. She said, 'Right, Fargo.'

'It's just this game,' Jaime said, feeling the surrender in his voice. 'That's all, isn't it? We're not going to use these, are we?' He touched the pommel of the sword at his belt.

Fargo and Zee exchanged a grin.

'You done a morph before?' Fargo said.

Jaime shook his head.

'So it's a fair trade. You give us the tramp, we let you play the game. Just a game, like we said. Riandra, tell him.'

'It is,' she said, giving Fargo the smile that Jaime wanted for himself. She glanced at Jaime and sniffed.

Despite Riandra's reassurance, Jaime didn't like the way Fargo had said, *Give us the tramp*. He shrugged and told Fargo again, 'I don't see him. he isn't there today.'

The old man chose that moment to get up. No, Jaime thought, beginning to realise what he might have done, telling Fargo about the old man who lived in the alley with his precious bundle. Fargo was crazy as hell.

As the old man rose laboriously to his feet, the heap of tatters rolled away from him like the camouflage it was – the blanket of plastic offcuts and shredded sofsteel, of visthene and rag all stitched and soldered together into the thick rug that cloaked him all the time. It was his bedding when he slept, his clothing when he woke. It was his anonymity and his cloak of invisibility.

He was on his feet now, swaying groggily, and the blanket was a heavy cape swinging in the warm wash of aromatic air from the vent shaft. He blinked once and then stood quite still, suddenly alert, a curled and grimy hand hooding his eyes as he squinted at the group of kids standing in the alley's jaws. The vent blew at his shoulder, its usual low hum raised to an anxious whine by his proximity. Jaime was suddenly hyperconscious of the sound. Swags of rag fluttered around the old man's face, and the flakes of metal in his cape clinked like wind chimes.

Jaime wanted to say something to him, to warn him, but it was clear that the tramp hadn't recognised him, and Jaime suddenly didn't want to identify himself, to have to start making explanations. And anyway, there was nowhere for him to run, except into the arms of Fargo.

Fargo was muttering at Jaime, shoving the bLinkers towards him, and Jaime quickly threw his head back and pressed them over his eyes, as if doing so would take him away from what was going to happen, instead of drawing it closer. He squeezed his eyes closed, holding the hard eyeLids down until they caught, and then, bLinkered, he looked again.

Everything had changed. He was in the game. He lurched forward with the new perspective, then steadied himself. Fargo had already drawn his sword, the blade glinting warmly in the torchlight from the dungeon walls, the great rough blocks of dark stone fused with slashes of grey mortar. The jutting torches were lodged in rust-scabbed iron mounts high on the walls. Only a vague grainy texture gave away that the torches and their mounts were pure software and couldn't be touched, just like the gloomy high stone ceiling that buried them deep underground.

At Fargo's shoulder, Zee slashed his short heavy sword through the air, whooping wildly and scraping the blade's tip harshly down the dungeon wall, drawing sparks.

Not knowing what else to do, Jaime drew his own sword, the blade he'd hired for the game today from Real Skills. Riandra had the same weapon. Fargo threw a glance of scorn at Jaime for the light, thin blade, and Jaime could almost see the thought in his head. A woman's weapon. Jaime noticed Riandra registering that look and copying it.

Fargo caught Zee's eye and cleared his throat, then cried out, 'Let's go to battle! To gold and glory!'

Zee crashed his sword into Fargo's raised blade, and Riandra did the same. Fargo waited, staring hard at Jaime until he touched his blade reluctantly to the other three.

'Okay!' Fargo yelled.

Uneasy now, Jaime looked up and down the street where Roco and Agamemnon, the remainder of Fargo's pack, stood at the street's open ends to left and right, each about twenty metres away. Only the street was a long, claustrophobic dungeon corridor now and the ash-strewn gloom of the afternoon was transformed into murky underground light. Roco and Agamemnon were signalling all clear with their daggers.

Fargo brought his sword down and took a pace into the dead-ended corridor. As always, Zee was at his side. Riandra was behind them, seeming nervous. She avoided Jaime's eye. Programmed torchlight swirled, throwing everything into rippled light and dark. Jaime noticed the hard, long look passing between Fargo and Zee, and thought, That isn't part of the program.

The old man at the corridor's end took a slow step forward, squinting. 'Who's there? Jaime? Is that you?' His voice was faint and querulous.

Jaime couldn't bring himself to answer. Since he'd come across him a few months back, he'd grown to like the old man. He didn't like the idea any more that he'd sold him to Fargo for an afternoon's gaming. He didn't like himself for telling Fargo about the bundle the old man protected as if it was treasure, building it up to Fargo so Fargo would let him play the morph along with Riandra. He decided he didn't like Riandra any more either.

'Give up your riches and surrender, and we may be merciful, evil one,' Fargo said. His voice sounded tinny and pathetic to Jaime.

The old man stopped in his tracks, though. He stood suddenly upright, and was tall and straight. 'You've come,' he said flatly.

Jaime thought he must have misheard. The old man was acting as if he had been expecting them. He was taking Fargo seriously. Jaime wondered if the program had taken words from the old man's mouth and fitted them to the game, like it had buried them all deep underground with torches on the walls and the light changed to suit, but he was pretty certain that morphs didn't do that. In fact, he was sure of it.

It had surprised Fargo and Zee too. They stopped, but only for an instant. Fargo grinned and said, 'Yeah, we've come. And we're gonna fucking kill you and take your stuff.' He raised his sword.

'No,' Jaime said, then closed his mouth, staring at the old man, not believing it. In a single smooth movement the old man had swung his cape back and drawn a sword from a long scabbard. The scabbard was black and smooth and the silver sword that came from it was a swift lick of ice. There seemed to be lettering chased into the flat of the blade. Jaime peered at the sword and scabbard. Neither was even faintly grainy.

This was insane. The old man's sword and scabbard were real.

Jaime looked at Fargo, who just went on grinning. Maybe he was surprised, but he was crazy enough not to be. Game crazy. Once he was bLinkered, he was there. And Zee was right in there with him.

Jaime threw a glance at Riandra. She was holding her sword ready, not looking at Jaime. She had no idea. She probably thought it was all part of the game.

Fargo stepped forward, weaving the tip of his blade in a fine figure of eight. He wasn't scared at all, the adrenalin coursing through him. Jaime had seen Fargo fight in the demos at Real Skills. No one ever beat Fargo with a sword or with anything else. He even sliced the shit out of the

Douglas Fairbanks animats. This crazy old man wasn't going to make him sweat.

'You won't have him,' the old man said suddenly, taking a few paces up the corridor. 'You won't ever have him.' He brought up his sword and stretched it out towards Fargo's extended blade. Jaime wondered what the hell the old man was talking about. He had to be even crazier than Fargo.

Fargo moved forward easily, not pacing but sliding his feet evenly over the ground, his balance rock steady. He stopped again and waited. Seconds passed, a minute. Jaime noticed a stream of ants flowing over Fargo's boots, heading for a wedge of rotting pizza. The tip of his blade was just a few metres from the old man's.

'Give it to us,' Fargo said, his voice brittle with excitement.

Jaime could see the bundle now, back in the far corner. The program had incorporated it, morphed it into a grainy wooden chest riveted with brass. The old man had always tried to conceal it from Jaime, but the way he'd shielded it with his body had only drawn attention to it. Why had the old man called it *Him*? There was clearly nothing alive there. The bundle wasn't moving. And if the bLinkered software had detected life it would have morphed it into something living.

It was something dead, then. God, the old man must really be insane. He had some dead animal there, rotting away in the warmth of the pizza vent.

'Give it to us,' Fargo said again, edging forward.

Jaime reached out to touch Fargo's arm. 'Let's go. He's mad. Leave him alone.'

Zee swept the flat of his blade to meet the point of Jaime's elbow. Jaime screamed with the sudden pain, dropping his sword to the ground as the old man tilted his head and muttered, 'Jaime? Is that you?'

Jaime was on his knees, hugging his throbbing elbow. He looked up through tears to see Fargo already down the corridor, slashing his sword down in a sharp arc to take out the old man's blade while he was distracted.

Except that the blade wasn't there to be struck. The old man had backed a step even more smoothly than Fargo had advanced. Jaime couldn't believe it.

Away down the long corridor to his right, Jaime heard a shrill cry from Roco at the lookout point. Fargo had the old man backed against the end wall of the alley. The vent shaft to the old man's left, morphed into the neck and head of a stone-carved dragon, blocked Fargo's right-handed swing. Fargo backed, dropping his sword a fraction, trying to tempt the old man clear of the obstruction.

'Leave him alone, Fargo,' Jaime called, trying to ignore the pounding pain in his elbow. He tried to pick up his sword, but couldn't. His hand was tingling and there was no grip to it. He looked around desperately. 'Riandra, do something.'

She was looking from Fargo to Jaime and back. She wasn't going to do anything at all. He wondered what he'd ever seen in her.

Zee was at Fargo's side, sniping with his blade at the old man's legs, but getting nowhere. The cape of stitched tatters was draped down to the ground, and for some reason Zee's honed blade was just glancing off it. Zee swore, his voice rising in confusion. The program accommodated the new information smoothly, the leather jerkin and trousers that it had given the old man morphing into a cape of shining mail.

Ignoring Zee, the old man advanced towards Fargo. Fargo backed quickly, then abruptly stopped, ducked and swept his sword up and into the old man's chest. The cape had opened fractionally with the advance, and the blade flew perfectly towards the gap. Fargo cried out, 'Hah!' and then suddenly screamed in pain.

Jaime didn't see how it was done. The old man was faster than Fairbanks in the old vids they kept playing in the arcade. His sword was already down again, and Fargo's blade was arcing up out of his hand and blurring through a fake torch to zing against the wall. It fell clattering at Riandra's feet. She dropped her sword beside it, her mouth wide.

Fargo was holding his wrist, shaking his head and staring in disbelief at the old man, who was panting slightly. He took a step towards Zee. Zee backed away.

'Fuck you,' Fargo said. He let his twisted hand fall to his side and brought something out of a pocket. The program had trouble with it, running through a few vague shapes before deciding on a small, cocked crossbow.

Jaime opened his mouth to yell something, but another voice beat him to it.

'Drop it, kid.'

Jaime turned round sharply to see someone new at the mouth of the corridor, someone unquestionably real. The man was pointing an identical weapon at Fargo. His legs were spread slightly and set firm, and he was holding the little crossbow with two hands braced against each other. He was wearing a leather jerkin and breeches, courtesy of the program, but there was a look on his face that took Jaime right out of the zone.

'I said drop it. That's twice. I won't go to three.'

Fargo knelt and placed his weapon carefully on the ground, not taking his eyes from the tiny black bolt pointed at his head.

'Fine. Now kick it away.'

Fargo stood slowly and drew his foot back. He kicked the weapon with deliberate awkwardness, and it spun to crash loudly into the wall just to his right.

Jaime was suddenly aware of Zee, standing against the opposite wall, reaching for a pocket, and instinctively yelled, 'No!' He threw himself back into Zee, who fell over, a tiny dagger dropping from his hand. The man at the alley's mouth had turned briefly to cover Zee, and was still turning back as Fargo dived for Zee's weapon, raised it smoothly and extended the blade in a fluid stabbing movement to the man's chest. A killing strike.

Except that it didn't get there. From nowhere, the old man's sword intercepted Fargo's straightening arm. There was hardly any force in it, but the sleeve of Fargo's thick jacket opened in a new fold and slid down his bare arm towards his wrist, reddening rapidly.

Fargo slumped against the wall, holding his arm and swearing. Blood was oozing through his fingers and beginning to run along his sword from the hilt to the tip. Zee was just staring at him. With the fight over, the old man had sheathed his sword and was looking uncertain, not seeming to realise that Jaime had been one of his persecutors. The man who had come to his rescue was touching his shoulder softly and talking to him.

'Are you okay, Pi? Are you hurt?'

He got no answer. The old man had turned to pick up the bundle and was cradling it in his arms, rocking it and talking to it, his voice holding a gentleness Jaime had never heard from him before. 'Don't worry, it's all right now. I'm here. They'll never take you away from me. I swear they'll never take you.'

From the other end of the corridor, Agamemnon's end, Jaime heard a cry. Agamemnon was on his belly, screaming, Magnacled and writhing, and a rotund shape that filled the corridor was rising from his side and moving smoothly forward. In its wake the alley was restored to grimy life, the walls eaten by graffiti, the paving with its urban lichen of chewing gum and filter wraps. For a fraction of a second the advancing silhouette was a metal behemoth, a golem, but then the program disengaged from it and the trig came on behind a bow wave of reality. It had to be a 'fist trig, to do that. And after what had happened here, Jaime knew it was trouble for everyone.

270

He touched the bridge of his nose and rubbed his eyes, the bLinkers falling to the ground. He'd had more than enough of the morph. A tributary of the nearby trail of ants detached itself from the main flow and began to examine the limp neural tendrils.

Jaime took a pace forward and looked at the bundle in the old man's arms. Inside the swaddling of rags was a bulbous, bright orange shape moulded into a rudimentary body. It was weird. It was more than a doll. It looked vaguely like a child, but it was moulded and built from scraps of visgel.

The man at the alley's end looked at the advancing trig and caught Jaime's eye. He said quickly, 'Are you responsible for this?'

Jaime looked down. 'No. I'm sorry.'

'All right,' the man said, seeming to make a decision. 'Pi'll be okay. I'll take a chance on you. Come on. Be fast.'

It made no sense to Jaime. The man had to be a 'fist, the way he moved, talked, everything about him, yet he swept Jaime past the trig and away like he was scared of it. And the trig called out for them to stop as they ran past, the man yelling, 'We're unarmed. They shot us. We're going to GenMed for treatment.'

And before the trig could process that and react further, they were round the corner and gone.

The man pulled Jaime along, holding his hand like they were Magnacled together. He had a hell of a grip for an old man. And he was fit, too, dragging Jaime for miles, it seemed, down those streets. The Angel, Old Street, on into the City where the ash was thick and pulpy underfoot with last night's fall of toxic rain. Pi, he'd called the tramp. Jaime hadn't known the old man had any friends, but here was someone who even had a name for him.

'Okay, kid, here we are,' the man said at last, slowing down and letting Jaime's hand go. Jaime rubbed life back into it as his companion coded them into a great stone building, the very blocks as tall as Jaime. It was like some game again, except that the only grain was the grain of the stone itself, and that remained even when he squinted at it.

The man closed the heavy door behind them. It must have weighed a ton, but it moved smooth as swallowing. There was an echo in the vast hall that silenced Jamie, and he said nothing until they were in a small room wound up in corridors and far within the building. The room was windowless and lit by lines of bare bulbs strung around three walls of the place like they had been left by crazy men. Then he said nothing still, just stood and stared at a great maroon canvas roughly taped to the fourth, back wall. The heavy colour consumed the wall, threatening to engulf the room. Jaime thought he saw a door swimming there in the colour, a shimmering, misshapen door into a darker maroon beyond. He'd never seen a zone like that painting. It was beautiful and terrible.

'You like it?' the man asked, beside him. He was fiddling with some contraption on a table, an incomprehensible great machine covered with dials and polished chrome.

'No,' Jaime decided. 'I don't think so. What is it?'

The man laughed. 'It's a painting. I found it on the river bank. It seemed appropriate. The bankers who worked here liked dark paintings of pale men, but they're long gone now and they took their history with them. Good riddance.' He shook his head. 'That was the beginning of the end of everything, I sometimes think, when the economists were more valued than the ecologists.'

The guy was crazy. Maybe not quite as crazy as the tramp, but crazy anyway.

He was pouring water into the machine now. The coolant for some sort of ancient game machine, Jaime guessed. Where was the screen? He looked around, but there was just the disturbing painting.

'So, what were you doing with that crew of nils?'

'There was a girl,' Jaime began, and stopped. And that was it, he thought. He'd done all that, nearly got the old tramp killed, for Riandra who wasn't even worth it.

'Always is,' the old man said. Light from an overhead bulb caught the corner of his eye and the gleam of it took the edge off the seriousness in his voice. 'There's a girl, or there's a boy.' He seemed to go inside himself for a moment before saying, 'And now?'

'That's over.' Jaime was surprised at the harshness of his own voice.

'For the moment. You'll choose better. You'll learn. Not all of us make the same mistake all our lives.' He glanced across at the maroon door as if it might suddenly open for him, or maybe close. 'Choosing wrong when you're young, it's better than choosing right when it's over.'

No, he was just as crazy as the old man in the alley. Jaime started to back towards the door, the real door. The man was standing in front of the maroon one on the far wall, the bulbs surrounding him springing him free of all shadow, leaving him hovering before the shining canvas, as if he might float away through it at any moment.

And this place was crazier than any zone, Jaime thought. He cleared his throat. 'I've got to go now. I've got people waiting for me. They know where I am. They'll come looking.'

'Like who, Jaime? Who's looking for you?'

How did he know that? And his name. Had Jaime told him his name back at the alley? Had someone else said it?

The machine was hissing like some sort of motor now, leaking air. The man didn't seem troubled by it. 'You live alone, Jaime. I know where you live. The orphans' home might be interested in that information. But you're pretty good at moving around, aren't you?'

'Look, I really gotta go.'

'Okay. But if you need someone, I'm here. Pi's not much good to you. He's not much good to himself. You know where I live now, and no one else knows that. So.'

As if that was a big deal. 'Fine. Look, I'm going now.' But Jaime stopped at the door, had one last look at the old man standing there, and the shining machine that was starting to give out a really good smell. He couldn't quite name it. It was like something familiar, only far, far better.

Maybe he did like that thing on the wall. There was something about it. Something about the confrontation of terrible hope. Even though there was no hope.

PART THREE
REACTIVE

TWENTY-SIX

The girl had a slight limp, her left foot leading her right and her body moving in a faint roll as she crossed the floor towards him. The café was almost empty, just him and a couple of other people sitting at their coffee in the corners. This was the tenth place he'd tried in the area around Madsen's old room in Islington. He was getting fed up with the taste of coffee, the smell of it, even talk of it, and he was near to giving up.

'Can I get you something else?' she said.

'No, that was fine,' Auger said, giving her an apologetic smile. He made a point of glancing at the name tag pinned to her blouse. 'Hi, Ursie. Tell me, are you the owner of the place? I need some help. I'm with Community.'

She stiffened, adjusted her balance a fraction, a boat in rough water. She knew what that meant. He was a tax inspector. 'Co-owner,' she said, her voice suddenly clipped. 'With my dad.'

'Fine. We're checking coffee imports. You're registered as an importer?'

'We have a licence. You want to check that?'

He took a pen from his pocket and reached for a notepad. He let her see the pad, then slipped it away again, letting her register the gesture, and smiling. But he kept the pen in his hand. 'At this point, no. I'd like to keep this friendly. A few days ago, a routine check picked up a small anomaly on your throughput. There's an excess of coffee ordered and supplied over what you claim to have sold. I did some back-checking and found what seems to be a steady excess, over a period of several years. I just need some clarification. We're concerned about black market sales.'

'We don't service the black market.' She glanced at his pen. From the kitchen behind her came the drawn hiss of an espresso machine. Her voice rose over it. 'Our customers like their coffee strong. That's all it is.'

He smiled, careful to be easy with her. She wasn't particularly worried. No more than anyone would be with the threat of Community hanging in front of them. 'That doesn't quite explain it. This excess only began a few years ago, and it began suddenly. Two years ago, in fact. And three months. Mean anything?'

He paused, sipping from the cup, watching her. For the first time, she looked away from him, and his heart beat. None of the others had even blinked at that one.

'Hold on,' she said, staring towards the kitchen. 'I'll be back in a moment. There's an order ready.'

He watched her go, noticing her sea was getting rougher. She was gone five minutes. 'I thought you said there was an order?' he said when she returned.

'I was mistaken.'

He nodded. 'You should be careful of mistakes.'

She folded her arms. 'Is that a threat of some kind?'

He shook his head mildly and put the pen away. Don't screw it up, Auger, he told himself. Stir it, don't spill it. You're just a tax man. 'No. Of course not,' he told her. 'I'm just here to give you a warning that you may be at risk of an investigation.'

She shrugged. 'Fine. We don't deal in cash. Everything's declared. You can send in your men. They won't find anything.'

'Okay.' He smiled at her and decided to take the risk. Push her hard, see which way she'd fall. 'They'll be here tomorrow morning. You know, sometimes all that turns up is a member of staff pilfering. You had anyone start with you that time back?'

'No one. There's just me and my dad. And I told you, everything's declared. You can pay for your coffee now.'

Maybe it hadn't been such a good idea to come, but there was no knowing. Had the guard at the desk looked at him any differently today?

Troy Gordo was usually a good judge of what lay in the eyes, and behind them. With that beacon of ravaged skin on his face, he had suffered their gaze all his life. He had learned early how to read eyes. Their curiosity, their disdain, their shock, revulsion and pity. He had learned how to change that look to one of attraction, though. Not caring what their owner felt about him, just wanting the softness of their eyes on him.

That was what Rox had promised him all along. A cure for his face. A true cure. Not a drug cocktail with a thundering side-effect hangover, not a glistening mask of plastic microsurgery, but a fresh face. And she had chosen him well as her recruiter. He was a charmer, and he was motivated. Every new recruit to the project, Rox told him, was a step closer to his cure.

It hadn't concerned him too much when Haenson had died. Rox had told him it was an accident, and he had believed her. It wasn't murder, so why not call it suicide? Why compromise the project? And when Merchant had followed Haenson, he had swiftly accepted that it was a tragic glitch. It had almost been easier, the second time. Almost confirmation of the status of the first death as an accident.

He hadn't expected it to happen to Astrid. He tried to convince himself that he hadn't expected it to happen again at all, but he had realised that his reluctance to recruit her had been a suspicion that the other deaths were more than pure accidents. And in the end he had only drawn her into it for a reason to see her again, knowing she would see nothing else in him.

And now Astrid was in a coma, too. Was she going to die, like they had?

He opened the elevator doors. Rox was standing there, waiting for him.

'You told Auger about Astrid, didn't you?'

He hesitated, unsure whether she was guessing. Then he said, 'Yes. Why not? He would have found out anyway. How is she?'

'That isn't your concern, Troy. She's a volunteer. Just like you.'

'I'm more than—'

'You're the same, Troy. We just pay you a little differently, that's all. What else did you tell Auger?'

'Nothing. Nothing at all.'

'Are you sure about that?'

'Why?'

'He's gone. Disappeared.'

Troy looked at her. Was she worried about Auger? Or about what Auger might be doing? Gordo had a faint suspicion that he was out of his depth here.

'Never mind, Troy,' Rox said. She seemed to have dismissed the problem of Auger. 'We'll carry on with the experiment. Something slightly different today. Something you'll enjoy, I think. A bit of a break from the grind.'

'What is it?'

'A breakthrough, in many ways.' She was walking him through the department, past the CrySis pods they usually laid him down into, to a pod set alone against a wall. 'Here,' she said, opening a slim case and passing him the bLinkers they contained. 'I think we've solved your problem. Permanently.'

He stripped off his clothes and laid himself down, closing his teeth on the rubber block and taking a deep breath as he went under. The pod closed over him.

It was as if he was swimming through galaxies, swimming for ever, and then, eventually, he awoke. He felt her touch on his hand, and knew it was her even before he lifted his head clear of the gel and opened his eyes.

'Astrid.'

'Troy. Thank God.' There were tears glittering in her eyes. She caught her breath and wiped her eyes with the back of a hand. 'I thought I was alone here.' She stood back to peer at him. He could feel the gel at his throat like a heavy necklace. 'You look wonderful. It worked, didn't it?'

He raised his fingers to his face, and she bent and covered them with hers. Soft under his palm and above. His skin just like hers. 'What happened?'

'I just woke up.' She shook her head, frowned. 'Before that, I don't remember.' She touched the butterfly valve at her wrist. 'I was on a drip. I took it out. There was no one here. It's the middle of the night. I saw the light in this pod and came over. I hoped it would be you.'

He glanced at the window and saw the dark sky. One day? More?

It didn't matter. Whatever Rox had been trying to do, it hadn't worked. She was responsible. She had been using him. He knew that now. But if he had been guilty, at least Astrid hadn't died too. Now he could locate Auger, tell him the truth, make amends.

'We have to get out of this place, Astrid. Now. God, I thought you were going to die.'

He pulled himself clear of the pod, the gel hitting the floor in clumps, and stooped to gather up his clothes. Astrid was wearing a thin blue surgical shift. He could see her body beneath it, pressing at the material, almost ghostly. She came forward to stand against him, shivering, clutching at him, in sudden tears. He dropped the pile of clothes, and they were falling together on the bed at their side. He pushed away the tubes and wires littering the bed that she had ripped away from herself, and groaned as she pulled herself on top of him, her thighs sliding as she encased him, reaching behind her back to release the shift that fell away and slid to the floor. Then he laid himself back and stared at her, as if for the first time. The pale night light in the room made soft shadows on her face and neck and down the cleft between her breasts as she rose and fell over him like a rising tide. He felt the swell of her and let it take him over.

'Your face,' she murmured, reaching down to stroke it. 'So beautiful.'

Rox looked down into the CrySis pod and murmured, 'I wonder where he is right now.' And then picked up the clothes and walked over to a burnbox. She dropped the shirt into it first, then methodically everything else, while she talked into a small comms unit.

'I don't think there was any major harm done. The project's more or less complete, anyway. Yes. Well, he's here now, under control.' Listening intently, she glanced down at the pod, at the bLinkered eyes beneath the gel. 'Okay. It shouldn't be too hard. Say he was called away to some family crisis. Tell Ferec to arrange the details. Then we need a 'fist report detailing a vehicle crash *en route*. You can do that, can't you? That should do it.' She dropped Gordo's last shoe into the box. 'Then arrange for the pod to be collected. It can go up. No point wasting him.' She started to walk away from the burnbox, then stopped and went back, tugging the bLinker case from her pocket. She glanced briefly at it, before tossing it into the bin after Troy Gordo's clothes. 'Personal heaven,' she murmured.

'Come on,' Troy hissed, pulling her through the lobby area. The guard wasn't there, probably having a piss. 'It's clear. Quickly, Astrid.'

The glass doors opened for them, letting them into the night. The air felt unaccountably good. He took a lungful of it, his heart bursting with joy. She was alive, and they were altogether.

Somehow he knew that everything was going to be all right.

The café closed at six. The girl came out ten minutes later and locked the door carefully, silhouetted for a moment against the light inside, then vanishing as the light extinguished. She was almost gone before Auger's eyes became accustomed and he caught her walking quickly off, her limp balanced by the bag in her hand. This had to be the one, he thought. It had to be.

He followed her easily after that. She wasn't thinking of being followed, her head full of tomorrow and the inspectors from Community. Dark began to fall as she walked. It was a solid darkness, this. No moon, no stars. There was silicon in the day's dust, and as the streetlights came on, they bloomed globes of frosty light. Auger was wearing a full-face mask, ancient and cheap, but the filter was as good as any and there were nighteye lenses fitted. Ursie stood out ahead of him like a flame in the wind.

Now and then Auger could smell the coffee. It wasn't the stuff she'd served him in the Has Bean. This was high-grade stuff. Auger was still twitchy with all the caffeine he'd had over the last few days, but the smell of this was another country. The aroma was like a line reeling him towards her. He had to force himself back, keep himself clear of it. He wondered what that bag of it was worth.

She stopped in the park and sat down. Auger walked straight past her, head up, a passer-by, taking one last gulp of the coffee's perfume. The sky above was a sea of ink.

He kept going for a minute. He'd given her a plausible story, but Madsen had to be good to have kept clear this long, and he'd be wary. Auger slowed, went to the side of the path, unzipped his flies and openly looked around, then slipped into some bushes, nothing more than a nervous pisser. He dropped to his knees and pushed on through the undergrowth, crawling along until he could part a brush of leaves to see the bench clearly.

After ten minutes, a man came to sit by her and they began to talk. They were friends, obviously. This wasn't just a transaction taking place. Auger watched them talk for half an hour, his knees soaking up water and his joints and bones beginning to ache. And then the girl passed the man the bag. He made to give her something from his coat, but she waved him away. His gesture and hers, the offer and its refusal, seemed routine. It wasn't just today she was refusing to be paid.

He stood up from the bench and so did she, and they hugged briefly, touched hands and then parted. The man was holding the bag now.

Auger pulled himself out of the bushes and followed him. A tall man, starting to stoop, a fedora on his head, brim down. Long dark coat, belted tight. The guy was good, too, changing speed, doubling back, checking and checking again, but he wasn't expecting a tail, probably hadn't had to lose one for years. And the story Ursie would have told him had been plausible, even to the warning Auger had given her. If it had been him they were after, Madsen would be thinking, there wouldn't have been a warning. So as far as Madsen knew, it was unfortunate, and he was just taking home the last bag of coffee he'd ever get from Ursie. That would be what was going through his mind as he checked half-heartedly for a tail. The story, not the tail.

Still, Auger thought, Madsen was good. He might have lost Auger if he'd been thinking about it.

The City surprised him. But the way Madsen drew him there was a new way, unfamiliar to Auger. And at the last moment Madsen nearly flushed him, seeming to be arrowing home in the open, then speeding just enough to fade away between a pair of dead streetlights and disappear around a corner, only to turn back as Auger accelerated thoughtlessly, and coming straight at him with the fedora in his hand. Staring directly at Auger, his gleaming bald head where the fedora had been. It was all Auger could do not to stare right back at him, not to break stride and stop dead in his tracks. All that did it was that he was not even thinking of Madsen in that instant, that he was thinking, in the City, of Astrid so close at GenMed. Of Astrid, and not of Jay in her ward. So he let Madsen pass by and ducked into the gloomy doorway of an ancient bank, and picked him up again a few moments later as he returned.

The Bank of England. Auger chuckled to himself at that, seeing Madsen leaning in to push open one of the high, heavy doors. The times he must have walked past Madsen's home without knowing. Maybe Madsen had seen him pass, had wondered who he was, what he was doing. And all the time been there.

Madsen left the door ajar, and Auger at once felt completely stupid. He walked across the broad and empty junction and climbed the stairs to follow Madsen inside, closing the door behind him. It was surprisingly light on its hinges, and entirely noiseless.

Inside, watching Madsen shrug off the coat, he said, 'When did you spot me?'

'I didn't have to, Auger. I knew you were going to be there one day. I've been waiting. I was just checking you weren't tailed.'

'You knew?'

'Sherry was a friend of mine. I never told her I was still around, but I always kept an eye on her. So I knew about you. I was patched in that night, like you were.'

Madsen. It had been Madsen, the last man there. 'I—'

'You wouldn't have made it in time, Auger. You took the right decision. I live closer, and I was too late. Trouble with Sherry was that she'd set up her firewalls and beartraps a few years back and hadn't updated them since. And I knew how she was wired from back then. So I could patch in without her knowing and keep an eye on her, which was okay, but with a bit of effort anyone she was linked to could trace her back. And that wasn't okay.'

Picking up the bag of coffee, Madsen carried on, moving into the building. Auger stayed with him.

'There's always someone with a better system, Auger. I was pretty sure I was going to be too late to save her, but I had to save you and me. At least she kept her comms with us on autonomous lines and drives, otherwise they'd have had us all the same night. But given a few minutes at her screens and they'd have had you and me too, sure as hell.'

A kitchen. Madsen stroked a hand across his head. 'You know, I never really believed anything would happen to her. Her rapist was never going to come back. She was paranoid, but it turned out she was just paranoid about the wrong thing.'

'They were from GenMed, the men who killed her,' Auger said.

'Yes. I destroyed everything. I made sure there was nothing left to connect you or me with her. GenMed's hiding something big, Auger.'

He stopped. 'So I figured you'd be coming after me, sooner or later. I wondered how you'd go about it. I needed to know how good you were.' He grinned. 'And I wondered whether I'd left any loopholes. I guess I did. See what I mean about systems?'

He was hauling the bag of coffee on to the table. 'I suppose I'd better freeze this. Last me a month, probably. Ursie thought she was giving me the last of it ever.'

'I'm sorry for worrying her.'

'Don't be. She's strong, Ursie. Once told me she'd turn me in to Community herself if I stopped accepting the coffee. Friends, huh?' He gave Auger a mock grimace. 'But we'll drink some now. Why don't you sit down?'

Auger sat, looking at Madsen fussing with the coffee. He had a machine there, a Gaggia, spit-polished and gleaming. He had friends, too, that he could pretend to complain about. And he was a dead man. And Auger was alive and felt there was no one for him, just a wife sinking into the quicksand of the past, and Auger himself not knowing how to let her go, how not to be dragged down with her. And Astrid, for whom he felt responsible, and for whom he was feeling something more, he realised.

The machine drew breath and began to hiss and snort.

'Okay, tell me,' Madsen said.

'Father Fury.' Just saying his name somehow stopped Auger.

'I saw that,' Madsen said. 'On the holocast. Fury was always dangerous. But don't blame yourself. There was nothing you could have done.'

'Not that. I didn't mean that. I meant you. Maze. Your leaving CMS.'

Madsen shrugged it away. 'That wasn't anything to do with Fury. They used him to bury the case and scapegoat me. Fury was a psycho but he wasn't ever connected with Maze. He didn't kill those Vets, didn't even launch them on a suicide track. You've seen the original psych report on him?'

Auger shook his head. He hadn't seen anything on Fury prior to the Maze case. The whole report was blocked. 'No,' he told Madsen. 'Fury . . .' He took a breath while Madsen scrutinised him evenly, his hand going up again to his gleaming skull and scratching at it. 'Before Hyde Park, and after you left CMS, I thought Father Fury was responsible for a terrorist attack. A mass murder.' Auger tried to make it a report, a briefing to a fellow officer, hoping it would be easier like this. 'An incendiary device was set off at a religious ceremony. About a hundred people were killed.'

He was about to choke off, but Madsen interrupted him, and he was grateful for it.

'In Cherry Tree Wood. I heard about that. It was a private ceremony. No one ever claimed responsibility for the bomb. It was a wedding, and the only survivors were the bride and groom. The device went off as they were leaving in a 'flite. It must have been terrible, I remember thinking that.' He looked at Auger, waiting, making it plain he knew.

'It was.' That was all Auger could say.

Madsen caught the hard silence and took a shot into it. 'You think that device was meant for you? Or was it a general warning to CMS, to leave Fury be? That's what you're thinking?' He broke off.

'It was, for a while.'

The Gaggia was screeching. 'You ready for coffee, Auger?'

Even the small kindness threw Auger, and he found his eyes stinging. 'The last guy I drank coffee with is dead,' he said.

From the sink Madsen glanced back at him. 'Don't start making connections,' he said. 'Not that kind, anyway.' Madsen got on with the coffee for a minute, then said without turning round, 'He was a friend?'

'An informer. And a friend, I suppose. A friend.' He thought of Fly in that jungle, and saw him so alone there. And himself standing in the kitchen doorway, at the edge looking in. And flashed from there to Fly's bLinkered view of Fury as the Final Church went down into the rift, taking Fly down with it. And himself jerking away from Fly's whirling scream. Exiting. Escaping.

Madsen was handing the coffee to him, saying, 'You have to know when to quit, Auger. When just to pull out, to give it up. That's one of the things you need to learn. There are two things, and that's number one.' He raised the coffee to his lips, but didn't drink. He moved it under his nose, taking the aroma in, smiling gently to himself, and said,

'Trouble is, it never seems to stick. You have to learn it again every time.'

Auger followed Madsen, smelling the coffee. There was nothing, and he looked at Madsen who was sipping from his cup, calm and peaceful, meeting Auger's gaze. Auger raised the cup again, and this time the delicate scent struck him. He almost laughed with sudden pleasure. He'd been expecting the stiff jolt of caffeine that Fly's coffee always gave him, but this was something different. He sipped it, expecting something insipid, but the fine flavour expanded in his mouth, making him aware of a sense of taste he'd forgotten he had ever had.

He swallowed. 'This is good,' he told Madsen.

'It is. It's very good, Auger. But I think that you and I both needed it.'

Auger drank the coffee with Madsen in silence, thinking. He couldn't recall when he'd last been able to think like this, quietly and still, but now it came to him. He almost forgot about Madsen sitting over there as he began to speak. He told him everything, Madsen taking it all in, his face set hard against Auger's story. There was something about Madsen that made Auger know he understood more than simply what Auger's words were telling him.

'I thought she'd be okay, though,' Auger said, finishing. 'She'd get over it. I thought that was as bad as it could get, everyone dead except Jay. But Jay was still alive, and we had each other.' He closed his eyes for a second. 'You know what I think sometimes now? I think it would be better if she had died.'

He found he'd finished his coffee. Madsen was at the counter, doing something there, his back to Auger. His shoulders were moving as he worked, and then he turned, holding a plate with bread on it, and a slab of what looked like cheese. Auger took it from him and began to eat. He realised he was starving. He chewed and swallowed, and it tasted wonderful. Madsen just watched him.

'And you thought it was Fury.'

'Until a few days ago. Well, I'd tried to reopen the file on him after you—'

'After I left,' Madsen said lightly. 'Yes.'

'I thought it had to be him. After the bomb, I was off for a month, and while I was off Sweet was given the case. By the time I got back he'd had it closed due to lack of evidence. I couldn't get it reopened. I tried to get Wisch to give it to me, but he said since Sweet had found nothing to link Fury with it, it wasn't a CMS case. And that was it.'

Madsen tilted his head. 'Well, if Fury did it, it wasn't to stop you or anyone else finding he was linked to the Vet deaths. More likely he was pissed at being linked with it in the first place. Like I said, those deaths at Maze had nothing to do with him. You said you'd tried to look at my case?'

'They wouldn't let me. It was a closed file. The word was you'd had some vendetta against Maze, and because of that, Fury had been able to cover his tracks. The whole case was a screw-up.' Auger finished the bread, wiping the crust around the plate to pick up the last of the crumbs.

'Not quite,' Madsen said. 'It wasn't Fury. But as soon as I realised they were starting to finger him for it, I knew it was time to go. I let them think I just knew I was going to lose my job, and left before they could ditch me. That way they'd think it was just job loss I was afraid of. I figured if I disappeared before they realised I was a loose end, I could cover my tracks better.' He smiled at Auger. 'Obviously I didn't cover them well enough.'

Pushing the plate away, Auger said, 'Well, it wasn't Fury this time either. I think it was GenMed. I think they've taken over from Maze, and I think for some reason they were trying to kill her. They didn't succeed, but what they achieved was good enough.'

He took the pack of photographs from his bag and spread them out on the table between himself and Madsen. For a few minutes Madsen just looked, moving the images about, getting an idea of the layout of the scene. Auger could see him working out where Tomasz had to be facing when each image was taken.

After a few minutes, Auger said, 'Recognise anyone?'

'No. Not from my time.'

'There's the pyrotechnician,' Auger said. 'He's clear of suspicion. Quite apart from being dead, of course.'

Madsen grunted. 'You had security, didn't you?'

'Of course. Everything was checked beforehand. I was paranoid. Wisch supervised it himself.' Auger shot a glance at Madsen.

'No, Wisch is okay. I'd trust Wisch.' Madsen indicated the pyrotechnician with a finger. 'Auger, your friend Tomasz was pretty interested in the fireworks guy, wasn't he?'

'Yes. So?'

'Well, don't you think that if there was anyone else unusual, he'd have shot a few frames of them? A curious guy like Tomasz cruising the whole scene with his cam?' Madsen waved a hand over the spread of images. 'Looks like he was everywhere, Auger.'

'Tomasz might not have spotted them.' Auger found himself being defensive. Madsen was talking like he had an answer, and Auger had the feeling it wasn't one he was going to take to. 'They may have brought the stuff in surreptitiously,' he said.

'Come on, Auger. An explosion that big?'

'Explosives don't need to be bulky.'

'They don't fit in the pocket of your tux either. Not if there's timers and the rest. And it had to be timers, Auger, or a faulty remote, didn't it? They missed you. They got everybody else, but they missed you. A suicide bomber wouldn't have screwed up like that.'

Auger went back to the images on the table.

'Describe the explosion to me, Auger,' Madsen said.

'I told you. I thought it was a rift at first, or else the fireworks. It was tremendous. I've never seen anything like it.'

'But you've seen explosions before, Auger, haven't you?'

'Not like this. Not from above.'

'Okay.' Madsen reached over the table and jabbed at an image. 'This was the last shot he took. Look at it.'

Auger examined it, wondering what Madsen was seeing there. But there was nothing, just the 'flite starting to curl away into the sky, and that look of bliss on Jay's face.

'I don't get it,' Auger said.

'The marquee was some way behind you. Away from your friend with the cam.' He tapped the disrupted image. 'The centre of it, the source, had to be the marquee, didn't it? But you said you thought it was a rift at first. And this frame must have been taken at the same time as the marquee went up.'

Auger shrugged. Then he got it and felt the hairs rise at the back of his neck. He murmured, 'It wasn't a point source, was it? That's why I thought it was a rift. It wasn't a fire tide spreading from the epicentre that hit Tomasz with his cam. It was a simultaneous, multiple source blast.'

Madsen started to gather the images together, shuffling them into a neat pile. 'You think Jay was working on Dirangesept?'

'Yes. I didn't know that at the time.'

'Maze was working on ways of killing the beasts. That research must have been taken over by GenMed. One of the things they discovered at Maze was that, under certain circumstances, psychokinetic abilities could be developed in the Vets who hosted beasts. These abilities turned out to be uncontrollable and almost invariably resulted in the death of the subject. The circumstances triggering these abilities were associated with phobias.'

Madsen was about to go on, but Auger lifted a hand and stopped him. He said, slowly, 'Phobias are extreme emotions. The last thing Jay said was how much she loved me, how this was the happiest day of her life.'

Madsen watched him, let him do the work.

'Extreme emotion,' Auger said. 'Not a phobia, but love. She was overwhelmed by love, and it triggered . . .' He had to stop for a moment, seeing it again in his mind, the fires blooming beneath the tiny 'flite; his world, and Jay's, destroyed. 'She did it, didn't she?'

'I think so. Yes, she did.'

Auger rubbed his eyes, thinking of Jay in her fugue of tears. 'Do you think she knows? Do you think that explains—?'

'Maybe. But probably not.' Madsen slid the pack of images back into their envelope and placed it on the table.

'That's what she was doing, then,' Auger said, sitting back as it hit him like a bolt. 'That was it. Her research at GenMed. It had to be. She was conducting neurological nano-based research, and she was self-experimenting. She always did that. She said the risk was too great to ask anyone else to take it if she wasn't prepared to do it herself.'

Madsen sighed. 'I doubt she knew the true risks. They'll have used her. Ultimately, she was just another guinea pig. Whatever she was using was probably an attempt to develop safe and controllable psychokinetic powers without exposure to the beasts. For D3.'

'But it hasn't worked, has it? It failed. They've got nowhere.'

'So?' Madsen rubbed at his head.

'Forget about Jay for a moment. The D3 project's still going. Why? It's bound to fail, isn't it?'

'They can't abort it now. The world's going to end anyway. It's displacement activity. It's fiddling while the world burns.'

Auger shook his head. 'No. I don't believe that. The Administration's stepped up its publicity. There's something they think will work.'

'If there was something new, they'd announce it. God knows, it would boost enrolment. All they've done is build ships and develop better autoids.'

'Then it has to be something they won't tell us. Something they can't tell us.' Auger sat back and nursed his coffee. Madsen went and made more, the Gaggia snorting like an unstoppable behemoth, then returned and sat with Auger again.

'So we have to find out what's happening in the research wing.'

'Yes,' Auger said, and he started to tell him about Astrid.

'Cathar,' Madsen murmured at the end of it. 'Always Cathar.'

The look on Madsen's face made Auger pause before saying, 'I have to get to her. I have a pair of bLinkers . . .'

Fly. Fly was in his mind again. He brought the bLinkers onto the table and left them there between himself and Madsen.

Madsen eyed them. 'Have you—?'

'Not yet.' He turned them over, the tendrils squirming over the palps of his fingers. He showed Madsen the passport nodule.

'Means nothing, Auger. Saves you from the hardware barbs. It's the software you need to worry about. Cathar's dangerous, Auger. More so than you can imagine. It isn't just another game. You can't go there. You'd have no chance.'

'I have no other chance. I have no choice. I have to do something.'

Madsen sighed. 'Do you trust me, Auger?'

'I don't know what to believe, Madsen. How can I know who to trust?' He stopped and looked at the man. 'Yes. I do trust you.'

'Give me the bLinkers, and then give me a day.'

He stood up. Auger did the same, then said, feeling unaccountably elated, 'Was there anything in that coffee, Madsen?'

Madsen grinned. 'Coffee. Water. I suspect the coffee was purer than the water, but otherwise there was nothing. The only other thing was the circumstances, but that's all there ever is, Auger. Circumstances. Everything else is just fact.'

Auger chuckled. 'But it was good coffee.'

TWENTY-SEVEN

'Okay, Auger, here are your bLinkers back. I've had a friend of mine take a look at them.'

Madsen put another pair of bLinkers on the table beside the first set. The two pairs of tendrils moved in unison. 'This is a symbiote. It gives you simultaneous split entry to the zone. In other words, two people can go in together with these, both covered by the single passport. You bLink together, you wake up in the zone together. It means you can have a partner who's your guide, who's been there before. Who may keep you alive.'

'A partner?' Auger pushed the two sets of bLinkers apart. 'You?'

Madsen shook his head. 'No, not me, Auger. Someone's got to stay here and hold the fort. And I've never been to Cathar. I can't help you there.'

'What do you mean, hold the fort? What's to hold?'

'Okay, you're asking for the downside now. These bLinkers are untraceable. Cathar's a closed zone, a research zone. Everyone that's in there, they know about. So you'll be setting off flares and sirens as soon as you bLink. My informant reckons you'll have maybe an hour in there. After that, they'll be starting to trace you. You have to be out, or they'll be here. I'll be watching you both.'

'So, who's my guide?'

Madsen raised his voice. 'Pi? Can you come in now.'

The door opened and a tall man came in on the wake of a sour stale smell. His cheeks and forehead were scored by the masks of a filter, and his skin beyond the filter line was eaten and blown with sores. In his arms he was cradling something, rocking it constantly.

Christ, thought Auger, the old beggar has a baby. Then the blanket slipped, and before the tramp could cover it again, Auger saw it was a doll made of visgel.

It was a beggar's hook, that was all. Please, help feed my baby. Auger wondered whether it worked, who would believe such a man could be caring for a child. He was holding it gently, though, protectively, as if Auger might be about to attack it. Auger revised his opinion again. The old man was just crazy. He'd had his doll so long he'd started to believe it was real.

'Auger,' Madsen said, 'I want you to meet my friend Pibald. Pi, this is Auger. Tell Auger about yourself.'

The tramp gathered himself together, holding the baby close, keeping it warm against his chest. It stank.

'I shouldn't be here,' he said, and lapsed into silence. His smell grew denser, curdling the airconned atmosphere. Auger kept his breathing shallow, skimming the top off the air.

'Where should you be, Pi?' Madsen asked him. Madsen seemed unaware of the stench.

'With my wife. With my child.'

'And where are they?'

The tramp looked up at Auger, and in his eyes Auger saw the hard, certain look that he saw every day in the eyes of the eager suicides.

'They're waiting for me in Cathar.'

'Go on,' Auger murmured, wondering what Madsen was playing at. Waiting there or in heaven, it was the same thing. He was another crazy with his eyes fixed elsewhere.

'I was in Cathar, years ago, and I met Jhalouk there. She was pregnant with my child when I was exiled. He'll be three years old now, and I've never seen him.'

'Him? A boy?' Auger wasn't interested, but the question asked itself, as if he was trying to bring the tramp back to sense.

Pibald looked at Auger with that certainty, though, saying, 'A boy. We knew. We were going to call him Fouane.' His head quite still, utterly sure, eyes open only slightly too wide. 'They need me. I know they need me.' He cradled the fake baby.

'Why were you exiled?'

'Not only me. All wakers. Calban seized control of Cathar. He caused the interface to be destroyed, so that we wakers could no longer reach Cathar. Cathar is undefended.'

He looked at Auger, and laughed. An edgy laugh this time. 'I know what you're thinking. This.' He lifted the swaddled doll. 'It keeps my thoughts with them, nothing more. You think I imagine it's alive? No. It's a symbol, a token. A representation. I'm not crazy. But I know what I know.'

Auger thought of the people who filled his days in Passive, the men and women who knew what they knew. And now here was another one, also seeking Auger's sanction to go to a place that didn't exist.

Was there any difference between them? Auger wanted there to be, for his own sake. He looked into the tramp's eyes and kept looking until he found something. But all he could see was that this one lived for his world, while they wanted to die for theirs. He wondered whether that difference would be enough.

'Thank you, Pi,' Madsen said. 'That's good. Would you mind leaving us for a few minutes?'

'Well?' Auger said, as the door closed, leaving only the smell of the old man lingering. 'This is the man who's going to keep me alive in Cathar?'

'Listen to me, Auger. Pibald was one of several people who went into Cathar when Maze was experimenting with beast-killing software. The player who used the name Calban was part of that. He's dead. If there's another Calban, it's a replacement. Construct or player. When Pibald talks of his exile, he means the closing down of Maze and of the zone at that time. He believes Cathar to be real, but that's no bad thing. He'll be focused. Jhalouk was a construct. You'll find constructs and players. Some of the players will be researchers, some will be guinea pigs.'

'Astrid.'

'Hopefully. And maybe others like her, too.'

'Troy Gordo,' Auger said. 'Though he could be part of the team. I'm not sure.'

'Yes.' Madsen paused. 'And there's one final category. There will be the Dirangesept beasts.'

Auger took it all in. 'Civil war in fairyland,' he said, trying to make it a joke.

'Cathar's killed a lot of real people, Auger. Take it seriously.'

'Am I safe, going in with your friend?'

'I don't know, Auger. But it has to be safer than going in blind. Go in with him once, at least. If he goes crazy, you can leave him behind next time. Remember, it has to be in short bursts, or else you'll be traced. And another thing. When you come out, you have to stay out for about six hours before you go back.'

'Six hours?' Auger shook his head emphatically. 'That's crazy. Why that long?' Thinking of Astrid.

'When you exit, you leave a lingering trace. Go back again too quickly and they can lock on to you more rapidly. A sort of law of diminishing returns. Sorry, Auger.' Madsen waited for the tightness to leave Auger's face. 'Hopefully you won't have to visit Cathar more than once or twice before you find her. If she's in a PVS, she's at least stable. We're okay as long as they don't decide to terminate her, and they could do that any time.'

Auger nodded.

'Good. Also, some ground rules. Be careful what you say and where you say it. They'll be monitoring the game. You have to assume everyone you meet is theirs. Give away as little as possible either to them or within hearing.' Madsen stood up. 'You still sure you want to do this?'

'I'm sure I'm going to. I'm not sure I want to.' He tapped his forehead and said, 'One last question, Madsen. You never broke into Rudd Merchant's room at GenMed, did you?'

'No. Why?'

'Someone did. Someone I know very well.' He closed his eyes, squeezed them tight shut. 'I just can't quite see them yet.'

Auger glanced around the empty warehouse. Madsen had made a good choice. Lots of exits, the place hard to locate. Safe, if anywhere was safe to bLink from.

Pibald was at his side, preparing himself. There was something different about him now. There was purpose. He was reflexively touching the hilt of the sword at his belt, drawing it a fraction out and slipping it back. It moved soundlessly, smooth as water. He glanced at Auger and said, his filter flattening the words, 'First, it won't be safe when we arrive. Calban's taken control of Cathar. He'll have the Hall guarded.'

'Madsen said Calban's dead.'

'This is Cathar, Auger. You listen to me about Cathar. Not Madsen.'

Auger shrugged. 'The Hall?'

'The Hall of Wakers. When you first arrive, it's where you wake up. When we arrived there, we were greeted and escorted from the hall. We have to assume it won't be like that this time. If Calban's taken Cathar he'll want the portal secured against assault. When you wake up, just stay quite still. Don't move at all. Just wait for me. I'll find you.'

'If you don't?'

'Count to a thousand. If I'm not there, they'll have caught me, or else we'll have woken up in different places. Though that's not likely, if we're going in together. Either way, if you get to a thousand, you're on your own.'

Pibald was crazy, but he was right. Maybe it wouldn't be Calban securing the hall, but whoever was running Cathar would be taking

294

precautions against hackers. It made sense to listen to Pibald. He'd go in the first time with him, then the tramp could go back to his alley and his visgel child.

'Okay.' At least he wouldn't have to suffer Pibald's stench in Cathar.

'Good,' Madsen said. 'Let's go.'

Leaning back on the thin coat spread on the ground beside Pibald, Auger saw the glance Madsen gave the kid who seemed to follow him around like Lethe trailed Auger. Jaime, he called him. A runt of a boy like she was a twist of a girl. Lost kids running after lost adults, he thought.

And then he glanced at Pibald, synchronising movements, and bLinked.

It came like sleep, like sleep and the waking from it stirred into one. Auger was counting without even realising it, had reached fifty before he knew it. He kept counting, kept his eyes closed, not daring to open them. There was such a silence that after a minute he wondered whether he was counting out loud, so piercing were the numbers in his head. Sixty-two, sixty-three . . .

Stale air, a smell of something rotten. Himself, unwashed, he realised. How long had he been here? A hundred and thirty-three, and thirty-four . . .

A sheet against his skin. He was naked. No, they were clothes he was feeling. He was dressed. But the clothes were loose, and the material unfamiliar. Three hundred and five, and six, seven . . .

Noise now, approaching feet. Close. Stopping by him. Someone lightly breathing. Watching me, waiting for me to give myself away. Four hundred and nine, and ten, is it Pibald, should I open my eyes? No, he'd say something. Keep still, keep still. Four hundred and twelve, and thirteen . . .

Still there, five hundred and twenty, twenty-one, I'm going to start shaking in a minute, and fifty-three, -four, footsteps receding now. Risk opening my eyes? No, could be more of them. Six hundred and forty, forty-one . . .

Only the rhythm of the numbers was keeping him stable. And the footsteps returned, a hand on his shoulder, shaking him.

'Time to wake up.'

He opened his eyes cautiously and looked up. A tall vaulted ceiling rose into a core of deep shadow. Auger sat up slowly and stared around. The room was big and gloomy. Along the walls were set a few small, square windows high and out of reach, with bright, almost luminous sky-blue blinds closing off the day. Dust trembled in the air up there.

Auger looked at the windows again. No. Blue sky. That was blue sky. The thought of it made Auger faintly dizzy. So real. Tatoro had been right about that. It was perfect.

Regathering himself, he looked down again and peered around. The room was full of beds, dozens of them, and bodies lying on them, but there was no one else conscious in sight. The room was quiet. There was just himself and Pibald.

'Was that you before? Christ, you scared the crap out of me. What the hell—?'

'Calm down. I was just checking you were okay and it was safe in here. That's all. And that you'd do what you were told.' He stretched out a hand and pulled Auger to his feet. There were sandals at the foot of the bed. Auger slipped them on, not surprised at them fitting, but noticing they were worn, as if he'd used them before, worn them for months. As if he'd woken up as he did every day to wear the clothes of every day.

'There's a guard outside,' Pibald said. 'Just the one. But, then, there's just the one door, so we can't avoid him. And he's a shade, too.'

'A shade?'

'Leave him to me. I'll deal with him. We're on the coast here. The harbour's straight ahead. If I remember right, there's a lane to the left, then a hillside. Follow the lane, you'll find a path, wait for me. Okay, take a run and go. Once you're through the door, roll and run. Don't look back, it'll slow you down.'

Auger gathered himself without thinking. The authority in Pibald's voice was total. Auger took a short run and threw his shoulder at the door, which splintered and gave. There was a stone step that took Auger off balance and he fell awkwardly, tumbling forward and down. A shape was over him, falling heavily on top of him and crushing him. He heard breathing in his ear and then an approaching yell and a thump and the weight was gone.

In sudden fear Auger pushed himself to his feet and looked to his left, breathing fast.

The sea? The sea shouldn't be to his left. Pibald had got it wrong, had forgotten.

No, Auger had been knocked aside by that, that thing. Left again, and there it was, a narrow lane leading up a hillside. The lane lined with trees. Sunlight. Safety.

At the start of the lane Auger hesitated and looked back. Pibald was struggling with something more than a head taller than himself. A shade. It looked human, but it was fighting Pibald in total silence. Pibald had its sword, he must have used Auger as distraction and taken it while it was thinking Auger was its only prey, and the thing's head was almost severed. Pibald was retreating, hacking at the thing whose stretch was almost as great as Pibald's reach with the sword.

Auger started to run back towards Pibald.

Pibald yelled, 'No! Get back.'

The shade stepped closer again to Pibald, who drew the sword back and allowed the creature to reach towards his throat. And then he swung hard, and the shade's head tipped away and fell heavily to the ground. The body slumped after it.

Pibald furiously motioned Auger on before slipping back inside the building. Auger was halfway up the hillside when he became aware of a crackling noise behind him. He looked back to see the Hall of Wakers in flames. A crowd was gathering there.

A few minutes later, Pibald was with him, his face blackened and gasping for breath. He stank of smoke, but he was smiling. 'We're in.'

Auger pointed down at the Hall. 'Why the hell did you do that?'

'They'll know anyway that someone has broken out. If I'd left the place as it was, they would have gone straight in and found my body gone. You, it doesn't matter. You're anonymous. But seeing me gone, they'd go straight for Jhalouk. This way we've a chance of getting to her first.'

Pibald had taken authority over Auger. Auger wondered whether to say something now, but decided against it. Jhalouk was a known quantity, a part of the game. If they could find her, she could be a source of information, at least until Auger and Pibald were identified by GenMed and they changed Jhalouk's parameters.

'Okay, let's go,' Auger said. He tried to make it sound a decision, but it came out more like acceptance. After they had climbed for a while, Auger said, 'What exactly was that thing back there? The shade.'

'I don't know. I think of them as living machines. Calban's soldiers. They feel no pain, don't talk, tire or turn tail. And they're strong. You can't outrun them. You can't wound them. They don't think, but they don't really need to. You have to decapitate them or pierce their heart.'

'Fine. I'll remember that,' Auger said.

Pibald was far fitter than Auger, striding swiftly up the track, and Auger wondered why that should be so, until he realised that Pibald was existing here on adrenalin. The lane became a path, lined with trees in full leaf. Pibald turned off down a thin track, and stopped at the edge of a line of trees, panting. He stepped back into their shade.

'Here we are. This is where she used to live.'

Auger noticed Pibald's slight hesitation. It was a small mud and brick shack with a square garden fenced off at the back. There was a scent of herbs and citrus fruit. A green door, paint peeling from the wood. Rich blue curtains at the windows, tied back with paler blue cord.

Auger held Pibald back. 'Let me go. Better you aren't recognised yet. What shall I say?'

'We're travellers. Ask who lives here. If it's her, I'll come out. If not, say we heard a woman with a child lived here. Ask if they know where she is.'

'Shall I mention Jhalouk's name?'

'No. Not yet. It might put her at risk.'

'Okay.' About to leave the cover of the trees, Auger hesitated. 'Is there any chance she's real, Pibald?' And seeing Pibald's face, he added, 'I mean a player, a guinea pig. Or else a GenMed researcher.'

Pibald shook his head. 'She's real, Auger. In here, everything's real. You even start to think otherwise and you're going to be dead very soon.'

Auger nodded. No point in asking Pibald, then. He was never going to be any more than a guide in Cathar. A map reader, maybe a bodyguard. Auger left the cover of the trees and began to approach the hut. He knocked at the door and waited. Maybe there was no one there. Maybe the program was deciding what to do about this.

The rustle of light footsteps rose behind the door and stopped silent, and through the uneven wooden slats a shape swelled and fixed. Someone inspecting him. He stood back, showing open palms, and waited on.

Whoever it was, they were in no hurry. Auger wondered. Not a player, he decided. The place seemed isolated, and a player was going to want action. Probably not a researcher either, for the same reason. So a construct, then. Part of the framework.

The first thing he saw was the yellow of her eyes.

The badge of the construct. The Catharian. He felt instantly foolish. Madsen had told him that. So much information, and he'd forgotten the basics. But then he felt fine again. He'd figured it out right, that this would be a construct. Okay, then. Get the information and go.

Auger took a small step to the side, in case she was Pibald's woman, the construct he was obsessed with. If she was, it might at least clear his system. But there was no movement behind him from Pibald.

The woman said, 'Yes?' She didn't put much curiosity in the word. Auger had a strange sense of a life behind her words, a life he had interrupted. That his knock on the door hadn't summoned her into existence, and that after he and Pibald had left, her life would go on. Crazy. He examined her, the construct. She was short and plump, wiping sweat from her forehead with the back of a hand. Callused fingers. Brown hair spilling from a tie of cloth, the same material as her dress. A heavy brooch pinning the dress together, dragging at the cloth, pulling at its weave. It took his attention, the brooch, and he wondered if it was a clue, something in the game. But then he dismissed this. It was just an old brooch, a flower worked in bronze. Important to her, though, by its polish and the faded detail.

The woman had seen his stare. She pulled the dress tight and held her hand there, protecting herself. Auger realised what she was thinking and felt his cheeks redden.

And instantly caught himself – what she was *thinking*? Christ, much more of this and he'd be as crazy as Pibald.

'I'm sorry,' he said quickly. 'I'm looking for someone. I wondered if you could help me. They might have passed here.'

The woman interrupted him, saying, 'There's been no one up here for months, except me.' She was looking at him oddly. 'No one comes up here any more. Why should they? No reason. I haven't seen you before. Where are you from?'

Auger pointed vaguely behind himself. He felt oddly self-conscious, as if he was being watched and judged by this woman, and he felt stupid for reacting like this when this was just a game and she was a construct programmed with a certain range of information that she would or would not provide, depending on how her buttons were pushed.

'You look familiar,' she said slowly, intruding into his consideration of her. As if he could be familiar to her. Maybe she wasn't a construct after all. Recognising him? Or just probing? He looked more closely at her. The yellow eyes didn't have to mean a thing. Madsen's information was years old. The game had moved on. Technology had moved on.

She turned her back on him and stepped back into the shadows of the house. Auger realised he was expected to follow her. Was she showing trust? But, then, it could equally be a trap. So was she looking for trust in him? He hesitated a moment, glancing back at the bushes where Pibald was concealed, wanting a signal from him. But Pibald didn't reveal himself.

The entry to the zone had been a trap, back at the harbour. Auger tried to remember game setups, protocols. The first encounter no more than a hook, the second encounter usually a chance to gather information, to draw breath and take stock. So, safe. Why would Cathar be any different?

Auger had to stoop slightly to go inside. He raised his head to see there was no hallway, just a single large room taking up the entire floor area of the shack. Nowhere to hide.

It had been trust, then, and he had played it right by entering. Auger felt immediately confident again. He'd played games like this before, knew the tests, knew how to read them and how to work them. He was in and safe, and next time he could leave Pibald behind.

The woman was standing in the centre of the room, her arms folded. She looked quite solid there, lit by a fire in a hearth to her left, casting flickering shadows of herself across the room. She was as real, as solid as anything he'd ever seen, and it didn't matter a damn. Madsen hadn't needed to be worried. No matter how much was at stake, Auger knew this was just a game. He'd play it like it was life, but he wasn't going to let it prick him enough to make him bleed.

The woman tilted her head. 'Are you searching for the child? Is that it? You have the appearance.'

Child? The word surprised him. Making him think of Lethe, perhaps. Or Pibald, even. And then, finally, but in a way that jolted him like a fake fortune teller guessing a hidden truth, it made him think of Jay and the child she had been pregnant with. His child.

But it was just the woman's program. Anyone would get this response. 'The woman and the child,' Auger began, then cut it off. That was Pibald's quest, not his. He wasn't interested in any child in Cathar. 'Strangers,' he said, trying to remember the word here. 'Are there any new wakers? A woman? About twenty-five?' He tried to describe Astrid to her.

'Wakers are taken away,' the woman said without consideration, and then paused, squinting at him. 'But you, you have the look. And you're a waker, aren't you?'

'The look?' Auger said involuntarily. 'What look?'

She raised a hand and pointed at the wall to his side. Above a small cabinet was a picture in a wooden frame. A portrait. A man? On the wall, the indicating shadow of the woman's finger multiplied and faded in the firelight. Auger took a few steps closer to the painting. No, a child. A boy. The firelight animated the eyes and gave life to the young features. The paint was heavy, so full of texture that shadows were moving within the brushstrokes.

He stepped closer still, until he was facing the picture, then had to move to the side, as his own shadow was hooding it. The child still stared at him.

'Yes,' the woman said, her voice suddenly soft. She was standing beside him, glancing from Auger to the child's face. 'You have the look.'

He shivered. The child did have the look. It had his look about it, and more. It—

Behind him, the door jerked open, and the light of the day outside muted and dulled the gold of the fire. The portrait seemed to flatten and withdraw. The woman turned an instant before Auger.

Pibald was silhouetted in the doorway. 'Everything all right in here?'

'Yes. I told you to stay outside, Pi—' Auger cut the name off quickly. No point identifying Pibald. GenMed would probably have Maze's old records. Auger turned to the woman, but glanced at Pibald first, emphasising the words, making sure he was listening. 'I'm Bolt.' Stupid name, but the first thing to enter his head. Still, it was done now. He was stuck with it here. 'And Pi's my companion. Don't worry about him.'

'Bolt,' the woman whispered, nodding to herself. 'Yes.'

Pibald was at the portrait now, touching the face with his fingers, running them along the thick hard trails of paint and murmuring something to himself.

Auger looked at the portrait again. He still saw the resemblance, but no longer so strongly. Pibald was still fingering the painting, still muttering. As Auger went up to him, Pibald glanced from the child's face to Auger and back, and Auger heard it.

'My son. Look, it's my son.'

'Yes,' Auger whispered, not knowing what else to say. Of course it looked like Pibald's son to Pibald. Just as to Auger it looked like his own.

Auger felt he was getting the measure of Cathar. Cathar was not just a programmed environment. It was a true game. It had its story, the arcs of its action. And within that, the researchers had their objective. But Auger could only follow his own purpose within that of the game. He couldn't cut through, and if he tried it, he'd fail. Whatever Cathar was, the format was that of a game. And it had recognised him as a new player and locked him in by telling him he was special. He was The One.

But it had told Pibald the same thing, and they couldn't both be The One. So Cathar wasn't perfect. GenMed put its guinea pigs into Cathar one by one and kept them apart. That was how it worked. It couldn't cope with two players together. It couldn't adapt.

'Where are the wakers taken?' he asked the woman. 'Who takes them?'

'Calban, of course.' She gave him a peculiar look. He understood that asking the question was like asking what colour the sky was. 'To the island,' she added. 'In his search for The Child.'

The child again, Auger thought. The way she says it, The Child. That must be the game, then. Rescue The Child, win a free play. 'Thank you,' he said, and turned towards the door. 'Pi, it's time to go.'

Auger was through the door as Pibald stopped to say to the woman, 'If anyone looks for us—'

'No one was here,' the woman said serenely. She smiled. 'I told you, no one ever comes here.' The door closed behind her.

As they moved into the trees, Auger tried to break down the time they'd spent so far. Ten minutes getting out of the Hall of Waking, fifteen making it up to the hut, half an hour with the woman. Cutting it fine.

'Pibald, we need to think about—'

'I know. But we need to put some distance between here and where we leave ourselves first. So you'd better speed up. And you'd better think of me as Pi, too. All the time, not just when we've got company. Safer that way. Okay, *Bolt*?'

Auger let that go, but after Pibald had been going for at least five minutes, he pulled him up again. 'We've been here more than an hour, Pi. We can't risk being traced. We have to get out now.'

Pibald stopped. Behind him, a tree was whipped into life by the wind, a billow of leaves stirring into action. 'Fine, Auger. But what about *here*? You think you're safe now? They'll be after us right now, and when we're gone, they'll still be after us. I know you think this isn't real. Well, I'm not going to argue with you about that. But it isn't a game either. This is a hostile environment, and when we bLink out, you're going to leave *this* behind.' He leaned forward and gave Auger a sharp shove in the chest. 'Your body isn't a military trig. It gets burnt, you don't get issued another one. Or if you do, they're going to be better prepared for you next time. So we have to make it safe first.'

'Okay. Just a few more minutes, though.' Cathar was as real to Pibald as Earth, and maybe he was right. Maybe that was what was needed here.

'Are you a Vet, Pibald?'

'No.'

A hard, cut-throat negative, which meant yes, Auger realised. Pibald just didn't want to talk about it. The forest grew thicker as they went on, its floor remaining dry. Pibald kept them away from fallen leaves, avoiding disturbing softer ground and dodging spindly branches.

Auger ran through what he knew of the second project and its so-called Far Warriors. They'd mine and wire the surrounding area before bLinking out for rest, leaving their trigs down on the planet. Leaving Cathar had to be done with the same care. Pibald had to be a Vet. It hadn't been obvious before, but there was something about him, his language and that wary confidence, that gave it away here.

'I went down once,' Pibald said eventually. 'Just once.'

He picked up his pace and went ahead, talking as if to himself, and Auger made no effort to join him. Auger just followed closely, concentrating on trying to be as light-footed as Pibald. Pibald knew what he was doing. Tracing them wouldn't be easy.

'We were the scouts. There were six of us. The elite. The elite. That's what they told us, but what they meant was that we were expendable. We went down before the first wave. In single shuttles. It was a lonely drop. We didn't know if they'd be prepared for us, after the first project all those years before. We were hoping, expecting, that the beasts would have no memory of the previous time. That they had been no more than beasts, and that the D1 fiasco was just sour luck. So, the six of us were the first toes in the water, and we didn't know if it was going to burn us or freeze us.'

He stopped talking for a minute, walking in the forest's quiet fold.

'My autoid got nilled before the shuttle even hit the ground. They remembered, all right. Hot water, Auger, hotter than hell. They came through the hull, their claws ripping through it, through me—' He quickened his pace, cracking dry leaves underfoot like small explosions. 'I exited and never bLinked down again. I heard the beast in my skull. *Why are you doing this again?* It scared the shit out of me, that voice. But it was more scared than I was, Auger.'

He stopped talking for a moment, pushing low branches aside. 'So I was debriefed, shipboard. And the other five, too. Same thing had happened to them. None of us was going back down there. No way. We made that plain. We had no business there.'

The trees thinned into a grassy clearing. Pibald led Auger quickly across the open ground and back into the shadows. 'The techies played a little with the autoids, but it made no difference. We told them we weren't interested. They put us straight back into CrySis. No contact with the rest of the guys. They didn't want us disturbing morale. We were brought out of CrySis six months after everyone else back on Earth, when D2 was a dead subject. It suited me. There was no point in saying anything about it. I didn't want to, anyway. We were marked deceased on project records, and that was it. They told me to go away and start a new life. But what new life was there?'

'What about Maze?'

'They never knew I was a Vet. They took me on because of my scores, never questioned why they were so high.' He turned his head and looked at Auger with something that looked like amusement. 'You're wondering if I've got a beast.' He tapped his skull. 'Never seen it. Never heard it. Don't know. Does it bother you?'

Auger tried to say no, but the syllable came out awkwardly.

'Doesn't bother me,' Pibald said.

That's because you're crazy anyhow, Auger couldn't help thinking.

Still, he was acting sane enough here. Auger thought back to the Hall of Waking. What Pibald had done had made sense, firing it. But why had it been guarded? Was that part of the game, or had GenMed been expecting invaders?

They carried on until eventually the forest petered out at an expanse of grey rock. Pibald accelerated over the bare surface, calling, 'This is what I was looking for. Come on. Even if they trace us to the rock, they'll never work out where we left it.'

Auger caught up with Pibald and ran beside him. 'Do you know the island she was talking about, Pi?'

'Calban's island. He used to murder wakers there. Calban's a wizard, Auger. Some of the wakers could do magic, but Calban, he was something special.'

'But he's dead, Pi.' Madsen had said that. Calban was dead.

'You heard the woman,' Pibald said flatly. They were at the far edge of the rock now. Off to the right were fields of pale green set out in a pattern of grids. Pibald pointed. 'We'll follow the stone walls.' He set off, stopping to wait for Auger at a junction of fields. The rough, solid build of waist-high stone walls looked like it had been there for ever with its dusting of golden lichen. They clambered over it, careful not to pull away the foliage, and Pibald pointed again, this time to a small copse at the edge of a field. 'There. That fallen tree. It looks like it's been down just a few days. Lots of leaves still on the branches, and no animals yet. We'll make ourselves a hole beneath it. It'll do fine.'

'A hole? What will we dig a hole with?'

'Don't worry. I'll do it,' Pibald said.

And Auger watched as Pibald stood there by the toppled tree, silent, nothing moving but his lips. There was a noise, Auger thought, perhaps a squall starting to rise, but there was no breath in the air. And yet Pibald was now moving as if resisting a gale. And his chest was heaving as if the wind had been knocked from him.

And then it stopped, and Pibald slumped to his knees.

'Pi?' Auger felt distinctly shaky. He didn't understand this.

'You'll have to help me,' Pibald murmured. 'I'm not used to it.'

'What? What do you mean?'

Pibald nodded, and Auger looked to see a long, shallow hole excavated beneath the branches of the tree.

'I was never very good at it,' Pibald murmured. 'Quickly.'

Magic, Auger thought, pulling a blanket of leaves over them both. Pibald had no strength left even for that.

Just before they bLinked out, Auger said to Pibald, 'Did you trust the woman in the hut?' Not that it made much difference. By now Cathar's operators would know two unauthorised players had entered Cathar, broken free and were moving towards Calban.

'An hour and a half,' Madsen said. Auger could hear the anger held tight in his throat. 'That was too long. Let's go.' He pulled Auger up and Pibald after him. 'We have to get out of here now.'

Auger pocketed the bLinkers and struggled for balance. Pibald had struggled on his mailed blanket-coat and was picking up his visgel baby. He was still crazy. Maybe crazier still, now he'd been back to the source of it.

'Is it clear out there?' Madsen called through the tarnished metal wall.

Auger heard a muffled, 'Front's okay,' from the other side, and recognised Lethe's voice. And then a boy's voice giving the all-clear behind. Jaime.

'Then let's go,' Madsen said. He took the heavy door handle in two hands and leaned back on it until the steel doors of the warehouse started to move. He let the door go, its inertia still hauling the warped metal on, and pushed Auger and then Pibald through the widening gap and onto the street.

'Okay, everyone separate. Auger, Pi, we'll meet at my place in one hour. Jaime and Lethe, tomorrow morning. You've got six hours. Don't be followed. You got that?' Madsen didn't wait for an answer or look back as he crossed the street.

Auger went left out of the warehouse and kept going, fast. Out of the corner of his eye he saw Lethe slouching down a side road and away. Pibald was gone already, headed in the opposite direction. And the boy looked like he was following Lethe, despite Madsen's instructions. She'd spot him and lose him, though, Auger was sure of that. Lethe was the best street worker Auger had ever seen.

Across the street from the warehouse was a derelict factory. As soon as the others were out of sight, Madsen doubled back and made his way through the rows of rusting machines to climb up to the foreman's gantry. From there he made his way to the fire escape and worked his way up the corroding stairway to the flat roof. The roof was thick with dust, the dust pitted by the remains of dead birds and small animals. The atmosphere had made quick skeletons of them and then gnawed the bones down to toothpicks. Madsen pulled his coat tighter and yanked on the filter straps until the edges scored his cheeks before lying down flat at the rooftop's edge. There was a junction of streets beneath him, and a termite mound like an orange sarcophagus. Up here the air swirled and tugged at him. He didn't want to be up here for long. But, then, he didn't expect to have to.

Five minutes was all it took. Two road cars swerved round the termite hill and pulled up in front of the open warehouse door, and four men spilled out of each. Unmarked cars, no uniforms. Nothing to identify them. Madsen pushed himself back from the edge and left before they started to widen their search.

'You were following me.'

Jaime heard it but had no time to react before she shoved him hard in the back, pushing him to his hands and knees. He straightened and brushed the street debris from his gloves. She was standing in front of him now, hands on her hips. How had she done that? He'd lost her ten minutes ago.

'So?' He wanted to sound hard, but it didn't come out like that. He had no luck at all. Look at him. Turned around by a girl. He stood as tall as he could, and was nearly her height.

'So why were you following me? Or trying to.'

She was not as pretty as Riandra, but there was a liveliness to her, and a brittle hardness. 'I don't know,' he said, shrugging.

'Well, you're shit at it. And you're shit at checking your own back, too.'

He felt stupid, and felt it more when he saw her register that on his face.

'No point worrying about it now, it's a bit late,' she said. 'Anyway, there was only me behind you. I made sure.' She pulled the collar of her coat tight around her thin neck, and for a moment she seemed like she was the one who needed looking out for.

'What's your name?' he said, made briefly bold by that thought.

She squinted at him and muttered, 'Lethe,' as if she was giving something away.

'I'm Jaime.' He added a smile, but she wasn't interested.

'Your guy, Madsen, he told you to follow me?'

'No.'

'No, he didn't look stupid.'

'He isn't stupid.' Jaime wondered why he'd put so much heat into it, for the bald old man who meant nothing more to him than something to do for a bit of cash.

'Well, *you've* got a friend,' Lethe said, smirking at him. Jaime wanted to slap her face for that, but he was pretty sure he'd just end up flat on his back again.

She jerked her chin at him. 'You got some place to live? Got no folks, have you? I can tell. Little lost boy.'

He felt himself blushing. 'At least I've got a friend. You've got nothing.' She shrugged as if she didn't care, but Jaime could tell he'd hit her with that. 'What's it to you where I live, anyway?' he said.

'You haven't got the hostel look, little lost boy. I need somewhere to stay, so maybe I'll put up with you. Auger's got no idea where I am now. He's a loser. He's just heading to get himself killed, that's all.'

'Auger? Madsen thinks he's okay.'

She shrugged and pulled at the coat again.

'What's Auger to you,' Jaime asked her, and couldn't resist adding, 'if he's not your friend?'

'He did something, but he did it for himself, not for me. That's all. He doesn't care about me.' She sniffed under the filter, raised its seal and wiped her nose quickly with the back of a hand.

'So why are you here with him?'

'Maybe there'll be something for me at the end of it. I don't know.'

Jaime shifted his feet on the rough ground, the cold of the day seeping up through the soles of his shoes. 'Anyway,' he said, 'what makes you think you can just come and live with me?'

She lifted her chin, confident again, taunting him. But a little fragile too, he saw. Not like Riandra. 'I'll tell you what, little lost boy. You go home, and see if you can get there without me. And then maybe I'll teach you how to lose me. And the day you can lose me, I'll leave. Okay, little lost boy?'

'Fuck you, Lethe,' Jaime said, but into the wind. She was gone. He stood for a minute, the air swirling around him, until he was calm again, and then he set off. Follow him, would she? Scrawny, scratchy girl. He thought of Madsen, Madsen who had given him friendship and Jaime hadn't even realised it.

He doubled back, went through ruined buildings, and came to

Centrepoint. Lethe's face wouldn't leave him. 'Okay, follow me now,' he muttered into his filter. The tower was just a mountain of concrete scree now, and Jaime hauled himself up it, deafening himself with the hard avalanche he set off in his wake and blinding himself with the swarming dust. He scrambled down the other side and ran on, listening in vain for the sounds of pursuit as the scree settled, glancing over his shoulder and watching the dust heave in the air.

And nothing. She wasn't behind him. She wasn't even trying. She'd just been messing with him, playing. Only her face was still with him, taunting him. He ran on, filling his head with answers to her taunts as his feet pounded the cracked pavements.

And, of course, he opened his door and there she was. She just glanced at him and said, 'Looks like I'm going to be here a while. You got any food at all, or am I going to have to do that?'

'I think maybe I was followed back from the warehouse,' Auger said. He was rubbing his eyes. He'd never been bLinkered before for so long, and there was an ache in his skull. His shoulder was also still reminding him of Fly. He ate the food Madsen had left on the table for him without noticing the taste. He was so hungry that he probably wouldn't have noticed it even if Pibald hadn't been giving out his stench from across the room, where he was asleep on the floor.

'Maybe?' said Madsen.

'Maybe. Maybe I'm just twitchy. Next time put Lethe behind me. If there's anyone, she'll flush them.'

'Okay. In the meantime, and from now on, you stay here with me,' Madsen said. 'Gordo's dead. They're closing all the loopholes, cutting the loose ends.'

'Maybe they're panicking,' Auger said.

'Or maybe the research is complete and they're done.'

Auger felt himself tighten up, and Madsen must have seen it, because he said, 'Astrid's still alive, for now. They'd have announced otherwise.' He glanced across the room at Pibald, who was muttering something in his sleep. 'But you can't go back to your place. That's finished now. From now forward, you're as dead as I am. Pibald, too. What about Lethe?'

'She told me she's staying with Jaime. I don't think he knew it at the time.' Auger smiled at the thought of it. At least it solved his problem, although a part of him felt unaccountably hurt by it. He checked the time. 'When do I go back? To Cathar?'

'When do *we* go back?' Pibald said. He hadn't moved, but his eyes were wide. '*We*, Auger.'

Madsen gave Auger a look as he hesitated, and Pibald said, 'I did it all like you told me. I know what you're thinking, but you still need me. You can't leave me here now.' He shifted position, the mail of his cloak jingling. 'You think you know Cathar? Do you?'

'Three more hours,' Madsen said, when Auger let that go. 'Like I said a few minutes ago.'

Auger stood up, sat down again. 'This is crazy. The longer we wait, the readier they'll be. Here and in the zone.' And the more risk to Astrid, he thought.

'You go back now, and they'll be on top of you inside twenty minutes,' Madsen said. 'Why don't you just get some rest, like Pibald? Then you'll get your hour.'

TWENTY-EIGHT

Standing up to brush the leaves from his shirt, Auger said, deciding he may as well make peace, 'Why don't you tell me some more about Cathar?'

Pibald gave him a short look and started walking. 'You aren't interested in Cathar. I don't even know why you're here.'

Auger fell into step with him, silent for a moment. 'Okay,' he said. 'I have a friend who's at GenMed, in a coma. I think she's also in Cathar. I have to get to her.' He had a sudden vision of Astrid lying in a bed in the Vets' wing, only in his mind the Vets' wing was also the Hall of Wakers. It was as if everything was reversed, he thought. To wake in one place you had, in spirit, to leave the other. Except that it might not be in your power to do so.

'And that's your quest,' Pibald said. Auger glanced at him, searching for the irony that was in the words, but Pibald's expression was closed to him. 'Is that all?' Pibald said.

Auger shrugged.

'Okay, this is mine. Cathar is as real as anywhere I've ever been. As solid as Earth, as real as Dirangesept. But to me it was always a good place. The only one. I met a woman here, and she was going to have my child. But Calban destroyed all that. I was forced to leave Cathar and Jhalouk, my woman.' Pibald stooped to flick a stone from the sole of his boot. 'Tell me, Auger, do you have a dream?'

'Not like that. No.'

'If you did, maybe you wouldn't mock the dreams of others.'

'But they're dreams. They aren't real. What's the point?'

'They give you purpose. They give you hope.'

'Or death, Pibald. Heaven's a dream, and you have to be dead to get there. Sometimes you have to be protected from your dreams.'

Pibald looked and grinned at Auger. He waved a hand, taking in all of

Cathar – the sky, the land, everything. 'This is my dream, right? And who's protecting who right now?'

They were climbing now, leaving the fields and meadows behind and moving on to harder ground studded with black and cracked rocks. The only vegetation was a spiky herb with red-veined leaves that pierced the earth and the rocks with equal ease.

'Where are we headed?' Auger said.

'High ground. There's a bluff to the east of the village that overlooks Calban's island.'

They walked for what Auger reckoned to be about half an hour, climbing steadily until there were no more trees and no more bushes, only a rising slope of cropped grass beneath a flat blue sky.

And then ahead of them he saw an end to the bluff, an edge so straight and sharp it seemed etched against the sky. They drew closer to the edge, and the wind started to pick up around them, making it harder for them to keep their footing on the increasingly rough ground. Auger leant into the wind, pushing his feet on as if trudging against a river current. It was hard to breathe against the wind, and water stung his eyes. He could hear Pibald grunting with effort.

Who are you?

Auger shouted through the wind, 'What did you say?'

Pibald kept walking, head down. 'Nothing,' he called back. 'Keep going.'

The wind was whipping his hair now, and drawing tears from Auger's eyes.

'We're nearly there,' Pibald called, turning to cup his hands against the wind. And a few paces further on, he stopped dead and dropped flat to lie on his stomach, and waited for Auger to join him. 'Look,' he said, pointing.

The wind was driving deep into Auger's lungs. He had to drop his chin into his chest to breathe.

Before him was a heaven of uninterrupted, perfect azure. Beneath the seamless sky, the glittering blue sea appeared to extend for ever. And in the heart of the sea Auger saw what seemed a ragged-edged hole, a shadowless pit fringed with white froth. A black hole. An inexplicable fault. A program error.

'Calban's island,' Pibald whispered, or seemed to whisper. It was a shout, though, a shriek into the wind.

Black rock, Auger realised. Not a hole at all. It was simply absorbing the light, hurling away the crashing water.

'That's where they'll be,' Pibald yelled, and for a moment Auger believed him, that Pibald's woman and his child would be there.

But Astrid must be there, too, by the rules of the game. Prisoners were held in the heart of the tyrant's domain.

'Time's up, Pi,' Auger yelled. 'We need to exit.'

Pibald nodded.

They went down the slope hard and fast, pushed on by the wind, thrust away from the cliff's edge, from the sight of Calban's island.

Jaime made for home again after Auger and Pibald had come out of their zone. Two days now, and they didn't trust him like they trusted Lethe. Letting her tail Auger, and she hadn't spotted anyone behind him. They ought to give him a chance. There was probably no one anyway. Auger was nervous. Not like Madsen. Not like Pibald.

They were his friends. They cared about him. He spent a whole hour jinking and backtracking, thinking about it. About her.

He ran up the stairs, his thoughts burning, and then stopped. Something felt wrong.

As soon as he coded the door, he knew it for sure. The lock clicked at the third digit. He punched the fourth automatically and went in, furious with Lethe for screwing with his stuff again. She screwed with everything, rearranged his clothes, his books and vids, his games, his whole god-damned life. She cooked for him because she said he couldn't, and then when she'd shown him how to do it, she moaned that it wasn't as good as when she did it. Not that it mattered to him. It all tasted the same anyway.

'Who taught you to cook, then?' he'd asked her last night, after she'd pushed his meal aside. The question must have caught her off guard because, instead of telling him to mind his own business, she'd dropped her head and muttered, 'My mother.'

That had shut down the conversation pretty successfully for the rest of the evening. Lethe had sat down and read the same page of a book for two hours solid like someone had pressed the pause button on her, and Jaime had planted himself in front of a screen, playing games and watching vids.

Her mother. Jaime couldn't understand that. Mothers and fathers didn't do what hers had done. They loved you or they hated you. His had hated him, so they had left him on the street, a raggedy baby screaming for love. It was clear to Jaime that Lethe's father had hated her to have left her, and it was just as clear that her mother must have felt the same to have wanted her dead. So why had she taught her to cook? It made no sense.

But, then, Lethe made no sense. She loved her mother one minute, hated her the next. And it was the same with Auger. She didn't give a shit about him, but wouldn't walk away. She was weird as hell.

But what was even more weird was that Jaime was getting as messed up by the whole damn thing as Lethe was. He'd sat at his screen eyeing her all night, and she'd sat there staring at that damn book, and it was like nuclear fission between them. He could almost feel it.

He pushed the door open, pushed it hard with his anger. 'Christ, Lethe—'

He stopped. She was sitting in a chair facing the door.

'Looks like you didn't learn a thing, Jaime,' she said evenly. 'Got yourself followed home by your friends.' She jerked her head at Fargo, who was standing at her side, grinning. Her head was all she could jerk, everything else tied, hands behind her, ankles to the chair legs. Her face was red and shining, her left cheek swollen. 'You let these guys trail you? A purple elephant could have lost them with its legs hobbled.'

Fargo raised an arm and put another welt on her face, then touched his own with its fresh bruises. 'You got yourself a real ball-breaker here, Jaime. Got a pox-poor taste in women, you know.' He snapped his fingers and Riandra leant in to snuggle at his side. She had a vacant look and her cheeks were sucked in to the bone. Her balance didn't look too good. Jaime wondered what she was on.

She gave him a vague smile. 'Hi, Jaime. I'm with Fargo.'

'Hi, Jaime,' Zee mimicked from the other side of Lethe's chair. He rested his arm around her shoulders, then put his hand to the nape of her neck and squeezed. Lethe winced. She was looking steadily at Jaime.

Jaime couldn't meet her eyes. This wasn't even connected with Auger. This was his fault totally. It must have been yesterday, he'd been so cross with them all that he'd spent an hour blasting aliens at Real Skills on the way back and hadn't taken care coming from there to home. He'd seen Zee at Skills, too.

He looked away from Lethe and said, 'What do you want, Fargo?'

'I still want that tramp. We had a deal. I want to know where he is.'

'Any deal we had is gone. You broke it. It was a game. You were trying to kill him.'

Fargo touched his arm. 'He hurt me, Jaime. He owes me my honour. He owes me a duel.'

Lethe snorted, then started to laugh. Jaime waited for her to stop, but she took a breath and went on laughing.

Fargo glanced at her. 'Something's funny?' He slapped her, but she didn't stop, throwing her head back, cackling like crazy.

'For fuck's sake, girl, didn't you hear me?' Fargo hacked the stiff edge of his hand into the exposed hollow of her throat and she came forward, convulsing and vomiting. The chair rocked and teetered. Zee lunged, failing to grab the back of it as it tipped over.

It had to be now, Jaime knew. He threw himself to the side as Fargo realised it too, drawing the small boltgun and firing at him. He heard the missiles thrupping into the wall behind him like nervous footsteps as he rolled behind the cover of the room's small wooden table. Briefly out of Fargo's sight, he pulled up and came straight back out again the same way he'd gone in, fast and low, knowing Fargo and Zee would be expecting him the other side, and made for the long counter of the cook unit while Fargo was wasting bolts on the far wall. Misdirection. Lethe had taught him that.

Jaime was behind the cook unit by the time Fargo had realised and swung the gun back again. Head low, he reached up, pulled out the knife drawer and started fumbling through it, feeling blindly for the best to use as a weapon. His chest was thudding. Even if he could have examined the knives, he had no idea which to pick. Real Skills didn't cover opportunistic weaponry. The blades chimed together as he rummaged through them. He pulled one out at random by the blade, feeling it score his finger.

He crouched lower and peered cautiously round the edge of the unit. Fargo had begun to cross the room, heading for a clear shot at Jaime.

Jaime took a shuddering breath. The knife in his hand had a short, fat blade and heavy handle. Not a throwing blade, not a thrusting blade, and not a stabbing blade. Great. And it had a hopeless grip, too, made greasy by the blood oozing from Jaime's finger. His hand was shaking.

He chanced another quick look. Fargo was hard up against the wall, edging very slowly along it, the boltgun cocked and set at eye level. There was sweat on his forehead, and he stopped to wipe it away. He was in no hurry. He had the gun. Jaime crawled to the far end of the unit where a long crack in the wall had opened a space he'd never bothered to plug, and put his eye to it.

Zee was down on the floor with Lethe, but with her fall Lethe had come forward and away from the chair, and her arms were clear of the chair's back, although her wrists were still tied. Jaime saw she had wriggled her feet free of the chair legs.

Not realising she was already out of it, Zee was bent down, trying to right the chair. Lethe rolled hard into him, knocking him over, then wriggled herself into a crouch to jump, knees first, on to his chest. Lethe wasn't heavy, but all the air went out of Zee. He was wheezing in pain as she came down on him again, this time with more control, dropping her head and smashing her forehead into the bridge of his nose. He stopped wheezing. He stopped moving altogether, except for a faint rise and fall of his chest.

The silence drew Fargo's attention. He turned and saw Lethe squatting on Zee, and turned his gun on her.

Jaime stood up and yelled, showing himself but keeping the knife down, out of sight. 'Fargo!'

'Shut up, Jaime. First I'm going to kill the bitch, and then you're going to tell me where I find the tramp.'

He steadied the gun as Jaime threw the kitchen knife. It scythed awkwardly through the air and caught Fargo on the shoulder and bounced away. The weight of it did more damage than the blade. The gun fired, but Fargo's aim was spoiled and the bolt buried itself with a small, solid thud in the flesh of Zee's upper arm, flattening it against the floor. It made no difference to Zee. Zee was out of it anyway.

Vaulting the counter, Jaime hurled himself at Fargo. Fargo tried to brace himself, but toppled under Jaime, who heard himself as if from a long way off screaming, 'You leave her alone, you bastard.' Jaime hardly noticed the fists bouncing his own head back as he pounded and pounded at Fargo's face. 'Don't you dare hurt her. Don't you *ever*—'

Fargo's resistance faded, or Jaime stopped noticing it. There was a hand on his shoulder, light at first, then pulling at him until he stopped punching Fargo and leaned back, breathing hard. Fargo's face was all blood.

'I think you can stop now,' Lethe said.

Jaime stood up. His knees were shaking and his knuckles were tingling. He took a long breath and looked at his hands, and found he was holding them steady as rock.

It was never like this in games. Fist-fighting. He looked around. Riandra was still standing in the same place, still vaguely smiling. Zee was starting to groan, his groans turning to screams as he tried to wrench his arm from the floor.

Jaime glanced at Lethe's wrists, then at her, frowning.

She shrugged. 'I keep a little blade up my sleeve.'

'You could have—?'

'Probably. I wanted to see what you could do.'

'What? You wanted—?' He couldn't believe it. He was furious with her, more so than ever before, but then he was crying, and she was holding him. He relaxed slowly into her. It felt comfortable. A long time seemed to pass, and the strange thing was that at the end of it, all the tears seemed to be hers, and he was the one holding her.

He pulled up the chair and sat her gently down on it, and knelt beside her. Riandra was still standing there with the same stupid grin on her face, Zee was screaming and bubbling blood and snot from his broken nose and trying to rip his arm from the floor and Fargo was starting to come round. And Jaime was feeling as happy as he'd felt for as long as he could remember. He gazed around the wrecked room as if it was the last shining scene in a fairy-tale.

'What do we do now?' Lethe said, looking at him.

He looked at her. Lethe asking him what they should do.

Jaime thought a moment, then went to get his little vidcam. 'I know exactly what to do,' he said. Thumbing it on, he began to cover the scene. He went over to Zee and stood over him, the cam humming.

'What happened here, Zee? Tell the world the whole thing.'

'Fuck you, Jaime.'

Jaime kicked Zee's arm. It went into spasm on its little stake. Zee began to scream again. Jaime adjusted the recording volume and waited till he stopped, then pulled back his foot. 'What was that again, Zee? I didn't quite catch it.'

'Okay, okay . . .' and Zee started talking. Jaime stopped him when there was enough, then went to Riandra. 'Was that right, Riandra?'

Riandra giggled. 'That girl got Zee good. And you punched the shit out of Fargo, Jaime. It was funny.' She tried to hold on to Jaime, but he pushed her off.

'It would have been just as funny if he'd punched the shit out of me instead, wouldn't it, Riandra?' he said.

She nodded happily.

On the other side of the room, Fargo had got to his hands and knees. He was head down and retching. Jaime nudged him on to his back with a foot and let the cam take in his face.

'I'm going to put this vid on delay-send to Real Skills, Fargo. And I'm going to hold it back every day. But if I ever see you again – if *we* ever see you again – or if you try anything stupid, or if I just forget or wake up in a bad mood, they'll get it, and I just know they'll put it up on their big street screen. The ten-by-ten-metre one. You understand me?'

Fargo wiped the back of his hand across his face and nodded.

Jaime pushed Riandra to the door, and watched Fargo crawl after her. Then he went to Zee. 'What about you, Zee? Are you going to hang around? Three's a crowd, you know?'

'How can I go? I can't move. Get this thing out of me, you bastard.'

'No point moaning to me, Zee. It's Fargo's bolt, not mine.'

'We could take his arm off. That'd do it,' Lethe said.

'Very funny,' Zee said. His voice was stretched taut as wire.

Jaime shrugged. 'There's no easy way.' He knelt down beside Zee and caught a sharp scent of urine. He touched Zee's arm. There was hardly any head to the bolt, but what there was had sunk deep into Zee's flesh, pulling his sleeve into a deep dimple. Jaime tried to worm his hand under Zee's arm to feel the point where the bolt entered the floor, but couldn't get close to it. There was no gap. Zee's flesh was pinned too hard to the floor.

Zee screamed a little. 'Christ, be careful.'

'I can't get in to sever it underneath, at least not without damaging the floor,' Jaime said. 'And the head of the bolt's sunk deep in the wood, so it won't wriggle free. I think you're right, Lethe. We take off the arm.'

Zee howled. 'For Christ's sake—'

'Shut up, Zee, we're thinking,' Lethe said. She walked around Zee. 'It looks like it's just in the flesh. We could cut round it, I suppose.'

Jaime nodded. 'Like coring an apple. Good idea. Get some ice, make it a bit easier for him. I'll see if I can find that knife I threw at Fargo.'

Zee screamed, made a fist and pulled hard at his pegged arm and carried on pulling, and then screamed again as his arm slowly and then suddenly ripped free. He stood up and made for the door, cradling his arm. Jaime raised the cam to take a final image of them scuttling away, Fargo and Riandra leaning against each other, Zee moaning curses.

Just as they were about to vanish, Lethe called out, 'Hey, Riandra.'

Riandra turned round. 'Yeah?'

'You want to know something? You've got a really pox-poor taste in men.'

TWENTY-NINE

The dawn's first light was just coming as Pibald led Auger up towards the bluff again, but they didn't reach the edge.

They were collected at the high ridge of the cliff, as if they had been waiting for them. Between Auger and Pibald and the cliff's edge. Perhaps twenty animals, standing or sitting together as if they were a family unit instead of natural competitors, or predators and prey. The lion and the lamb, Auger thought.

Patiently waiting. They were staring at him, at Pibald, too.

Are you the one?

'What do you mean?'

Don't speak aloud. Are you the one?

They were wolves, some of them, and cats, and apes, and bears and things he couldn't name, and there were birds, too, eagles and hawks and more. Auger wondered which of them had said that to him.

'What the hell are they doing here?'

Auger glanced at Pibald, who was rubbing his eyes, and said, 'I was expecting you to tell me that.'

Are you the father? Is it you?

Pibald had to be hearing it, too. Auger glanced at him, but Pibald was transfixed, on his feet now and not moving, not answering.

'Dirangesept.' Pibald murmured. 'The beasts.'

'What do you see, Pi?'

'I saw cats on Dirangesept.' He was transfixed. 'But these are every-thing.' He took a long breath, held it, let it go. 'We all saw them differently. Each of us had a beast, it made itself what was closest to us, and we saw them all like that. Each of these must be someone's beast.'

'It could be the game, Pi. They could be constructs. Like the shades.'

'No.'

But Pibald had to be wrong. They were constructs, and the plot was running, telling each of them they were the hero, the quester. What had the voice asked them? *Are you the father?* Pibald must have heard that, too. He was locking into the zone even further, convincing himself Jhalouk was on the island, his child with her.

Are you the father? The words made Auger think uncomfortably of Jay, of the child she had been pregnant with. He shivered. The portrait in the woman's hut. It had looked like his son might have looked. Not just because it reminded him of himself, but because it reminded him of Jay.

'Come on, Auger. They're going now.' Pibald was touching his arm. 'And something's coming, too.'

The beasts, or whatever they were, were filtering away. A rumbling was sounding in the distance, and Pibald was staring in the direction of the noise.

'Shades.' Pibald was pulling at him now. 'They're after us or the beasts, and it isn't worth the toss of a coin to wait and find out.'

Auger could see them now. A crowd of maybe twenty shades running steadily in a long, easy gait, and in their wake some sort of cart pulled by some sort of horses. There was a dark-robed figure driving the cart on, a whip flailing at the horses' backs, white froth at their mouths. An empty cage rattled and bounced at the rear of the cart.

The beasts were moving away parallel with the cliff's edge, staying together, eagles keeping so low that their wingtips on the downbeat brushed the wolves' fur, and bears loping at the same speed as the big cats and the apes and all the others.

Seeing them go in that direction, Pibald ran down the hill towards the nearest stand of trees and kept running, Auger right behind him. At the trees they stopped, panting, and looked back. The shades with their following cart had made as much ground uphill as Auger and Pibald had made down, and were carrying relentlessly on. The hillside shook with their approach. A powerful scent of burning plastic blew in the air, making Auger gasp. He would normally have screwed up his nose at such a smell, but here in Cathar even this was somehow rich and wonderful. He was beginning to understand how Cathar trapped its players and made them believe in it. It was not simply more convincing than any other gamezone. It was more real than anything on offer in the real world.

Pibald sniffed at the air. 'Strong magic. I hope it's not aimed at us. That's Calban.' He dragged Auger down behind a tree. 'We won't outrun them,' he said, looking at the shades, who were nearly at the point from which they had descended. 'May as well toss that coin after all.'

The shades and cart were silhouetted now against the sky, and it was clear after another moment that the beasts were their quarry. Auger had the feeling, lying there watching the strange assortment of creatures run, fly and lope away, that they were almost being herded. That the operation was more to round them up than to capture them.

'They've gone,' Pibald said eventually, on his feet and brushing grass from his clothes. 'Let's go.'

He stopped just short of the lip of the cliff and stood against the lightening sky. Auger stood at his side and stared out. The island was as dark and its details as undefined as before, but there was no weather, no ruffle to the faint sea, which was a perfect pale blue.

'What if they aren't there, Pi? Your wife and child. Have you considered that?'

'They are.'

As if his certainty might make it so, Auger thought. And this being Cathar, perhaps it might. Here, anything might be. Death, too, if Madsen was right. Maybe so even if Auger didn't believe it. Maybe especially if he didn't.

The island was becoming clearer, its outlines given relief, its shades developing shadows and the sea around it growing a stubble of waves. Looking out over the bay, Auger saw himself with sudden clarity.

A gatekeeper. That was what Lethe's mother had called him. She was right. He was, and not only at Passive. With Fly. With Lethe, separating her from her mother and then taking no responsibility for her. With Oswell, too, and with Sherry. And with Jay, and everyone at their wedding, all the rest of the distant dead.

'And if they are, Pi? Then what?'

'I'll bring them back here.'

He looked at Pibald with his crazy certainty and knew that Pibald had it all before him in his head. Rescue, return, a shack somewhere along the coast. A family. Love, food, sleep, a life. All that time of waiting on Earth he had had it there, focused into that ridiculous orange visgel baby.

Who was Auger to judge him? So far Pibald had been right. Here he was, returned as he had known he would be. There was the tale of a child here, and maybe Pibald's certainty would make it his child. Madsen had told him there were people who could change the program immutably.

And he himself? What could he change, the gatekeeper? Could he believe enough in something to make a difference?

The mountains on the distant island were drawing themselves harder now, the sea gathering in rolls and swells, and there was a sting of salt in the air up on the high bluff.

Was Astrid over there? Astrid, who had believed in the need to act and had then gone ahead and done it while Auger had remained here – there – gathering information. Was Astrid on that none-too-solid island? Might she be if Auger believed it enough?

In front of him Pibald was pointing down. 'Down there, a boat.'

And with that he was gone, over the edge and out of sight. For an instant Auger thought he had leapt off the rim of the bluff, was probably soaring down with sudden wings grown from his belief, but when Auger followed, he saw Pibald scrambling down a narrow snake path cut into the grey rock.

Auger went after him. The wind whipped at his clothes as he descended the cliff face, and his feet dislodged small rocks that bounced out and flew groundward.

It was a long descent. On the beach there was abruptly no wind, and the only movement of the sea was a slow polishing of the ramp of sand. The boat that Pibald had seen was nodding at anchor a short distance out, and Pibald was already wading to it, the water slapping at his knees, his thighs, his chest until he was swinging himself aboard and beckoning to Auger.

The water was cold and hard, and Auger's thoughts were knocked out of him by the effort it took to fight his way forward. Pibald pulled him up on to the wind-etched deck with a hand, springing him clear of the bright water and on to the thudding boards.

This is it, he thought. It was as if something of Pibald's determination and absolute conviction passed to Auger with that joining of hands and lock of muscle. This was the start. The embarking.

Pibald was leaning over the prow, the flat of his hand tapping the water, and Auger was not faintly surprised to see the shell of a turtle rising from the sea a few metres distant. Pibald let the great brow of its head break the wavelets and lift into his palm. Auger watched him, wondering at the thoughts he might be having. The memories of another life.

No wonder he was crazy, Auger thought. No wonder, with memories of this, and then to have been removed to a life of that. Removed from Cathar, which seems eternal, to the Earth which was clearly not.

Pibald was swinging a leather harness over the side now, and the turtle was nosing into it.

'Whose boat is it?' Auger asked.

'Some fisherman. But the turtle was . . .' he paused, searching '. . . the companion of a man called Lile.'

Auger could see him remembering. 'Lile?' he asked.

'Yes. Lile lost a son and a wife. He hated wakers, blamed us all for it. Jhalouk and I, we'd come here and sit by the sea, and one day Lile's turtle came, and we knew he was dead.'

Auger watched Pibald thinking of Lile's lost family. The complexity of this place. Not an invented complexity, but the inevitable tragic complexity of everything that humanity involved itself with. No wonder Cathar had been withdrawn. It was a game like Russian roulette was a game.

A sudden jerk, the rope to the harness pulling up a line of spray, and the boat was moving away from the beach. The waves were coming in sharp-ridged now, breaking white several metres out. The boat nosed down into its own wash, fell briefly back, and the slack was taken up evenly by the turtle. Auger could see the movement of the solid spades of its flippers, and had a sense of its tirelessness. Such an ungainly thing to be so at one with the sea. And Auger behind it, at one with nothing at all.

Pibald glanced ahead at the island. From the top of the cliff it had seemed closer than it did now. 'The journey's at least six hours. We'll exit now,' he said, and Auger realised he'd completely lost track of time. 'The turtle will carry us safely enough.'

THIRTY

Still two hours before they could return again, and Auger couldn't sleep. He wondered how Pibald could, on the floor like that, swaddled in his mailed cloak and cuddling his visgel child. Auger's skull was humming. Unable to concentrate on anything, he watched the HoloNews channels on Madsen's screen.

The images were without end, on channel after channel. Service shuttles moved towards the fleet of ships like slow, glittering rain. The preparation for departure was all there seemed to be. It was fine by Auger, who sat in front of the screen, trying not to think about Astrid, and about the child he might have had with Jay. Had Jay borne the child? Had they terminated it?

He set the monitor to five-second channel jump, and simply stared at it all.

Every detail was available through the screen, and Auger sat and took it in. It felt like swallowing honey. He watched exterior views of the fleet, internals from the ships, interviews with individual Far Warriors, technological reports and updates. He listened to statistics on the numbers of Warriors, the nutrition they would be provided with via their pods, on the trigs and their weaponry, the beauty and suitability of Dirangesept for us all, the environmental damage being caused to it by the beasts . . .

There Auger nilled the autojump and remained watching the channel for a few minutes, taking in the detailing of that, and thinking, Now we're *saving* the planet? We destroyed ours, but we're saving theirs. Who believes that?

He sighed and flicked on through the endless channels of endless images, catching glimpses of the sleek rows of weapon-ready trigs filling the ships' holds, the ranks and ranks of CrySis pods packed on to decks that, once the pods were occupied, would drop their floors until the ceiling would prevent the pods even opening.

He stopped again, and this time he put down the control.

The voice accompanying the images was heavy and sombre. It was the Holohead's voice, although the Holohead was, unusually, not in the picture. 'With only five more days to go, these brave souls are the first of the Far Warriors to embark. They will not emerge from this hibernation until they attain their orbiting positions around Dirangesept, eighteen years hence.'

Five days to go? There had been no announcement, Auger was certain. Unconsciously he squeezed the screen control, shifting the choiceball under his palm, and inadvertently lost the picture. The screen greyed and he swore until it bloomed again. Five days. Suddenly just five days. He couldn't have missed it. Even holed up here, with Madsen, he wouldn't have missed it. Unless it had been when he had been in Cathar. But even so, news like this.

A noise beside him told him Madsen was there, and Auger only had to glance at him to see that Madsen had not known it either.

Madsen sat heavily beside him. Embarkation had been imminent for weeks, or shortly, or very soon, but there had been no date set. 'When we are prepared,' the First Minister had always stated, grimly, whenever the News Holohead had asked him. 'And I can tell you, we are very nearly ready,' he had added each time.

And now they were ready. Or at least, they were going. The cam showed it. They were filling the pods already. Warriors were entering their long sleep. Auger watched men and women, naked, shrouded in shimmering turquoise light from long, dim overhead bulbs, filter quietly along the metal floor of the deck. A few were chattering, touching hands as they stopped at their pods. Some were clearly withdrawn and tense, but the cam slid quickly away from those and favoured the many who waved at the cam or made hand signs of victory before they clambered into their pods and disappeared.

There was a swell of martial music in the background, as the voice murmured proudly, though they could not hear it on the ship, Auger was sure, 'We wish you well. You are our future. Our hope and our future.'

Almost abruptly, as if the image had shifted, the entire deck was apparently deserted. At Auger's side, Madsen grunted. The pods were full. The music faded.

In smooth unison, the pods began to close down like folding petals, until eventually they were still.

'And now . . .' whispered the voice, and Auger's neck prickled as the ceiling started to descend towards the CrySis pods. 'And now the interdeck floor will descend to permit access to the tank space for the oceans of fuel that will drive the sleeping Warriors to their far battle-field.'

The cam dropped to pod level, resting at the curved head end of a silver pod, and looking between two ranks of pods to the far side of the ship. From this perspective the pods resembled lines of shining eggs. The ceiling continued to slide down until it was almost touching the upmost curve of the pods' carapaces. As it stopped, the turquoise light blinked off, leaving each pod glowing with the palest luminescence. A faint hum sounded, and remained. Auger had a disquieting sense of claustrophobia, even to see the cramped deck on the small console.

After a moment, the voice resumed. 'The fuel stored in the seventeen interdeck tanks on each vessel will be all consumed in reaching Dirange-sept, and there the floors will rise again, and the Warriors too will arise for the final battle.'

A whispering, knocking sound of fluid hitting metal began to swell in the background as the tanks started to fill. The ceiling creaked and the lights of the pods dimmed further.

'What if something happens?' Auger murmured. 'They'll be trapped. The pods can't open with the deck down.' It struck him that going into space was like going underground. It was a huddled, tunnelled life up there in space.

'Change it, Auger,' Madsen said, leaning forward to touch his sleeve. 'It's almost time to go.'

Auger nilled the screen.

Their timing was good, bLinking into Cathar with the island looming. Auger leant back and looked up at the rock face rising hundreds of metres above them. He looked at Pibald, whose face was set. Calban's island seemed to swallow the sky, and swallow hope, too.

They came in at a little inlet strewn with rocks, the sea shattering against the black boulders, but the turtle was steady, pulling the boat towards a narrow strip of numbed water. As they passed through it, the sound stilled. Auger found himself gasping for air and realised he'd been holding his breath. Pibald grinned at him and slapped him on the back.

There was a tight, steep curve of shingle ahead, and the turtle drove forward towards it, at the last moment ducking its head to the side and disappearing under the water. A moment later its harness rose to the surface. The boat smacked into the shingle and rose sharply with its momentum, driving high on to the beach with a noise of bone crunching.

'This is it,' Pibald said, swinging a leg over the side.

Auger stepped into the water after him. It seemed colder than it had been on the sandy beach back on the mainland of Cathar. He forced himself on.

Maybe Pibald's right, he thought, pushing towards the shore. It's only what's true right now that matters. The fight is to keep it true, and if you die while it's true, then it's true for ever. Maybe it's all as simple as that.

Pibald was at the foot of another path at the end of the tiny beach, ready to start climbing. 'Are you coming, or are you going to stand there all day?'

The path snaked across the face of the cliff and curled sharply around a great bluff of rock, and they were suddenly almost drowned in noise and water. A vast narrow waterfall crashed down from so high above them that Auger had to squint to make it out. Pibald gave it a quick glance and carried on climbing up the flank of the falls.

Auger followed, peering up from time to time. The high sun caught the distant rim of the falls and made it a tongue of fluid chrome. It would take them hours to reach it.

The mist came at him like damp smoke as he climbed, entering his clothes and oozing into him. He soon lost sight of Pibald. The path jinked left and right around a huge boulder, the rock soaked as everything was soaked and sodden in the misty falls, and he looked up, catching his breath, to see, at arm's length, a rainbow half-sheathed in the rising wall of wet black rock like a scimitar.

'Are you still okay?'

Pibald's faint yell seemed to come from directly above, barely penetrating the deafening roar of water. It took Auger a moment to locate him standing there, far ahead on the steep path. Auger cupped his hands and yelled, 'Keep going.'

A rock slab to his right was as slick as ink. Mist gusted up from the fall's base, which he realised was now hundreds of metres below. The climb was exhilarating. The effort of it and the sheer overwhelming glory of the mountainside swept all thoughts from his head. The path opened briefly on to a wide, verdant ledge into which the falls had bored a deep pool, the sunstruck water crashing down and boiling there a few moments before spilling over the edge and carrying on towards the sea. Beside the pool the ground was bright and lush with thick, long, glittering grass. Tree trunks lay cracked and black, rotting into the earth.

He carried on up, coming through an arch formed by a vast shingle of stone lying elbowed over the path. A high overhang, dark and shadowed, let single drops of water fall into the brilliant light, and he opened his mouth to drink the sweet water. He wondered how long he'd been climbing, and realised that with no physical reference points he had no sense of time. And there was no sign of Pi. He must have carried straight on up, too impatient to wait for Auger.

Auger looked out at the sea again, and then across at the coast. The summit of the cliff from which they had looked down at Calban's island was far below him.

The island, this island, was climbing as Auger scaled it.

They know we're here, Auger thought. They're keeping us going, holding out against us and holding out again. They haven't located us yet, but know we're somewhere here and they're drawing us on, making it seem we're nearly, nearly there, so we forget the time, so we don't exit.

And Pibald took the bait, rushing on ahead, and I've lost him.

Auger tried his Exit word. Nothing happened. He said it again, feeling stupid, and still nothing happened. There was no choice but to carry on.

He buried his head in his hands for a moment, then stood up, feeling pain in his knees and aware of blisters on his feet, and then he forced himself on again. He kept his head down and climbed, hand over hand. Looking up was pointless. Sometimes there seemed no lip to the fall. The falls came like cloud tumbling down, the water slamming into the air and simply disintegrating.

Eventually he stopped looking, and he almost didn't realise it when he was there. He flopped over a ledge of rock and reached for the next and there wasn't one.

He lay gasping for a few minutes before standing up to survey the plateau. The water moved in a deep channel over the broad apron of rock, shimmying thickly towards the edge.

He stretched his legs and looked around. There were trees and great boulders here, and birds flicking through the air with luminous blue wings and scarlet beaks. Water dripped from the branches of the trees, soaked the rock. Auger had thought he was as wet as he could be, but now he felt the water sink deeper into him. It looked like it had rained here and would rain on for ever.

Ahead of him, the river divided into two arms embracing a small island of sparse trees and rejoined to narrow into the deep channel approaching the edge. About five metres before the edge, the water abruptly accelerated in a fury of white foam.

Auger's eyes were drawn to the edge, where the river funnelled more tightly still and swept out in near silence. There was nothing to be seen beyond that jet and its curling away but a faint rising spray and the sky. No land, no sea, nothing at all.

He turned from it and looked over the broad plateau. His eyes were drawn up yet again, and there was still distant and dizzying height beyond, white-rimmed mountains webbed by streams of snowmelt unthreading down flat plains of rock.

But his climb was over. There was no need to carry on. This was his destination.

'Auger!'

'I see you, Pi.' Auger came forward to the river's edge, looking across an arm of the river at the island where Pi was standing against a tree by the river's shore, his arms stretched behind him as if he was clasping it to his back.

There was no one else in sight. Auger screamed over the water at Pibald, 'What happened?' Then, 'It doesn't matter. We have to Exit, Pi. It's been too long.'

'No,' Pibald yelled. 'If we leave now, they'll kill me here and I can never come back. I'm not doing that. You have to free me. You have to help me.'

Auger swore. 'Pi, this is crazy.' It was endangering everything. Astrid. He stared at Pibald, then looked over the river more carefully. Whoever had caught Pi had gone again, probably in search of Auger. There was a scattering of trees over on the small island, but nowhere to hide. Auger cupped his hands and yelled, 'Free yourself, Pi. Use magic, can't you?'

'No, he can't use magic.'

A hooded figure, coming out from the trees behind Pibald. How could Auger have missed him?

So this was Calban, he thought.

The figure stopped at Pibald's side as if they were the two companions, and Auger the stranger, and called out, 'Who are you?'

He was slight, far shorter than Pi, and his voice was light too, hardly carrying over the rush of the river. Auger instinctively stepped into the shade of a boulder, not to be identified.

Who are you?

A gecko splayed flat on the rock. This time the voice seemed to have come from the lizard with its head cocked.

Are you the one?

'What—?' Auger began.

Not aloud. Don't speak aloud.

A beast. The gecko had to be one of the beasts of Dirangesept.

'Come out and show yourself, then. Come out, or . . .'

The voice hesitated and stopped. Or I'll kill him, Auger thought. His heart thumped as he worked it through. But that's no threat, as it's not Pibald you're after. And you know we're linked, and if he dies, I can Exit. So you're after me.

Auger backed further behind the rock. You're after me. Which is crazy. Which means—

It means I'm the one. But what does that mean? What the hell does that mean?

Auger thought he must be feeling dizzy, and leaned against the boulder, then realised the rock was starting to move towards him. There was a faint menthol smell in the air. Gravel crunched, crushed by the shifting rock.

Magic. Calban was using magic. Auger backed as the rock nudged him and started slowly to gain speed. Auger tried to shift to the side, then realised that this was what Calban intended, to draw him into plain view. He continued to back, and realised that the cliff's edge was closing on him.

You can stop it moving. I'll help you.

The gecko was still there, crawling over the face of the boulder as it moved, steadily maintaining its position in front of Auger.

I'll help you.

How?

But as he thought it, Auger found himself willing the rock steady. It slowed, and bumped to a halt.

'Who are you?'

Calban again. Auger gained some satisfaction from the uncontrolled rise in his voice. He hadn't expected Auger to be able to do that. Any more than Auger had. Auger peered carefully around the rock. Calban was facing Pi now.

'Who is he, Pibald? Oh, yes, we know who *you* are. You had to have been here before, the way you came out of the Hall of Wakers when you arrived. We didn't expect to have to go back that far to identify you. There's someone here who wants to see you. She's been waiting a long time, Pibald.'

Calban snapped his fingers and the trees revealed a shade holding a slender woman by her wrists. He managed it with one hand, yanking her arms behind her back. The woman had long brown hair that shimmered under the sun and moved with the breeze, and she was whimpering. She was straining against the grip of the shade, but there was no use in it. The shade seemed unaware of her presence even, staring only towards Auger.

As soon as Pibald caught sight of her, his attitude changed. He screamed and strained against the ropes. 'No,' he keened. He seemed to slump, calling out to her, 'Jhalouk! Oh, my Jhalouk!'

The woman said, 'Please, Pibald. Do what Calban tells you. For the sake of our son.'

And then, as Auger watched, another voice called from by his side, and he turned to see the same woman standing here, in the same sleeveless brown jerkin. He could smell her perfume as she called out, 'No, Pibald. Here I am.'

Pulling himself awkwardly up, Pibald stared from one woman to the other. Auger stared, too. The deep shadow of Calban's hood also turned to the new version of Jhalouk standing in the open beside Auger.

What was this? The woman didn't even exist and now there were two of her.

'Fouane is safe. This . . .' she pointed a slim finger at the woman by Calban '. . . is Calban's creation.'

Across the river, Calban drew a blade from the folds of his cloak and held it to the throat of that Jhalouk. 'I'll kill her. Decide now. I'm not playing identity games. I don't know what magic this is, but your wife is here, Pibald, and she is about to die unless you tell me the name of your friend.'

Beside Auger's rock, the woman took half a step forward and raised her hands towards Pibald. 'We have a house, Pibald. I painted it white, and Fouane comes fishing with me. He rides on the back of Lile's turtle. He knows all about you, Pibald. How much you love him and would be coming back to us again.'

'No!'

Calban took the woman from the shade and tipped her head back, then released it a fraction, so the woman could speak.

She gabbled frantically. 'We exchanged our vows by the sea, and lit a fire on the sand as the sun set. We sat by the fire all night, talking and holding each other and making love, and said that our love would last for ever. It would keep through the warmth of the day, and then we would lie together and make our own warmth through the night. Do you remember that night, Pibald? And our long walks through the woods and the fields of Cathar? Do you remember? I remember it all, Pibald.'

'You still doubt her, Pibald? I'll kill her, I swear it. Tell me who he is.'

Beside Auger, the woman took another step. 'I've told Fouane how you made and cherish that little image of him. How you speak to him through it, and how you think always of him.'

His beast, Auger thought in a rush of understanding. She is his beast. Only the beast inside him could know that. The rest, they could reconstruct from records. Only his beast would know this.

For a moment Calban slackened his grip on the woman, and there was a silence. Pibald stopped pulling at his bonds and looked at the Jhalouk held by Calban, and at the Jhalouk across the river. And then Calban spoke again.

'Tell me his name, Pibald, or I'll kill her.'

You must help him.

Auger looked at the woman that was Pibald's beast, but it hadn't been her.

It was the gecko again.

You are the one. Only you can help him against Calban. You are the one and the father. You must have the power, and you must use it now.

Auger looked across the river and saw Pibald looked towards him, his face set in the acceptance of failure.

'His name?' He was ready to give up, slumping against the tree. After a moment, he raised his head again slightly. 'Okay. I'll tell you his name.'

You must use it.

Not knowing what he was doing, Auger closed his eyes and imagined Pibald's hands freed. He was seeing them tied with cord, and the cord was slipping away.

Somehow the imagining made him feel briefly faint. It was somehow more than an imagining. It was a believing, even though what he was believing was a lie. It was an act of faith. And, despite everything he knew, despite all Madsen's warnings, Auger realised in that moment that he had been trapped by Cathar.

But Pibald's hands were free. He knew it.

'Yes?' Calban's voice shook with impatience. The hood jerked, as if Calban was sniffing the air, and Auger could smell it, too, sump oil and coriander. It was intoxicating. It was magic, and it was Auger's.

Pibald stood up against the tree, still holding his hands behind him. 'His name is Bolt.'

'Very well, Pibald.' And saying it, Calban slit the throat of the woman. As he did so, Pibald leapt forward to dive with a great splash into the water.

Calban pushed the woman's body away from him and yelled in fury at the shade, who jumped into the water after Pibald. Pibald was already swimming well, but the current was taking him swiftly down towards the river's junction with its further arm, and the meeting of streams was a crash of foam. Even so, it looked as if Pibald would reach this side before the current could drag him down that far.

The shade was moving steadily through the water, advancing slowly on Pibald, and seemingly without the same need to raise its head to breathe as it swam. It wouldn't matter. Pibald would be out in time. Neither the shade nor the river junction would catch him.

Oleander. Auger caught the rich scent as he saw the current becoming stronger and the river faster, and realised that Calban was responsible. Pibald was not going to reach the bank in time.

Auger looked up at Calban to see the dark cavity of the hood directed silently at him, as if in quiet triumph. Knowing that in Cathar, no one could beat him. The game was his game, the rules his to make and unmake.

It's not over, he said to himself, to Calban.

The river was carrying Pibald to its junction. There was nothing Auger could do about that. Anything he did, Calban could quickly undo. It had to be something else. Auger had to trust Pibald to cope with the river.

The shade was being carried, too, and would reach the junction barely behind Pibald. Auger watched the water, calculating, seeing the far stretch of the river as it joined this one. He glanced at Calban, at the darkness within the hood. The hood turned back to the water, ready for Auger's move. As if it was a game, Auger thought. But it wasn't a game. He knew that now.

Pibald hit the froth at the waters' meeting, and went beneath, and Calban's hood shifted abruptly, distracted momentarily by the scent of Auger's magic.

The waters seethed. There was no sign of Pibald. A moment later the shade went into the froth, and instantly, but too late, Calban saw the huge log carried along the far flank of the river judder as it struck the back of the shade's skull. The log Auger had toppled in.

Pibald was hauling himself on to the shore and starting to run towards Auger and Jhalouk. In the river the shade was still alive, flailing its arms, but the rushing water was almost at the edge of the plateau. The shade's body smashed into a rock at the very edge, and somehow its arms held there and clung to the rock, hauling it against the thunder of water as it slowly gained a better hold.

Pibald was with Auger now, yelling at him, 'Go. Let's go!'

'Wait.' Auger could see Calban's attention fully on the shade, helping it to safety. The air was full of magic. So much effort, he thought. There was only one explanation for that. It meant that if Pibald and Auger weren't immediately caught, Calban had no way of pursuing them. And Pibald was too exhausted to fight off a shade, and Calban wouldn't under-estimate Auger again. The shade had to be stopped.

Auger tried to slip the shade's hands from the rock, but it was no use. Calban wouldn't let him. He was too strong. The air was thick with the scent of oils and herbs, the spills of magic. Auger let the shade have the rock.

The shade opened its mouth as the rock came away in its arms, but the scream came from Calban, a high scream of fury as the shade was hurled off the cliff's edge, jetted out with the smash of water. Even out there, the creature seemed for a moment to be trying to scramble along the almost solid jet, but then the water began to break up and the shade dropped out of sight.

'We're okay now,' Auger said, starting to run. 'But we have to find somewhere safe to Exit from.' The rocks here were wet and slick from the mist of the falls, and this slowed them down, but it would make it almost impossible for Calban to track them.

It suddenly struck him that Pibald might not want to leave Cathar, now that he had found his Jhalouk. They were moving hand in hand. When Pibald didn't answer him, Auger called out, 'Pibald!'

'Yes.' Pibald sounded quieter than ever before. 'I know.' After a moment he said, 'Jhalouk? Where can we go?'

'I'll take you where you'll be safe.'

Auger wanted to ask Pibald whether they could trust her, but Pibald would say yes anyway.

You can trust us.

The gecko. On the sleeve of his shirt, hanging there as he ran.

THIRTY-ONE

Auger came out feeling nauseous. He tried to move, but couldn't. Tied down. Had he been captured? He moved his head.

'Hell, Auger, where were you?'

Madsen's voice. He sounded relieved and angry. 'Lethe, unstrap him. Pi, are you out, too?'

They were in a car, screeching through streets. Auger felt Lethe's hands fiddling at his waist and legs from behind and he was loose. He sat the seat forward, not quite feeling part of the situation, and tried to gather himself. The windows were sight-filters and the streets were drained of colour. Wan buildings arrived and faded. Masked pedestrians walked slowly by, heads down, as if in comas. He grabbed the handstrap to stabilise himself as the car swept round a corner.

'I'm okay,' Pibald said quietly, behind him.

Auger glanced at him in the mirror, sitting beside Jaime and Lethe. He was just staring out, holding his bLinkers in one hand, and after Jaime had released him from the straps securing him he just let the juddering of the car slam him around as if it didn't matter any more.

'They're behind us,' Madsen said tightly. 'You were in there far too long. We picked you both up and kept moving. Now all we have to do is lose them.'

'There was nothing else we could do,' Auger said. He saw Pibald glance at him, but in the bouncing vehicle he couldn't read what the look meant.

'Well, we're out now,' Auger said. But he was still thinking of Cathar. Of Pibald and Jhalouk.

Madsen was looking at a console on the dash, swearing. A Pacifist tracer screen, Auger saw. And he saw why Madsen was swearing, too.

Lethe said, 'What is it?' She was braced against Jaime in the back. Or simply holding him.

'Too late, I think.' Madsen glanced at Auger and said, 'They may have lost you in Cathar, but they've got us surrounded now. Closing in. They're locked on to the vehicle.' He slowed, punched the screen. Auger saw blue dots plugging every street around them.

'She's with me now,' Pibald said, almost dreamily.

'Pi?' It was Jaime, touching Pibald's arm anxiously. 'Pi?' The car screamed left. The dots on the screen reconfigured, still closing. Taking their time. The closest a few hundred metres now. Their screens would be giving them the same thing as Auger's. They were in no hurry. They were prepared for the car to stop, prepared to switch to a foothunt.

Pibald was saying, 'Jaime, if you've got someone you love, you stick with them. Make sure of it. I have my Jhalouk again, for ever. We found each other.'

Auger glanced at Pibald, whose face was grim and serious as he looked at Auger and quietly said, 'Thank you, Auger. You were my guide more than I was yours.'

He squeezed Jaime's hand, then reached forward and rolled into the front of the car, pushing himself between Madsen's seat and the door, forcing Madsen aside and taking the controls from him.

'Pi! What—?'

Pibald straightened the vehicle with one hand, clutched the bLinkers with the other. He said, softly, 'I know what's true, Auger.'

Madsen made to try and recover the controls, but Auger put a hand on his shoulder and said, 'No.'

Licking his lips with a tongue almost as dry, Pibald said, 'I'm going to slow down at the end of this street. When I say, get out, all of you. It's our only chance.'

The street flashed by, tilting wildly. Our only chance. Auger noticed that play of words.

'Pibald?'

'Don't cry, Jaime. Things only end if you're still there afterwards to know it. Otherwise they go on for ever. The truth is what you die knowing. I'll be with Jhalouk and our son, and I'll be with you, too, Jaime. Always.'

He took the car round another corner, sweeping through mists of ash, slowed down, and then said, 'Now.'

Auger opened his door and tumbled out, Madsen following him. Lethe came from the back, yanking Jaime after her. Auger caught a glimpse of Pibald setting the bLinkers over his eyes as the doors closed.

The car accelerated away from them. Ahead of it, in the ashen street, a huge termite mound straddled the kerb, almost glowing with the visgel secreted there by the termites. In profile it looked like a great church, a cathedral. Pibald was still gaining speed as he hit it. The car exploded in orange and yellow flames.

On the tarmac Lethe hugged Jaime, who was starting to weep, his tears bright in the light of Pibald's funeral pyre.

'Come on,' Madsen said quietly. 'They'll have registered him bLinking in, then his trace vanishing at the same time as the crash. He took the symbiote to Cathar. He knew he was dead when he bLinked. They'll assume everyone's dead here, at least for a few minutes. We need to slip through the net before they start to think otherwise.'

Moving away, Auger whispered to himself, 'Thanks, Pi. I won't forget.'

Three hours. Madsen and Auger had pushed and pulled at it, and three hours was the agreement. Madsen had gone off to find another place to bLink from, and Lethe and Jaime had gone to talk and find some comfort.

Waiting for him to return, Auger sat in Madsen's great room in the old bank and stared at the screen, hoping it would take away his thoughts again.

The News opened with a view of the fleet. The drizzle of shuttles was now a two-way thing, and light coruscated in the darkness. Auger noticed a disturbance in the main field, and took a moment to locate the source of it.

In the centre of the screen, a star was moving purposefully forward, advancing directly to the cam and stretching into the shape of a man as it came, until Auger recognised it as a vacsuited spacewalker. It looked disabled, and Auger thought for a moment that it was a spinning corpse loosed from some hull. Half the helm, one side of the walker's body, an arm and a leg seemed to be sliced away.

Not sliced. The body was just in total shadow. It was the Holohead floating in a vacsuit that threw him into half-light. Behind him was the fleet.

The Holohead flicked back his helm as if without thought and raised his gloved hands to his throat, giving out a soundless screech as pressurised air burst away, then spread his hands again and chuckled. 'Don't worry, folks. Remember − first, I'm not real . . .' The universe faded around him, and his studio assembled itself where the universe had been. 'And second, I'm not there.'

McCrae, standing by his side, smiled at the Holohead.

'Though I could be,' the Holohead added, grinning.

'Which?' McCrae asked him. 'You could be which?'

The Holohead arched his eyebrows at the cam. This was not scripted, Auger understood.

'I could be there, Doctor,' the Holohead said. He made to move on, but McCrae stopped him.

'How, if you're not real?'

'My projection could be there,' the Holohead said, showing irritation now. 'I was using "not real" in a sense of not human, not in the sense of nonexistent. If we might carry on?' The Holohead winked at the cam and added, 'That is, "we" in the sense of you and a theoretical I.'

'Of course.'

'Now, tell me, Doctor, how do you feel about the schedule for your Leaving? I understand that Minister Maxenham has brought forward your date.'

'I am, of course, grateful to the Administration, and the Minister for Faith in particular for donating the ships to us. It places a great burden on us to be prepared in time, but God will speed our hands.'

'Would you tell us some more about the date?'

'The Minister has decreed that we must set off simultaneously with the D3 project.' McCrae seemed reluctant to say more, and the Holohead looked to his other side. 'Minister Maxenham, you seem to be here almost as often as I am myself. You've recently taken the post of Stability as well as Faith. Perhaps now you're after my job.' The Holohead's eyebrows jumped.

'No, NH, no one else could do your job. Dr McCrae understands how difficult it is to arrange these things. We on Earth unfortunately don't have the facilities at our disposal that his Master has.'

'I wasn't—'

'If I might finish, McCrae,' Maxenham said sharply. He waited. The cam went to McCrae's face and stayed there until the expression on it faded. It was the first time Auger had had the slightest sympathy for the preacher.

'Now, then,' Maxenham said mildly to the Holohead. He adjusted his position slightly, and with the tiny shift it was as if McCrae had vanished utterly. 'Our resources on Earth are limited. We were relying heavily on Nugel, and were let down by the previous Minister. A simultaneous departure of the two fleets will allow us to keep energy loss to a minimum. Dr McCrae understands this, I think.'

He waited again, and this time McCrae stepped quietly into the deepening silence. 'Yes, of course I do.'

'Good. We are fast-routing the new, easy-to-use Understands, and berths on the ships allocated to Dr McCrae's ministry are nearly all taken.'

Maxenham leaned forward to look directly at McCrae across the Holohead. He drew a piece of paper from his pocket, and held it out to the preacher. 'I thought you might like to sign this yourself, Doctor, live and on air.'

'What—?' McCrae reflexively took the paper from Maxenham and opened it out. He stared at it. His lips went thin and white.

The Holohead tilted his head to see what it was that Maxenham had passed to the preacher. 'It's an Understand, Doctor,' he said. 'You look like you've never seen one before.'

'Oh, he's seen them before,' Maxenham said. And then, to McCrae, 'My records indicate you haven't signed one yet.'

McCrae stared at the Minister. He said nothing.

'Well, Doctor, you are going, aren't you? The leader of your flock?'

'Yes,' McCrae whispered. The paper rasped in his hand.

'Dr McCrae?'

The preacher looked at the Holohead.

'Take the pen.'

He opened his hand, his face quite blank.

'No, not from me, McCrae. I can't pass you a pen. I'm not real, remember.' He smiled a small and very human smile, Auger thought, and leaned back. 'Take it from the Minister.'

'Yes. Yes, of course.'

As McCrae signed the Understand, Madsen's voice came from behind Auger. Auger nilled the picture.

'It's time, Auger. I've found us a deserted house. There's even a bed. You can be comfortable.' He sounded tired. Auger wondered how he sounded himself, rising stiffly to his feet.

'Good,' Auger told him. 'Let's go.'

Lethe was standing there, too, and Jaime, his cheeks shining.

Auger looked at the three of them and thought of everyone who had died or otherwise gone away. Jay, Fly, Oswell, Astrid, Pibald. And all of them in some way for him, because of him. He had failed them all.

'You don't need to come,' he said. 'Tell me where, and I'll go. I'll see you back here afterwards.'

Lethe was looking at him like Jaime had looked at the flames of Pibald's car.

'We're coming,' she said.

Madsen and Jaime both nodded.

THIRTY-TWO

Pibald's body was there as Auger sat up, lying beside him as if in peaceful sleep. Auger hadn't expected that. He went over to touch his cheek, murmuring, 'Goodbye.' The warmth was leaving Pibald. Straightening again, Auger looked around, half expecting to see Jhalouk there.

She's gone, too. They were together.

The small cave was dark and low, and he had to stoop to leave it, as he and Pibald had had to stoop to enter. It gave him a pang of sadness to think of it. The memory of the crash in which Pibald had died, with its explosion and brilliant flames, was less solid than this gloomy cave in Cathar with its quiet corpse. It was easy for Auger to imagine Pibald reunited somewhere with his love. He recalled what Pibald had said just before the crash. The truth is what you die knowing.

Outside, it was late afternoon in Cathar, and the light was starting to fail. The great mountain face into whose base the caves were set was stroked by shadow. With the mountain at his back, he looked out over the plateau. The river was a distant murmur and a faint slur of mist. The plateau was so high that it might have been another world. Beyond its edge was just sky.

A program, he told himself. Cathar had got to him, as Madsen and Pibald had said it would. Just a program.

The little gecko scuttled over the ground ahead of him, leading him along the foot of the cliff face. There were natural caves set into the rock every twenty or thirty metres. After a while, the gecko stopped at the mouth of a cave larger than the others.

This is the place.

The gecko flicked its tail and vanished into the darkness. Auger took a few paces into the mouth of the cave, and shadows closed over him. There was a faint chill breeze coming from deep inside. Aircon, he thought immediately, but of course it wasn't that. It was air channelled through the cave from an air hole beyond.

And it wasn't that either, he thought, catching himself. It was the program. All a program. Nothing of it was real, not even the voice of the gecko, the beast, in his head.

I'm real, Auger. Be sure of that. I may not be here in the way you are, but I am real. I'm as real as you.

Auger glance at the tiny, unblinking lizard splayed against the crumbling rock. It moved forward with the same deliberate, mechanical action that Larry used as he paced the walls of Auger's room. It looked like an antique toy, a painted clockwork thing of beaten tin. His beast.

He looked into the central darkness of the cave. It took his eyes a few seconds to accommodate to the deep gloom, and he saw that beyond its mouth, the rock opened out into a vast chamber, the walls seeming to shiver with the windblown motion of damp, drooping mosses. The floor glistened with water. Auger took another step, keeping to the wall. The gecko padded beside him and Auger put his hand on the rock, waiting. The gecko ran along his arm so swiftly and lightly that Auger felt its voice more heavily than its physical presence. It steadied itself on his shoulder. The warm touch of its feet was reassuring.

Now he saw why the gecko had brought him here. The cave was filled with low beds, and many of them were occupied, though not all. For a moment he thought this was another Hall of Wakers, but it clearly wasn't. The people lying in the beds seemed not to be fully present. They were as if poor holos, adjusting awkwardly on the beds as Auger moved and his perspective changed. He felt he could almost see the pixels shifting to accommodate the sleepers to his angle of view. It was as if it didn't matter whether or not they were totally visualised. As if the connection between them and this place wasn't quite true.

'I don't understand,' Auger whispered. He moved forward. With the stillness of the sleepers and the apparent life of the stone cave, it was as if the proper order of things had been reversed.

He began to move among the beds, not knowing why, and then stopped.

Astrid was lying there. She was wearing a roughly woven brown shift that covered her from shoulder to thigh, and she looked to be in light sleep, except that her body shimmered in a light that wasn't there.

Auger felt he could wake her with a touch, but he hesitated a moment and just went on looking at her. She seemed to become more actual as he gazed at her. The perfect curve of her neck at her shoulder, the softness of her slumbering half-smile. The memory of her voice was in his head, the recollection of her touch.

'Astrid,' he murmured, and he gently touched the back of a finger to her lip. She was solid. 'I'm here. Let's go.'

He didn't know where he was going to take her, but at least he had found her. She was with him.

She didn't open her eyes. She didn't move.

'Astrid?' He took her shoulder and shook it cautiously, not wanting to give her a shock.

Still nothing. She looked beautiful there, in the half-light of the cave, but she didn't move.

'Astrid.' The cave stretched his helpless voice into a hiss.

Something outside the cave threw a shadow on the floor and Auger instinctively moved to the side and crouched in the lee of a slab of rock. The entrance to the cave was darkened and almost filled by a strange, broad silhouette, and the outward breeze, its free passage interrupted, moaned. Auger pushed himself back hard against the wall.

The cave became lighter again as a low rumble sounded and grew. The noise grated against its own echo. Auger slowly made out an iron-wheeled cart, and on the cart a tall, fine-meshed cage that rocked as the cart came forward. There were shapes inside the cage – something or things, alive. It was hard to see what they might be with the cart shaking and the mesh so fine and in the half-light.

A team of eight shades were bent over in harness, pulling the cart. And there, in front of the procession, was Calban.

Auger pulled back as Calban strode to the nearest bed and stopped, standing with the flat of a hand on the forehead of the man lying there. The cage was brought up until it was close enough for Calban to touch the bars, which were of some coppery metal, with his other hand.

Now Auger could see inside the motionless cage. Animals. A few apes, dogs, big cats, a few birds perched on the haunches of the others. Smaller animals, too, on the floor of the cage. They were packed inside, Auger saw, but there was no clawing at each other. Even so, Auger could sense their fear. They seemed to huddle together as far from Calban as they could get within their cage. Beasts of Dirangesept.

Calban bowed his hooded head.

Auger didn't notice it at first. The light didn't change, but the cage appeared to become better defined. Then behind the mesh, the animals started, it seemed, to melt away, though it was hard in the gloom for Auger to make this out clearly, and his attention was slightly distracted by

342

the sound made by the gecko as it shifted on his shoulder and ran down his arm and away.

Calban's body stiffened, and Auger noticed the same tang of magic that there had been before. Where the beasts had been, there was a shivering stream of dull green luminescence that bulged into Calban's hand. Calban stiffened further, straightening, and the luminescence was leaving him through his other hand, was lighting the forehead of the sleeping man who jerked faintly and even groaned, but didn't wake up.

The scent was gone. The cage was empty. All of the beasts had disappeared.

Calban motioned the shades away, and remained. He stood up, a slight figure, and the sleeves of the robe fell to cover those boyish hands.

There was something about the way he moved, turning towards Auger in the shadows. He knew Auger was there. He had known it all along. But Auger wasn't thinking of that, wasn't thinking he had been discovered. He was thinking about Calban.

They were not boyish hands. Not boyish at all.

Calban was a woman.

Dr Carroll. Calban had to be Rox Carroll herself, the director of the research wing.

Auger came out into the open, an uncontrollable fury rising in him. 'What is this? What are you *doing* here? What have you done to them all?' His voice cracked into a yell that slammed around the cave. 'What have you done to Astrid?'

Calban didn't move. No surprise, no fear. No reaction at all.

Auger reached out and wrenched back the hood, almost expecting it to fall away and reveal nothing at all, the cloak collapsing to the ground empty, a magician's trick. But Calban was solid, and the hood fell in thick folds about Calban's shoulders to expose her face. She was as still as Auger suddenly was, but she was smiling at him.

'Cy,' she said. 'I wondered.'

Auger looked at her and looked again. Then he whispered, as if speaking her name could make him believe what he was seeing, 'Jay?'

Jay. He stood and stared at her. Cathar seemed to fall away from him as he reached out automatically to take the hand she had lifted. He didn't know where he was any more, except that he was with Jay again. She hadn't changed at all, he thought, and knew that was a lie.

But her smile was the same. It was the same tired smile she gave him every night when she arrived late, blaming the work he knew he always came second to. And it was a smile that reminded him of the way they had been together.

'What's going on here?' he said. He felt drained of everything, sucked dry of it all.

She shrugged the way she always shrugged when he asked her about her work. The shrug said, You wouldn't understand, Cy. He had always let it go, but this time he shook his head.

'No, Jay.' His voice was a rasp that sent an echo juddering along the dark, cavernous walls. 'You have to tell me. I know what happened at our wedding.' He stopped. Did *she* know? Did she know what had happened? Did she know she had done it?

Her face told him she knew, though. She knew it all.

'Emotion,' she said. 'I regret that, Cy.'

He waited for more, but she closed her mouth, and he saw that she had said as much as she was going to say. As far as she was concerned, it was over with that small phrase. It was an experiment gone wrong, a side effect, an error. And Auger saw that that was how she felt about him, too, now. Regret.

Unable for a moment to say anything else, he said, 'What is this?' He made a gesture around the cave.

'It's a test bed, if you like.' She smiled at her pun. 'I was always part of the D3 project. I was self-experimenting, of course. I knew you wouldn't like it.'

'You knew? You knew all along?' Auger felt nauseous. 'I thought we shared everything,' he murmured, half to himself. He was staring at her and realising he had never really known her at all. No, that wasn't so. The driven, determined part of her had always been there, but it had been tempered. Now it was not.

'It was part of my work,' she said. She looked surprised that he could have reacted as he had, and repeated it, almost rebuking him. 'This was my work. And more than that . . .' adding as simply as an afterthought, 'it was for the future of the planet. Of us all.'

Auger said nothing, still trying to connect this Jay with the woman he had loved. Examining him, she looked more amused than anything else.

'What we were trying to do was vital to the project. We thought we could use neuro-nangines to duplicate the empowering ability of the beasts of 'Sept, without the unfortunate side effects that seemed to come with it.'

'Self-destruction,' Auger said.

'Emotion,' she said, and he wasn't sure if this was part of her explanation or a further reprimand to him. 'The power seems to come from the centres of emotion. The nangines were in place to prepare the ability, but I hadn't found a way to release the power.'

'Until our wedding day.'

She looked at him, suspecting him of an accusation perhaps, but he was just wondering how she felt, telling him this. It seemed simply to irk her.

'It was hardly deliberate. I didn't expect it. I was weak back then. Now I am not. Now I am free.'

He looked at her, wondering what she meant by that.

'The nangines were programmed to close everything down in the event of uncontrolled activity, protect the brain, but they reacted too late, and then rather too efficiently.' She held up her hand and inspected it, turning it over and back, as if it was to blame for something. 'It's irreversible, unfortunately. My emotional centres remain in control of my externally conscious self – I'm there, too, by the way, Cy, and thank you for visiting me recently.' She frowned vaguely. 'It's an interesting experience. I observe, but I can't participate at all. It's like watching an experiment from within.' She made a face. 'A rather boring one, though. It's a relief to be here.'

She was quite without emotion, he saw. Her nangines had effectively sawn her in two, the outwardly conscious half in helpless fugue, in her time-frozen room in GenMed, and this half, merciless and emotion-free in Cathar.

But doing what here?

'You were pregnant with our child, Jay.'

Did she know that? Maybe not. Maybe he could shock her free of this.

'Yes.' She seemed to brighten. For an instant Auger thought it was at the notion of their child. It was a piece of knowledge that made Auger feel both empty and full at the same time when he considered it. His child.

'Yes,' she said. 'That was an unforeseen benefit, Cy. Every cloud has a silver lining, eh? Once Rox discovered I could still communicate with her in Cathar, we discussed what should be done about the pregnancy. I felt it would be a shame to waste the opportunity to take my experiments further. We consulted with Dr Saffer, and we decided that we might nangineer a child of potential superintelligence.'

She waited for Auger to collect himself. It took him a while. Nangineer? Had Jay said that? His *child*? His fists were clenching and he had consciously to relax them. He wanted to strike her down. Instead he said, as calmly as he could, 'Why?'

'Why?' She seemed genuinely surprised. 'What question is that? Because we thought we could. And because we wondered what question the answer would pose.' She tutted at him, a teacher with a backward student. 'Experiments are only ever pointless until they are completed, Cy. Then they have their meaning.' She sighed, summoning a way to penetrate his dimness. 'What we got from going to the Earth's moon in the first place, all those years ago, was not simply that crisp footprint in the dust. That was never an objective, that was just newsprint. The true purpose of it was all the information we obtained out of discovering how to plant that footprint.'

'And what did you get from nangineering your – our – child?' He tried to damp his voice down, but she didn't even notice his tone.

'What did we get, Cy?' She smiled, and for a moment he thought he had broken through to her. Her child. Their child.

'What we got was victory, Cy. Certain victory for D3. We regained our future here in Cathar. Here.' She spread her arms.

Auger looked around, seeing the cave with its blurred sleepers, the cage empty of its beasts.

'I don't understand.'

'You should be proud, Cy. Your son is the centre of this.' She tapped her head. 'You – we – are right now in his skull. To all intents and purposes, our child is the computer that houses us. Cathar is within him.' She waved a hand in a grand gesture. 'His brain is beyond the capacity of even the beasts to comprehend. I share his genome, so I share his basic neuronal pattern to a degree sufficient to remain, in Cathar, superior to the beasts. Beyond that, my nangines render me impervious to their invasion.'

'And that's why you wore the hood, too,' Auger said, seeing it at last. 'They could still get some little way into the child's brain, and some little way into yours, too, and if they saw your face, it would perhaps tell them more about the relationship between you.'

She smiled. 'Very good, Cy. You were never a fool.'

But it wasn't him, knowing that. It was the beast inside him. And she didn't know about its presence. And that was why the face of the child had been so familiar to him. The beasts in desperation had created it from the information they had, and managed to work it into the zone. Pibald had taken it to be his own child because he had so wanted it to be, but Auger had seen it as his child because it had been his child.

He was the one. He was the father.

His child. He felt anger rise again, but pressed it back. 'That doesn't explain it all, Jay.'

'No. The child is the computer, if you like. I am the operator of the program. The shades are neurological tools, nangine-constructs. They are synaptic sequences made illusory flesh.'

'What does the program do, then? What do you do?'

'That, Cy, is the most beautiful thing of all. That is the true fruit of all our research.' She put up her arms and threw her hood back as far as it would go, and with that gesture Auger realised that this was the end of the experiment. Auger had done nothing by his arrival. The breeze blew gently, and the cave shimmered.

'When the Vets come into this zone, their beasts are released. I use the shades to marshal them, to collect them and to transfer them . . .' She glanced at the sleepers in the cave, and pointedly at Astrid, smiling at Auger. 'Where they are trapped. You see, one of the problems we confronted was that the beasts can leave their hosts and return to Dirangesept if they can accommodate to the brain in which they are housed. They become the key to its lock by comprehending everything about the lock. But with the nangines, we can constantly adjust the parameters of the lock, and they can never escape.'

She made a gesture. 'As you saw, each of these nangineered hosts can hold quite a number of beasts. It's an efficient process. And once freed from their beasts, the Vets can Exit the zone.' She looked up into the darkness. 'Our son is a clever boy, though not much use apart from his brain, sadly. He can hold a great many hosts.'

Auger waited, but Jay just smiled at him.

'And?' he said.

'And that is all. That is all there is, Cy. That is the end. Now, the zone is clear. We are done here. Exit when you are ready. It was good to see you one last time.' She turned and left.

Auger went over to Astrid and stared down at her. She didn't move in her sleep. He shook her arm. She was warm to his touch, but she didn't respond.

He tried to imagine her awake, but nothing happened. He tried to see her eyes open, to see her sitting up, but nothing changed. 'I can't help you. I can't do it,' he said, and despite it being no more than a whisper, the words rumbled in a low echo. He was on his knees. 'I don't know what to do, Astrid.'

He looked up at the cracked stone of the cave's ceiling. It was wet and shining. He brought his head down and thought of Astrid, of Jay and her betrayal. It should be simple, he thought. Love should be simple. Honour should be straightforward. It should be the stuff of a gesture, a sign.

Auger needed a gesture, a route that was direct. It had to brush aside the network of nangines in Astrid's brain as if they were cobwebs. It had to be possible – he had to *believe* it was possible, with both logic and desire.

Astrid was here, in some sense. She had to be. Jay had passed a cage full of beasts, who were here, in Cathar, into the convolutions of her brain. So she was here.

Yes. She is here.

Auger looked down and saw it there, the lizard, on the stone bed beside Astrid's head. It stared at him with those unblinking eyes. He could feel its gaze inside his skull.

She is here. She holds many of us.

What can I do?

Only you can do it, Auger.

And the lizard fell silent. Auger wanted to shout in frustration, but he forced himself to carry through the thoughts. Okay, the magic will work. She is connected to here. I can connect to her, just as Jay did. I just have to work out how.

He looked at her again, then knelt and took her hand in his. It was limp and lifeless, but it was warm.

The lizard skittered up his arm and stopped again on his shoulder, fastidiously adjusting the pads of its feet. Auger felt its approval, some-how, or its reassurance. He was doing something right.

With his other hand he brushed a strand of hair from her cheek, and then left his hand gently on her cheek. He noticed that his hand was trembling, his fingers almost fizzing.

My son, he thought. Help me. My child I do not know. Can he sense me?

Auger leaned forward and there was a barrier, it seemed, between their faces as without thought he dipped his head towards Astrid's. A breeze that became a wind was baring his lips and exposing his teeth, and yet her face remained still and serene. Her eyelids were softly closed. She was aware of nothing.

He felt himself pushed back, and tried to force his way forward again. The lizard ran back down his arm in a thrill of movement and made a small leap to stand, its tail in a faint curl, by Astrid's head.

You can.

Auger opened his mouth to yell in frustration, but the wind cracked into him and opened his lungs in a gasp. The wind grew and flattened his eyeballs, squeezing water from the corners of his eyes.

You can.

Auger clamped his mouth shut, clenched his eyelids and snorted air from his nose against the gale, and pushed forward again. He was thinking of Astrid, but differently now. Not from logic, but remembering the flutter of her touch, the melody of her voice, the shine of her lips – and her lips were there and his were meeting them in a gentle crush, a kiss—

—and her eyes were open and the wind was gone.

She looked up at him. He could see himself in her eyes, and even tiny images of the gecko that was at her shoulder.

'Astrid,' he whispered.

'Auger?'

And then there was a gasp from her, and she seemed to dissolve in front of him.

'No!' he yelled. He tried to grab hold of her, but he was grasping smoke. 'Astrid!' His vision blurred, and he thought it was the zone until he wiped the water from his eyes.

THIRTY-THREE

Lethe said, 'I've got an itchy feeling,' and stopped there abruptly.

Madsen looked up at her as Jaime said, 'What do you mean?'

'Like there's someone else here. Watching us.' She swivelled her head, looking around the place, but Madsen, following her movements, could see nothing, just the scratched and pitted walls of the derelict house whose hull they were squatted in, and Auger laid out and bLinkered on a discarded mattress with a ghostly motif of rusted springs, and Jaime squatting motionlessly beside Lethe as he had been for an hour now. The small portable air scourer set on its telestalk was groaning and starting to fail, and Madsen was beginning to taste the atmosphere again.

'Madsen?' Jaime said, but Madsen said nothing back. He was concentrating on Auger, whose eyes were jumping beneath the bLinkers. It looked as if something was in his skull and trying to break out through his eyeballs.

Madsen checked Auger's pulse, which was running fast and slightly weak. Lethe saying she felt itchy like that didn't help Madsen's frame of mind. Not after Pibald. But he trusted her. If she felt itchy, he felt stung.

'Maybe a tramp. But it could be the 'fists,'' he whispered without glancing at them. 'We've been here far too long. They'll be closing in. I don't know what the hell he's doing there. He should have Exited by now.'

'Can't we pick him up and take him?' Jaime said. 'Like before?'

'No point. Pibald with the symbiote blurred the signal. If he's alone in there, as long as he stays bLinkered, moving's no use. Once they're locked on to his set, we may as well start throwing up location flares.'

Madsen looked up at Jaime. 'You two don't need to worry, a couple of kids hanging around the wreck of a house. Better go, though. As long as I'm here to explain it.'

'We're not leaving you,' Jaime said, his voice coming out hot. 'Lethe?'

She said nothing, unusually not backing Jaime up, and Madsen looked towards her.

She wasn't there.

'Lethe?' Jaime swivelled so hard he nearly fell. His voice broke altogether. He yelled, 'Lethe?'

Madsen looked at him, not knowing what to say.

'I'm going to find her,' Jaime told him, controlling the suddenly wild syllables with difficulty. His feet slipped in the brick dust and he almost lost balance, crashing towards the ruined doorway. Adjusting his respirator, he paused there and glanced at Madsen, obviously realising it looked like he was just running. 'I'm coming back.'

Madsen watched Jaime disappear, then went back to Auger, who was making little body movements, jerking and twitching. It was an uneasy, creased sleep he was in, not the usual calm bLinkered state. 'Come out, come out, wherever you are,' he murmured. 'This is far too long, Auger.' He glanced at the monitor on his wrist, thumbed it. A small beep sounded and he swore. He thumbed it again, trying to source the signal, but there was nothing else. The screen remained as clear as hope. Above, the scourer stuttered and recovered, delivering Madsen a choking breath of dust. The filter warning light on its stalk started discreetly to flash.

'They're coming in shielded this time,' he told Auger, as if Auger was likely to respond. 'Must have guessed I had a tracer last time. And they're nearly in place, but not yet. They aren't quite sure. That wasn't a transmission leak. That was to flush us out.'

There was a lance of pale sunlight beyond the doorway, gilding the settling brick dust. Lethe and Jaime needed to keep their stories simple if they got themselves caught. Madsen considered it. They'd been messing around in here, the pair of them, working the mattress. A couple of guys had come in and they'd hidden themselves, watching as one of the men bLinked, and then the other man had spotted the kids and scared them off. Lethe would spin the story, that was for sure, she was tough as sin, but Jaime was a different matter.

Madsen smiled at the thought of him. He was a good kid, even if he had more sense of honour than common sense. He needed Lethe. But she needed him, too. Madsen had seen that, though he didn't quite understand it.

There was no sun in the doorway now. The filter warning was flashing more brightly. Madsen shook Auger's shoulder in frustration. 'Come on, Auger. Come back.'

He waited on, until the doorway darkened with a double silhouette. He knew it for Lethe and Jaime before their faces came into view. They were holding hands. As they came inside another shape loomed behind them.

It would be a 'fist autoid, he knew, shepherding them in, and he was thinking that at least the kids had given him up instead of trying to be heroes.

But it wasn't an autoid behind them. It was just a lone, small man carrying a small black bag.

'I need to see Auger,' he said, just as if it was an appointment he was keeping. Dropping his mask, he slipped past Lethe and Jaime, seeing Auger there, and Madsen frowned a question at them.

'It was him,' Lethe said to Madsen, nodding her head. 'Those times. We were bugged. We must have been bugged all along. That's why I could never tag him.' She sounded disgusted with herself.

Jaime took her hand and told Madsen, 'He wasn't following us at all. He was trailing the signal. Me and Lethe had no chance.'

'We'll be surrounded very soon, I think,' the man said evenly, and glanced at Auger. The sight of him seemed to draw a small smile from the man which he held a moment before adding softly, 'He's been in too long.'

'He says he's not a 'fist,' Jaime said. 'He says he's a friend of Auger's.'

The man was kneeling beside Auger now. He looked up at Madsen and said, 'That's right. But I don't know if he'd think it right now. I'm responsible for him being where he is.'

The cave was still there, and Auger himself, and the gecko too, but Astrid was gone. Auger groaned and reached a hand to his eyes, feeling more lost and alone than he ever had before, and Exited Cathar.

He looked up, nothing but Astrid in his mind and the knowledge that he'd stayed too long in Cathar for safety, and knew he was either hallucinating or in another zone. Or maybe he was dead, since he was seeing a dead man. He was seeing Fly.

'Auger, listen to me,' Madsen was saying.

He turned to Madsen, barely able to think. First Jay, and now *him*. But Jay hadn't been back from the dead.

'There's no way out of here for you, Auger,' Madsen was telling him. 'We're going to have to leave you. Tell them you'll cooperate. Tell them anything. Just stay alive. We'll get to you. Get them to talk. We'll be listening. We'll know where you are.'

Auger nodded, hardly hearing it. He coughed and raised his filter. Above him the air scourer beeped, whined momentarily and was quiet.

'Listen. It seems you've got a bug, Auger. Subcutaneous, biocompatible. It's a transmitter, a frequency skimmer. Skims too fast for a passive scanner to register it, and detects active scanners and skips behind their fields.'

And stings like hell, Auger thought.

'Under your left shoulderblade. You've had it for—'

'Yes.' It was like swallowing ice water and feeling it fill his gut, cold as dead stars. Fly slapping him on the back. Planned. The whole thing planned.

In Merchant's room, he'd known Auger was there all along. He'd just gone there to make sure Auger didn't lose interest.

He whispered, 'Why?'

Fly bent down, speaking quickly. 'I'll get the rest of us out, Auger. I've got a record of a conversation between Vinz and Sweet, when they killed Oswell. I got it when I was following you at the time. Sweet's one of the team here. I'm sure I can persuade him to let us through.'

And Fly was gone again, with Madsen and Lethe and the boy, and Auger was alone once more. The springs of the mattress dug into him.

It was Vinz Szolty at the head of them, when they came a few minutes later. He stepped delicately through the strewn bricks, and waved the trig forward.

'You've been playing truant, Auger. I'm terminating your employment.' He smiled, watching the trig haul Auger to his feet and fit Magnacles to his wrists and ankles. 'But I don't think you need to worry about that, Auger.'

'You're going to kill me like you killed Oswell?'

'That was an accident. You know that. No, you're going to see the Max. He wants to talk to you. First.'

The trig gave him a shove in the back. Unbalanced by the Magnacles, Auger sprawled forward and with an effort picked himself up. He rolled his shoulders and felt his pulse race – not at the fall, but out of fear that the bug might have been damaged. But after a moment there was the itch of it again, and for the first time it held some reassurance for him.

He started to walk, thinking about Fly. His father had been a Far Warrior. He had told Auger that. But it hadn't been Father Fury who had been responsible for his death, like Fly had said. It had been Dr Carroll's research. Fly's father had been one of her – and Jay's, he had to remember that – guinea pigs. He had left the bLinkers for Fly, and Fly must have finally used them, gone to Cathar and found his father in the cave. And then his father had died.

But Fly would have seen images of the child in Cathar, and he would have been keeping an eye on the research wing too, and seen Jay coming and going, and if he had followed Jay, he would have seen Auger as well. He would have spotted the resemblance. He would have identified them as the child's parents.

Stumbling out on to the street, shoved by the trig, Auger glanced left and right. A few people standing curiously, watching the play of events. No sign of Madsen or the others. No sign of urgent conversations among the 'fists, of other prisoners. Fly had done as he'd promised, so far.

The trig pushed him forward towards the black custody vehicle with its red lights smouldering in the ashen afternoon.

So, Fly had realised Auger and Jay were involved in the zone. And then? Well, it didn't take too much effort to work it out. He had probably nearly been caught using those bLinkers. But what could he do? He wouldn't have dared go to the 'fists, or straight to Auger, even after what had happened to Jay, in case Auger was part of it too.

But Auger would have been his only chance. He would have had to risk bringing Auger into it, and maybe he needed to disappear himself, especially if they had nearly caught him using the bLinkers.

So he had worked it all through, and carried it out perfectly. He had used Fury to get to Auger, and then Auger to get to the killers of his father.

Hustled along the street, Auger didn't feel any anger, though. Fly had had no choice. And Auger, in the end, had been doing his job.

The trig pushed his head down and shoved him into the darkness of the vehicle's cage, transferring the Magnacles to the fat central restraint bar. His eyes gradually adapted to the dimness of the vehicle. There was nothing to see, though. Just bars and the metal bench.

In a while, Vinz squeezed inside and sat down opposite him, smiling happily, and pulled the doors closed on them. The aircon hummed, sucking ash from the tiny cocoon, and Vinz passed a scanner down Auger, head to toe, slowly, taking Auger's gun and then sitting back with the small pushJect vial that Auger had forgotten about. Troy Gordo's nangine vial.

'What's this?'

'An asthma drug. It's a fast delivery device. You've seen them before, haven't you?'

Vinz's face was empty, trying to read Auger's. 'Maybe.'

'Sometimes I go into respiratory failure. I have an environmental allergy. I could die without it.'

Vinz raised the vial towards Auger, leering. 'So I can check it on you now, then. It won't kill you.' Leaning forward with it.

'Yes. Except it's a monodose, and I only carry one.' Auger pushed out his elbow against the grip of the restraint, offering his arm to Vinz. 'So if I go into shock later on and need it then and it's gone, you'll tell Maxenham what you did, right? And he'll understand, right?'

Vinz sat back and nodded, examining Auger for a long moment, then slipped the vial back into Auger's pocket. He breathed deeply and folded his hands around the bar and said, 'What the hell.' He smiled, relaxing, and stretched his arms along the back of the seat. 'The Max is really looking forward to seeing you again, Auger. Almost as much as I'm looking forward to showing you in.'

Auger shrugged, the movement reminding him of the itch on his shoulder.

THIRTY-FOUR

Vinz stood in the doorway staring from Maxenham to Auger and back. Maxenham made a gesture for Auger to sit, then said to Vinz, 'Thank you, Vinz. You can go now. I'll call when we're ready for you.'

It wasn't what Vinz had been expecting. He scowled.

'Vinz.'

Vinz tried to slam the door behind him but it was too heavy and too well damped. It gently ushered him out.

Maxenham sat behind his desk. Mahogany, Auger guessed. The minister's office smelt of wood and leather. Of permanence. The chair swivelled as Maxenham inspected Auger.

'Vinz is a rough tool. He won't be refined, nor would I want him to be. I won't apologise for him, though I regret the need. He didn't damage you, did he? Didn't take anything apart from your hand weapon? He was instructed not to.'

'No.' Auger patted his pockets, checking the tiny pushJect vial. A small victory. Hardly a weapon, but nevertheless the vial was vaguely comforting.

'Good. Sit down, Auger. Please.'

Auger walked across the room towards the window. Real glass. The whole building was that well stabilised. Through the pane of real glass he could see the rest of the Administration complex. Stability. Safety. Economy. All the Ministries, and towering above them here, behind the illusory veneer of the ancient parliament, was the Administration Centre.

'Stand, then.'

The chair wheeled round and Maxenham said easily, 'I didn't realise you were the husband of our star researcher. No one saw fit to tell me that until now.' He sat back expansively, as if a treaty had been signed and the rest was champagne. He went on, lightly, 'What do you think of the world, Auger? Hmm? Come on, man. I could bring out the weapon I have here in my drawer and kill you now and no one would ever know it or care. Tell me what you think. How long will we last?'

'A year, five years. I don't know.' Auger looked at the painting of Maxenham on the wall, set beside but a fraction lower than the painting of the Administrator. The portraits of the other Ministers were set slightly apart from these two in a further line along the wall, visibly beneath Maxenham's level.

'That's right. You don't. Hope comes and goes, doesn't it?'

'Nugel went. And the Cultivation Net's a fraud, isn't it?'

To Auger's surprise, Maxenham simply nodded. 'Yes. The Net and Nugel – they're just nodes of hope and despair. Leavenings of the mood. We do our best, but when it becomes apparent that they will fail we use them as we need. They, and the Leavings, help us manage the population.' He caught himself at Auger's look. 'Perhaps I exaggerate, but not much. Technological advance, it's something like evolution. For each advance, each useful development, there are uncountable failures. Our scientists have a rather morbid expression for it. Do you know what they say? The more rapid the advance of technology, the shorter the EOS gap.'

'The EOS gap?'

'The time between Eureka and Oh, Shit.' Maxenham pushed himself energetically out of the chair. 'Let me show you something.' A screen flipped upright on his desk. He swivelled it to face Auger and moved round the desk to join him. He touched the screen's base and said, 'Tokyo.'

Auger watched the picture rise into view. Buildings, people, all swimming in ash.

The Minister keyed again. 'New York. And Moscow.'

'So?'

'A year ago the screen would have looked the same nilled as nined. The ash is settling, Auger. The waters are stabilising, perhaps withdrawing. The end is not, after all, nigh. The Earth will gutter on a while longer, it seems.' He touched the screen off. It flipped away into the desk. 'A few years back, it was thought that D2 was our last hope. When this Administration started to discuss D3, we imagined it would be our final desperate flourish. But it will be successful, and when it is, we shall be here to depart.'

He came close to Auger and made to put a hand on his shoulder. Auger shrugged him away.

'Why are we fighting, Auger?' Maxenham retreated to his chair again. 'We're on the same side, aren't we?'

'You're encouraging suicide. You're murdering people in the name of research.'

'We're embarking on a war. War requires desperate measures.'

'A war to destroy the entire population of another planet so that we can take it over. Not to live side by side, to share.'

'To share?' Maxenham chuckled at the idea. 'We aren't a species that shares. We aren't capable of it. If we could share, we could live peacefully on Earth. There would be no fundamentalists, no socialists or capitalists.' He grinned at that. 'No. Our politics, like our religion, is greedy. Our faith is not self-sufficient.' He sighed to himself, then almost murmured, 'What do you know about faith, Auger? Do you believe in God? Any God? Anything?'

'I don't believe in anything you'd understand.'

'Well, let me tell you something about faith.' His arm waved languidly. 'No, not my Ministry. Religious faith. There is a gene for it.' He searched Auger for a response. 'All right, no, that's not quite true. It's not a lie, but it's simplistic. It's a gene combination. But let's call it a gene, a faith gene.'

Maxenham smiled at Auger's expression. 'Yes. I still find it astonishing. But listen. Early genetic research was based on twin studies, and one of those studies examined pairs of twins brought up in vastly different religious and atheistic environments, who quite independently and for no developmental reason at all developed powerful religious faiths. Every other factor was eliminated. It was – it is – genetic. Faith is genetic.'

Maxenham steepled his fingers and peered at Auger through them. 'Bizarre, isn't it? If you have the gene, you are programmed, actually programmed to believe in God.'

He tilted his head, examining Auger. 'It makes sense, in Darwinian terms, doesn't it? Faith has a survival function. Those with religious beliefs live longer than those without. It's the reassurance of a God, perhaps, the sense of belonging, and relief from the stress of thinking yourself alone in the wilderness.' He glanced at his own portrait on the wall. 'We at Faith understand this. Faith is more important now than ever before. A common religious belief makes a community and binds it together. Belief in an afterlife and a judgmental God makes a community responsible and makes self-sacrifice possible in its defence.'

A light on the small comms unit on Maxenham's desk began to flash discreetly. The Minister leaned forward and said something Auger couldn't make out, the machine pushing a hiss of interference towards Auger and raising a tiny glittering holo to flutter before his lips.

'It makes for religious wars and suicide bombers, too,' Auger said when Maxenham was done. 'And Father Fury.'

Maxenham nodded indulgently. 'You can't have everything, Auger. But don't you find it slightly ironic that science has revealed a mechanism by which we can believe passionately in something that any rational scientist would dismiss out of hand?'

'Where is this going, Maxenham?'

'Self-sacrifice.' The Minister sat forward now and leaned his elbows on the desk. 'Fundamentalist terrorism made use of it, and it almost destroyed the Earth. But now it will save it. The future of the Earth, Auger, depends on faith. Dirangesept will be conquered by faith.'

Auger shook his head. 'I don't understand.'

'Oh, come on, Auger. How do you imagine that D3 is going to succeed where the previous projects failed? Hmm? Weapons are no use.'

'By draining the beasts into the heads of the Warriors,' Auger said. 'Jay's research. She told me.' He suddenly saw that that could not be all. There had to be more to it. 'What else?'

'What else,' Maxenham said. 'Let me tell you. There may be up to a billion beasts on Dirangesept, if our calculations are correct. As you realise, they can't all be transferred into our Far Warriors. And if they could, what then would become of the warriors? Can we use and discard our heroes like that? Hardly.'

He gazed at the window for a moment. 'No. The same technology will be used to transfer the beasts on into further containers. We will pass them on from the warriors, and return the warriors to Dirangesept, and repeat the process. We have hardware and carriers capable of containing far more beasts than the warriors can hold.'

Maxenham looked keenly at Auger, a teacher with a bright pupil.

'Your self-sacrifice,' Auger murmured softly, realising it. Maxenham was talking about McCrae's seekers of heaven. They were to be the carriers of the beasts. All along, they had been intended for this. They were destined to be nothing but war fodder.

Auger felt dizzy at the enormity of it. His hand was in his pocket, gripping the small glass vial. He made himself release it, afraid he might crush the thing. For a moment he considered rushing at Maxenham with it, but he didn't know what it would do, and anyway he would never get out of the building.

'Exactly.' Maxenham looked pleased. 'McCrae's congregation will be the ultimate hosts to the beasts. His heaven-zone, which we helped him develop, is the equivalent of Cathar. The personal zones will be controlled by the augmented brains of Dr Carroll's nangineered babies. Your child was the first of what will be thousands by the time the armada reaches Dirangesept. Each baby can monitor and control a thousand hosts, and each host can contain a thousand beasts. To each ship, a million beasts. Eventually every beast on Dirangesept will be decanted into those ships.'

He was staring right through Auger now. 'Our Far Warriors will be at little risk. They will bLink into their autoids and go down to the planet, and they will bLink out again as soon as a beast infests them. Back in the ship, they will bLink into a host's zone, and the beast will be transferred. The whole process should taken ten minutes, from beast contact to host receipt. Allow an hour's turnaround . . .' Maxenham clicked his fingers. 'As soon as the process is safely under way, the evacuation of Earth will commence.'

Auger was still taking it in. He said, his voice sounding like a whisper, 'And the hosts? What about them?'

'Once they are filled to capacity, it doesn't really matter. They can fly eternally through space, or they can die. Either way, they have their heaven.'

Auger went to the window. Far below him was the ground. Too far to jump. Too many people. He put his back to the glass. Even through his jacket, it felt cold.

Maxenham rocked on the chair, staring at the ceiling. 'You can help us, Auger. Until you turned up in Cathar and raised the issue, we hadn't considered the fathers of our babies. Dr Carroll and your wife – no, she's not your wife, I keep forgetting – they feel that your help could be very useful.'

'I thought the research was complete.'

'Research, it seems, is never complete. Scientists are irksome. No, the research will even continue on the ships. We still need more mothers and babies. Not that we'd ask you to embark, of course. But it makes it far more straightforward if our participants are fully cooperative. Jay, for instance, is using Cathar as her zone, but our other mothers, her equivalent on the ships, will be in zones that they can, well, that they can understand. The beasts will seem to present a direct threat to their babies, and they will respond by disposing of them into our hosts. Not all our mothers are as efficient as Jay, unfortunately. However, a mother *and* a father working together—'

'No,' Auger said. 'I won't be part of this.'

The Minister made a fist and examined it, opened his hand again. He said mildly, 'No? Really? Consider your friend Astrid. I gather she has recovered.'

Auger's gut turned over. 'How much does the Administrator know about this, Maxenham?'

Maxenham burst out laughing. 'The Administrator! Auger, what do you know of politics?'

Auger looked at him. Nodes of hope and despair. That was all it was. Even if Maxenham wasn't lying about Astrid.

'No,' he repeated.

The Minister stood up. 'Think about it. Your refusal won't change things. It won't stop the project or affect its success. It would just make it less simple. Your assistance, though, would save you and your friend.' He patted his palms on the desk decisively. 'Now, I have arrangements to make, Auger. This is a busy time. Tomorrow it all comes together. The fleets depart. Speak to Vinz. He'll take care of you. Either way.'

THIRTY-FIVE

Madsen looked away from the screen for a moment and said to Fly, 'McCrae looks calm, doesn't he? You definitely told him the whole thing? Everything Maxenham told Auger?'

Fly's expression didn't change. He could almost have been asleep, Madsen thought. Dreaming. Hardly stirring, Fly softly said, 'I told him. I told you I told him.' He shrugged. 'Maybe that's what faith does for you. It gives you certainty, and certainty gives you calm.'

'Do you have any faith, Fly?'

Fly still didn't look at him. 'I have what I need.'

Madsen couldn't sit still, though. He had no faith, no calm, no certainty. He got up and stretched his legs, and couldn't hold back a yawn, even though he was beyond exhaustion. He hadn't slept since the 'fists had taken Auger, two days back. Why the hell had Auger said no to Maxenham? Stupid, stupid.

On the screen, McCrae looked almost beatific in his rich red robe. It was impossible to believe he knew what Fly was supposed to have told him.

Madsen couldn't work Fly out at all. He had wondered at first where Fly's calm might come from, and decided there was no real calm there, not a jot of it. Madsen figured that Fly was constantly simmering just below the boil. That calmness was just the lid he pressed down on it.

'Is it just ignorance that you have?' Madsen threw that at Fly's composure, wanting to needle him. Wanting to make him know how Madsen felt about Fly using Auger like he had, even if there hadn't been an alternative. 'Ignorance gives you certainty, too.'

'Well, McCrae isn't ignorant any more, is he?' Lethe said, coming over to touch Madsen's arm. 'Will you two stop scratching away at each other? You're like kids.'

'Maybe he just didn't believe it,' Madsen said to Fly, ignoring Lethe. 'Maybe this is all a waste of time and we've blown the whole thing.'

After that, no one said anything for a while. Madsen sat down again. Jaime and Lethe went back to their subdued chattering. Fly still looked half-asleep, though his head was straight and still, and his back like a rod.

Auger's mouth was eggshell dry. He ran his tongue around it, but that made no difference. His head throbbed.

Vinz reached a skinny arm through the bars and lifted Auger's head by the chin. 'Wakey-wakey, Auger. This is your final alarm call. The Project's about to depart. You might as well see it.' He squeezed Auger's neck sharply. 'A final treat.'

It was cold here. It was very cold. Auger pulled himself stiffly away from Vinz and rolled himself over on to his elbows. The tiled floor was freezing against his bare skin. He looked out through the bars. To either side, the walls of the long room were lined with shelves, the shelves arranged with squat glass jars whose curves caught the high strips of light and distilled the neon to brilliant points. In a few of the jars there seemed to be movement, but that might just have been miniature reflections of Vinz, who was stalking around the room, waving his arms.

'The mortuary,' Vinz told Auger, though Auger hadn't said a word. 'Save us bringing you over later. My idea.'

There was another faint light source that Auger hadn't immediately noticed. A glowing pale blue rectangle, set high on the far wall beyond Vinz. It was a screen, angled down, its bright yellow cable falling to a socket in awkward loops. On the floor below the screen were three steel dissection tables on wheels, set in a row. Two piles of clothes lay on one of them. One of the piles was Auger's. He didn't have the energy to consider the other.

'It's an odd thing, don't you think?' Vinz said to Auger. He was talkative, exuberant. 'Why have cells in a mortuary? There's only dead people and doctors here. Any idea?' He waited a moment, and then turned fractionally away from Auger and said, 'How about you? You're a doctor after all. Can you tell us?'

'To p-prevent organ looting.'

Auger jerked his head at her voice, and Vinz laughed. 'Ah, I thought that might perk you up, Auger. I gather from Dr Carroll that you two are . . .' He leered at Astrid and made an obscene gesture. 'A poignant moment, then, Auger. Love and death. No, Dr Remarque, it's nothing to do with organ looting. That's the story Ferec gives out, and it's a sad reflection on us all that it's quite plausible, don't you think? No.' He rubbed his hands against the cold. 'Let me tell you why there are cages in the mortuary.'

He paused for their attention, going over to one of the dissection tables and rapping the polished steel with a knuckle. The steel frame boomed in the frigid atmosphere, and the light from the jars shivered. 'Human vivisection,' he said. 'Criminals are occasionally terminated in here. Not so often as to draw attention, of course. People are squeamish after all. They'd rather not know about extended executions. Administration researchers bid for termination control on behalf of their projects. Dr Carroll has used the facilities here in the past. And so has your wife, Auger. Did you know that? Did she tell you?'

'Go to hell, Vinz,' Auger said, standing up, moving as far towards him as he could before the bars brought him short. Two paces. The bars were like rods of ice folded into the palms of his hands. Vinz took two paces back, then smiled.

'There's n-no point, Auger,' Astrid murmured. She was sitting on the floor of the cage adjoining Auger's, hugging her knees, and every few moments she shivered. She was as naked as he was. She tried to smile at him, but the cold shook it away. She put a hand to her face, and he saw that the tips of her fingers were white as frost.

'That's absolutely right. No point at all,' Vinz said. 'The researchers call this place Securicorpse, I hear. Morbid sense of humour, medics have.'

Auger was at the bars dividing the two cages now, reaching an arm through them, reaching towards her. She stood awkwardly to her feet and stumbled to him. He was cold enough, but her hand was stiff with it. 'Are you all right?' he asked her, knowing how stupid the question was, but not knowing what else to say to her.

'N-no,' she said. 'But it d-doesn't seem to matter quite so m-much.'

'Oh, so sweet,' Vinz said, and turned away. The high screen flared brightly to life, hurling shadows across the dead room. Vinz looked up at it, his back to Auger and Astrid.

'Wait,' Auger told Astrid. He crossed his cell. There was a pale blue sheet crumpled up in the far corner. It was dry, but it was thin and so cold that it crackled as he shook it out.

Astrid was standing away from the icy bars, hugging herself tightly and shivering, watching him. He wrapped the sheet around himself tightly, drawing breath at the cloth's bitter chill and the faint chemical stink that came from it, and realising that it had probably last been draped over a corpse. The sheet leached the heat from him, but after a few minutes against his bare flesh it had to be a little warmer. He unwound himself from it and passed it to Astrid through the bars. She had some difficulty in even gripping it with her fingers, but managed eventually to wrap it partly around herself. Then she started to feed the rest back through the bars for him to wrap himself.

'No,' he said. 'You use it. You need it more.'

'Don't be st-stupid,' she told him. 'We can use each other, t-too.'

He understood. Against his chest, the material gave insulation from the coldness of the bars, and he found he could stretch his arms far enough between them to hug her and be hugged.

'That feels g-good, Auger,' she said, and looked at him. This time her smile held. 'If a bit late.'

Vinz came over to the cells, his boots crunching across the tiled floor, and rapped his knuckles on the outer bars. 'Oh, a lot late, actually,' he said. 'In fact, way too late.' The transmitted thrill of the rapping through the bars shook Astrid and Auger as if they were one soul. 'Now, do you two want to pay attention to the last thing you're ever going to see, or don't you?'

The audio came up. Auger couldn't help but look.

On the high screen, McCrae was talking easily to the News Holohead, whose quiff was jumping like crazy. McCrae looked entirely unruffled, as if the day was promising nothing more unusual than three synthetic meals rounded off by a sleep.

'This 'cast is on every single screen,' Vinz said. He grinned at Auger and Astrid. 'Every screen in the world is carrying this.'

'So, Doctor, heaven is aboard those vessels,' the Holohead was saying. Behind him and McCrae was a dusting of stars and a great tracery of ships falling back into its own dizzying perspective. The separation of the two fleets was hard to make out now. There was just a slightly exaggerated interval between two of the ranks, and a subtle difference in formations of the ships to either side of this.

McCrae started to say something, but the Holohead held up a hand to interrupt him.

The Administration fanfare sounded, and the Holohead bobbed cheerfully upright.

Madsen moved forward, tipping his chair on to its front feet. 'Now,' he murmured. He glanced at Fly, who still hadn't moved.

On the screen, McCrae put his hands on his knees and pushed himself unhurriedly to his feet as Maxenham strode into view, his eyes sparkling more brightly than the stars that were his backcloth. His right hand jetted out to clasp McCrae's, his left smoothly folding over the preacher's in a grip that said that this was more than two men of power meeting. Maxenham shook McCrae's hand forcefully. The handshake was a gesture of partnership, but not of equal partnership. McCrae's arm shook, too. McCrae shook.

Maxenham released the preacher and turned to the Holohead. The Minister was almost as chiselled as the Holohead today. He looked calm and cool, his skin glistening with health, his glittering eyes full of cheer.

'This is a historic occasion,' the Holohead said, and paused, nodding. 'A day to remember.' He turned to the cam and spread his arms. 'I have with me now the two men responsible for this day. It is not an exaggeration to say that they are the architects of our future.' He bowed his head and made a gesture to the cam. 'Of *your* future. Minister Maxenham, of the Department of Faith, and Dr McCrae, of the Congregation of Heaven.'

At Madsen's side, Fly clicked his tongue. Behind the Holohead, a few of the ships were beginning to spit needles of flame and shift position. More followed, stirring restlessly, and the vast grid adjusted as if a mild breeze were starting up. The Holohead turned to look. 'Not long to go now. Minister Maxenham, how does it feel to be at last announcing the leaving of D3?'

'It humbles me,' Maxenham said. 'All I have done is my job and my duty. I am a servant of the people, and of the Administration. I am a cog. That is all.'

'Thank you, Minister. Dr McCrae, you have a few last minutes here on Earth before your shuttle takes you up there to be with your flock on their long journey. Do you have a message for us before you leave for your long heaven?'

'Yes – excuse me.' He took a small silver box from his pocket and held it up apologetically. 'Indigestion, I'm afraid.' He popped a tablet into his mouth. He had to swallow a couple of times to get it down his throat, almost gagging. His Adam's apple jumped.

'Nerves?' suggested the Holohead. Beside him, Maxenham smiled.

'I shall be going to heaven, yes, to answer your first question,' McCrae said. 'But, no, I am not nervous in the least.' He stroked the sleeves of his robe.

Madsen glanced at Fly. 'Suicide pill?'

'Maybe.'

Madsen felt abruptly flattened. He realised they had no guarantee that

McCrae would expose the plot. Maybe he was just going to kill himself and let the secret die with him.

'Maxenham,' McCrae said. His voice was a croak, and he cleared his throat with difficulty.

Madsen leaned further forward in his chair, and noticed Fly doing the same. Lethe and Jaime stopped talking and came over to stand beside Madsen, holding hands.

'I know it all, Maxenham,' McCrae said clearly.

Madsen let out a sigh of relief. This had to be it. The preacher was going to tell the tale.

The Minister smiled. It was impossible to read the smile on that chiselled face.

'Ah, the prophet speaks,' the Holohead said, chuckling. 'Will you tell us the word of the Lord?'

'No. I would not presume. The Minister knows what I mean. Don't you, M—'

McCrae vanished abruptly from the screen, and Maxenham too. The Holohead seemed frozen there, still in space, with the great fleets now micro-manoeuvring behind him, ships aligning themselves for departure and shuttles buzzing more urgently.

'What?' Vinz said. He took a step towards the screen. 'What the hell—?'

Auger felt Astrid tense through the bars. The cloth binding them tautened. She whispered to him, 'What was McCrae talking about?'

'His congregation. They're going to use them for D3, as hosts for the beasts. McCrae must have found out. Fly probably told him. I imagine McCrae was about to spill it. But the 'cast must be on live delay. They've pulled transmission.' He pulled Astrid closer. The bars between them weren't even faintly cool through the sheet now. 'It's pointless, though,' he said. 'Wasted effort. But there's nothing else McCrae can do.'

'No,' Astrid said. 'That pill.'

'Maybe he was intending to kill himself on air.' It didn't bother Auger what McCrae did. It didn't matter any more. 'Maybe make some sort of protest.'

'No,' she said flatly. 'He's not going to make any protest.' Her voice was rising and she struggled to level it. 'They don't realise it. They think they've covered it, but they're wrong. They don't know what they're dealing with.'

Through the bars Auger felt the tension in her, but he couldn't see the cause of it. She was overreacting. He said, 'What do you mean?'

'Don't you remember what I told you about schizotypy, Auger? He won't just kill himself. It wouldn't be enough. He'd have to do more than that.' She shook him, jolting her words home. The bars between them rumbled.

'Don't you see? *He* hasn't been betrayed. *God* has been betrayed. And McCrae is God's direct agent. And the gestures of God are not merely symbolic. If McCrae didn't have a plan, he wouldn't be there now.'

A discreet buzz began to sound in the mortuary, quickly becoming more insistent until the room rang with it. Vinz, who had been standing and staring at the screen, swore, reached for his pocket and made for the door. It slammed behind him, leaving a brief mournful echo. The buzzing left with him.

Madsen looked around, aware of a bone in his neck clicking loudly in the silence. Fly, Lethe and Jaime were locked as still as the Holohead on the screen.

'What do we do?' Jaime finally said. He sounded flustered, his voice tiny.

'We wait.'

Music came on in the background, a soft and lethargic variation on the Administration fanfare in strings and horns. The ships continued their slow line dance. The Holohead smiled serenely in the centre of the screen, saying nothing.

Lethe said, 'What's happening now?'

'Everything. Nothing. They're wondering what the hell to do. They haven't got long. It depends on whether McCrae's set anything in place to force their hand.' He glanced at Fly, who was as impassive as ever. 'You were the one who saw him, Fly. You told him. What do you think? Did he say anything to you?' Madsen waited. 'Fly?'

Fly said nothing.

The music faded, and McCrae came into view again beside the Holohead. The preacher was looking pale and unwell. But so was Maxenham on the Holohead's other flank.

In the top right corner of the screen a message box blinked on and kept blinking.

Urgent! Open This Now!

Maxenham's features seemed rounder and weaker, Madsen saw, and his eyes had more of the rat than the hawk.

'They've jettisoned Maxenham,' Fly said, echoing the thought that had come into Madsen's head. 'Yes!' He stood up and clapped his hands together. 'Yes!'

McCrae was having trouble speaking. His face seemed to blur with pain and he bent abruptly and awkwardly forward. His cheeks bulged and for an instant he seemed about to vomit, but instead he pulled himself up and said, quite clearly, 'I have personally sent this message, Maxenham, with the full details of your secret scheme, directly to the Administrator himself. He is horrified and appalled by what you attempted to do behind his back.'

The preacher's voice exploded in a cough that spewed him upright, and he faced the cam again. 'The details of your scheme have been disseminated over the broadcom. You can't block the message.' His voice was slurred now, but still clear. 'It's too late. In a few minutes, everyone will know what you are intending to do with my congregation, Maxenham.'

'That first part,' Madsen whispered, almost to himself. 'McCrae didn't say it. They morphed him and pasted it in. They're trying to damage-limit. That's why they brought him back. They're still running on delay. They're making certain Maxenham takes it all himself.'

'Are you all right, Doctor?' the Holohead was saying, leaning solicitously towards McCrae and putting an arm seemingly around his shoulder. The cam closed in, leaving Maxenham barely in shot at the edge of the screen.

McCrae shook his head, then looked sharply at Maxenham.

Auger pointed to the screen with its message box as Vinz came back into the room. He couldn't resist it. 'Every screen, Vinz,' he said. 'Every single screen in the world.'

'Shut up, Auger. McCrae's an irritant, that's all. It's fixed. He's under control now.'

'No, he isn't,' Astrid said. She started to unfurl the sheet from around her, but it was wound tight, and bound to her and Auger with sweat. 'Vinz, you've got to get through to the studio. McCrae's going to do something. I don't know what—'

'Save it,' Vinz said. 'There's nothing he can do. McCrae's just a psycho.'

'Vinz won't listen to you,' Auger told her. 'Anyway, what *can* McCrae do?'

'I told you, I don't know, but there will be something, and whatever it is, it's going to be big.'

On the screen, McCrae was slumped in his chair and croaking, 'I'm going to heaven, Maxenham. And you're going straight to hell.' He made a face of pain and touched his neck. 'Acid. I've swallowed acid.'

Vinz laughed. He looked at Astrid, visibly relaxed. His voice dropped a notch. 'There you are. He's just going to curl up and die. That message of his, we can handle that. This just makes it easier. An on-screen psycho-suicide doesn't exactly give his message credibility. He's cooked. Problem solved. The Max'll survive it. You just watch.'

Maxenham's face bloomed with fury. He walked directly through the Holohead and picked McCrae up by his collar.

The Holohead shuddered and went bright green. He adjusted his jacket and said, 'Hey, Minister, that wasn't polite. You walked right through me. I feel *queeeasy.*'

Vinz swore at the screen, but this time he sounded in control. 'Goddamn Holohead. A goddamn AI with an attitude, that's all it is.' He banged a fist on the nearest trolley. The clothes on it jumped. 'I kept saying tighten its goddamn parameters, but no one ever listens to me.'

Maxenham wasn't listening to the Holohead. He shook McCrae and then pushed him back into his chair. He looked down at him and said, 'Then you've just saved me the trouble of finishing you off myself. You're insane. Eat your acid and die in agony, McCrae. Take your time. I'll enjoy it. You think you've destroyed me? You don't know a thing.'

McCrae belched. A cord of black spittle ran from his mouth and dripped on to the red of his collar. 'No.' He breathed unevenly, belched, then gathered himself. 'I know this. There's a kilogram of MagmaX in my stomach. You know what that is? Right now, the acid is burning through to its biodetonator.' He winced and clutched his gut, and groaned, then managed to control himself again. 'A few seconds after that, the bio-detonator will be set off by my stomach enzymes. You're going to hell, Maxenham.' He belched again, a ragged spume of vomit arcing on to Maxenham's cheek. Maxenham recoiled. McCrae collected himself one last time and said, 'Vengeance . . . vengeance is mine.' He smiled and raised his arms high. There was a look of glory on his face.

MagmaX, Auger thought clearly. A kilogram of the explosive would destroy the whole of London. They were all about to die. Astrid had been right about McCrae.

For a moment there was perfect silence on the screen and in the mortuary, and then Auger yelled, 'Vinz . . .'

Vinz turned round. He started to say something, then stopped and cocked his head.

370

Auger felt the rumble in his chest before he actually heard it, and by then his legs were trembling. The trembling travelled up to his skull.

In unison, the dissection tables started to roll towards Vinz, who put out a hand to balance himself as floor tiles exploded and the ground began to rear and crack, but the trolley he was reaching for slid away again, crashing into the wall.

The shock wave swelled. Auger heard the rattling of his teeth. There was pain in his eyeballs, and he saw Astrid separate into two. He blinked, and she multiplied further, merged and parted again. He tried to yell and had no idea if any sound had come out. Astrid was hardly more than a blur. The ground felt as thin as paper under his feet and began to rip. His footing went, and he and Astrid, still bound together by the sheet, slid down the bars that separated them. The air filled with noise and smoke. There was a sensation of everything expanding, and then there was nothing.

Madsen felt it coming a fraction of a second before it happened. The air shivered like jelly, sucking at his cheeks and ears and eyeballs. The breath in his lungs left him in a slow groan, and his balance deserted him. He watched the window bubble inward and then out again, the sofglass colouring in ripples of indigo and mauve as it buckled and corrected, and a wave of heat and low sound crossed the room. Jaime yelped, the sound seeming to come from a far distance, and the floor and walls juddered. The overhead lightbar fizzled, faded and came back, and with it the picture on the screen. The distant booming rose and then was abruptly overhauled by an almost physical crack splitting the air. Madsen was deafened by it. At the same time he felt himself lifted towards the ceiling and for an instant held there, suspended. And then, with astonishing lightness, he was released again to land on his hands and knees.

It seemed for ever before the noise slackened. Madsen felt sick and dizzy. He looked at his trembling hands, then put his head down between his legs until the blood came back and he could sit up without feeling nauseous.

Lethe and Jaime were at the window, rubbing at the sofglass. Across the room, Fly was saying something to them, but Madsen couldn't hear a word of it for the rumbling echo of the explosion. And then Fly's voice came through to him, as if Fly himself was on delay.

'Can you see anything?'

'Dust,' Lethe said shakily. Madsen rubbed at his ears, trying to make time synchronise itself again.

Wallowing on its visgel bed, the building slowly settled. The floor and walls groaned. Madsen felt sick again. A small cloud of brown dust spilled into the room from the corner of the window and then dissipated as the sofglass flowed to seal the leak.

'Christ,' Lethe whispered from the window. This time the word arrived with the movement of her lips. Auger looked and saw her there almost in silhouette, the sofglass gleaming pale yellow now, but the yellow wasn't in the glass. It was distant fire shining through the dust.

The screen was glowing in the corner, a neutral jade. Soft music played.

'He did it,' Madsen said. 'That was it.' But as he said it, he knew there was something wrong. Something about what had happened didn't quite make sense.

Fly stood up and stretched out his arms. 'Maxenham's dead.'

Madsen turned to him. 'Maxenham? What——?'

'Shut up,' Jaime yelled. 'Look!'

The screen was colouring up again and the music fading. A frame of deep Administration green edged the picture. The Holohead was there once more, and grinning happily. 'Temper, temper, huh?' He shook his head. 'Boy, I felt really nauseous there. Did you see that? He walked right *through* me. Brrr.' The Holohead shuddered. 'Well, I said this was a day to remember, didn't I? I won't forget this for a while. Two ministers off to meet their maker in one go. But not your old NH.' He winked at the cam. 'Maybe that's because I've already met mine – and a very pleasant tech she is, too.'

The Administration fanfare blasted again. The Holohead's face contorted. His eyes crossed and he rubbed his cheeks vigorously. He seemed to fray at the edges and then fix again. 'Oops. Sorry about that. Inappropriate reaction. I think I was hysterical there.' He winked and smiled. 'And I don't mean funny-hysterical either. I——' His face froze. Music started and stopped again. The screen faded back to jade and stayed there.

Madsen became aware of the silence and the glowing rectangles at either end of the room. The yellow and the green. Everyone was staring at the dulled screen. Lethe and Jaime had their backs to the window. Somehow it was more of a shock to see the screen lifeless, the Holohead without a joke.

The Administration fanfare repeated, the screen bloomed and the Holohead cracked back into action. 'Hello,' he said, tilting his head. His colours were sharper and his quiff bounced energetically. 'I think I now have a *very* special guest.'

'Thank you, News Holohead.'

Madsen whistled.

'Who's that?' Lethe said.

'The Administrator,' Madsen told her. His voice died away. The Administrator was taller than the Holohead, and looked somehow both more and less actual. He was grave, yet with the set of his features he was entirely reassuring. Madsen knew the whole image was as sham as the Holohead's, but for the moment it didn't matter.

'Thank you, Holohead. None of us was prepared for that. Not even you. There is no shame in that.'

The Administrator turned smoothly to face the screen, and said, 'Friends.' He spread his hands, palms upward, and held them there. It was the gesture he was known for. They were broad hands, the lined and seasoned hands of a manual labourer, but at the same time long-fingered and expressive. The Administrator's hands had universal appeal and almost perfect approval ratings. They expressed experience, honesty, trust and sensitivity.

And then, astonishingly, his poise seemed to fail him. 'My friends. My friends and companions. My . . . my friends.' His voice was deep and resonant, but there was no disguising a faint tremble. Despite the augmentation of his image, it was plain that the Administrator was shaken. He lifted his arms, then helplessly let them drop again. He was scrambling for words. 'This is unspeakable. A terrible, awful tragedy. I . . . we all, all of us, have been betrayed. The Minister for Faith, Minister Maxenham, has grossly breached the trust we placed in him. I had barely been informed of the situation when Dr McCrae detonated . . .' His voice trailed away entirely.

At his side, the Holohead sighed in sorrowful understanding.

The Administrator nodded his head in acknowledgement of the Holohead, rallying himself. 'There has been a tremendous, unimaginable loss of life. We don't yet know how many. Tens, perhaps hundreds of thousands of people . . . Perhaps another degree of magnitude still.' He raised his head again, eyes suddenly sparkling with fire. 'We shall, of course, recover from this terrible tragedy in time. But right now, the vital thing is that we do not allow ourselves to be defeated by ex-Minister Maxenham's treason.'

He squared his shoulders. 'The fleets shall depart on schedule.' He stood taller, outgrowing the screen, and the cam pulled back to contain him. Muscles rippled under the granite-grey of his suit. 'Maxenham's computers are already being disconnected by technicians under my personal command, and his traitorous associates will soon be rounded up.' The Administrator made a fist almost as big as the Holohead's skull and held it still as rock. 'They shall escape neither justice nor righteous wrath.'

The Administrator took a breath before going on in a softer voice. 'And I give you my own personal assurance that Dr McCrae's congregation, in their leader's absence, will, as is their inalienable right, set off safely on their long heavenward trail. McCrae's action shall not taint them any more than Maxenham's plot shall ensnare them. They will be free from all further contact with the Earth. I, your Administrator, guarantee that.' He thumped the great fist into his palm, stronger again now. 'They shall have their heaven.'

His jaw was set, his eyes gleamed. 'And the Dirangesept project shall set off on their own great journey in the certainty of victory. Now . . .' He set his face firm and paused a few beats. 'Now is a time for unity and strength.'

The Holohead straightened himself and beamed. There were vast tears in his eyes, and he let them fall from his cheeks. 'Administrator, if I might say this, I am *honoured* to be here today. I announced at the beginning of this holocast that today was a historic occasion, but I never believed it would be as – well, as *emotional* as this.' He wiped his eyes. 'On behalf of your viewers, your people, I should like to thank you. I am more proud than I have the words to express. I—'

Madsen nilled the screen.

'Now what?' Lethe asked.

Fly said, 'Maxenham's gone. So has most of South London. Maybe GenMed, too.' He went to his small case. The aftershock had thrown it to the floor. He picked it up, clicked it open and pressed a few keys, waited, then looked at Madsen. 'Nothing from Auger's bug. It could just be the dust blocking the signal, but . . .' He shut the case and said, 'Let's go. No time to waste.' He waited, but no one else said a thing or moved. Madsen caught Lethe and Jaime looking at him.

'May as well,' Madsen said eventually. There seemed nothing else to say.

At the street door Madsen put on his mask and maxed the filter until every breath etched his teeth with carbon and mint. Then he pulled open the door. No one met his eye.

Outside, the street was totally silent. The door swung closed behind Lethe, who was last out. They stood still, the four of them in a little clump. Madsen noticed Jaime shaking his head and putting a hand to his ear, and Fly started to speak but stopped after the first syllable.

There was no sound at all. No motors, no voices. No panic. It was as if what had happened was too much for even panic to be sufficient response.

'Come on,' Madsen eventually whispered.

There was no wind, just a strange, violent, aimless swirling of the air. There was dust, as always, but this dust was thickening. Madsen felt it gathering in his pores, caking his sweat. He touched a finger to his scalp, and it came away brown. Everyone's hair was turning the same brown. Madsen walked ahead, and after a few minutes he stopped at a deserted ferryflite beached in the middle of the road, its rotors drooping.

'We'll take this,' he said, pulling the curved door wide. 'There's not going to be much in the sky for a while.'

The 'flite rose awkwardly, then stabilised. Madsen thumbed auto, and the AP's voice stirred itself. 'Where to, guv?'

'GenMed,' Madsen told it. 'You have the co-ordinates?'

A snort. 'Does Bow church have bells?'

'Not any more. Max velocity.'

'Hang on a tick, guv. No can do. I'm set at fuel economy priority. You want me to override that?'

'Override everything,' Fly said, leaning past Madsen. 'Just go.'

'Everything? Do me a favour. You want me to override speed restrictions, guv? And air lanes? You sure about that? If I do, I have to send out a Pacifist alert, and it's the pokey for you, guv.'

'I think the 'fists'll have better things to do,' Madsen told it, pushing Fly back into his seat. 'Override everything. Including the cockney.'

The whine of the motor stretched up a fraction as the ferryflite tilted forward and accelerated, and the small dashboard screen filled with words.

PACIFIST ALERT EXTENDED. AND IT WASN'T COCKNEY.

The air was dense with dust as they rose, but as they flew south it became almost impenetrable. The 'flite flew into the heart of it, and the tone of the rotors changed.

For a while no one spoke. In the spin and swirl of dust, time and gravity seemed to be suspended. Madsen looked around. The internal lights of the 'flite glimmered, settling a flat light on everyone's face. 'Lethe. You okay?' She nodded shortly. 'Jaime?'

Jaime took Lethe's hand in both of his, and whispered, 'Yes. We're okay.'

'What about you, Fly?'

'I'm fine, Madsen. Don't worry about me. Let's get to GenMed.'

The 'flite banked, and the dust momentarily cleared beneath the machine, giving Madsen a glimpse of the corner of a building too close for his liking and a view down its flank to the ground. The wall was cracked and open. The crack carried on into the ground and kept going down.

The dust closed again and they flew on. The silence, Madsen grew aware, was not total now. Once he had become accustomed to the grind of the rotors and the drone of the engine he started to notice muted noises in the distance. Cracks and rumbles, like distant rifts. Grating and tearing sounds like machine screams. The air felt like jelly, buffeting the 'flite.

Jaime said, 'What's happening?'

The screen lit up with words.

THERE IS CONSIDERABLE MAGNETIC INTERFERENCE. I SEEM TO HAVE DRIFTED TOO FAR SOUTH. YOU WILL NOT BE CHARGED FOR THE OVERSHOOT. I AM CORRECTING MY READERS.

'We're south of GenMed,' Fly said, his voice low and muffled. He had his nose to the window's curve, his hands cupped at his eyes. His breath clouded the glass at his mouth. 'We're over the dead zone now. Can't see much.'

I AM NOT RECEIVING LOCAL BEACON INFORMATION. NOW COR-RECTING TO SATELLITE.

Madsen looked at Fly, at his reflected face distorted in the glass. 'What exactly did you say to McCrae, Fly? What did you tell him?'

Fly straightened. 'I told him the truth, Madsen. What do you think? What else did you expect?'

'Did he tell you what he was going to do?'

'I told him, "You've got to let the truth out. You've got to tell it." ' He shook his head at Madsen. 'It wasn't me that did this.' He went back to the window again, ghosting the glass with his breath.

The sounds were more frequent now, and closer and sharper. Madsen felt as if they were travelling through space, or else deep in the sea. There were no reference points. The dust was a different colour too, no longer brown or sulphur-tinged, and he puzzled over that for a moment. It wasn't environmental or atmospheric dust. It was grey, but not that fine grey of common atmospheric ash.

No. Madsen gripped the edge of his seat as he realised what it was. They were flying through the fabric of London, and all around them were pulverised buildings. Above them and below, ahead and behind, and to their left and right. They were moving through houses and shops and offices and churches, all suspended in the air, all ground to dust. And people too, in the air all around them, all dead, thousands and thousands and thousands of them. This was crematorium smoke.

ROTORS SUFFERING PARTICULATE DAMAGE.

A harsh crack sounded below and in front of the 'flite and it immediately banked and rose, and as it did so, the sharp wash of its blades cleared a perfect column of air directly beneath Madsen. As if in a spotlight he saw a wall collapsing and caught a glimpse of a human body tipping sideways through the column of air and a turning head and the wide, direct stare of an eye. A blue, blue eye. It blinked, as terrified as Madsen. As the rest of the sudden body aimlessly flailed, the head seemed to turn deliberately towards Madsen, as if he and this miraculous person about to die were perfectly synchronised, their faces moving in parallel. Its mouth opened as Madsen's mouth opened, and the dust closed again and it was all gone.

'What was that, Madsen? What did you say?'

'It— Nothing.'

What had the Administrator said? Hundreds of thousands? From the holocast studios in Croydon to GenMed, to the Thames, with that as a radius there had to be more than a million dead.

But why GenMed? Why might GenMed have escaped? He looked across the capsule. 'Fly?'

'What?'

'What makes you think GenMed's escaped?'

'I don't know if it has. I'm hoping, like you are, aren't you? What do you mean? What are you getting at, Madsen?'

Maxenham's gone. So has most of South London. Maybe GenMed, too. That's what Fly had said. Sandwiching South London between Maxenham and GenMed. And *Yes!* when he'd realised Maxenham had died. He'd wanted Maxenham dead more than anything. And he'd wanted GenMed safe. And for some reason he expected it to be.

'Nothing, Fly. I'm twitchy.' A kilogram of MagmaX, he remembered now. McCrae had said he'd swallowed a kilogram.

MOTORS CLOGGING. STABILITY FAILING. DITCH OPTION SUGGESTED

'How much further?'

K2.1 2.0 1.9 1.85 1.83

'Is there anywhere safe to ditch?'

There was nothing on the screen for a moment, then,

MAP INDICATES NOT, BUT

SCANNERS INDICATE NOT

Fly said, 'What the hell does that mean?'

The ferryflite was dropping. The rotors were screeching.

SCANNERS AND COMPASS DO NOT SYNCHRONISE. SATELLITE INDI-
CATES LOCATION, BUT RELIABILITY UNQUANTIFIABLE

'What does the satellite indicate?'

NOW ABOVE GENMED

'Put us down. Gently.'

NOW LANDING

The dust washed up and scratched at the 'flite's window, and the machine wallowed uncertainly for a moment and then dipped back and fell.

'Shit,' Lethe said.

The rotors slowed to a steady thump, and then stilled. The machine was down.

GENMED

POSSIBLY

Madsen cut the motor and pushed the door. Heat came in, and rolling dust. 'Well, this must be at the edge of the blast zone. You were right, Fly. I don't know what we'll find, though.'

Fly had his case open. He said, 'I've got a signal. Auger's bug's still active. It's close, too.'

'Does that mean he hasn't been killed?' Madsen asked, stepping out cautiously into the swirl of air. The ground was firm.

'It means he hasn't been atomised.'

Madsen could see railings, which meant that they were in the 'flite park at the front of GenMed. Out of the corner of his eye, he caught the screen flickering.

HOW WOULD YOU LIKE TO PAY?

A hand grabbed his jacket and a man yanked him away from the door of the 'flite. The man's face was streaked with grime and his hair glistened with blood.

'Out! Out! Get out, all of you.' He was screaming and crying. 'I'm taking this 'flite.'

Lethe and Jaime had to force themselves out past the desperate man in rags. Fly followed them, stumbling at the door. Madsen reached out to steady him, and instead Fly passed him the tracer for Auger's bug, saying, 'You've used one of these before?'

Madsen nodded as Fly jumped down from the 'flite.

On the ground, Fly started to say something more to Madsen, but the crazy man had thrown himself into a seat and was screaming, 'Go! Just go!' and pulling the door closed as the 'flite rose unsteadily and was gulped by the swollen air. Fly shrugged instead.

'Let's keep together,' Madsen yelled. He looked around.

The air was full of screaming. People were running around in the opaque dust, dashing into view and swerving away again. Someone ran straight into Jaime, knocking him over, then got straight up and ran off wildly.

Like ants, Madsen thought. They were like ants with their nest kicked over, except that ants had purpose. This was just chaos. This was the edge of the abyss, and it was crumbling away.

He tried to get his bearings. The cobbles under his feet were arranged in an arc, and he knew the arc pointed him towards the colonnade. He opened the tracer case. 'Come on,' he said, increasing his pace, and then slowing down again as through the dust he saw a vague shape ahead, a tall and motionless orange-cloaked man standing on a podium in a cage of railings.

A guard. GenMed was operating under emergency regulations.

Madsen slowed down, prepared to retreat into the dust, then stopped to stare at the figure. It wasn't a guard. It was a termite mound with the head of a man. It was the statue of GenMed's founder on its plinth, all but consumed by the termites.

The case was beeping. 'It's okay,' he said, turning to the others. 'This way. Let's go.'

Lethe and Jaime nodded. Fly had vanished.

Auger picked himself up and found that his right ankle wouldn't take his weight. The cloth had ripped with the explosion and Astrid had been thrown across the cell. She wasn't moving.

Across the room Vinz was lying under one of the trolleys, and coming to. He tried to push it away but didn't quite have the strength, and it fell back onto him. He looked around and saw Auger, then looked up at the ceiling above Auger. The expression on his face altered slightly.

It took Auger a second to realise what Vinz had seen. The ceiling of the mortuary had dropped with the explosion, bowing and parting the bars of the cells. Vinz grunted and tried to roll out from beneath the trolley as Auger forced himself through the bars and ran towards him, tiles cracking under his feet. There was glass too underfoot, and a stink of formaldehyde from the specimen jars smashed on the floor.

Vinz was on his feet before Auger reached him. He wiped a bloody hand across his mouth, then reached into a pocket and drew a small sharplight.

A noise behind Auger made him turn. Astrid had crawled from her cell after Auger and was coming slowly towards them. She looked dazed. Vinz leaned on the trolley and said, 'I'm going to kill you, Auger, but you'll see her die first.'

He raised the weapon. Astrid stopped and shielded her eyes as the sharplight's bright dot roamed over her face. She opened her mouth to scream, and the shining dot slipped inside.

'Say bye-bye,' Vinz said, and stepped forward but lost his balance as he squeezed the trigger, his foot sliding on a bleached, gilled foetus lying released from its jar. The sharplight threw its long gleaming needle into the cell behind Astrid and whipped it left and right as Vinz fell. The bars of the cell split and the ceiling groaned and collapsed, billowing dust from the cells.

Auger hurled himself at the trolley as Vinz got back to his knees, ramming it into Vinz and knocking him sprawling among the shards of glass and wilted specimens. Auger's clothes had spilled to the floor and he grabbed his jacket to wind round his fist, searching wildly for a fragment of glass to use as a weapon.

Vinz was steadying the sharplight again. There were no shards of glass long enough to be of any use, so Auger threw the jacket at Vinz, who fended it away easily and took aim once more at Astrid. As the jacket fell, there was a small separate sound on the floor and a flash of reflected light that caught Auger's eye and distracted Vinz again for an instant.

Troy Gordo's small pushJect vial was rolling towards Auger. He scooped it up and threw himself at Vinz, who raised his arms to fend him off. The cartridge punched into Vinz's forearm and Auger fell awkwardly to the ground. Vinz Szolty winced as the vial dropped. He crushed it under his foot, then kicked Auger in the ribs before he could roll away. Auger pulled himself into a ball against the pain as Vinz kicked him again.

'Okay, Auger. You first, then.' He raised the sharplight, but for some reason he didn't fire it. He frowned and looked at it. 'Trigger's . . .'

The sharplight shot its needle out, but it was directed hopelessly wide of Auger. Vinz seemed to slow down, as if the cold of the mortuary had got to him. His arm stiffened, and then his shoulder. The needle of light swayed wildly across the room, leaving curls of smoke drifting from the walls. 'What . . . is . . . ?' As he looked slowly at Auger, his neck locked too.

Auger got to his knees, staring at Vinz.

The freezing seemed to radiate across to his left shoulder and down his other arm, and he began to run for the door in a strange silent panic, the light beam like a stick held out before him. After a few metres his gait grew awkward, then his hips arrested and he slowed and managed to lumber around to face Auger again, and his knees locked. Making no sound at all, he fell heavily to the floor. The light drove, hissing, into the ground. His head cracked a tile. His feet twitched a little, and then he was still. Staring slightly to Auger's right, he looked no more than mildly startled.

Astrid helped Auger to his feet and said, 'Was that Troy's cartridge?'

'Yes.' He winced, feeling his ribs. 'Will it wear off?'

She shook her head. 'He hasn't the bLinkers to control or reverse it.'

'Is he going to die?'

'It's highly selective. I think it only acts on peripheral connective tissue cells. He's still alive. He's still healthy. Lungs working, heart pumping. If he dies, it'll be of starvation or dehydration. Not very quick. Not very pleasant.' She stumbled over to Vinz and knelt and tapped the rock of his hand. The sharplight was still drilling its needle into the ground. The needle trembled as she tapped his hand. 'We can't do anything for him, even if we wanted to. Can't penetrate that to get a line in. Forget him.'

She started to gather her clothes from the floor, dressing herself quickly. Auger did the same. He felt that there had been something between them for a few minutes before the explosion, and that now it had gone, and he didn't know what to do about it. What she had said to him had been distorted by fear and relief.

Her voice broke the silence in his head. 'Auger?'

They were both dressed now. Her clothes seemed like armour, sealing her away from him. The beam from Vinz's weapon was fading as the charge failed, and the room darkened slightly.

'Yes?' he said.

'Thanks.'

'That's okay.'

'I've got to go now, Auger. I've got to help.' She stood up and touched his cheek with her lips, then moved her lips to his and held them there, soft and warm, for a moment.

'This'll have to wait. I'll see you later, Auger, won't I?' At the door she turned and said, 'You know, I would have expected McCrae to do more damage than that, given his ego.'

'Would you?' He stopped, and murmured, 'Yes. A kilogram.'

She waited. 'What do you mean?'

'Didn't he say he'd swallowed a kilogram of MagmaX? That much would have destroyed most of London.'

'That would have been more like it.' A shrug. 'Thank God he made a mistake. No. Not God. Luck.' She jerked forward and said to someone Auger couldn't make out, 'Hey, look out,' and was gone.

'Who was that?' Madsen said, watching Astrid disappear, and then, more softly, 'Auger.'

His face seemed to break. Caked dust cracked away with the smile. 'It's good to see you, Auger.' Lethe and Jaime swept past him into the mortuary as Madsen looked around, his gaze stopping at Vinz. Lethe and Jaime were already examining him, pushing him, rolling him to and fro as far as they could. He clattered on the smashed floor but didn't break. 'What happened to him? Is he dead?'

'Apparently not.'

Madsen looked around, suddenly urgent again. 'Is Fly here?'

'Fly? No. Didn't he come with—?' And then Auger saw what was in Madsen's head, and it all made sense to him. 'The research wing.'

Madsen turned and ran. Auger started to follow him, then stopped. 'You go ahead, Madsen. He may have finished there by now. He may already have moved on.'

Madsen looked at him. Auger said, 'She was my wife, Madsen. That's still a part of her. And he may not stop even there.'

'Go, then.'

For a moment Auger thought Jay had returned from her fugue. She was crying, but her hysteria was in context. Fly had a gun to her head, the slim solid barrel whistling softly. A sonic weapon.

'What are you doing, Fly?'

Fly pulled up the gun, turning it on Auger. The ready tone dropped to a faint hum that scratched at Auger's skull. Fly jerked his head at the door behind him. The door to the back room Auger had never entered. 'In there,' he said. 'I told her why I was doing it. She killed my father, Auger. She and your wife.'

'She isn't my wife,' Auger said. He went carefully round Fly. In the other room was a CrySis pod and monitoring equipment. The pod was open and a woman's body was sprawled over the side, her head down and submerged in the gel, her hands trailing on the bottom as if she was casually searching there for something.

'Dr Carroll,' Fly said from behind Auger. Auger knelt and made to haul her out, his bruised ribs squeezing sudden pain into his chest, but Fly touched the gun rod to his neck and said, 'Leave her.'

'What are you doing, Fly?'

'I'm finishing it. There's just your wife now. I'm sorry, Auger. I would have told you if I could, but by the time I knew I could trust you, I couldn't risk exposing myself. You can come out of there now.'

The shivering coolness of the gun withdrew from Auger's skin, and as Auger stood slowly to his feet he became aware of another CrySis pod in the corner. A small one, its cover down. Occupied. There were words on the casing. CATHAR – MAIN UNIT

Forcing his thoughts from the meaning of that, he said, 'You gave McCrae the explosive, didn't you, Fly? I doubt McCrae would even have known about MagmaX. You set this up, even this.'

'I had no choice. I'm sure he would have got it himself if I hadn't. And he wanted more. I told him it was enough to destroy the whole of London. But I wasn't going to let him kill you if I could help it. He was a preacher. He didn't know a kilogram from a kilobyte. It was just a bellyful of swallow-bags as far as he was concerned.' Fly looked at Auger anxiously. 'We're friends, Auger. Aren't we? We've been through so much.'

Jay was weeping and clutching at Fly's arm. 'Who are you? What are you doing? Don't you know what's happened? Everyone's dead. Our wedding! All dead.'

Fly cracked the weapon across her skull and she fell back on the bed. He trained the gun on Auger again. 'Aren't we friends, Auger?'

'We were, Fly.'

'What does that mean?' He glanced at Jay, who was keening to herself, clutching the pillow to her face and rocking on the bed. The pillow was reddening. There was a spray of blood on her wedding dress.

The door opened and Madsen was standing there. Fly moved the gun quickly to Auger's temple and held it there, saying, 'Give us a moment, Madsen, will you?'

Madsen looked at Auger. His eyes flicked from Fly to Jay, taking it all in.

'We're friends, Madsen,' Auger said, keeping it light. The singing gun was trembling, and he wasn't sure if it was Fly's hand or the weapon shaking. 'It's okay. Fly's overwhelmed by all of this. He'll be okay. Take Jaime and Lethe, and see if you can find Astrid. We'll be finished here soon.'

Madsen said, 'Ferec's dead in his office. There's no sign of Dr Carroll. You sure it's okay?'

'Dr Carroll's with us,' Auger said. 'I'm fine.'

'If you say.' Madsen backed away.

'Close the door behind you,' Fly told him, then nudged Auger across the room and locked the door.

Auger gently pushed Fly's gun away from his head. Fly's hand dropped to his side. 'The MagmaX,' Auger said. 'It wasn't me you were saving. It was GenMed. McCrae told you where the interview was taking place, didn't he? In Croydon. You gave him enough MagmaX to leave GenMed just clear of the death zone.'

'I had to be sure, Auger. I had to be sure Maxenham didn't get away with it. You don't know him, Auger. But this is almost the end of it.'

'The end, Fly? You've killed—'

'Not me, Auger. McCrae did it. You saw it. He knew what he was doing. He knew exactly. And all those people Maxenham was going to kill, all McCrae's congregation. I saved them, didn't I?'

'That didn't matter to you, though, did it?' Another thing struck him, Fly talking of congregations. 'Father Fury,' Auger said. 'You couldn't have escaped the Final Church without him. He must have known, too. You let them die to give you your cover, but he escaped, didn't he?' Auger remembered Fury's last, taunting quote. It went on, Auger knew, *And if thy right eye offend thee, pluck it out and cast it from thee: for it is profitable for thee that one of thy members should perish, and not that thy whole body should be cast into hell.* Fury had even told Auger he wasn't going to die.

Fly brought the gun up again, but this time it was aimed at Jay. It changed tone again, rising in pitch as Jay cowered, holding up the pillow and crying, 'What are you talking about? Who are you? Don't you know what happened?'

The barrel of the gun dropped momentarily as Fly made to grab the pillow from Jay, and Auger threw out his arm to knock Fly's aim adrift. The turning gun whined and a cloud of plaster floated from the wall. Jay screamed as Auger followed up and wrenched the weapon from Fly's hand.

Behind him Jay was still screeching as he adjusted his grip on the gun's rubber stock. The barrel seemed to buck and he squeezed his hand to steady it. He saw Fly register his awkwardness with the weapon as he said, 'Turn around, Fly. Face the wall. Hands high.'

Fly half turned, then ducked and stretched out to grab at Auger's ankle. Auger pulled away, catching his foot against the corner of the bed, and fell. As he raised the gun his ribs cracked and in the pain he hesitated. Fly was immediately on him, pulling the gun from his hand, breathing hard.

'I'm sorry, Auger.' And Fly looked sorry, too, holding the gun steady at Auger's head, settling to fire. The barrel's black nib quivered and shifted in tone. Auger's eyeballs shook, disintegrating Fly and reforming him again. Auger couldn't move. The needling sound was a vice holding him. Fly's voice barely penetrated the rising note. 'I really thought we were friends, Auger. I thought you'd understand.'

Jay yelled and Auger saw her dive at Fly, something glinting in her fist. Auger tried to pull away as the gun's whine corkscrewed into his skull and lodged there, rising and rising until it became his scream and he lost consciousness.

The room seemed to be shivering as Auger shook his head to clear it, but the noise was Madsen banging on the door. Auger crawled across the room to let him in.

Fly was lying on the floor, the last centimetre of the handle of a scalpel blade acting as a conduit for the blood pumping from his neck. Jay had found his carotid.

Auger left the body there and gently settled Jay back on the bed, trying uselessly to soothe her. She was sobbing against him, adjusting her wedding dress, rubbing in puzzlement at the blood on it and on her hands from the wound where Fly had hit her with the gun. She had forgotten the cause of it already. She had probably already forgotten flying at him and killing him to save Auger's life.

'What's happening, Cy? I don't understand. I love you. Don't leave me, please.'

Madsen sat with her, motioning Auger away. 'I'm from Pacifism. We're investigating the situation, Ms Auger. Don't worry. It's under control, now. Leave it to us.'

In the back room again, Auger lifted the cover of the small CrySis pod. The body of a child floated there. His child. Auger reached in and gently gathered the boy in his arms, supporting the great skull in the crook of his elbow. The respirator tube fell from the child's lips as he came clear of the gel, and he tried to mouth something, staring at Auger. His skin was red and weeping and his brown hair thin and patchy, but his eyes were blue and clear, and as he looked at Auger he smiled a weak smile that made Auger's knees buckle. Above the pod a monitor was beeping and readouts flatlining, counts going to racks of nils. Red letters flashed over a grey screen. ZONE DOWN.

The boy reached up and touched Auger's cheek with the soft tip of a finger and whispered, 'Are you the father?'

'Yes,' Auger said in a whisper. 'Yes, I am.'

And then he went with his son and showed him to Jay. Both to the Jay who had saved his life and to the other Jay within.

'This is your mother,' he said softly. And then, 'This is your child.'

For a moment she quietened, gazing at the child. Her look was uncomprehending. Then Auger bent down and kissed her for the last time, looking into her eyes, knowing that the Jay who had done this was trapped in there for ever now, and that the other Jay would not remember this kiss in a few minutes' time. 'Goodbye, Jay,' he said.

Madsen held the door open for him. In the corridor Jaime and Lethe were standing waiting, arm in arm.

'What will happen to her?' Madsen asked Auger.

'I suppose eventually she'll wander outside and see the destruction. She'll probably think it's part of what she knows, which is not too far wrong. She's a medic. She'll help. Maybe it will help her a little.'

Jaime and Lethe were looking at the child in Auger's arms and at him, and realising what Fly had realised all that time ago, in Cathar. Jaime made a small laugh and Lethe's face opened into a grin. She put out a finger and the child clutched it tightly. 'Well, well, Auger,' she murmured.

'Let's go,' Madsen said. 'Astrid's waiting.'

As they walked away from the room and the sobbing began to recede, Auger smiled down at his child and said, 'We'll take care of you. You're safe now.' He thought of this child and then of Astrid. Astrid who was host already to so many. He thought about it with sudden hope, this strange new family of his. It was a fragile thing and damaged, but so was everything.

A thought struck him and he said to Madsen, 'You once told me there were two things you had to learn, and the first was when to get involved. You never told me the second.'

Madsen said, 'I think you've found it out. It's when to forget, Auger.'

The neuro unit was behind them now as they approached the ward's sterile veil, and the lone sobbing could not be heard. The chimes of the veil tolled them through. They walked on. In front of them was all the pain and shrieking of the world.

EPILOGUE

He woke up as he always woke up now, drawn from a sleep so deep and dreamless that the night might not even have existed, to an immediate awareness of her. And to the feel of her warm hand cupping and playing almost absent-mindedly with him, steadily massaging him to stiffness, and then when he was hard a bounce of the mattress and the duvet billowing and sighing, and her slight, warm weight settling comfortably upon him, her fingers guiding and feeding him into her, tight and almost chafing for a delirious moment, and then contained deep and secure, Astrid riding him, kneading him, developing a rhythm that she could always maintain for longer than he could withstand it. It was a perfect way to wake up. It was always perfect.

Despite the temptation to gaze at her, he pretended still to be asleep, as if she was having no effect on him. Eyes closed, he yawned ostentatiously, and she giggled and lifted her hips and dropped them until he yelped and laughed with her, and finally opened his eyes to her bobbing grin.

Astrid. He could still hardly believe she was with him. And for how many years now? He had never even dreamed of such contentment, such happiness.

The alarm chirped. Keeping him carefully inside her, she leant off to the side to nil the clock's chime. Across their bedroom the square of filtered daylight through the sofglass was golden in his eyes until she straightened again and the silhouette of her head and shoulders centred there, bobbing, as if she were swimming in honey.

'I've taken the day off,' she murmured, as if reading his thoughts. She was still rising and falling, flexing, squeezing him, drawing his breath irresistibly into her rhythm. He felt as if he too were swimming in honey.

'Yes?' he said briefly, concentrating.

'What shall we do?'

'Uhhh.'

'What would you like to do?'

'I. Don't. Knooow.' He groaned.

She laughed. 'I don't think you're paying attention.' She dug her hips down again. Her silhouette flowed in the window as she leaned forward and pressed her hands on his shoulders. 'I don't think you're listening to a word, are you?' She grinned, nudging him with her hips to emphasise her point.

'Nuuhhhh. Uuuuhhh.'

'Okay. Do you want me to stop?' She lifted herself a fraction.

'No! No no no.'

She came down again, slowly, giggling. He pushed up to meet her as she fell forward now, out of control with laughter, and he rolled her over and drew on top of her and began himself to move, taking the rhythm over, looking into her eyes and saying, 'I know. We'll take a picnic, go somewhere out of London, find ourselves a quiet field.' He cupped her face in the palms of his hands. 'Where shall we go, then?'

'Uuuh.'

'Now who's not listening?'

He watched her eyes lose focus as he moved, steering them both to the end of it and then collapsing beside her, the two of them glowing with sweat in the soft morning light from the window. It was going to be a fine day again.

'Mmm, this is heaven,' she said.

He laughed. 'You always say that.'

'It's the truth.'

Shadows faintly clouded the room and he raised his head and looked at the square of sofglass to see shapes moving there, silhouettes behind the glass. He lifted himself to his elbows.

Animal shapes. A wolf, or a large fox perhaps. No, he saw it had to be a wolf, its large head dipping and turning. His breath caught. He thought he had seen shapes there yesterday morning, but they had disappeared before he could look more closely. This time they remained. He made a sharp gesture at the window and they pulled back, the shapes shrinking and losing focus, but after a minute they approached the window again.

He threw off the bedcovers, and was aware that the room was slightly cold. The heating must have nilled itself. He went to the window and rapped a knuckle against the sofglass, the pressure eddying reds and pale greens across its surface. A nose touched the window from the other side, bulging it inwards, a violet cone with a black tip.

Instinctively he stepped back, then punched the thrust-up nose with his fist. It withdrew, and a muted yelp penetrated the rainbowing sofglass.

'There,' he said aloud, conclusively.

But after a moment the nose returned, and behind it was the faint form of a bird, the bird perched on the wolf's shoulder, its wings half-opened and trembling as it struggled for balance. And nudging up against the wolf was some large insect, rearing up, its abdomen a magenta mound on the sofglass, exploring the pane with the palps of its feet. Six crimson bulges shifting across the window. It struck him that the animals were acting together, or at least were not affected by the presence of each other, of other species. That was strange. There was something else arriving too, he saw, enlarging and defining itself. A cat perhaps, springing to the sill. It pressed its nose to the glass beside the wolf and the spider-thing, and the sofglass bloomed with colour.

He raised his fist, uncertain which of the creatures to strike first, then lowered it again. He didn't know what to do.

'Did you say something?'

He turned round. Astrid was standing there, a towel wrapped around her, glistening wet hair coiled high on her head.

'Look,' he said.

She came to his side. He could smell the scent of soap on her. Lilacs. She pulled the towel tight. 'Oh, Troy,' she said.

The sofglass bulged again in several places. A beak, a snout, a number of paws pressed hard against it. Colours radiated wildly across the stretched surface.

Troy watched the distorted pane, waiting for it to yield. In panic he reached for Astrid. She seemed oddly insubstantial, suddenly.

A claw came through the window, curved, silver, and all the colours vanished as the sofglass split in a long, ragged, diagonal tear.

ACKNOWLEDGEMENTS

Thanks to the Azzurri writers, including: Simon Campbell, Susan Clegg, Anita Dawood-Nasar, Kate Grunstein, Richard Hughes, Margaret Laing, Steve Mullins, Annemarie Neary, Sam Patterson Jr, Joanna Pocock, Mike Roberts, Elise Valmorbida. Especially Sam, and also Nick Doughty, who are particularly in our thoughts.

Also Dr Graham Pickup for biannual conversations about schizotypy (though he is in no way responsible for my wilful and probably woeful misinterpretation), Tina Levy, Adam Roberts, Simon Wooden, Antony Harwood. And Simon Spanton for more than just fine editing, but also for having, well, faith.